UNOFFICIAL ROSIE

UNOFFICIAL ROSIE

An omnibus of
Unofficial Rosie
and
Rosie Among Thorns

ALAN McDONALD

WARNER BOOKS

A *Warner* Book

This omnibus edition first published in Great Britain in 1993
by Warner Books

UNOFFICIAL ROSIE omnibus edition
copyright © 1993 by Alan McDonald

Previously published separately:
UNOFFICIAL ROSIE first published in Great Britain in 1988
by Futura Publications
Copyright © 1988 by Alan McDonald
Yesterday © 1965 Northern Songs, under licence to
SBK Songs Ltd, 3–5 Rathbone Place, London W1P 1DA
ROSIE AMONG THORNS first published in Great Britain in 1989
by Futura Publications
Copyright © 1989 by Alan McDonald

The moral right of the author has been asserted.

A CIP catalogue record for this book is
available from the British Library.

ISBN 0 7515 0956 6

Printed in England by Clays Ltd, St Ives plc

Warner Books
A Division of
Little, Brown and Company (UK) Limited
Brettenham House
Lancaster Place
London WC2E 7EN

UNOFFICIAL
ROSIE

Chapter One

It was one night in Liverpool that Rosie Monaghan had the idea. The month was September. The football season had just begun, which was a sort of Merseyside New Year: the only beginning there was to celebrate these days.

Earlier that evening a full moon had hung, big as a football, over the serrated rooftops. For some reason Rosie had become intoxicated with the idea that it was, like a star in the east one thousand nine hundred and something years before, some kind of a celestial navigation aid. Believing it to be suspended over her house and her house alone, she'd steered her first unsteady steps home by it after closing time.

Now the bloody thing was hiding from her behind a cloud. *SPOT THE MOON*, she imagined saying to the lamp-post she was leaning against. *The moon has been erased from this picture of the night sky. Use your skill and judgement to place an X where you think the exact centre of the moon should be* ...

That wasn't her best idea, though. Not by a long chalk. She levered herself away from the lamp-post and lurched off, picking her way through the broken glass that would have glittered like starlight if someone hadn't vandalized the streetlamps. She, Roisin Theresa Monaghan known as Rosie, was going to become a private detective. That was her real idea. 'Down these mean streets,' she said out loud, 'a woman must go.'

But first she'd have to find her way home. The trouble was, Rosie was as drunk as a lady. She'd been in one pub or another since lunchtime celebrating her recent reduction to the ranks of the immoral minority (ah, but growing all the time) of the unemployed. NATIONAL FOODS SHED 200 JOBS had said the second headline in the *Echo* two months before (news priority that day having gone to a sex murder in West Lothian). Now it had come to pass: redundancy. 'Here I am, shed,' said Rosie to the gloomy tenements she was stumbling through. 'And why not? Down these mean streets? If in doubt . . .'

If in doubt, what? A gang of kids was trying to set fire to an enormous rubber tyre in the centre of the tenement courtyard. Their faces glowed like witches over a broth. A couple of quarter-Alsations yelped at the bonfire and at Rosie. Acrid smoke hung over the landings. Something in the unchill air made her shiver. Shadows of men interested in her money or body suddenly lurked in every passageway and she realized she was lost. With a clatter of heels she hurried back through the archway into the street.

Why hadn't she taken the bus? Too late now, Rosie. And the moon was still hiding from her so she hailed a taxi.

'Y'all right, queen?' asked the tired cabbie's face in the driving mirror as they drove south to Rosie's home.

'Fine,' she said to the man's eyes. 'Fine.' She was fumbling in her handbag to see if she had enough cash for both the cab and the teenage girl from across the street who was minding the kids. 'Have you seen the moon?'

'Not lately.'

'Nor have I,' said Rosie, her purse now in her hand, the reason forgotten. 'But I'm fine. Redundant. Fine,' and she burped loudly.

'Everybody's doing it,' said the cabbie. 'I was made redundant myself. From Plessey's.'

'Really?' enquired Rosie politely. The lights of the city kaleidoscoped by and she had a brief delusion of the beauty of her home town.

'I blame the microchip,' said the mirror's eyes.

'Me too,' said Rosie with renewed vigour. 'And the microfiche. Even with microsalt and vinegar they just don't taste the microsame.'

They'd stopped at a traffic light. 'You wha'?' asked the cabbie. He turned to look at her. His face bore a strange resemblance to Humphrey Bogart. Or was it Robert Mitchum? Elliott Gould? If in doubt . . .

6

'Artificial food in the leisure society,' she explained patiently. 'I charge twenty dollars a day plus expenses. Shame about the moon,' and she closed her eyes against the cabbie's inquisitive gaze. Suddenly she remembered why she was supposed to count her money. Then, inexplicably, her purse and handbag began to slide very slowly to the floor and so did she. As a police siren blared importantly past with a flash of blue lights and a twinkle of uniforms, she fell literally and resoundingly asleep.

Chapter Two

The morning after, the idea didn't seem such a good one. The morning after, nothing seemed so good. There were bags under Rosie's eyes like kangaroo pouches; a strange clinging fur had grown inside her mouth and stomach; and within each of her temples tiny circular saws had been implanted overnight and were busy grinding her pleasant memories of the night before up into little pieces. The only memory that perversely remained intact was of being carried in by the taxi-driver and Jennifer who'd been minding the kids and was trying to persuade Rosie to stop singing 'O silver moon'.

'Ugh,' said Rosie, contemplating a bowl of cornflakes.

'Were you drunk, Mum?' asked eleven-year-old Bob. Not a musical child, he was proving the point by banging his spoon rhythmically against the side of his cereal bowl in time with the adverts on the radio.

'Please stop doing that.'

'Were you drunk, though?'

'I was — celebrating,' Rosie replied carefully, wondering where she'd gone wrong with his upbringing. The last straw had come only a week ago, when he'd gone to comprehensive school for the first time and enjoyed every minute of it. Why wasn't he artistic and unusual, the little sod?

'Was it fun, Mum?'

'It was, I wouldn't call it, yes but, well it wasn't exactly,' said Rosie, wrenching the spoon out of his hand with a motherly smile. The bloody child even liked seeing his father on alternate Saturdays. Perhaps it was something to do with penises. 'Time you were off.'

A little later she shuffled blearily into the F-to-M entrance of the Unemployment Office and signed up with the leisure society. Hesitating over 'Occupation' she finally settled on 'shorthand-typist', meticulously noting down her typing speeds and RSA qualifications. Well, they'd only laugh if she put down 'private detective', wouldn't they?

She looked into the eyes of the girl behind the counter and knew they wouldn't have laughed at anything she said or wrote.

It was a long walk home but maybe it was good for her health: the rain wasn't all that heavy. Besides, it didn't seem right somehow to drive to the dole and back, even if your car was only a blue 1969 Mini that you were hanging on to till it became a collector's item or fell to pieces, whichever came first. She knew from past experience that that was the sort of thing employed people got very huffy about: unemployed people enjoying little luxuries like keeping dry when it rained. There were certain standards you were expected to live down to, as a member of the leisure society.

Her head pounded all day in time with the washing machine and next-door's television as she pondered her idea. Why didn't she just go the whole hog and turn to crime? Thirty-three was probably too old to start on the game, even if she'd fancied it; her nerves wouldn't stand bank robbery. But something genteel — like fraud — would be nice. Or drug-smuggling might suit her, what with all those foreign trips. Mm, she'd always fancied travelling ...

Yes, crime would be logical. Unfortunately Rosie thought most crime was morally wrong. This wasn't something she liked about herself; it left her feeling ill-equipped for the modern world. But she'd always been a goody-goody child and had never outgrown such foolishness. Oh, she'd have a drink out of hours and buy the odd packet of bleach that had fallen off the back of a lorry like any normal human being. But mostly she played by the rules and disapproved of the criminal classes: thieves, murderers, politicians. She even, when the car wouldn't start or she couldn't afford to feed it with petrol, insisted on paying the right bus-fare. 'The buses belong to all of us,' she'd say, proudly clutching her 25p ticket, while her friends laughed at her and looked anxiously out of the window for inspectors.

So private detection seemed the best bet. That way she could get a sniff at a life of crime without actually having to taste its bitter flavour in one of Her Majesty's jails. That way, too, she wouldn't have to dress up in a blue uniform to do her detecting, and then have to tell people off for speeding or being black or thrusting their chins at police officers' fists. Perhaps, she admitted to herself, she'd have to cut her detector teeth on less important cases — the odd seedy divorce, the occasional runaway teenager — but she could probably graduate from that without too much difficulty to fraud and kidnapping and so on: including of course, murder — that speciality of private detectives everywhere.

Now that she'd decided on her future it would be nice to tell someone. The kids, she considered, should have first preference. Bob's spoon-banging had eliminated him from the privilege, but she could still tell Carol when she came home from school. Carol was two years younger than Bob and was, Rosie hoped, going to be a top criminal when she grew up — or, failing that, a successful businesswoman, since that more or less amounted to the same thing. At four o'clock Carol rushed in, all smiles. Rosie kissed her long brown hair, and framed with her hands the face that was so like a smaller version of her own, even down to the little bump on the bridge of the nose. 'Had a good day?' she enquired maternally.

'Yeh,' said Carol enthusiastically. 'Listen to this, Mum. Mandy Baker learned me.'

With the utmost consideration for Rosie's hangover, Carol had chosen that very day to satisfy a long-cherished ambition; she'd learnt how to whistle. Rosie could just make out the phantom of the intended tune behind the banshee wail: *All things bright and beautiful, all creatures great* —

'Please stop doing that,' said Rosie with quiet desperation.

'It's whistling, Mum.'

'It's a — beautiful noise,' Rosie acknowledged. 'In the right place at the right time. In a torture chamber, for instance.'

'You wha'?'

'Isn't it a nice day to play out, though?'

Well, the rain wasn't all that heavy, and anyway Carol was soon across the road in her friend Marie's house — demonstrating her whistling, Rosie expected. She crossed her daughter off her list of possible confidantes and settled down to making the tea.

Later, after spaghetti on toast and television and home-work, the two cherubs were at last tucked up in bed, whistling to each other across the house, when Jerry came round. 'I've had an idea', she said to Jerry over the lager he'd brought. 'About my life.'

'I've had a terrible day at the office,' said Jerry.

Rosie loved Jerry. She loved his soft hands, his soft heart, his soft features, his soft voice talking about his soft desk-job at the Corporation. Listening to another catalogue of bureaucratic woes, she felt the urge to clasp his soft head to her breast and ask him to live with her.

The problem with Jerry was that he was too soft. Some-times she wished he'd reveal to her his latent ambition to rule the world, or his sordid bigamous past, or his private desire to be bound to the bedhead and whipped with the flex off the bedside lamp. But he never did. Jerry was unashamedly glad he had no secrets from her. He was proud of his softness.

And Rosie was proud she'd never quite suggested he moved from his flat round the corner.

Jerry's account of his day seemed to take almost as long as the day itself. 'If in doubt,' Rosie managed to say at last over the third can of lager. 'That phrase has been going round my head since last night.'

'Mm hm?' said Jerry.

Rosie shrugged, resigned to not remembering its mean-ing. 'I've had an idea,' she said instead. 'About my life.'

'Great,' said Jerry, smiling up at her from the cushions at her feet. 'Would you mind if we had the telly on? There's this programme I want to watch about the arms race.'

11

Rosie decided not to tell Jerry about her idea for now. After the programme he half-suggested he might stay the night and she said she still had a hangover.

Strangely it seemed to dissipate as soon as he went.

She didn't even tell the woman in British Telecom the following morning about becoming a private detective. She'd gone there to make the first investment in her future: a telephone answering machine for when the important clients called while she was out signing on, or at home but on the loo. She was in fact ready to share her secret with the saleswoman, but when she launched gaily into 'I'm going into business on my own account' the woman switched on the briefest, falsest smile Rosie had ever seen — even including her ex-husband's smile when she and Jerry had met him and his new wife at the Odeon that time — so she decided not to bother.

It was only, therefore, the great anonymous world which first got to know of Rosie's idea. They read about it, whoever they were, in the Classified columns of the *Echo* and the window of Khan's newsagent and general store:

ROSE MONAGHAN
INQUIRY AGENT
Reasonable rates. Confidentiality
guaranteed. Ring 471-5243 now!

'Down these mean streets a woman must go' she thought of adding, then decided to reserve the motto for the letter-heading she'd invest in once business got going. Now, for the first time in her life, she felt mistress of her own destiny. She anxiously awaited her first call.

Chapter Three

For the next month the phone never stopped ringing.

That was because it never started ringing.

No, that's an exaggeration. There were three calls related to her new life. One came while she was at home, from Polly who'd worked at National Foods with her. 'Have you seen the *Echo*?' asked Polly's nasal tones out of the black telephone.

'No.'

'It's got your phone number in it,' said Polly. 'And your name. Well I said to our Kath, I said, look someone's put Rosie's name in the *Echo* as an inquiry agent, I mean, it must be someone's idea of a joke I said, but it might be embarrassing so I thought ...'

'Have you got work, Poll?' said Rosie curtly.

'Two nights in a bar, y'know, nothing to worry the Social, so I thought someone ought to tell you, I mean, what if someone really rang you up and ...'

Rosie bit her lip. 'It's perfectly serious,' she said.

'Oh,' said the black telephone. 'You mean you're really ...?'

'Really,' said Rosie.

'Oh,' said the black telephone. 'Oh.'

'Oh,' said Rosie, replacing the receiver.

The other two calls came while she was out. Rosie played them back with trembling hands on the answering machine.

The first was from Bob and Carol who now knew, to justify the machine, that their mother was 'going into business on her own'. Carol's crackly voice just about drowned out Bob's giggles: 'Hello Mum. We thought we'd call to cheer you up because nobody was ringing you.' There was a break for whispers and throat-clearing. Then they whistled in unison down the wires *Yesterday* by Lennon and McCartney because they knew how much she liked the song.

13

Rosie was touched by her first recorded phone call.

Rosie was irritated and unnerved by her second recorded phone call. A moderately well-spoken man said he would like to enquire into the wetness or dryness of whatever was underneath her knickers (assuming she wore knickers, he hastened to add) and not only that, but — She erased whatever else he wanted to enquire into.

Time began to slip away from her. The moon got gradually smaller, then gradually bigger. Never again did it seem to be suspended directly over Rosie's cosy little terraced house. She menstruated and received giros through the mail. No-one called to offer her work and she began to think that maybe she'd have to go back to typing men's boring and banal letters and getting told off when she improved them. Meanwhile she somehow managed to fritter away the hours — cooking, cleaning, washing clothes, shopping, arbitrating in disputes between small people, taking Carol to the dentist and pretending she loved the sound of his drill — doing all those little things unemployed people who are also women and mothers do to while away their unemployed time.

She also frittered time away with Jerry. Many hours with Jerry. Many hours in bed with Jerry. Rosie may have told herself she loved Jerry for his softness, but when the rest of her life wasn't going well she knew what she really loved him for: because he was so good in bed. Soft, in bed, he wasn't. Gentle, he was. Unselfish, he was. Unhurried, he was. She'd lie there on the flowered sheet, the kids safely tucked up in bed, the world safely locked outside the windows, and she'd feel wonderfully relaxed, and think about all the things you weren't supposed to think about when you were making love — tomorrow's shopping list, her lack of employment, the future of the world — and know none of it mattered as long as Jerry made all the nerves dance and sing inside her body.

Sometimes she'd stare at him, in the living room in the evening, in his crumpled bureaucrat's clothes, while he told her about his terrible day at work, and she'd wonder if this was the same man who made her feel like singing *Zip-a-dee-doo-dah* at midnight.

14

It was one midnight when the moon was just past new and she'd just been singing *Zip-a-dee-doo-dah* to herself that she finally got to tell him about her new career. 'A what?' Jerry asked faintly, exhausted from his labours of love.

'An inquiry agent. A private detective,' she murmured intimately, tenderly picking scraps of dirt out of his navel as they lay entwined together.

'Experience?' asked Jerry vaguely.

'I was a store detective, love,' said Rosie. 'For six months, when Graham left me. I learnt a lot then.'

'Oh yes?'

'Yeh,' she affirmed, transferring attention to her own navel. 'I felt sorry for the shop-lifters, that's all. They seemed nicer people than the shop managers. But I'm more ruthless now.'

'Mm,' said Jerry, who was beginning to sound as if he wasn't listening.

'And I've been a temp in a solicitor's office. I'm sure that legal experience will stand me in good stead.'

Jerry didn't even reply to that. He'd dozed off. Humph, thought Rosie. What was so unrealistic about the idea? People with thousands in redundancy payments set up little shops and businesses; people with £453.26 just had to cut their cloth. Maybe he thought it was an unsuitable job for a woman? She'd show him. You've got to take risks in this life. If in doubt, do it. If in doubt ...

Absent-mindedly twining a pubic hair round her index finger, she finally remembered how the phrase finished. *If in doubt, have a man come in through the door carrying a gun.* Oh dear. That was Raymond Chandler's advice. That was what happened to private detectives. Males of the species proved their higher intelligence by beating the hell out of you. Then you had to prove your heroism by beating the hell out of them. Oh dear. She should have gone to those self-defence classes when her friend Margie had wanted her to. Tears pricked at Rosie's eyelids as she contemplated the ceiling that needed decorating and the idea that maybe wasn't such a good one after all.

Even Jerry's snoring didn't soothe her to sleep that night. The next day she went to see Margie: also a single

15

parent, a fellow-member of the leisure society, a good friend and a living accusation. Margie was fair where Rosie was dark; good-looking where Rosie was just this side of plain in a good light; competent and determined where Rosie was chaotic and inclined to uncertainty. Margie immediately gave her her first lesson in self-defence — 'Always carry an aerosol: doesn't matter what's in it, red paint's as good as poison' — and didn't altogether dismiss the inquiry agency. 'Might as well try anything,' was her comment as she opened a bottle of home-made wine.

Rosie had once tried to follow Margie's instructions and make her own elderberry wine. The contents had exploded all over the airing cupboard and ruined several sheets and towels.

Still, she decided to take her friend's words as encouragement. 'I'm going to retrain,' said Margie, 'as a computer operator. That's where the future is: Silicon Valley.'

'Get away,' said Rosie, 'don't you take a 38C as it is?'

'No,' said Margie, 'I mean —' Then she looked at Rosie and laughed. They raised their glasses and Margie proposed a toast. 'Here's to us and the future. Private detection — or bust!'

But even Margie's encouragement didn't keep up Rosie's spirits for long. Soon the full moon came near again, and there were still no cases for Rose Monaghan Inquiry Agent, and it was melancholy autumn. Rosie knew because leaves were browning on the trees the Corporation had planted in front of the decaying walk-up flats round the corner, and Bob kept campaigning to stay up late on Saturday night to watch *Match of the Day*. And Rosie kept feeling wistful; if only my bloody ex-husband's maintenance would arrive on time for once, if only I had a job: autumnal, impossible dreams.

She'd already written her first letter of application for a typing job and was just thinking about sending one of the kids out to post it when the man telephoned. She had to be summoned from the baked beans on the stove to talk to him. Telling Bob to turn down the television, she pressed her ear to the receiver pessimistically. 'Mrs Monaghan?' enquired a cultured voice.

'Close,' said Rosie, anticipating research into her underwear.

'I saw your advertisement and I wondered if we might meet?'

'CRACKERJACK!' said Bob, Carol and the television simultaneously. All three of them ignored Rosie's finger-to-lips gesture. 'Yeh?'

'About a job you might be able to do for me. Confidentially, of course.'

About a what? 'Of course,' said Rosie, her voice suddenly as smooth as vinyl silk. 'Of course. Of course.' About a what?

'You are the — inquiry agent, are you not?'

Am I not? 'Of course, of course,' said Rosie's stuck groove, her gesticulations at the TV volume becoming a wild, unheeded semaphore. 'Sorry, I'm just back from an assignment.'

'Mm. Quite. Good,' said the cultured voice. He named the place and the time and himself: Mr Andrew Stephenson, who'd be wearing a grey polo-neck and drinking scotch. He looked forward to meeting her.

'So do I,' said Rosie. 'I mean, you. Tara now. That is, goodbye.'

She stared blankly at the telephone and wondered what the smell was. 'CRACKERJACK!' said TV and children for an encore and Rosie joined in this time. 'CRACKERJACK!' she shouted, louder than any of them.

She went over and turned the set down then went to the sideboard for the letter applying for the typist's job. 'What are you doing, Mum?' asked Bob.

'I'm tearing up an envelope,' said Rosie, sniffing the air. 'I think the beans are burnt.'

Their faces clouded: 'Oh, Mum!'

But soon they were smiling as she added: 'Who's going to the chippy, then?'

Nothing was too good for her family, now that she was really in business. She even agreed to two helpings of curry sauce as she began to wonder what she could wear to meet her client — her client! — and where the hell the Atlantic Crossing was that she had to meet him in.

Chapter Four

As it turned out the pub wasn't that hard to find. She simply went out into the street and there was Billy from Number 29 just emerging from beneath a fifth-hand Jaguar; Billy who knew every alehouse within a ten-mile radius and had the paunch to prove it (how he fitted his body under the cars he mended was an everyday miracle). He told her the pub was 'over the water' and tapped the underside of his nose with the back of a greasy forefinger.

'Over the water' meant the Wirral, through the Mersey tunnel and across the river, and when Rosie got there (after only four wrong turnings, A-to-Z in hand, up sub-suburban avenues and country lanes) she saw what Billy meant, with the nose. The Wirral itself was posh; the Atlantic Crossing was posh for the Wirral. There were expensive cars parked outside and expensive bottoms parked within. Slung below the low white ceiling were genuine oak beams for you to bang your head on. Rosie looked round expectantly. Half the clientele seemed to be wearing grey polo-necks but none of them was drinking scotch. Andrew Stephenson was late.

Which was a shame, because Rosie had planned and executed her entrance so carefully — flouncing in through the door to the lounge bar, her black patent pseudo-leather bag swinging at her shoulder, her best red dress still warm against her skin from its last-minute ironing — all to follow her new motto for private eyes: *If in doubt, have a woman come in through the door carrying a handbag.* That was going to be her way: the peaceful way. None of that nonsense about men and guns. None of Rosie's problems were going to be solved by physical violence.

Assuming, that is, any of her problems were going to be solved at all.

Still, as she parked her not-so-expensive bottom in a

corner, with a slimline orange to nurse, she had a feeling things were going to work out. The car had started first time; she'd left Bob and Jerry playing intense knock-out whist for used matches while Carol watched something rivetingly unsuitable on the box; she'd practised 'How d'you do, Mr Stephenson?' half-a-dozen times in front of the mirror till she thought she'd got the half-smile about right. Yes, all the portents were good.

'What'll you have?' said a cultured voice in her ear.

She looked up, startled for a moment, at the grey polo-neck who'd somehow materialised from behind her. What've you got? she wanted to reply. But instead, rehearsals forgotten yet the style still in place, 'Vodka and orange please' she murmured in her most cultured voice and switched on the half-smile.

Unfortunately Andrew Stephenson missed it. He was already at the bar, busy being tall and erect and suave, ordering the drinks with an effortless combination of smiling eyes and condescending mouth. His hand smoothed back flecks of gold dust in his hair that had been cunningly camouflaged as grey streaks. As he turned with the drinks, even the wrinkles that criss-crossed his face looked sketched in for the camera that must be hidden somewhere, filming the telly advert they were performing in.

The vodka he brought was a double, with a slice of real orange perched among the ice cubes. 'Sorry if I kept you waiting,' said his down-turned, unsorry mouth. 'Something came up.'

Your John Thomas? asked Rosie's renegade voice. 'That's all right,' she said out loud. 'I only just got here.'

That little lie set her up nicely for the other little lies to come: so somehow she managed to fill out her store detection and temping for the solicitor into a few spurious cases for Rose Monaghan Inquiry Agent, and gulped her double vodka too quickly, and wondered if she'd over-emphasised the divorce case she'd invented on the spur of the moment. Call-me-Andrew looked like divorce to her, but how did you judge? Maybe he just looked bored and impatient for her to finish her self-introduction.

19

'I'm in the public service,' he said at last. 'But frankly, Rose — may I call you Rose? — it's not what it was: the public service. Local government.'

'Ah, the Corpie,' said Rosie before she could stop herself.

He frowned a little, as if she'd just used a swear-word. 'Mersey City Council, that's who I've given the best years of my life to,' he said, crinkling his eyes to indicate that the best years were actually still to come. 'When I went into the public, ah, the Corporation as a young man: it was different then. There was a sense of decency, a certain idealism in being a public servant. We cared. It was our job to care. There was a consensus among us which cut across divisions.'

'Yeh?' said Rosie, trying to cut across the stare of a man with a fat cigar and a naval moustache across the room.

'But now all that's changed, Rose. Politics has become a question of extremes. Some of my fellow public servants have become openly political themselves. And the idea of service, the word itself has become a dirty word.'

'Yeh?' said Rosie, who thought it was a dirty word and wondered how and when he was going to bring the conversation round to divorce.

'Another?' he said abruptly, but it wasn't really a question; he was already halfway to the bar before she could tell him to skip the vodka this time.

Looking around, she noticed for the first time the prints on the walls: the *Lusitania*, the *Queen Mary*, passenger liners full of waving arms and laughing faces from Liverpool's heyday: ships long since scrapped and the metal turned into machines that did the work of five people or into corrugated roofs for shanty towns somewhere. While the liners went with the name of the pub, the Atlantic Crossing, yachts would have been more apt for Rosie's affluent fellow-drinkers. Or speedboats maybe. I'm just a little sprat to them, she thought to herself, these people live on their smart little island and fish me out of the pond for dinner, and that one over there with the moustache, pretty soon he's going to wander over and ask me if I've had any good plankton lately ...

Another double vodka arrived. The hand that set down

the drink had a gold signet ring gleaming on the little finger. 'And there's corruption,' said the voice that went with the hand.

'Yeh?' said Rosie.

Andrew Stephenson was an islander too, though not it seemed from this particular one. She'd seen no casual greetings to anyone, no little nods across the room. 'Corruption,' he said. 'True, there've always been bad apples; the greedy are always with us. But nowadays it's almost an accepted part of what goes on. The tiny deceit, the small back-hander. I find that very sad.'

'Me too,' said Rosie, wanting to be polite.

'I've tried to keep above all that, you see. But now I simply can't pretend it isn't there any more.'

'No,' said Rosie.

'You see, I'm in refuse,' he continued, catching her off guard so she had to choke back the laugh. 'I'm in the administration of refuse disposal. The detritus of our lives. Shit,' which sounded like the first word he'd really meant. 'The administration of shit: that's my business. If you'll pardon the phrase.'

Business or shit? Rosie stopped herself from asking, thinking they were both pretty dirty and unavoidable. And it looked like he wasn't working round to revelations of his private life and she felt a bit disappointed, stifling a yawn, as he droned on:

'... Council, in its wisdom, has been reviewing the collection of refuse. Its political leaders have considered the merits and demerits of allowing petty bureaucrats such as myself ...'

Petty? thought Rosie: I wouldn't accuse you of being that.

'... to remain in charge of the men who are prepared to handle other people's rubbish, but who also have an unfortunate propensity to join trade unions. So the politicians have decided they want an inferior job done more cheaply. Not in so many words, of course. The catch-phrase is: privatize.'

That sounded so near the title of Rosie's new occupation that she woke from a reverie about cruising on the *Lusitania* fishing for yachtsmen and tried to recall what

21

he'd just been saying as he went on:

'Accordingly the Council has sought tenders from a number of contractors who believe they can make a profit out of, out of ...'

'Shit?'

'Quite,' said Andrew Stephenson, frowning again. 'And, as is customary within our fine democratic traditions, certain inducements are available if any councillors are prepared to smooth the path towards providing this, ah, public service through private enterprise. It's depressing.'

He seemed to mean that too. He drained his scotch with one swallow and looked hard into it for evidence of how depressing it was. There was a pause. 'And me?' said Rosie.

'And you. You're just starting out in this business, aren't you?'

'No, as I said —'

'You exaggerated your experience a little, didn't you, Rose?'

'A bit,' she confessed, 'but how ...?'

'I made some enquiries about you.' He was avoiding her eyes. A hearty laugh resounded from across the room. 'This is a delicate business, Rose. And frankly, all the information I could obtain about you was lack of information. Perhaps this really isn't the job for you.'

'Oh, but, Andrew,' protested Rosie, awkward with his first name but not sure what else to call him, 'I'm sure I would, could, no not for me,' because he was on his way to the bar again, a drinker this one, soon returning with another scotch, and that yachtsman still gawping at her in between wiping the beer off his moustache, and surely Andrew Stephenson wasn't going to have led her on and now ...?

No he wasn't. 'But then,' he said enigmatically, 'there are advantages to your inexperience.'

He was a fisherman all right. Rosie had the feeling he was reeling her in now as, suddenly decisive, he took a photo from his pocket and set it before her on a fake-veneer table. 'Here's the job. This chappy's Bill Jones. He's the managing director of a company called Streetclean. This Thursday he'll be staying at the Centre Hotel and trying to make a few new friends on Mersey City

Council. The meeting to discuss privatization is next week, you see.'

'Mm hm?' said Rosie, trying to get her brain working through the alcohol. It was one of those passport-sized photos you got in station booths: a glimpse of dark jacket and stripy tie beneath a face that looked to be late graduating to shaving and ought to be called Tristan or Julian Something instead of Bill Jones. Younger than me, thought Rosie. Managing director.

'What I want you to do,' said the cultured tones across the table, 'is to watch and follow him. If he makes contact with any of the people in here,' placing a packet of photographs on top of the image of Bill Jones, 'you're to make a full written report of what goes on. If anything is passed from one to the other you're to take a picture if possible. With me?'

'It's all a bit cloak-and-dagger,' said Rosie, full of fear and doubts and alcohol drunk too quickly. 'If you know somebody's paying somebody off, why don't you just tell the boss? Or the bizzies? — the police,' she explained to his questioning eyes.

'The boss might be one of the somebodies. And the, er, the police would need evidence. Evidence is what you're going to provide, Rose.'

'I'm not a dab hand with a camera,' she said, wishing he wouldn't keep calling her Rose. 'I mean, if they were to meet somewhere dark ...'

'Just do your best,' he replied. Him and his condescending smile. 'And as for your terms ...'

'Twenty pounds a day,' just stopping herself from saying 'dollars'. 'Plus expenses, of course.'

'Of course. There's a small advance tucked in with the photographs. I'll telephone you on Wednesday night to make sure you're all set. And now I'm afraid,' checking the digital watch at his wrist that looked like it doubled as a personal computer, 'I should already be elsewhere. If you'll excuse me ...'

'But where do I get in touch?'

'You don't. I'll contact you,' said Andrew Stephenson, and he was standing over her, and there must be a

23

thousand and one questions she should have asked but here he was shaking her hand with his soft, surprisingly damp grip and saying, 'All the best,' and there he was, gone: most of his last scotch untouched.

Rosie drained her vodka. Sneaking a look inside the packet of photographs she glimpsed a brown gleam of tenners, four or five of them. A small advance. She tucked the money into her handbag.

On an impulse she changed course on her way out and went over to the yachtsman with the cigar and the fixed stare. Little globules of beer hung from his moustache. 'Better luck next time. With the fishing,' she said to him, treating herself to a quick glance at his astonishment before turning for the door.

Her exit was only slightly marred by a glancing blow to the temple from an oak beam as she turned, but it was worth it for the way he dropped his cigar. Once she was recovering from her slight dizziness at the wheel of the Mini, and the engine had deigned to respond to her twist of the ignition key, she permitted herself a rub at her sore head and a sigh of relief. 'Fishy business,' she said out loud, shaking her head to try and swish vodka out of her brain. Some bureaucrat coughing up fifty quid or so of his own money? To get flimsy evidence of corruption from a novice private detective?

'And you're the minnow, Rosie. The little sprat. Still, it's a job,' she said to her image in the windscreen, pale among the dead flies illuminated by streetlights. She winked to herself as she put the car into gear.

'How did it go?' asked Jerry as she came in. He was smiling cheerfully up at her from the floor, reading an Agatha Christie.

'Fine,' said Rosie. 'I'll just pop up and see how the kids are.'

'I'm afraid that Bob, you see, the game of knock-out whist, he —'

'Lost,' said Rosie, already halfway up the stairs, trying to think what game Andrew Stephenson might be playing with her that he would feel he had to win.

Chapter Five

'So I read in the *Echo*,' said Mike Bracewell's cheerful voice on the answering machine, 'that you've gone into the inquiry business. Maybe I could put some bread-and-butter work your way. Or maybe you could just turn it down over lunch and I could charge it to expenses nonetheless. Either way I'll be in my old haunt at half-past twelve.'

Success breeds success: another motto for Rosie. Well, why not look at it that way? Even though his call, coming the day after her vodkas in the Atlantic Crossing, was just a happy accident? Mike was the solicitor she'd temped for, a few summers ago. He was the only one of her ex-husband's old schoolfriends who'd made good; and the only one who'd not assumed, when their separation became common knowledge, that it was either all her fault or that she was now sexually available. Rosie concluded it would only be fair to let him treat her to lunch.

Besides, hearing his voice made her feel better that morning. Preceding him on the machine had been another message from — she assumed — the underwear-researcher. This time, though, he'd gone underwater, or at any rate that was what his breathing reminded her of: the soundtrack for a Jacques Cousteau film about the habits of divers and dolphins. She listened right through to the end and almost managed a smile when he sounded as if he'd drowned. Then he spoiled it all by letting out a long deep sigh, very much alive, before hanging up.

And earlier, in the queue in Khan's shop for playing cards to replace the ones Bob had torn up after last night's game, her spirits had been depressed by meeting Edie from next door but one. This was unusual. Edie had had seven children, three husbands and two operations on her womb. She could generally be relied on to declare that the world was getting better all the time, now that all her children, husbands and operations were out of the way. Rosie, brooding on Andrew Stephenson, asked her: 'Is the world getting more corrupt, d'you think, Edie?'

'Yeh, it is,' Edie unexpectedly replied.

'You reckon?'

'It's this stuff, isn't it?' said Edie, rubbing a dirty pound note between thumb and forefinger. 'It's what everyone thinks they want. Oh, and people who haven't got enough should have more, but they shouldn't let it rule their lives. And them with more money than sense: they still want more of the stuff.'

'I never knew you felt like that.'

'Not sure if I do,' said Edie with a sudden smile. 'It's just, like, our Karen's back at my place with her two 'cause she didn't pay the rent to the Corpie and her feller gave her a black eye for it. Ask me another day, eh?'

Still, by lunchtime the sun had come out to brighten the cold October day, and when Rosie found a parking meter in town that wouldn't accept her money she thought maybe things were looking up. DEAR WARDEN, METER JAMMED, she wrote happily on the note she tucked under the wipers, and walked up the hill between the tall buildings of the commercial district. She half-expected to see the staring yachtsman from the night before; he and his smart islander friends probably commuted here every weekday and looked down from their pseudo-marble offices on people like her who were just passing by.

In the downstairs café that called itself a bistro she felt on equally foreign ground. She peered anxiously for Mike's balding head among the clatter of la-di-da accents and plates bearing food fit for rabbits or the trendy middle-classes.

He waved to her from a window table. 'You're looking even younger if anything,' he said through a mouthful of quiche lorraine as she settled herself down.

'You need a hair transplant,' said Rosie, wanting to

look at the world as it was. His hand went up instinctively to comb a few brown hairs across his baldness and she smiled.

And really she wanted to ask him what he thought about the trends in corruption but it had been a long time so they talked about less important things — like mutual friends and how they felt about their lives. 'I wonder where I belong,' said Rosie, feeling some true confessions coming on. 'I mean, here's me, brought up in Norris Green in a council house and all that. But I don't belong there any more. All 'cause my da was a socialist who turned into a foreman and my mam made me learn shorthand and typing and then I married a salesman.'

'Still selling, is he?'

'Still a salesman,' said Rosie precisely. 'Aren't you in touch?'

'Not since he told me his wife's black eyes were his own business.'

'I'm sorry ...'

'And as for you,' he said regardless, 'now that you're in business for yourself ...'

'But I don't belong here either,' she said, pushing away her plate of carrot and kidney bean salad that had seemed a good idea at the time. 'Not like you do. Not like all these do. So what's this bread-and-butter work you're going to put my way?'

Mike offered her a cigarette. No thanks I've given them up, she said secretly, accepting one. 'Process serving,' he said. 'It's what most of you high-flying detectives do: process serving. In between arranging divorces and solving murders and uncovering corruption in high places, of course.'

'Of course.'

'Writs and notices to quit and nice friendly bits of paper like that,' Mike explained, watching her for a reaction. 'You serve them on people who don't seem to keep the same hours as postmen. I've a couple you could do straight away.'

'I'll give it a whirl,' said Rosie, noticing her hand was shaking as she flicked ash off her cigarette. There was a

27

flat fee for the job and advice from Mike to charge a tenner an hour for her regular services. Mm, and that explained the size of Andrew Stephenson's advance perhaps and she tried belatedly to find out Mike's views on trends in corruption but he didn't want to be drawn:

'Stolen cars and petty larceny and wives suing husbands for maintenance: that's my field. I leave the big crimes — you know, bribery, murder, conveyancing — to the senior partners. On a big case, are you?'

'The biggest,' said Rosie, her hand still shaking. Was this what the rest of her life was going to be like? Serving writs and jokily lying to people and pretending to be proud she was her own boss? Just another way of going round and round and round?

Chapter Six

Still, it might turn out at this rate to earn her some kind of a living, and some kind of a living was the best Rosie thought she could hope for. But she couldn't do it all on her own. All through collecting the papers at Mike's office and smiling grim long-time-no-sees at the secretaries who were still perpetual motion letter-machines, Rosie's mental image of the wrongdoer she had to serve the first writ on grew more and more monstrous. By the time she was gulping in the fresh carbon monoxide of the street again he'd become enormous: a six foot seven prize-fighter, standing bare-chested in a doorway, showing her his tattoos, while a fragment of paper quivered in her puny hand.

She found a phone box. WARNING, said a notice on the door. NEW ELECTRONIC CALL BOXES HAVE BEEN VANDALIZED.

She found a nice old-fashioned call-box and dialled. Waiting impatiently through the purring of the tone she could feel her heart bumping against her spare rib, and a lunchtime kidney bean groaning against grated carrots in her innards. So this was fear. 'Margie?' she said at last to the pips, forgetting to put the money in. 'Margie?'

'DHSS Special Investigations,' said Margie at the other end.

'It's me, it's Rosie,' feeling this was no time for little jokes. 'Look, I've got this appointment with the heavy-weight champion of the world and I wondered if you'd hold my hand?'

'I went out with a boxer once,' said Margie. 'His fists were the only hard thing about him.'

'I'll pick you up in ten minutes.'

Of course, the boxing champion might not be a violent

man at heart. He's probably very kind to stray animals, she said to herself as she scraped up through the gears out of town. Think of yourself as an alley cat and you'll be okay, Rosie.

'So where's the fire?' asked Margie as she bent her gangling frame into the Mini's passenger seat. 'Who's this heavyweight boxer?'

'Well he might not be,' Rosie admitted as her foot slipped off the clutch and she scrunched the gears again. On their way up to the North end of town she explained apologetically what the job was but how it was deeply moral really getting men to cough up maintenance to their deserted wives and Margie didn't seem to mind — if silence and running her hand through her curls was not minding. 'Thanks, Margie,' said Rosie.

Tony Asu, the well-built man who was kind to stray animals, lived in Mason Row, which showed a nice friendly barracks-like face to the approaching world. Rosie parked the car by a line of new trees, each sapling encased in its own little post-and-wire fence against the dogs and vandals. Mason Row itself didn't need a fence round it: it was built like a wall, a four-storey wall of flats flanking two other walls called Mason View and Mason Place. In the centre stood a sculpture of children's play equipment: a pit, climbing bars. No children played there. Instead they dodged in and out of the buildings, pursued by a pack of dogs, or kicked a football against a gable wall marked NO BALL GAMES ALLOWED.

'Smashing little area,' said Margie as they stepped into a stairwell that smelt of stale urine. 'Can't understand people buying their own homes, looking at nice rented places like these.'

Rosie's shoes clattered loudly on the concrete steps. The bare brick walls of the staircase were scrawled with names and LIVERPOOL FC and pictures of sex organs and DENNIS KELLY IS INNOCENT and NO POPERY. The two women clanged along the third-floor landing, ducking a line of washing, and Rosie knocked on the door of 23C that would have been half-glazed if the glass hadn't been replaced by a piece of cracked hardboard streaked with maroon paint. A pale indeterminate face peered briefly round drawn curtains. The door opened, hooked on the security chain, and a girl of seven or eight peeped out. 'Yeh?'

'Mr Asu. I've come to see Mr Asu.'

The door banged shut. A dog barked. Rosie joined Margie at the balcony rail. 'You can see,' said Margie, 'what the architect had in mind, can't you? I bet it looked nice as little wooden blocks on snooker-table grass.'

Rosie nodded, wishing she hadn't given up smoking and that it was just wooden blocks on snooker-table grass.

'Yeh? What is it?'

A woman in curlers. Through the crack allowed by the chain Rosie glimpsed a tired face above a pink housecoat. 'I've come to see Mr Asu,' said Rosie with feigned determination.

'Never heard of him.'

The woman was closing the door. Rosie to her own surprise wedged her foot in the opening. 'I'm not from the Assistance. Nor from the Education neither,' she said, not liking the taste of the words in her mouth. 'I just want to see Mr Asu.'

The woman went away. Faint voices. Rosie took the writ out of her bag; Margie moved up behind her. The chain was taken off, and a man with light black skin stood in the doorway, just buttoning a white shirt. He was small and thin and didn't look like he was much into boxing. 'Mr Asu?' Rosie asked doubtfully.

'What can I do for you, girls?' he said with warm distrust.

'You can have a read of this,' said Rosie, thrusting the writ into his hand and turning to go.

'Hang on a bit, queen.'

His hand rested on Rosie's arm. He read through the notice. After a few moments he released his grip and a mysterious fluttering in her neck stopped fluttering. 'After money again, is she? Fuck that. Fuck her.' He tore the writ into two, four, eight pieces, and stepping past Rosie he scattered the fragments over the edge of the balcony.

'Nice job you've got,' he said as he went back into the flat and slammed the door.

Neither of them said anything as they went back to the car. Rosie leant on the bonnet; rust creaked beneath her. She looked out across the city. In the sunlight the river looked almost blue. In the middle distance she could just make out the Liver birds, stuck on the top of their building, forever wanting to fly away. 'Maybe this isn't the job for me,' said Rosie.

Margie gave her an awkward hug. 'I might be able to get you on this course for computer operators. Starts next week.'

Rosie shook her head and got into the car. 'I think we'll skip the other writ,' she said quietly, and turned down Margie's offer of a cup of tea. 'But look, Margie, the fee for this job was —'

'Don't be daft,' said Margie. 'Just remember me in your will, all right?'

All Rosie wanted to do was get home and do something about her new life quickly — like, cancel it. But somehow it had got round to four o'clock and although Carol was at a friend's for tea Bob was already home, brooding over knock-out whist and watching Play School. 'You're too old for that,' said Rosie, switching it off. 'And I just want to make a phone call, love.'

Bob didn't move.

'A private phone call.'

He got up sulkily and went to the door.

'By the way,' she said to his hunched back, 'I got some new playing cards. But if you tear them up again it's coming out of your pocket money.'

Bob turned to her fiercely. 'I'm never going to play with Jerry again. He cheats!'

'Oh, but I'm sure,' began Rosie but he was already gone and up the stairs and she wanted to go after him but first there were things to do. *Nice job you've got*. Mr Asu had done her a favour really: he'd made her decision for her. She began rehearsing her resignation speech to Andrew Stephenson: 'Rose Monaghan here. I'm most terribly sorry, but ...'

She called up Mersey City Council and asked, very clearly she thought, for Mr Andrew Stephenson, but they put her through to Mr Ronald Stephenson in Environmental Health. He was very friendly and said he'd put her back to the switchboard and the line went blank for three minutes and she dialled again and her resolve to pack it all in was already weakening. 'I want Mr Andrew Stephenson,' she explained patiently. 'He's in, er, refuse.'

So the woman said it must be Cleansing she wanted and Rosie didn't challenge that even though she'd had a bath that morning, but the line was engaged and when she finally got through the man was sure he could help her and was it a complaint? If he could just have her name and address? 'No,' said Rosie, getting a bit flustered. 'I want Mr Andrew Stephenson. He's in the administration of sh, er, refuse.'

Ah, administration, could she hold the line for a moment? And there were clicks and whirrs from outer space on the line and was it her imagination that one of the clicks said 'Coward' to her and why was she giving up on private detection so easily?

Administration had never heard of Andrew Stephenson and they transferred her to Personnel. 'Can you tell me what department Mr Andrew Stephenson works for?' asked Rosie, a bit grumpily now, her breathing beginning to sound oddly like the underwater man's. But once Personnel had established it was a personal matter, no, they couldn't divulge that kind of information over the phone, if she'd care to write in perhaps?

'Can you confirm he works for Mersey City?' asked Rosie in desperation. But no, if she'd care to write to them explaining the reasons for her enquiry . . .

'I've changed my mind,' said Rosie, banging down the telephone. 'Again,' she added to the empty air.

She took a deep breath and wondered why the room had gone misty. 'Bob!' she called. 'Bob!'

When she got to his room he was sitting hunched on his bed, trying to pretend not to shake with sobs. 'I used to like Jerry.'

Bob's room was misty and Rosie realized she was

almost crying too. 'Never mind,' she said, sitting beside him, 'let's go and put some nice hamburgers on for tea.'

'I don't even like hamburgers!'

They sat together for a couple of minutes till they could both safely pretend he hadn't said that. Rosie stared vacantly at the poster of THE CHAMPIONS OF EUROPE and told the voice that was still whispering 'Coward' in her inner ear to shut up.

A little later they stood, red-eyed but smiling, together in the kitchen. 'Real meat, you see,' she said to him, taking the mince out of the fridge, 'none of your frozen rubbish,' and she could tell he was feeling better when he failed to insist that he preferred frozen ones. Soon he had the new cards laid out on the dining-table, playing himself at knock-out whist, planning his revenge.

Rosie stood over the cooker and shook her head at herself. In the shimmering air over the frying-pan Andrew Stephenson's condescending smile drifted back to her. She was glad she hadn't resigned from him just yet. He was even beginning to interest her a bit. What, she wondered, thinking back, were the advantages in her inexperience that he'd spoken of? And was it just bureaucratic confusion that she hadn't been able to get through to him? Or was he not what he'd made himself out to be at all?

Chapter Seven

On Wednesday Rosie managed to occupy the daylight hours with none of the things she should have been doing. Instead she cooked three meals in advance for the first time in living memory, all the while composing in her head a guilty list of the tasks she was putting off:

1. Serving the second writ for Mike.
2. Reconnoitring the Centre Hotel.
3. Finding the camera.
4. Deciding what to wear in honour of Bill Jones.
5. Making arrangements for Bob and Carol tomorrow in case the job went on into the evening.
6. Worrying.

By half-past five she'd decided to work backwards through her list, and was getting nicely worried. The sense of panic was just beginning to challenge pride in her cooking for first place in her emotions when the telephone rang. She switched off the TV and, ignoring all resistance, banished the children to the kitchen for their delicious toad-in-the-hole and delectable non-packet mashed potato. It warmed her heart to hear, against the phone's persistent ring, their gratitude for all the effort she'd put in:

'Why can't we have proper sausages? On their own?' asked Bob.

'This potato's got lumps in,' said Carol.

Rosie slid the kitchen door shut on the praise they were so cleverly disguising as protest, and relieved the telephone of its torment.

'All set?' said the smooth tones of her first client in her ear.

'Just about, but —'

'Good,' said Andrew Stephenson. 'I'm afraid I haven't got long.'

Haven't got long what? 'Yesterday I was trying,' Rosie began but he was in brisk form and she didn't know quite what she wanted to say so she let him sweep on:

'Our friend Mr Jones is arriving at Lime Street at 10:30 in the morning. I suggest you pick him up there in case he makes any moves before checking in at the hotel. Got everything you need?'

'Yeh,' said Rosie, who was getting used to the lies of business pretty quickly. 'Which department did you say you worked for?'

'I'm sorry, it's a bad line,' he said. 'I'll be in the café at the Pierhead at 10:30 on Saturday morning. Bring me your report and what photographs you can get developed by then. All right?'

'Eer, yes, but —'

'Fine. See you then,' said Andrew Stephenson, and hung up.

That meant it was really going to happen. It wasn't just a mad fantasy she'd dreamt up over a hot stove. And there wasn't time to stop and think about the bad line that was as clear as silence to Rosie's ear, because she had to hunt for the camera (filed under knickers in the chest of drawers for some inscrutable reason, as she discovered after a half-hour's frantic search and thank God there was still half a film left in it); and find a self-defence aerosol to hide in her handbag (she settled on Johnson's Wax Polish since she rarely got round to actually using it on the furniture); and make arrangements for the kids for tomorrow (Carol would have tea at Marie's and Bob at his new friend Jason's and Jennifer over the road would round them up at seven and let them stay up late just as Rosie always asked her not to do); and decide what to wear (no, the red dress would be too conspicuous, and trousers might be too unrespectable for the Centre Hotel, so yes the grey blouse and the mauve skirt); and deal with the children's stomach-ache (maybe their delicate stomachs just weren't used to real food); and even though Jerry had

36

had another terrible day at the office she needed to talk about herself so she said curtly to his complaints:

'Why don't you look for another job, then?'

'How can I be sure that'd be any better?' Jerry replied mournfully. 'Maybe it's the same everywhere: people afraid to make decisions, hiding behind rules and politicians, quietly fiddling their expenses ...'

'Is it more corrupt than it used to be?' asked Rosie, seizing the opening.

Jerry was able to offer her considerable insight into the issue. 'No,' he said. 'No.' He thought a bit and shook his head. 'No.'

'Mm hm?' Rosie prompted hopefully.

'Mm,' said Jerry.

That seemed to be it on corruption. Still, Rosie had her next question prepared: 'How d'you follow somebody, d'you think?'

'What?'

'I've got to follow this feller tomorrow. I tried it out with two women in the Co-op today but I knew where they lived anyway. So how's it done, d'you think?'

'Well,' said Jerry, stroking his chin to show how carefully he was considering the problem, 'you just — follow them, I suppose. Sometimes you follow them from in front, of course.'

'Sorry?'

'That's what Starsky and Hutch used to do. And Charlie's Angels. Makes sense when you think about it.'

'Mm hm?' said Rosie.

'I mean, you wouldn't think somebody in front of you was actually following you, would you, now?'

'Er, no,' agreed Rosie, sure the logic would come to her later.

Sooner rather than later the conversation veered round to Jerry's day again and mercifully Carol came downstairs complaining of stomach-ache so Rosie, guilty at her relief that her child was in pain, took her upstairs and read to her and pleaded the need for an early night when she came back down.

It was only during the doorstep goodnight kiss that

Rosie remembered her other question. 'Jerry,' she said softly into his ear, 'do you cheat at cards?'

He denied everything. He looked a bit offended, in fact. 'So why did Bob think you were cheating?' she persisted.

'He caught me at it,' Jerry acknowledged ruefully, tucking up his collar against the cold night. 'I was trying to fiddle the cards so he'd win the last game. But he spotted it.'

'But you're,' no, don't call him a bad loser, Rosie, 'you like to win yourself.'

'Oh, I was already winning the series. I just wanted him to feel better. G'night then.'

In bed Rosie stared sadly at the wallpaper overhead that was only waiting for her to close her eyes before it peeled away from the ceiling. Why she asked herself, hadn't she murmured into Jerry's ear, 'I've changed my mind, stay with me tonight,' instead of asking him about the knock-out whist? Why wasn't he here now, tonguing and massaging away her fears that he was lying to her about the cards? Why wasn't she holding him close and humming *Zip-a-dee-doo-dah* quietly to herself, instead of shivering here alone, worrying about whether Andrew Stephenson was lying to her about Mr Jones and corruption in medium places?

Rosie couldn't think of a good reason. She just knew it was the way you were supposed to live your life: to worry about important things, and not enjoy yourself too much in case it got out of hand.

Maybe her Catholic upbringing was to blame.

Never mind, no, look, don't get upset. Jerry doesn't lie to you and Andrew Stephenson's just a job, she told herself, casting her eye again over the clothes and the *A-to-Z* and the aerosol and the camera all laid out for the morning like holiday packing. Everything was ready and she was sure she wouldn't be able to sleep all night for the worrying and the anticipation.

The next moment she was sound asleep.

Later, Rosie dreamed. She dreamt of a creature with two faces, one in the usual place, the other concealed beneath its hair so it could follow people from in front.

The front face was Jerry's; the one at the back was Andrew Stephenson's, and he and she were at opposite ends of this big ocean liner, and he kept shouting at her that he was a bad line but she could hear him perfectly clearly. She marched towards him, handbag swinging — if in doubt — through crowds of people with la-di-da voices. But as soon as she got near he was nowhere to be seen. She looked around in panic, knowing he was out there somewhere, following her from in front, cheating someone at cards.

Rosie woke at 4.00 am and wondered what it all meant and why he was still shouting at her in such a curiously child-like voice.

It was Bob that was shouting for her. I'm never going to make toad-in-the-hole again, she resolved, fumbling wearily for her dressing-gown. 'It's all right, I'm coming,' she said, drawing no comfort from the fact that she hadn't fancied the meal herself. I should suffer myself what I inflict on my children. I should let Jerry cheat me at cards too.

Rosie paused at the doorway, while Bob groaned 'Mum' in his best groaning voice. She knew what she should really do. She should pack all this in, and marry a 95-year-old millionaire with a house in Hertfordshire or Connecticut or maybe both, and live happily ever after, selling off the odd Old Master when she needed the price of a year's meals.

Bob was still groaning. *Mañana* she'd start looking for millionaires. But as for now:

'It's all right,' she said with a deep breath. 'It's all right, love, I'm coming.'

Chapter Eight

Laden with guilt, trying to shake it off her shoulders along with the raindrops, Rosie drank a cup of plastic tea and wondered how she'd ever meet a sugar-daddy with this way of life and watched the Lime Street Station signboard in case it decided to tell her that the train from London Euston was anything other than 30 minutes late.

She'd counted on neither: the guilt, nor the rain. The guilt, inevitably, was to do with the children. Bob had appeared hollow-eyed at breakfast and had dutifully forced down half a slice of dry toast. She'd known he was really sick when he hadn't banged anything against anything for the whole meal. Carol had tried to get in on the act by demanding to stay off school but Rosie, touching the pink flush of health in her daughter's cheeks, had dealt firmly with that.

She'd dithered about Bob, though, until the school-gates, him sitting in the back, pale and silent as a piece of melamine furniture. Then with sudden decisiveness she'd swung the car round and wondered who the hell she could leave him with.

'I want to go to Jason's,' said Bob sullenly.

But she didn't even know Jason's mother, he was such a new friend, so she tried three women she did know but two of them were out and the third was getting ready for a coffee morning with the Young Wives of St Barnabas. 'I want to go to Jason's,' Bob kept repeating.

So finally Rosie presented herself with a pale child and embarrassment to Jason's mother, a big smock-shaped woman in a big woman-shaped smock: 'I'm awful sorry,' said Rosie, 'but I've got to, you know, go for a job sort of thing, d'you think you could, do say if you can't ...?'

Jason's mother could, and Rosie hugged Bob goodbye. She was beginning to see why there weren't more women

40

private detectives in the world. What she needed was a slave: someone to run errands and mind the kids and do all the drudgery — a wife, that was the word she was looking for. Rosie needed a wife.

She wasn't sure what the neighbours would think, though, when they were introduced.

As for the rain, that stole up on her really sneakily. When she'd left the house just after ten, the sun had smiled benevolently down out of a cold, cloudless sky, like a kind father; by the time she got to the station it — just like a man — was nowhere to be found. Instead rain had begun to patter like tiny feet on the Mini's roof.

Rosie's preparations hadn't included the possibility of rain. A search of the boot — accompanied by a fiercer, drenching downpour — had revealed a plastic mac of some antiquity and no rain-hat. So now, the thirty minutes' delay duly elapsed and the train snaking in, she stood feeling soggy and nervous next to a man with a notice saying H WILSON: BEATLE MUSEUM, hardly able to hear herself worry for the din of people and trains and machines that were rebuilding the station so that her city might wear a more elegant face to the approaching world.

She'd never realized so many people came to Liverpool from the capital city. Could they all be company liquidators and experts on urban deprivation and football spies? Who else might they be? She was finding it hard to keep her footing against the stream of people, when Bill Jones suddenly materialized from under someone's armpit less than five yards away. He was unexpectedly small and seemed a bit lost and persisted, in the flesh, in his resemblance to a Julian or a Tristan rather than a Bill. His pair of innocent blue eyes scanned the crowd. Rosie felt herself blushing as his gaze seemed to rest on her for a moment. Then she was hurrying after the dark blue suit, rolled umbrella and smart brown leather suitcase, sorry that she'd never know if the ex-Prime Minister really was visiting the Beatle Museum, or just a namesake.

She'd gambled on parking outside the Centre Hotel, just round the corner from the station, and that indeed was where the suit and suitcase propelled their bearer under the now un-rolled umbrella. Rosie eased off her scruffy mac at the swing doors of the hotel and tried to make it look half-way presentable over her arm. As her quarry checked in and disappeared into the lift, she settled damply into a chair that seemed to let her body sink into it for ever. She smiled coolly at the receptionist and took a copy of *Cosmopolitan* out of her bag.

A minute later a smart woman in a fur-lined jacket sat beside her and took a *Cosmopolitan* out of her bag too. Rosie gave herself a pat on the back for melting so well into the scenery.

What with her trial run at following people from the Co-op two days before, and Jerry's helpful suggestions on the topic, she felt, when Bill Jones went out and strolled down into the city centre, practised and confident. And yes, it was easy enough. He went to Boots and bought himself a cheap packet of razors; in Smith's he spent five minutes at the Crime and Thriller rack and invested in another fictional exposé of the CIA; she watched him calmly from War and Horror. On the way back up the hill, her hair pasted down to the sides of her head with the rain, she even successfully experimented with following him from in front. She started, however, to get a crick in her neck from the half-turning round, and dropped behind him again.

Then, feeling blasé, she almost lost him outside the hotel. Instead of going in through the swing doors he got straight into a white Cortina that said GODFREY DAVIS in the back window. With her car facing the other way Rosie had to run for it, then brave a taxi-driver's vivid references to sexual activity as she turned the Mini round in the narrow street.

Somehow she'd assumed it would be easier to follow him in the car than on foot. It was harder. He drove aggressively, nipping in and out of lanes, overtaking in the narrowest of spaces, seeming to enjoy the chorus of horns and expletives that followed him. Rosie peered anxiously through the rain swirling over the windscreen and drove across two red lights with her heart stuck in her throat somewhere en route for her mouth. It was like falling in love, she decided, pressing on the horn before remembering it didn't work as two foolhardy pedestrians stepped out almost in front of her. Like falling in love: frightening and exciting at the same time — but mainly frightening.

Soon the main road was scudding out through the suburbs — tall council flats to one side, little semis with gardens to the other — and Rosie realized where they were heading. Towards Mersey City, one of those places that didn't really exist except in the bureaucratic mind; like its neighbour Knowsley, it was really a straggle of what had once been villages, now merging indistinguishably into one another in a blur of houses and closed-down factories and failed new towns. She kept her eyes on the white Cortina and her foot planted firmly on the accelerator, praying that the car's fragile engine would hold up against the strain.

In the centre of the biggest village, that nowadays called itself a town, he took the signs for the multi-storey car-park. Rosie waited at the entrance for another car to come between them before following him into the concrete beehive. She found a space on the level below him, ready for the departure, and with a clack of heels hurried across to the EXIT: PEDE TR ANS sign. The immaculate brown hair of the pedetran she was after was just bobbing out of sight down the stairwell, and she slowed to a walk.

Emerging into the shopping centre, twenty yards behind her quarry, she was just complimenting herself on her self-evident natural ability at this kind of thing when an old man lurched off a plank seat and began burbling incomprehensibly at her. Bill Jones disappeared round a corner as she fumbled in her handbag for her purse. 'Try the Sally Army,' she said finally, brushing off the old man's importuning hand, pushing past him.

When she got to the corner Bill Jones was gone. She looked for him in boutiques, in tobacconists, in shoe shops, in Woolworth's, and even, with mounting panic, in the record shop that was blaring out rock music. Finally she tracked him down in the pub at the end of the street; a modern plastic place with modern plastic seats, modern plastic tables and modern plastic customers. Rosie ordered an orange juice, guaranteed to contain fifty per cent modern plastic ingredients, and looked around in the murk. Bill Jones was at a corner table, having a half of modern plastic bitter with a gaunt-faced man. Rosie sat in shadow by the door and surreptitiously checked her packet of photographs. The gaunt man didn't seem to be among them, as far as she could tell in the sickly orange light.

Still, there was no harm in making sure. She felt in her handbag for the Olympus Trip: the camera had been Graham's last gift to her before he'd decided she was 'boring, in and out of bed' and had announced this to the street one drunken midnight. Like Graham in and out of bed, the camera worked automatically. She'd already imagined what she'd do. She'd casually lift it in one smooth movement and press it to her eye and click the shutter and casually lower it into her bag in one smooth movement and nobody'd be any the wiser. That, at any rate, was the theory.

The practice went fine — till she had to click the shutter. The frigging thing wouldn't work. She lowered it into her handbag and looked around. Nobody seemed to have noticed. She cursed quietly. The frigging thing wouldn't work if the light wasn't good enough. Like Graham again, she thought bitterly: he could only get it up with the bedside lamp blaring in her face.

She fumbled with the out-of-sight camera, setting it manually on some arbitrary numbers and wishing she'd stuck out the course of night-classes in photography she'd once started. She took a deep swig of Britvic orange and repeated the operation: lift, look, click — it worked! — lower, wind on, look around. She sighed with relief.

'Aren't you gonna take one of me, queen?' said a voice to her left.

The voice had a big smile to go with it, and big broad shoulders, and big hands grasping a tiny pint of bitter. 'Sure,' said Rosie, jumping back into her skin. She took out the camera and snapped him. 'Have you got a bit of paper?'

'Yeh,' said the man, squeezing his big hands into the little pockets of his jeans, pulling out an old giro envelope. 'What for?'

'Write down your name and address and you could win a major prize.'

'Straight up?' said the man, shaping the letters laboriously on the paper with a stubby pencil.

Bill Jones was on his way out and Rosie got up to follow him. 'A weekend for two in Chipping Sodbury,' she said, dropping the man's envelope into her bag and hurrying out before he could ask her about the second prize.

When she emerged into the rain, Bill Jones was already stepping into a doorway a few yards down. It was one of those sit-down hamburger restaurants where the length of the menu tries to hide the fact that you can have burgers, burgers or burgers. 'Small cheeseburger, no chips,' Rosie said to the waitress in the stars-and-stripes uniform. Over by the window Bill Jones shook hands with a shabby man in his sixties, she'd guess, and sat opposite him. She recognized the lunch guest — round and ruddy-cheeked, bushy grey eyebrows — one of the Andrew Stephenson portrait gallery. And also, curiously like someone else she knew: who did he remind her of? And how was she going to get a picture this time? Plus, did she have time for the pee she'd been craving for the last half-hour?

In the Ladies Rosie reset the camera to automatic and tried to stop herself from worrying. After all, it wasn't illegal, was it? — No, Rosie, just immoral. Come on, which of the deadly sins is this? — Must be one of them or you wouldn't be shaking like a girl in the queue for the confessional.

She tried to wash away the fear by splashing water over her face but it didn't do the trick and as it turned out there was only an electric hand-dryer. She bent awkwardly till her face was under the nozzle and got a quick blast of hot wind. Just then another woman came in and Rosie smiled an upside-down smile and decided not to bother trying to be witty for once.

She ate the cheeseburger fast and paid the bill while ordering a coffee. She kept glancing nervously around her, worrying. It felt as if everyone in the restaurant was looking at her — everyone except Bill Jones and his lunch-partner, who were deep in conversation. How could she possibly take a picture? Why hadn't Andrew Stephenson supplied her with a camera disguised as a brooch or a rollerball pen

45

or something? Didn't he watch James Bond films?

Inspiration struck her as she lifted her coffee cup to her lips. Leaving it undrunk, she draped her mac around her and went out into the precinct. There were seven or eight frames left on the film: good, good. Standing beside the window of the restaurant, she took a deep breath. Casual, Rosie, casual: Try to look arty for once.

One more breath, and she began to take pictures in a sweep around her. I was just trying to capture a typical street scene, Your Honour. Click: stunted tree with overflowing litter bin. Click: back view of two young mohicans. Click: doorway of restaurant. Click: Bill Jones and the man with the eyebrows. Click: the old drunk again with his arm outstretched towards her ...

'Is it something to do with my face?'

But the drunk wouldn't stop burbling and his hand was on her arm and she was beginning to attract attention. She retreated backwards into a shop doorway; the drunk followed. 'Okay,' she said, proffering ten pence. 'Be sure not to spend it on a cup of tea, now.'

The lunch across the street didn't last much longer. Just as the two men got up — and who did the older man remind her of? — there was some kind of argument, with Bill Jones offering an envelope, the man with the eyebrows reluctantly accepting it, Rosie going Click! and looking guiltily around her. Then Bill Jones was coming out alone and the rain was starting up again and Rosie hurried after him.

Back at the multi-storey she drove out first, then let the white Cortina go by. Soon they were heading back towards Liverpool and she was wishing she'd decided to give up giving up cigarettes. She imagined inhaling one now; the smoke, pausing briefly to coat her lungs before coursing along her bloodstream and unfastening all the knots her muscles were tangled up in.

On a stretch of open road between traffic lights she decided it was time to try following from in front in the car. So she eased out past the Cortina and tried to pretend to herself that the speedometer wasn't really registering that many miles per hour. Just as she pulled back across to the inside lane, the car lurched. She swerved for a moment. Bump, bump, bump went the nearside tyre. She slowed down and the white Cortina trailed spray past her.

'Oh, great,' said Rosie out loud.

Of course the rain had just come on heavier as she got out of the car. I've got a flat tyre, she remarked to herself with incredible diagnostic skill, as she wrestled with her plastic mac. As she kicked the offending wheel and walked wearily back to the boot, she saw that a car had stopped up ahead and was reversing. So some knight in shining armour had stopped to rescue her? So, no, she wasn't averse to that.

But it was a white car. Surely it couldn't be ...

It was a white Cortina with GODFREY DAVIS printed on the back window. Rosie bent to get the tools and the spare tyre out of the boot. Please, God: just a little earthquake, please ...

Her prayers went unanswered. Well, what could she expect? Not having gone to church since she was old enough to know worse?

'You don't want to get your hands dirty with all that,' said the surprisingly cockney voice of Bill Jones. 'I'll do it, love.'

I'm following you and you're not supposed to know what I look like so please go away, said Rosie's anguished voice on some other planet. 'Really, I'll be fine,' she said helplessly as he took the tools out of her hand and began to lever off the hub-cap. 'You'll get your suit ...'

'Tell you what. Why don't you hold the brolly?'

'It's very kind of you,' said Rosie, holding the brolly. 'But perhaps you've got an appointment ...?'

'Loads o' time,' he said cheerfully. 'I'm Bill, by the way.'

Oh really? 'Veronica,' said Rosie. 'Terrible weather, isn't it?'

Bill Jones was one of those men who believed in talking while he changed the tyres of damsels-in-distress. So he expected her friends called her Ronnie and he was just up from the smoke on a bit of business and he thought the humour of Liverpool people was a-may-zin and Rosie said 'Yeh?' and 'Really?' in her humorous Liverpool way.

47

Resolutely avoiding his eyes, she wondered when she was going to wake to the view of the ceiling that needed decorating, to the knowledge that it was all just a silly little nightmare.

She didn't wake up. As she slept on, he'd finished changing the wheel and she was laying a cunning trap for herself by saying, 'If only I could repay you in some way ...'

'Tell you what,' he said, straightening up. She followed him round to the boot: 'I'm free tonight,' he said. 'How about a drink?'

Well, okay, maybe she was awake, but how about the ground swallowing her up? Was that so much to ask, God? 'I'd love to ...'

'Great.'

'... but it's the kids, you see,' as his glance flicked down to the bare third finger of her left hand. 'I doubt if I could get anyone to mind them.'

'Maybe I could call you and see?'

'Er, no,' said Rosie unnecessarily loudly, 'I'm not on the phone y'see.'

'Give me a buzz then, eh? If you're free. Bill Jones at the Centre Hotel. Bye for now, Ronnie.'

'Wha'? Oh yeh, and thanks a lot.'

Ronnie, no, Rosie sat in the driving seat and clutched the steering wheel till her knuckles gleamed yellow but it didn't stop her shaking. The white Cortina drove off with a hoot and a wave. She couldn't bring herself to turn the ignition. How could she possibly follow him any more? 'Veronica'?

To pass the time till her muscles unfroze, she said over and over to herself a five-letter word for what men like to kick around. 'Balls,' said Rosie. 'Balls, balls, balls ...'

Still, it had been a nice career while it lasted. She unpeeled her fingers from the steering wheel and turned the key. 'It's all your fault,' she said to the car angrily, banging the dashboard with her fist. 'D'you hear me?'

The car didn't reply. It ticked over, in mild reproof. 'All right, I'm sorry, take me to the nearest tobacconist,' she said, and it drove her gently away.

Chapter Nine

'I'm no good at it,' Rosie said glumly to Margie the next day.

'Give it up for Lent.'

'That's months away.'

'Just what I mean,' said Margie. 'Give yourself time.'

'The trouble is,' Rosie admitted, 'I like it. I like being a private detective. Well, making out I'm one. I mean, it's scary and I don't know how to do it but it's, well it's just, you know, me against the world sort of thing.' Then, reflecting on torn-up writs and knights in shining Cortinas: 'But the world's winning.'

'Give it up for Lent,' said Margie firmly. 'Not before.'

That was the trouble with Margie; optimism. Rosie had rung her two hours before, flustered by the breakdown of the twin-tub that was almost as old as her and hadn't worn so well. 'Come and use my automatic,' Margie had said. On arrival Rosie had told her all about going to collect Bob straight from her 'assignment' in a haze of guilt and cigarette smoke and him having recovered perfectly and giving her hell all night when she'd needed some peace and quiet. 'Just his way of showing affection, I expect,' Margie had commented coolly.

Now Rosie had told her the whole story of the 'assignment' — following Bill Jones from in front and the photographs and the flat tyre — and what did her closest friend say to her? 'Give it up for Lent,' she said. 'Not before.'

'Thanks Margie. Sorry about me.'

Rosie loaded her damp washing into the big black laundry bag and drove home to hang it out. She stopped just short of her house, though, at the sight of two tree trunks in a pair of trousers protruding from under a seedy

Jaguar. She wound down the window and asked Billy if he could fix the flat tyre in the boot for her.

When he emerged and she repeated the question she could see from the way he wiped his hands on his overalls that she was in for a big production. 'You want to change this car,' he said, running his expert hand over the bluish rust through which little flecks of the Mini's original paintwork were occasionally visible.

Rosie got out to look at what he was looking at so she could pretend not to have noticed it before. 'Yeh,' she said, shaking her head sadly. 'But I can't really afford to run it, let alone change it. Just fix the wheel, will you, Billy?'

He put his arm round her and she knew a deal was in the offing. The combined smell of grease and under-arm was deadly, but somehow she smiled sweetly and held her breath as he said in his most worldly-wise tones:

'Here's what we do, Rosie. A feller I know drops your heap of rust into a dock for a tenner. Then I get a mate to certify it was in A-1 condition. You pick up the insurance, and I get you a nice little set of wheels through the trade, with enough cash left in your hand to pay your new premium and buy me a pint as well. How does that sound?'

'I'll think about it,' said Rosie, extracting herself from his pungent embrace, exhaling with relief. 'D'you think the world's getting more corrupt, Billy?'

'Nah. It's always been the same.'

No it hasn't, said Rosie silently to the wall as she struggled later with her report to Andrew Stephenson:

Mr Jones lunched with a man in his sixties of shabby but respectable appearance with big grey eyebrows who was included in the photographs you supplied ...

No, time was when you could have put your shirt on shabbily respectable old men with bushy eyebrows not being on the make. Or maybe it was just that Bill Jones's lunch-partner had reminded her — now she remembered — of her dad. Rosie's dad had never fiddled anyone in his life. He'd even regarded hire purchase as a complicated fraud perpetrated on honest working people by banks and, through some mechanism she'd never understood, absentee landlords. 'If you can't put the cash down,' he used to say in his pithy way, before cancer of the bladder got him three months after he'd retired, 'if you can't put the cash down, don't pick the thing up.'

He certainly wouldn't have approved of serving writs and following people for fifty quid. 'Sorry, Dad,' said Rosie, wrestling with the trickiest bit of her report:

> ... when unfortunately my car got a flat tyre and Mr Jones, seeing my distress, stopped and offered his assistance. I could not see any way in which I could reasonably refuse ...

She finally finished it at two in the morning. Her head seemed only momentarily to have liaised with the pillow when Bob was sitting on the edge of the bed fully-dressed and it was Saturday morning. 'Come on, Mum, eight o'clock,' said Bob, as if that was something to celebrate.

Saturday. Graham day, Andrew Stephenson day. 'Today's cancelled,' she said to Bob but he wasn't having any:

'We're going to the safari park,' he said excitedly.

'Throw your father to the lions if you get the chance,' said Rosie.

She immediately regretted it. She didn't want to poison him against Graham. The children should grow up in an environment where they knew their parents to be friends who had simply gone their separate ways.

At least, that was what Graham said. And she did need the maintenance.

But it was always so bloody complicated, Graham's Saturday. He wouldn't collect the children from her house, their old house, not wanting to see the neighbours who might remember him for his drunken midnight monologues. Nor would he let her deliver them to his present home. He didn't want his present and former wives to get together and talk about him (or at least, that was Rosie's theory). So her Mini and his this-year's-model had to rendezvous in Newsham Park, with Bob running out ꝫeagerly to meet his father, and Carol sitting in the back saying, as she did this morning, 'Can't I stay with you today?'

'I've got to meet a man,' said Rosie sadly, grateful she had a real excuse today. 'About a job. Sorry, love.'

Carol narrowed her eyes as Graham came to the window waving a bit of paper. 'Sorry about the maintenance,' he said. 'Here you go.'

Rosie stuffed the cheque in her bag and waited for Carol to spend her statutory five minutes getting out of the car. 'Saw Mike the other day,' she told her ex-husband to pass the time. 'He was asking about you.'

'I wondered when you two would get together.'

'What d'you mean by that?'

Graham bent his face close to hers as Carol slammed the car door grumpily. 'He always fancied you.'

She frowned at his aftershave. 'Get away,' she said, 'he was the only one of your friends who still spoke to me and never actually ...'

'Exactly. That's how I knew he really fancied you. Because he didn't do anything about it. See you at five, eh?'

Rosie pulled away quickly from the ritual kiss and started the car. She didn't have to listen to his nonsense any more. She gave Bob a last wave and Carol a blown kiss as she drove off, with a screech of the tyres to match the silent screech in her brain.

Chapter Ten

She was nervous, that was all. That was why she'd felt impatient with Bob and angry with Graham. That was why she'd got to the Pierhead so ridiculously early, with the newly-printed photos burning a hole in her bag because she hadn't dared to look at them yet. That was why she was shivering, leaning on the rail watching nothing bob up and down on the Mersey: nervousness. It wasn't cold, after all.

Oh yes it is, said the wind whipping up into her face off the river.

So she pulled on her woollen gloves, the ones with the unmended holes left over from last winter that almost made them fashionably fingerless, and forced herself to look at the pictures. She set aside for later the miracles of light, colour and composition that recorded the family's caravan holiday in Wales. Two of the others were blank but for a vague orange glow; somewhere in that darkness Bill Jones and the gaunt man and the big one who thought he was in line for a major prize were hiding from her.

But the rest of the prints were clear enough; including the drunk with the outstretched hand, looking strangely sad, and the stunted tree in the shopping precinct, looking strangely beautiful. And yes, the two vital ones were there: eyebrows, frowning; then eyebrows receiving envelope from Bill Jones, frowning again.

And yes, the shabby man that belonged to the eyebrows did look like her Dad, or at least how her Dad might have looked if her Mum hadn't been around to force him to smarten up occasionally: well-meaning, blinking, uncertain. Along the rail from her now a young father held his blue-coated kid up to look at the water and

53

yes, Rosie remembered coming here with her Dad when she was only that high and that wrapped up against the wind. They'd have just done the round trip along the docks (derelict and crumbling now, or being turned into museums); they'd have descended from the overhead railway (long since gone, where only cars rushed by now); then her Dad would be pointing and telling her about all the boats (where now there was only blue-grey water and the chugging ferry).

No point in getting sentimental about it, though. After all, the same Dad had locked her out at 1.00 am at the age of sixteen, blisslessly unaware that her real sexual education was happening in the afternoons round at Rory McTigue's; the same Dad had invested his main hopes for the family's future not in Rosie but in her brother Paddy, who'd been out of jail a year now and was earning a steady living receiving stolen goods down the South End. Maybe the interest in crime was in the genes somewhere?

No point in getting sentimental about it, then. But she was; about her Dad, and therefore about the man with the eyebrows. Now, as she watched Andrew Stephenson get out of his silver-grey Volvo a hundred yards away she felt a flush of irrational distrust towards him, her client; because he'd represented himself as Mister Clean and the man like her Dad as Mister Dirty Hands.

Silly. She told herself that, as she let Mister Clean wait for her this time, in the grotty Pierhead café. Silly. This was just a business arrangement. Not something to let your feelings get tangled up in. Silly.

Inside the café she nodded to Andrew Stephenson's almost imperceptible twitch of greeting, and insisted with a wave of her hand on buying her own plastic beaker of coffee before joining him at the table by the window. She looked out at the landing stage. A party of Japanese tourists was waiting to board the ferry, cameras at their shoulders, being confusedly guided by a drunken old man who was, Rosie guessed from the waving of his arms, telling them how marvellous it all used to be and the price of a cup of tea these days.

'Nice day for it,' she said finally, placing her brown

envelope with the report and the photos in it on the stained formica table. 'Here you go.'

He wanted to know how it had gone. The problems. 'It's all in my report.'

'Tell me about it.'

She avoided his condescending eyes. Down below, the tourists had boarded the ferry now. The drunken old man was still there, gesturing and explaining to no-one. 'Tell me about it.'

She told him about it. In a steady reasonable tone she told him the unsteady, unreasonable story: about the gaunt man in the orange light of the pub, about the shabby man with the eyebrows in the hamburger restaurant. She lit the cigarette she'd promised herself she wouldn't have till the interview was over and told him about the flat tyre and Bill Jones stopping and she was blushing and puffing furiously on her cigarette and he was smiling.

He laughed. It was a bit like a death-rattle. 'I take it you didn't follow him any further, then?'

She stubbed her cigarette out on the dirty saucer that did for an ashtray, and didn't deign to reply to that. He smiled smugly. Tapping her envelope importantly on the table, he seemed ready to go, to dismiss her. Out on the landing stage two policemen were escorting the drunk away. They're taking away my Dad, Rosie thought crazily, they're taking away the man with the eyebrows ...

'Who are you, then?' she asked grumpily.

'I've told you who I am.'

'Who d'you work for?'

'Really, I don't see ...'

Still smiling that fixed smile of his that pricked at her skin, he was getting up to go. She didn't mean to raise her voice but it got louder of its own accord somehow: 'I just want to know why I'm doing what I'm doing. Is that so much to ask?' His shrug only riled her. 'I mean, you don't work for Mersey City for a start, do you?'

The random dart, much to her surprise, hit a nerve. He sat down and frowned at her. 'Rose,' he said, patient father to irrational daughter, 'you were given all the information you needed, and rather more money than you deserved, to do a little job for me. You've completed the work — badly, I may say. I really feel under no further obligation to you. Goodbye.'

Tara, cock. Thanks for the lecture.

He was right of course. His departing back was right: this was the end of their business arrangement, and his lies were his own responsibility.

Yet as soon as he was out of the door she was up and after him. Come on, Rosie, you've got up his nose and that'll be something to savour after his fifty quid's run out: what more d'you want?

She wasn't sure. Confident it would come to her, though, she hurried across the windy plaza to the Mini and steered into the traffic behind his Volvo. He drove at a leisurely pace; she, feeling experienced at this kind of thing now, kept a car or two behind him as they drove up the hill past the Anglican cathedral.

He didn't go far. Soon they were opposite the open green of Sefton Park, and the Volvo was pulling into the shadow of a block of high-rise flats. She stopped the Mini by the roadside and watched as he went in and waited for the lift. As soon as he stepped out of sight she was out of the car and walking across the tarmac as quickly as she could without actually breaking into a run. The entrance door was hooked up to an entry-phone and momentarily she thought she was going to be frustrated. But the door gave to her touch; luckily someone had vandalized the lock. She watched the lift flick up through the floors: 7, 8, 9.

Nine. That was all she wanted to know.

Or was it? A mile down the road, in the queue at the chippy, it didn't seem much in the way of knowledge. Okay, so she could look up all the residents of the ninth floor in the register of electors or something, but if his name wasn't Andrew Stephenson — and, having maybe lied about his work, why not his name too? — then how was she going to know which resident was him?

Besides, the flats didn't seem the sort of place he'd live in. Smart, yes, nice location, yes; but owned by the

Corpie, no room in the back garden for the little boat to take sailing at weekends, no mortgage to link up to a little life insurance for the comfy retirement. Not, in short, quite Andrew Stephenson's style.

When she went back the Volvo was still there. She parked in the road again, just by the car park entrance so he'd have to drive past her if he was going anywhere. What are you trying to discover, Rosie? — I'll know when I find out, was her own unhelpful reply. Shrugging, she took out the *Cosmopolitan* she still had with her, and settled down to wait.

She'd reread the problem page three times and even the adverts for make-up and vaginal deodorant twice before he emerged, alone. This time he seemed in more of a hurry and the Mini's engine groaned and complained at her as it set off in pursuit. 'Come on, you owe me one,' she said coaxingly. The engine groaned again in reply.

Once more she was on the main road to Mersey City, and the Volvo put on speed. Her foot pressed down to the floor, but that didn't stop the silver-grey blur ahead becoming more and more distant. Rounding a bend she saw, as she flashed past, the Volvo taking a turning to the left. Her brakes screeched; screwing up her courage and her face, she reversed the car fifty yards back up the busy road to a chorus of passing horns, and followed him into the Council estate.

It was like the estate Rosie had been brought up in: semis, half-brick and half-rendered: roses and hedges and respectable working-class folk cleaning their cars on a Saturday afternoon. Andrew Stephenson turned sharply into a cul-de-sac and stopped; she went past, head averted, and turned round. He was carrying something that looked like her envelope. He stood in the porchway of a corner house, waiting for an answer, looking around. Rosie ducked down. When she dared to look up again he seemed to have given up: he was walking back down the shrub-lined path to his car. She checked the name of the road — Quarry Avenue — and restarted the car.

Rosie took a gamble on him returning to the flats. She drove off ahead, foot down hard. She didn't see him in the rear-view mirror once she was back on the main road: maybe he'd got held up at a light; maybe she'd made a wrong guess and if only she'd stuck behind him she'd have found out where he really lived. Coming into Liverpool she took a turn to the left and wove up back streets to try and keep her lead, if lead it was. The car kept groaning and complaining but she put on a show of not worrying: 'I know you're only trying to make me sweat,' she said to the dials. They stared back at her non-committally, for all the world as if the car didn't really have a mind of its own.

The Volvo wasn't in the car park to the flats. Attempting the air of a woman with all the time in the world, she locked the car and strolled nonchalantly — well, slowly — over to the entrance. Would he come? Would he come? She pressed the lift button and hoped no-one else wanted to go up for a minute or two, holding it there.

The Volvo swung into the car park. She got into the lift and pressed for the eighth floor. Once there she had a brief outburst of panic: where were the stairs? And what if he saw her? But she found the staircase through a door that looked like it ought to have led to a store cupboard, and clattered up to the next flight.

Either it'd all taken longer than she'd thought, or Andrew Stephenson was in a hurry. When she emerged from the staircase, just to check whether the lift was in motion yet; it was already arriving at the ninth floor and she had to retreat quickly behind the fire door that led to the stairs. She propped the door open a little with her foot and heard the lift doors wheeze open and — heavy breathing coming up behind her? Startled, she turned to see a ginger-haired man in a tracksuit running up the stairs, gasping. His tired eyes stared at her out of a red, exhausted face. 'Good luck in the Olympics,' Rosie whispered and pulled the door open, just in time to see Andrew Stephenson inserting a Yale key in a door along the corridor. She held back for a moment till she heard the door close. Then, with a deep breath, she went along the corridor to check the number. Fancy seeing you here, I was just visiting a friend, she imagined saying unconvincingly.

But he didn't come out, and the number was 906, and she made no excuses and left.

And all there was time left to do was to drive to Newsham Park and wait for Graham to turn up. He was late as usual. When he finally arrived, blaming the football traffic as usual for his delay, she just nodded to him, too tired for conversation, steeling herself for the journey home and the evening ahead. 'We had a great time,' said Bob, waving energetically to his departing father, 'but Carol kept ...'

Carol sat in the corner of the back seat, staring vacantly out of the window. 'I hated it,' she said. 'I don't want to see him ever again.'

Why couldn't one of them ask her what she'd done with her day? I had a really great time, you see, I followed this man ... 'He's got rights, love,' she said sadly to Carol. 'We'll have a good talk about it tomorrow, okay?'

Driving home, she felt the excitement draining out of her. As soon as she was with Bob and Carol, she seemed to have no energy left to expend on herself; it was like milk, flowing and flowing to her children but there was never enough for them: as they grew older they wanted more and more and it satisfied them less and less and where was the space for her, Rosie Monaghan? 'I had a really good day,' she began determinedly, 'I —'

'So did we,' said Bob, 'do you know what we saw? We saw ...'

And he chattered away about baboons and Graham and lions and trains, and Carol shrank further into her corner, and Rosie looked straight ahead, fixing her gaze on tomorrow.

Chapter Eleven

But by the time tomorrow came, the excitement all seemed a bit foolish. When Jerry came round in the morning with the papers, she couldn't think what it was she'd lain awake half the night imagining she'd eagerly recount to him. Instead, once he'd finished his serious reading of the *Sunday Mirror* and was about to flick through the pictures in the *Observer*, she announced: 'I really ought to serve this writ.'

'Writ?'

'My great new career, Jerry. I serve writs. It's my contribution to the welfare of the human race.'

'Mm,' said Jerry, hastily offering to stay behind and look after a sulking Carol. Rosie wished he hadn't; she didn't really want to visit another midget boxing-champion-and-bad-payer without somebody there to hold her hand.

She needn't have worried. The ground-floor maisonette in Speke where the man was supposed to live was boarded up. Turning with relief from peering through a crack in the ply sheeting — nothing but debris and floorboards — a large blonde woman with a face like the poodle she held on a straining leash was smiling at her. 'I was just,' said Rosie, 'I was only ...'

'Terrible, isn' it?' said the woman in an unexpectedly Scottish accent. 'People move out and half an hour later the kids are round, wrecking the place. This lot don't even steal the stuff to sell it, you know tha'? They just smash it up. Terrible waste.'

'Yeh,' said Rosie. 'They don't even teach them burglary properly these days.'

The poodle stopped yapping and looked up at Rosie doubtfully. Its owner tried to smile as she turned away with a 'Come on, Vixen.' Rosie said a cheerful tara and went back home.

Lunchtime was cool. Carol wouldn't eat anything, and Bob was out, and Jerry was relentlessly cheerful. 'Talking of great new careers,' Jerry said when Carol had gone back to her room and yes, Rosie had mentioned that about three hours before, 'I've decided to take your advice. Why don't I get a new job, you said.'

'Did I say that?'

For answer Jerry kissed her hand; all soft and romantic. Rosie could never understand it; kissing hands. Her pudgy knuckles felt like the least erotic part of her entire anatomy.

'So I've put in for a transfer.'

'Like footballers do?' said Rosie, surreptitiously wiping the back of her hand.

He ignored both words and gesture. 'Tourism division,' he went on. 'I mean, it's the only growth industry in Liverpool these days.'

'Apart from law and order.'

'Yes, well, you've boxed that off, haven't you? So I thought, that's for me, tourism. Liverpool, city of the Beatles and the great days of the steamship and all that.'

'And the slave trade,' said Rosie, 'don't forget about the great days of the slave trade.'

Jerry looked at her askance and turned to the crossword. She looked at him askance and turned to the pile of Friday's washing to iron.

'Stupid of me really, worrying about it, my case I mean,' said Rosie after half an hour's sweat seemed to have made the pile of ironing grow rather than diminish.

'Mm hm?' said Jerry, who'd now turned to the adverts for winter holidays in Switzerland. 'Have you ever been skiing?'

'Don't be daft,' said Rosie. 'You see, I followed this feller I did this inquiry for, 'cause I wanted to know who he was. What he was up to. What, like, purpose I was fulfilling, doing this job for him.'

'It's a job you did for the money.'

Rosie cocked her head with a flash of insight that even

61

made her lose interest in the fascinating creases in Carol's school blouse. She put down the iron and looked hard at Jerry. 'Like you: even when you hate your job, you enjoy hating it. It all means something to you. Whereas me, I'm just one of the ignorant plebs who should count themselves lucky to have a job at all and not ask silly questions like, what's it for? Isn't that right?'

Jerry finally responded with his usual answer to Rosie's unsolvable problems; he got up and held her very close to him and stroked her hair and told her it wasn't worth worrying about. She embraced him in return. Maybe I am a bit bored with Jerry, she thought as his tongue intruded into her mouth. This was supposed to be the sort of thing she liked him for, and she wasn't liking it.

It was his being clothed that was the problem. It was the naked Jerry she was really fond of. In his cord trousers and oversize sweater he looked all crumpled and boring. For a moment she considered taking his trousers down in one swift movement; then decided it would be a bit forward of her, and picked up the iron again.

'That's the way forward, tourism,' said Jerry, nodding to himself, and went back to his newpaper.

By the next morning she'd decided to put blinkers on and move one step at a time. First she called Mike and asked him for more work.

'I'm not sure,' said Rosie, feeling the urge to flirt with him after what Graham had said, but unsure how you went about that down a few miles of electrified cable, 'I'm not sure that serving writs really brings out my full potential, Mike. How about a nice juicy divorce instead? Or the missing daughter of a local celebrity? Or a half-a-million blackmail demand?'

'I'll let you know the minute one comes up,' said Mike kindly. 'I might have another couple of writs for you in a week or so.'

'Great,' said Rosie, and confessed how well her process serving had gone so far. When Mike advised her to trace the second man, and suggested a little brusquely that if she couldn't work out how to do that for herself she'd never make a private detective, she finally, reluctantly hung up and permitted herself, for the first time in a day and a half, to acknowledge that she should do something about Carol and the cause of her sulks.

'He's your father,' said Rosie to her daughter with cool matter-of-factness.

Carol was absorbed in a book about upper-class girls' schooldays. What did she see in the stuff? Was she actually reading it at all or just hiding between the pages? 'I don't care if he's Prince Charles,' said Carol. 'I don't want to see him.'

'Why not?'

'Just don't.'

'That's no answer.'

Shrug.

'Okay,' said Rosie, tidying the clothes strewn over the floor of Carol's room on to a chair. 'I'll talk to him about it. No promises, mind.'

'Ta, Mum,' said Carol, pretending not to be pleased.

But pleased she was. For after tea Rosie came down from giving Carol's room a proper clean-out to find the two of them, her and Bob, giggling together and the little red light burning on the answering machine. 'Who said you could play with that?' said Rosie, who always felt on the edge of laughter when she was trying to be stern.

'It's this man,' said Bob, laughing.

'On the machine,' said Carol, laughing.

'Time you two were getting ready for bed,' said Rosie, just managing not to laugh.

She'd forgotten to listen to the machine for three days, and here he was, the heavy breather, sporting a fake German accent: 'I'm lonely you see, Fräulein,' he was saying, 'perhaps you too lonely are. Ven I think of you, frigging yourself all alone ...'

'Dirty bastard,' said Rosie to the machine as she wiped the tape clean, and 'Don't let me ever catch you playing with my messages again,' she said to the children when they came down in their pyjamas, wondering if Bob knew what frigging meant.

'Mum,' said Bob at that precise moment, in his best questioning voice, and Rosie's heart sank, 'Mum, what —'

'Don't ask.'

Carol butted in brightly: 'We only want to know what this mysterious business of yours is that all these people phone you up about.'

Rosie sighed with relief and hugged them to her. 'Your mum's become a private detective,' she announced proudly. 'What do you think of that?'

'Exciting,' said Carol, whose face said she thought it was silly.

'Silly,' said Bob, whose face said he thought it was exciting.

'So far,' said Rosie, 'it's been both.'

Finally they went to bed, Bob persuading a reluctant Carol to act the Watson to his Holmes in an imaginary adventure, and Rosie curled up with the evening paper. She was leafing idly through the pages so it took her a few minutes to notice the article on page five, let alone realize its significance:

MERSEY COUNCILLOR DIES

Thomas O'Meara, 67, a prominent member of the Mersey City Council, died yesterday at his home in Quarry Avenue, Marksfield.

Mr O'Meara was a lifelong member of the Labour party and a local councillor for 22 years, the last six as Chairman of the Refuse and Cleansing Committee of Mersey City ...

... Mr O'Meara had been in poor health for some years, and had recently recovered from heart surgery. He was unmarried.

Poor old bugger. Quarry Avenue? The pulse in Rosie's neck was pumping. Refuse and Cleansing? It might just be coincidence, though. She stared sadly at the picture above the story: the heavy eyebrows, the ruddy cheeks, the tie askew. Perhaps he didn't really look that much like her dad, perhaps that had been an illusion of the light in the hamburger restaurant. Perhaps his death wasn't really anything to do with her. In poor health for some years ...

Nevertheless, that pulse in her neck still giving her the signal, she thought she might pop out to Quarry Avenue tomorrow and have a look around. After all, she'd been there recently herself; very recently indeed; and so had a man with a silver-grey Volvo ...

Chapter Twelve

First thing, though — after delivering the kids to school —
she made herself try to find James MacLeish the midget
boxing champion.

Her search only lasted one phone call. It needed more
rehearsal, she decided as she replaced the receiver. When
the Housing Department had asked her who she was,
she'd found herself saying 'his wife'. That was her fatal
mistake. Being married to someone didn't entitle you to
their forwarding address: you needed to be a closer
relative, like the DHSS or the Electricity Board, to be
permitted that kind of information.

So she drove out to Quarry Avenue and sat in the car
for a while, at the entrance to the cul-de-sac, wondering
what to do. It was quiet there in the late morning. A
mother pushed a pram wearily, but resolutely smiling, up
the road; an elderly man waited for his dog to shit among
the mulch of autumn leaves on the grass verge; a young
man gawped at Rosie as he patrolled the drives delivering
leaflets about double-glazing. He dropped one in her lap
through the side window, winking, startling her out of her
fixed stare at the house Andrew Stephenson had visited:
the tidy, unexceptional corner house; net curtains and
dug-over flower-beds.

It might all, of course, be coincidence. Her client might
have been visiting, quite by chance, a different house in
the road where the man had lived, the man who'd been
Chairman of Refuse and Cleansing and had shared a
hamburger meal with Bill Jones and reminded her of her
Dad, the man who'd since died. It wasn't likely, but it was
possible.

The only way to find out was to ask. Rosie strode, with
every appearance of relaxation, up the pathway and rang

the two-tone bell. She stood under the porch, admiring the neat view Thomas O'Meara probably used to admire when he left the house in the mornings. Unmarried, it had said in the papers; so she was confident of no reply. Then, she thought, she'd try the neighbours. Excuse me, she imagined saying, my Dad was an old friend of Thomas O'Meara's, I just wanted to know if —

A large red-cheeked woman with a full head of permed grey hair opened the door. 'Oh,' said Rosie, nonplussed, 'I'm very sorry to intrude but I understand ...'

'I weren't expecting you so soon,' said the woman in a thick Lancashire accent. 'Come in, though.'

The hallway was dark with patterned maroon wallpaper. 'I think I should explain ...'

The woman spared her the trouble: 'That's all right, love, they said on the phone. Thought you'd be later, that's all. Tell you what, why don't you have a look through his papers? Get an idea of what he had to cope with? And I'll get us some tea.'

'But I,' said Rosie feebly.

She was left alone in the dining room. At least, in most houses it would have been the dining room. Here, the table was strewn with papers. There were two filing cabinets and a bookcase where the sideboard should have been. Volumes about socialism lined the shelves, and names and titles familiar from her Dad's old collection of books: Shaw and Wells and Ruskin and self-improvement and Palgrave's *Golden Treasury*.

She leafed through the papers strewn around the table. A well-thumbed copy of *The Ragged Trousered Philanthropist* lay open at page 269; apart from that there were letters, newspapers and agendas and minutes of party meetings and Council committee meetings and Council meetings and God-knows-what-else meetings. Rosie had just spotted a prospectus from STREETCLEAN LTD: PUBLIC SERVICE THROUGH PRIVATE ENTERPRISE when the woman came in and suggested they'd be more comfortable in the parlour.

The parlour was a startling contrast: light and airy, and antimacassars on the backs of the chairs, and the woman

67

smoothing down the flowers that patterned her dress and saying, 'Aye, this is my room. I never could abide mess; and Tommy were a messy man. A good one, mind. But a messy one. Elsie, love, he used to say to me, don't tidy me up. I know where everything is, he'd say, and it may look like a dog's dinner to you, but it's the way I work. Sugar?'

The tea came in china cups with pictures of faraway places on them, and there were digestive biscuits on a plate of the same design. 'I don't think I can do this,' said Rosie, surprised to hear the words out loud.

'No, you mustn't worry,' said Elsie, pushing the biscuit plate towards Rosie. 'I said to the bloke on the phone, I said, I quite understand. I mean, it's for his memory, isn't it? And I think it'd do me good to talk about him, I mean we've lived together all our lives, cradle to — well, except for his war service like, so what would you like to know? Do have a biscuit, love.'

It was like being dropped blindfold into a maze. Rosie didn't know where she was. She didn't know whether she should try and get out, or fumble her way further in; every possible move seemed a wrong one. With a sigh she took out her notebook and pencil; it seemed to be what was expected. In for a penny; in for twopence. Another sigh, and she said, 'Tell me about his work on the Council, then.'

So it was as Rosie had begun to presume, that Elsie with the big arms and bosoms and ruddy face was the dead man's sister. And yes, he'd been a 'good man' and a 'dedicated man' and a 'selfless man'; but also something of a political wheeler-dealer. He'd been a signalman and holder of so many offices in the National Union of Railwaymen that Rosie stopped writing them down after the first four or five; then there was the ward Labour party, the district Labour party, the constituency Labour party, delegate to the annual conference of the Labour party ...

And there was this woman, old and bereaved now, who'd done her little job in the local newsagent's and kept house for him, year in year out, burying her life in his, defending him to all and sundry in life and now in death: 'It was his life, politics,' she said, topping up Rosie's tea and nudging the biscuits towards her again. 'What paper did you say this were going to appear in?'

'Er, no,' said Rosie, screwing up her courage, 'it's been very kind of you to talk to me but ...'

'Now I remember,' said Elsie, not enlightening Rosie. 'Old-fashioned socialist, our Tommy; the solidarity of the working-class and unity is strength. Out of fashion now, eh? That's me and our kid; out of fashion. I used to call him that, y'see — our kid — if he got a bit too big for his boots, like ...'

Elsie's garrulousness suddenly subsided. She stared into space, the folds of her face settling into sorrow. Suddenly the birdsong from outside, and the ticking of the clock and of Rosie's heart from inside, became very loud.

'Tell me,' said Rosie, 'tell me about something he'd been working on lately. An issue. An example.' Elsie was still staring vacantly. 'I think he was very involved in this problem about,' deep breath Rosie, 'about the bins going private?'

'He were a good man,' said Elsie, biting her lip. Then she sipped her tea and leant forward and was bright-eyed again: 'He were right worried about that. The bins. They're trying to destroy everything we've fought for, that's what he'd say. The bins are the thin end of the wedge, you wait and see. That's what he said. In fact he was supposed to see someone about that the day he — well, the Sunday, y'know, but they can't have turned up, can they?'

Rosie's shorthand tapered off into nothing. 'D'you know,' she asked, hearing the quiver in her voice, 'd'you know who he was expecting?'

'No.'

'Not a man,' pushing her luck, 'not a man called Andrew Stephenson?'

'Never heard the name. I were at church, you see. Tommy give all that up years ago. God. Wonder where he is now, eh?' She frowned at Rosie; then smiled again. 'Excuse my moods,' she said, 'the doctor give me these pills. Don't know whether I'm coming or going. Never liked pills. Tommy had to have them, for his heart, y'know, I told him to take things easy but he wouldn't listen — I suppose that's what he'd gone upstairs for, his pills, oh love what a sight he was,' and suddenly the tears were flowing and Rosie went and put a thin arm around the woman's fleshy neck. 'He'd fallen down, y'see, all bruised and bloody he was, down the stairs and his heart gave out, the poor lamb ...'

'I must,' said Rosie, her thoughts racing into patterns she didn't want to acknowledge to herself, 'I'm sorry, I must go.'

Elsie, swallowing hard, nodded and showed her out. Rosie looked up at the staircase. Two struts in the banister were broken and the carpet at the foot of the stairs had been taken up. Because of bloodstains? Pushing away the idea of belatedly explaining herself to Elsie, she found herself instead seeing a man going up the stairs, painful step by step, for his pills in the bathroom; a stumble, a fall. Or — what if somebody else had been there, up on the stairs, and ...?

'I keep making myself look up at them,' said the old woman. 'I were at church, you see ...'

They were at the front door. 'I'm awful sorry.'

'I'll survive, love.'

'No, you see, all the time you've been talking to me and I'm not, I'm not —'

In front of the house a Mini of far fewer years and less rust than Rosie's had drawn up. A neat young woman was getting out of the car, shorthand pad in hand, looking towards them. 'I'm sorry,' said Rosie, giving Elsie a quick peck of a kiss on the cheek before rushing down the path. At the gate she nodded to the smart new visitor and dashed across the road, praying that the car would start first time.

It did. As she reversed out of the cul-de-sac, not daring to look back, she felt tears pricking at her eyes to match Elsie's. Once out on the open road she eased off the speed, but her mind was still accelerating. If only. If only he hadn't reminded her of her Dad none of this would have happened. She wouldn't be sitting here now, driving auto-matically through the late-morning traffic, thinking about a dead man who'd surely had no great need of Bill Jones's money; a lifelong socialist who'd thought privatizing the bins was the thin end of the wedge; who'd been expecting somebody on the Sunday just before he died; died of a heart attack and a fall down the stairs? What if the heart attack and the fall had happened the other way round? What if ...

Soon she was sitting in the car outside her own front door, and someone had said hello to her through the car window but by the time she realized it was Marie's mother from up the street the woman had gone. Yes, and something else had passed by Rosie. In Elsie's parlour, among the antimacassars and the patterned tea-cups, there she'd sat, pretending by default to be a journalist, and something had brushed against her and moved on. Fear, that was what it was. Guilt at her deception; then, fear at what might have happened to Tommy O'Meara.

She had to do something. Okay, there were the children to collect and deliver and feed and pacify and be concerned about, and maybe she'd go to the Council meeting on Thursday — the decisive meeting Andrew Stephenson had spoken of, and she'd seen the agenda for it on Tommy O'Meara's desk — but for now ...?

For now, important matters like suspicions of major crimes would have to wait. For now, she had to remind herself to do the simple things. Like, how to get her body out of the car and down to the shops for tonight's dinner before the shops remembered it was early-closing day.

Chapter Thirteen

Next day she tried the library but Andrew Stephenson eluded her. The electoral register for Flat 906, Dahlia Towers recorded one Helen Thackray and no-one else. She could watch the flats again and wait for him to turn up, but where would that get her?

So what else could she DO?

Rosie decided to go along with a flash of inspiration she'd had in the middle of the night which she'd then, briefly, thought worse of in the morning. She went and declared her earnings from private detection to the dole. It was something. It was simply the right thing to do, she told herself. Oh, and maybe she was also trying to work off some of her guilt at deceiving Elsie O'Meara — she wasn't sure of her own motives herself.

She just had to DO something.

Or, alternatively, do SOMETHING.

Everybody thought she was mad. 'You're going to what?' Jerry had said: and she'd always regarded him as a moral person. And when she bumped into Polly outside the DEPARTMENT OF UNEMPLOYMENT, as some graffiti writer had renamed it, she tried physically to stop Rosie going in. 'Are you coming up to your period or something?' Polly asked, fumbling for a rational explanation, her hand on Rosie's arm.

'It's like the buses, Poll.'

'...es?'

'...rs to all of us.'

'...n screw out of it, yeh.'

...Polly's hand and marched into the ...atiently in the queue and told the man. ...surprised. And it wasn't too painful: ...oney for the days she worked.

72

Once the deed was done, news of her lunacy spread fast. Round at Margie's late that afternoon for a birthday party in honour of Margie's eldest, Rosie's best friend said to her, 'It's not true, is it, Rosie? That you went and gave money to the government?'

'It's true.'

'They'll only spend it on themselves, y'know.'

'Margie,' said Rosie seriously, 'I thought you were my closest friend. I thought you'd understand.

'You're one of life's innocents, aren't you, eh? I understand that.'

Rosie didn't feel very innocent. She felt guilty as hell. She'd composed and torn up half a dozen beginnings of letters to Elsie O'Meara in the past twenty-four hours:

> I just want to say sorry for butting in on your grief — specially as I am not who you thought I was. But I can only assure you

That was where all the attempted letters stopped. What assurance did she have to offer? That Tommy O'Meara had reminded her of her Dad? That she would get at the truth but she didn't know how? That she suspected ...?

Rosie spent most of the party hiding in the kitchen, handing out plates of sausage rolls and drinking more than her share of the homemade wine for the grown-ups. Bob kept hanging round her, with his 'I'm too old for this kind of thing' air; she kept just biting back snappy remarks at him. Then, when Margie came in for a break and Bob had found a friend to talk to about the serious things in life she finally couldn't stop herself, she let her suspicions come tumbling out:

'He might have been murdered.'

'You what?'

'This man I saw last week. He had a heart attack. But he might have been murdered.'

Everything should have gone very quiet. The party should have suddenly hushed at her words and all eyes should have turned on her. Instead someone suddenly turned the music up louder in the living room, and

Margie took her hand and said, 'You been hitting the vino hard or something?'

'I mean it, Margie.'

Her tone might have made Margie take her seriously if it hadn't been for the laughter: an earthquake of laughter that shook Rosie, not because it was funny but because it was crazy, a crazy cracks-in-the-earth self-evidently mistaken idea. For what evidence was there? Only evidence that pointed the other way: a photograph that might be of Tommy O'Meara taking money from someone in Streetclean Limited, a photograph of a man with such a solid reputation for civic virtue that what could be more likely to bring on a heart attack than his taking a bribe?

'You're having me on, aren't you?'

'It's all daft,' said Rosie, 'I just butted in on this woman's grief, that's all —'

'Hey, ease off,' said Margie, and Rosie stopped pouring herself another glass of wine and choked back her laughter:

'It's the lies, Marg. Pretending to be who I'm not, and not knowing what I'm doing —'

'I don't know what you're on about, Rosie.'

'Nor do I. Sorry. You'd better get back to your party.' Rosie looked round the kitchen for something to eat to soak up the alcohol, now she'd given all the sausage rolls away. 'And how's the exciting new world of computers?'

'Exciting. New,' said Margie, 'like being in a foreign country. It's a different language. I mean, they don't use words any more, they use numbers. And they're not even the numbers you and I use to check how much they're fiddling us by at the supermarket. Just yes and no, they call them numbers, you see, yes and no.'

It was Rosie's turn to be confused. 'What about maybe?' she asked. 'Don't computers have a number for maybe too?'

Margie shook her head as she went back into the party room.

When Rosie drove the kids home later there was a faint mist in the air. She wasn't drunk, she insisted to herself, just light-headed. It was the light-headedness and the mist that made all the streets eerie and unfamiliar. Cars and houses glowed with a faint orangey greyness, each very distinct and separate from one another, all shadows and maybes.

Don't kid yourself Rosie, she said to herself as the twenty-mile-an-hour journey finally ended at their front door. You're drunk all right.

So she had two cups of black coffee and packed the kids off to bed and told them: 'I'll just be next door if you want me.'

'Next door?' asked Bob.

'At Dave and Janice's.'

'But you never go there.'

No, she didn't. Next door was a gloomy looking place, one of the few rented houses left in the street; peeling dark green paint and a rent-man who still came on Friday nights. It was gloomy inside too. Dave, in his early twenties, had been out of work for two years, so there was always an atmosphere of despair in there and Rosie preferred to know her neighbours through the walls, for the sound of the day-and-night TV and faint shouting, to actually stepping over the threshold.

But tonight she had a purpose. Tonight she'd thought of something else to DO. 'I just want a word with Dave,' she said to Janice at the door, startled for a moment to see her neighbour bulgingly pregnant. She saw her on the street most days but they didn't really notice one another; they nodded and passed by.

'It's a bit of a mess.'

'That's all right.'

'If you're sure you don't mind ...'

Dave was in vest and blue jeans, watching the telly. In his arms lay their eighteen-month-old with a dummy in her mouth, staring at Rosie the way her parents stared at the television. 'Hiya Rosie,' said Dave, his gaze flicking on to her for a moment before refocusing on the screen, where rich Americans were falling in and out of love and business arrangements.

The room smelt of the baby; sick and piss and nobody

who could be bothered to clean it up. Janice took the child from Dave and failed to persuade Rosie to have a cup of tea and 'Dave,' said Rosie, 'you used to be on the bins, didn't you?'

'Got the sack.'

'Sounds daft I know,' said Rosie, struggling against the jarring voices from the TV, 'but I'm looking into something that's to do with the bins. So I wanted to know how it worked, the fiddles and that. How it's done.'

'Didn't get the sack for that,' said Dave, turning to her. 'I got my cards for getting pissed on duty and knocking out the foreman.' He smiled for a moment. 'It's a joke really. He tripped up on his way to hit me and I couldn't get my fist out of the way in time.'

So, in among Dave's macho bravado, Rosie learnt about the fiddles. 'Nothing big,' he said. 'I mean, it's a Scouse tradition, isn't it? Fiddling. My old feller was an AB, y'know, seaman. You wouldn't believe the stuff went out of those docks every day. Every day. Police, customs, they were all in on it too, like. It's a tradition. Moonlighting on other jobs, finishing early to get to the pub, selling off the valuable rubbish, all that sort of thing.'

Rosie shuffled uncomfortably on the edge of the suspiciously damp armchair and thought about the administration of shit. Janice reappeared from upstairs and there was the faint sound of crying from overhead.

'So did the same sort of thing happen in Mersey City?'

The same but worse, according to Dave. 'Of course,' he said, 'they're talking about handing it over to a private firm, right? Won't stop the fiddles. There'll just be less wages or less fellers, won't there? Just means a worse job. I mean, you mustn't get the wrong idea, from me telling you the angles. It's a shitty job, and people are always yelling at you, but most of the fellers like to see it done right, for the people, y'know. Is that what you wanted to know?'

No, somehow it wasn't. And Rosie felt ridiculously angry. The more she sat in their house, the more she wanted to shake them, by the throat if necessary, and tell them not to be so bloody apathetic.

But later, reflecting on it in bed — vaguely wishing someone else was there to share her pillow with her — she saw Dave and Janice's attitude was the rational thing. There was nothing to hope for in their position, so why hope? It was the way everybody else seemed to want it; that there weren't any jobs for a few million people like Dave and Janice, so they should give up hope. They'd only get disappointed and angry and start a revolution or something if they started thinking the world might be any different. Better, far better to curl up in front of the telly, and shout at one another sometimes, and if you were Dave do a little job for peanuts on the side sometimes, and if you were Janice get knocked up or knocked about sometimes. That way you'd fit in with what the world expected of you. *Is that what you wanted to know?*

No, it wasn't. Wanting to feel she was doing something, something for Elsie, something about the truth, instead she'd just learnt something about her neighbours' lives. And the ache of shame at lying to Elsie was twinging in her stomach again. And there were too many memories of things she hadn't done — phone calls she hadn't made, kind words she hadn't said to the kids, times she hadn't popped in on Dave and Janice, explanations she hadn't given to Elsie O'Meara — for her to let an absurd idea like the possibility of murder stop her going to sleep.

She lay awake, thinking about the possibility of murder.

Chapter Fourteen

'I'm trying to trace a man called Andrew Stephenson.'

The man behind the ENQUIRIES card beamed at Rosie in a public relations sort of way. 'Yes?'

'Yeh,' said Rosie, forgetting her manners for a moment. 'That's correct. He works for you. Or he used to anyway. I think. Worked for you, Mersey City Council.'

'That's us,' said the man, looking over Rosie's shoulder for the more interesting enquiry that might come through the door any minute. 'And you are ...?'

'I'm with Collins, Hutchinson and Macmillan. Solicitors. From whom he may learn something to his advantage, sort of thing.'

Mike had taken some persuading to be a party to the arrangement. She'd had to promise faithfully to have served the other writ by next Monday. In return she had, however, wrung out of him the promise of another lunch-date on expenses.

But as it turned out nobody actually checked back. When she said 'on behalf of Mr Michael Bracewell' to the second man who came to the counter, the name of a professional man had turned out to be sufficient in itself, and Rosie glimpsed fresh possibilities in the world of fraud and deception she'd plunged herself into — well, dipped a toe in.

Not that it was of any practical use this time around. Mersey City Council had never heard of Andrew Stephenson. 'Oh well,' she said to the man as she turned to go, 'Bang goes the villa he'd have inherited in the South of France.' She couldn't resist making his jaw drop a bit further into his collar and tie: 'Quite apart from the beach place at Malibu. California, y'know.'

Today, to avoid thinking about obscene six-letter words beginning with m—, Rosie was concentrating on the little things in life. Like obscene five-letter words beginning with m—. Money, for instance. Sometimes she thought there must be an invisible hole in her purse that it slipped through; sometimes she thought the hole was called Bob-and-Carol. Already it seemed a bit rash to have told the dole about her earnings, now she was busy recycling them back into the economy in search of her client and his real business. Still, it had eased her conscience declaring her earnings. She'd have that to comfort her when they declared her bankrupt. And meanwhile she was going to have to become a good saver, that was all. Thrift, self-help; hadn't they made this country great?

She had, therefore, resolved never to buy another packet of cigarettes. She'd also brought a packed lunch, planning to eat it on the seat opposite the hamburger restaurant in Mersey City for old times' sake. When she came out of the Council information office, though, rain was falling like in Noah's day so she had to sit in the car, steaming up the view of a derelict warehouse and the METER ZONE sign she'd carefully parked this side of, munching her jam sandwiches.

She arrived half an hour early at the Town Hall, dripping and still hungry. The building was a slimmed-down version of the 19th Century municipal palaces of the bigger Northern cities: all stones and pillars and carved gargoyles. She had to push her way past the wet coats and soggily suggestive remarks of a crowd of men outside, holding placards that read PRIVATE SERVICE = POOR SERVICE and FIGHT THE CUTS. Thinking she must be in the right place, she went up to the police-man at the top of the steps. He stood under the shelter of the entrance. To speak to him Rosie had to stand just under a drip from the genuine 19th century gutter. Plop, it went on her shoulder.

'I'm a member of the public,' said Rosie brightly.

'So am I sometimes,' said the face above hers. 'But right now I'm a policeman.'

'Really?' said Rosie, looking up at him. She was old enough to be his mother, if she'd started early. 'Where do I go, then?' she inquired maternally.

'Wherever you like,' replied the policeman, looking over her head at the crowd behind her. 'It's a free country.'

She wasn't altogether sure she agreed with him there, but this wasn't the time or place. Plop, went another drip on her left eyebrow. 'For the council meeting. Where do I go?'

'Not with the co-op, are you?'

'No,' said Rosie winningly, 'I'm with Barclays.'

The policeman looked down his acne at her for a moment. Then, without a word, he walked past her on towards the crowd of men. Just as she was about to point out her rights as a taxpaying member of the public who even declared her earnings to the dole, a strong hand gripped her elbow. 'So there you are, Angela,' said a voice in her ear. The hand began to push her up the steps.

The man had been a shadow beside her during her talk with the boy policeman. His face was very black and smiling; his body was clothed in a damp brown suit that looked as if it had been pressed with a steamroller. His grip was very strong. 'I'm sorry,' said Rosie, 'I'm not ...'

'Oh yes you are,' said the man, smiling fiercely. 'It's all right, Angela. Afternoon.'

This was for the benefit of the two security men who stood in the marble hallway at the foot of a wide wooden staircase. 'Not with the co-op, are you?' said one of them.

'No, I'm with —'

The black man squeezed her arm and interrupted: 'We're just members of the public,' he said, and they were through.

'But ...'

'I'll explain,' said the man in an undertone, 'when we're inside. Sorry if I hurt your arm, love.'

· Rosie gingerly removed his hand with her free one and wondered how many bones were broken. 'Why does everybody want to know the name of my bank?'

The man just shrugged. They went into the public gallery and he guided her to two seats on the front row. It was like being in a box at the theatre, Rosie thought, never having been in a box at the theatre. Down below were polished seats and desks in a wide semi-circle, and people milling around inconsequentially, and a chatter of voices like the monkey-house at the zoo. 'So this is it, then,' said Rosie.

'What?'

'Democracy in action. Where our rulers rule.'

'Nah, that's all done in London,' said the man. 'I'm Martin, by the way.'

He shook her hand as they sat down; her hand stung. He didn't know his own strength. 'I'm Angela.'

'Not really?'

'No,' admitted Rosie, 'but it's as good a name as any.'

He apologized again for his hand on her arm. 'But I'm with the MCC, you see. Not the cricketing version, of course.'

'Of course not,' said Rosie, who thought cricket was like pornographic films: one of those curious things some men liked to watch.

'The Mersey Cleaning Co-op. MCC. They're trying to stop us all coming in: except for a deputation. So we have to come in incognito, like.'

Rosie smiled politely and saw why the boy policeman had looked at her funnily when she'd said Barclays. She looked around her, trying to take the place in. She hadn't expected it to be so posh: chandeliers glittering over the main area, close enough to reach out for and swing on, if that was what you fancied; above, a blue dome the shape of a woman's breast pointing its nipple towards the sky. And down there, among the men in suits and the chatter of the monkey-house — hadn't she seen that gaunt man before? Hadn't she tried to take a picture of him, drinking a glass of scotch, his face bathed in orange light as he talked to ...?

'D'you know who that is?'

The black man called Martin had to put on his glasses to follow the line of her pointing finger. 'Andrew McLachlan. Met him, have you?'

'Seen him somewhere,' said Rosie cagily. 'What's he do?'

'He's the leader of the Sames. That's how I know him.'

81

'The Sames?'

Martin expounded his novel theory about party politics to Rosie as she watched the gaunt man making deals down below. You could divide the political parties, he said, according to how much public money they wanted to be spent. So conservatives were Lesses; socialists were Mores; the middle-ground were the Sames.

'I suppose you're a More?'

'I'm a socialist, yeh. But y'see, Angela — sorry about your arm, y'know — us in the co-op, we're a load of binmen who want to take over the Refuse and Cleansing: if it has to be taken over, like. And even the Mores don't want to know 'cause they reckon socialism's got nothing to do with working people actually running things.'

The crowd was filling up in the gallery. Martin kept giving surreptitious little waves of welcome to people; Rosie kept looking over her shoulder to see if Andrew Stephenson had turned up. What would she say if he did? Fancy meeting you here? I got caught in the rain, you see, and do you come here often? Committed any m—s lately?

'What about the others?' she asked to pass the time.

'The Lesses don't want us 'caus we're a load of no-marks who want to invest our profits in Mersey City instead of in the Cayman Islands. And the Sames'd have us if only we were as dirt cheap as Streetclean. So here we are.'

The meeting was about to begin. Rosie had thought everything would suddenly be hushed. But the chatter went on, and it was only after half a minute that everyone seemed to realize they were supposed to be observing a minute's silence for 'a widely respected member of this Council, Thomas O'Meara'.

Once some incomprehensible business to do with minutes and points of order had begun, Rosie whispered to her neighbour: 'Did you know him? Tommy O'Meara?'

'He was all right in his way,' murmured Martin. 'Saw him the day he died, actually.'

'You did?'

'Yeh. Personally he'd have loved to help us but he

82

couldn't carry the party with him, that sort of crap. But he was straight with us. Said he was seeing somebody from the other side after us and he'd tell them straight too. And I believed him. Must have died not long after. Just think, eh.'

Rosie was thinking. 'From the other side?' she asked unexpectedly loudly.

'Sh,' said Martin. 'Streetclean. They'll get the contract now he's not here. There was only one vote between the Mores and the others. It only went out to tender 'cause a Labour feller was in hospital. So one vote makes all the difference, y'see.'

'It does?' said Rosie, feeling dizzy.

And the business below droned on, with people wandering about and nobody seeming to listen to anybody, and Martin said they wouldn't get round to discussing the bins till six o'clock, and Rosie had to get back for the kids. 'You're gonna miss the demo,' said Martin in amazement. 'We're gonna disrupt the meeting, y'know.'

'What good will that do?'

'None. But we'll all feel better and get our names in the papers.' Martin smiled, handing her a scrap of paper he'd scribbled on in the margin. 'Here, have a leaflet. It's got my phone number on, if you ever fancy being Angela again, like.'

He winked at her. She rubbed her arm and struggled past the knees and out on to the staircase. On the steps of the Town Hall she stopped, pulling on her anorak, trying to argue herself out of buying a packet of cigarettes. She was also praying for amnesia. *One vote makes all the difference.* Suddenly there was another six-letter word to go with m—: motive. Not to mention, opportunity, even though that didn't begin with m. Suddenly she didn't want to remember anything about the bins or Andrew Stephenson's condescending smile or the tears streaming down Elsie O'Meara's face. Suddenly she had a tremendous urge to be a shorthand-typist again.

No chance, Rosie. In the midst of her doomed prayers two men materialized from raindrops. They were waiting to cross the street, in smart brown coats and animated conversation, sharing an umbrella. Andrew Stephenson and Bill Jones: her client, and the man he'd paid her to follow. They were heading for the Town Hall. They were sharing a joke. Rosie knew what she had to do. She had to go up to them, and demand to know who they really were, and whether one or both of them had been to Tommy O'Meara's house on Sunday afternoon. Yes, she knew what she had to do. So she —

She ran away. She ran, as fast as her heels would carry her, down one street, blindly down another, another. She ran till she could hardly breathe. A light glimmered in the distance. She stumbled the last few yards to her gleaming objective:

'Packet of cigarettes,' she said hoarsely to the man in the kiosk.

'What brand, love?'

'Any,' gasped Rosie. 'And some matches.'

She leant against the wall, coughing as she inhaled the smoke, the untipped cigarette already soggy from the rain, wishing she'd not prayed for amnesia after all.

Oh, she remembered Andrew Stephenson and Elsie O'Meara and the black man from the MCC all right. She'd just forgotten where she'd left the frigging car.

Chapter Fifteen

Of course when she found the Mini, after a three-quarter hour search in the rain for a view of a derelict warehouse and a METER ZONE sign, the stupid machine wouldn't start. 'Damp on the plugs,' it tried to whisper to her through the whine of the starter motor, but she wouldn't listen:

'Stupid machine,' she said.

That was a mistake. The engine whined, groaned, coughed and refused to start. She'd flooded it. It took another ten minutes to calm down; then another ten to find two passers-by willing to push it through a few puddles till it jump-started.

At last she was driving home. And finally — in between worrying about how late she was — Rosie knew she couldn't put off the thought that was loitering at the back of her mind any longer. She'd have to go to the police. There was no alternative. She knew exactly what she had to do: again.

And this time she really must not run away.

But a flurry of minor irritations intervened. First she had to find Bob and Carol, who'd arrived home and disappeared again while she'd been taking her refreshing shower in Mersey City. Then there was the tea to cook and clear up after, and Carol pestering her about Graham; so then there was Graham to call and arrange to see on Saturday afternoon. And then, just as she sat down to collect her wits, there was commotion in the street: for while Rosie had been sampling the unexciting world of politics a real-life crime had taken place in the house opposite. Crabby old Mrs Jameson, out all afternoon complaining to somebody about something, had returned home to find her house burgled. Rosie thought that everybody who'd ever met the grouchy old so-and-so must be suspected. But she forbore to say as much to the neighbours on the doorstep. She just listened to everybody's theories about the kids in the next street but one, and regretted ever opening the floodgates of Dave's reminiscences about life on the bins as he told her again about the market for waste paper, and watched the blue lights flashing on police cars that were lined up in the street to remind Rosie of what she had to do.

She was still discussing the rising crime rate with Dave and with Edie from up the road — more cheerful with life now her Karen had recklessly gone back to her husband in Belle Vale — when Jerry turned up. 'Nice surprise,' said Rosie.

'What?' said Jerry. 'We're going out. For a drink. Nine o'clock Thursday, we said.'

That bloody amnesia again; why didn't it hit the right targets? 'Couldn't get a sitter,' she lied hastily, hoping he'd take the hint and go home.

'That's okay. I'll get us something from the offie.'

She couldn't tell him about it. She wanted to, but she couldn't. It sounded absurd to her as soon as she imagined saying it; *I had this flat tyre, and a woman thought I was a journalist, and then I met this black man from the MCC...*

Was she just afraid he'd laugh at her? No, it was the opposite somehow. She was scared he'd listen too seriously, and make lots of excessively intelligent comments, and take it all away from her. It was her story; her incredible, frightening, secret story. She'd choose her moment to tell him. Tomorrow night, maybe. She'd arrive at his door, and tell him how it had all unfolded before her when nobody else realized the truth; how she'd told the police, and watched as their reactions changed from scepticism through interest to astonished belief; how they'd thanked her in the end and arrested the men responsible — how, against all the odds, her private detection had turned into the glittering, triumphant uncovering of a murder.

So she let him rattle on about the opportunities in tourism — an interview for his transfer was already fixed for next week — only half-listening as she planned her speech to Superintendent Barlow in the morning, till suddenly she heard him say:

'Are you tired of me, Rosie?'

He looked up at her with mute, sad appeal. Why did he always seem to be sitting at her feet? 'Just tired. Full stop. Don't mind me. Let's just — take all our clothes off, eh?'

Jerry looked a bit surprised at that — shocked, even — but he didn't say no. He didn't actually say anything.

He just took off his clothes.

Well, Rosie excused herself an hour or so later, humming her favourite song to herself, men stayed warm longer than hot water bottles now the cold weather was coming on.

So it wasn't until the next morning, Friday, that she presented herself at the police station in Mersey City ready to initiate a Major Inquiry. She waited patiently in the queue. There's no hurry, she said in her imagination, I only want to report a murder. The constable behind the desk was explaining what a summons for speeding meant to a deaf, mentally retarded Asian man. At least, Rosie assumed he must be deaf and mentally retarded; she couldn't think of any other reason why the constable might be shouting so loudly.

At last it was her turn. 'Bloody wogs,' said the constable with a smile of welcome for Rosie's breasts. He looked up at her face and held the smile.

'I want to report a,' said Rosie, then stopped and leant forward, conscious of the queue behind her. 'It's confidential actually, I wonder if...'

'Don't you worry,' said the constable with a wink. 'Just take a seat.'

After ten minutes of staring at posters advising her to watch out for her handbag and to cancel the milk when she went away, a young policewoman guided her to a bare interview room and Rosie realized the confidentiality stuff had been a mistake. 'Tell me all about it,' said the police-woman across the desk in a warm, human sort of way.

'It's not rape,' said Rosie quickly.

'I quite understand ...'

'It's not even the heavy breathing on the phone.'

The policewoman smiled a warm, human smile. 'No, of course, but it is ...'

'No, no, it's nothing sexual at all, in fact. In fact, it's a murder.'

'Oh,' said the policewoman, her eyes not lighting up in surprise and interest. She opened her notebook. 'And you are?'

Roisin Theresa Monaghan, born, alive, occupied, clean driving licence, unmarital status and yes to children, stared hard into the black-pencilled eyes of the police-woman. 'Thomas O'Meara: that's the man who got murdered. I got made redundant from National Foods, y'see. So I decided I'd become a private detective.'

'Uh huh?' said the policewoman, writing it all down.

Rosie told her everything. She kept smiling at the policewoman, but it didn't have any effect. The black-pencilled eyes flicked up at her coolly between notes in the little black book. Every now and then an 'Mm?' or a 'Yes?' or an 'Uh huh?' drifted across the room, but they didn't seem to signify anything. Still, there was nothing for it but to plough on. So Rosie told her everything.

Well, almost everything. 'See, I met this feller, my client so to speak, in the Atlantic Crossing' ... *and*, she didn't say, *there was this yachtsman with a fat cigar* ... 'then I followed this Bill Jones and I took, well I'd been told to so I took these pictures' ... *until I had this flat tyre but don't mention that no* ... 'so it turns out this client of mine doesn't work for Mersey City like he said so I followed him to this flat' ... *where I met this man training for the Olympics* ... 'and the way it looks to me, this old councillor' ... *who looks like my dad but maybe that's not relevant* ... 'might have fallen or he might have been, well, been, well, I happen to know you see that his vote was crucial from this feller Martin' ... *and one of your colleagues knows the name of my bankers now* ... 'so Tommy O'Meara might have been murdered' ...

Enough of the truth for a lowly policewoman, Rosie felt. She was pleasantly surprised at the nice logical pattern her words had made on the air. And maybe when she finally did get to see Barlow himself she'd feel freer to colour in the whole truth and be a bit embarrassed by it.

Nothing happened for a long time. She was left alone in the bare room. There weren't even any posters to read on the yellow walls. The windows were of frosted glass so she couldn't look out. There was a Newcastle Brown Ale ashtray on the table, full of stubs, but she'd given up cigarettes again.

After twenty minutes she began to understand why so many people had carved their initials on the table.

After twenty-five minutes a prematurely-balding young man in plain clothes and regulation black shoes came in and said he was Detective Constable Hickey and would she like to put him in the picture?

'But I just told ...'

'If you'd tell me again, in your own words,' he said affably, looking her up and down. 'It's amazing, the details that sometimes slip your mind the first time around.'

So she began at the beginning again, and ended at the end, not forgetting the middle — straining her memory, to make sure she left all the same bits out of her story. He seemed identical to the policewoman, apart from the clothes and the eye-liner: 'Um,' he said, and 'Ah' and 'Yeh?' as the mood took him, betraying no reaction. Once he asked her to show him the photo of Bill Jones and Tommy O'Meara in the hamburger restaurant, and she said she'd given the copy she'd kept to his colleague: that was the emotional highlight of the interview.

'Won't keep you a minute, love,' said Detective Constable Hickey, and went out.

He hadn't lied to her; he kept her several minutes. Then several more minutes. She'd just dug an old nail-file out of her handbag and was carving her initials on the table when the policewoman came in with a coffee and a sorry-to-keep-you-waiting. 'Thanks,' said Rosie, pretending to tidy up her cuticles.

The policewoman went out. Rosie drank the coffee. Somebody had accidentally dropped a bag of sugar into it but she forced it down all the same. Several minutes passed. Then several more minutes. She carved her initials in a different place on the desk, upside down from where she was sitting this time for the intellectual challenge of it. She began to feel hungry.

D C Hickey came back with an older man in plain clothes. She could tell he was a superior officer because he didn't bother to introduce himself, and placed a big lined pad of paper in front of him instead of the little black notebook the mere constables had used. 'Known Martin Brown long?' he asked, looking at a doodle on his pad of paper.

'Who?'

'Martin Brown.'

'The man with the phone number,' said D C Hickey from the doorway.

'Oh, him. I only met him yesterday.'

'Ever been a member of the Workers Revolutionary Party?'

Rosie looked at the older man in puzzlement. 'The only parties I go to are children's parties.'

'Don't get smart with me, love.'

'You what?'

'Communists, International Marxists, Militant Tendency? Ever been a member of any of them?'

'What's all this got to do with Tommy O'Meara?'

'You tell me,' said the detective, looking up at her for the first time. D C Hickey was looking at her too, from the doorway; he didn't look so affable now. Suddenly Rosie felt nervous.

'I'm just trying to find,' said the man opposite her, holding her gaze till she looked down, 'trying to find a motive for your coming in here and wasting the time of two constables and a detective sergeant. That's me, by the way: Detective Sergeant Murdoch.'

That's me, thought Rosie, looking down at her initials on the desk. R T M. Reporting the Murder.

'Well?'

'I'm just,' said Rosie quietly, 'waiting for the fog to clear.'

'So are you involved in this campaign about the bins, or aren't you?'

'Look,' said Rosie as indignantly as she could manage, 'I came here to report my suspicions of a murder.'

Detective Sergeant Murdoch laughed. He looked over his shoulder. Detective Constable Hickey laughed, right on cue. 'I've checked your story, love,' said the sergeant, tapping a biro on his pad importantly, 'and it doesn't make any sense.'

'I'll go then,' said Rosie, afraid she was going to cry and getting up to leave but the sergeant got up too and put out a hand:

'Not so fast,' he said with an edge to his voice.

Rosie sat down again.

'So I spoke to Martin Brown. Your black friend,' he continued, with that same smile the desk-constable had given her breasts when she'd first arrived. 'He was in here last night, actually. Mister Brown. Under arrest. For disturbing the peace at a Council meeting. Go to that, did you?'

'Er, well, for a bit . . .'

'Thought so,' said the sergeant making a note. 'But you've never been a member of any left-wing organization?'

Only the Catholic Church and that was a long time ago, Rosie might have said but didn't; she could feel all the fight draining out of her.

'So I rang up your friend Martin. Your black friend. To remind him about his bail conditions, sort of thing. And I asked him about you. In passing, as it were. And he'd never heard of any Roisin Theresa Monaghan. But he had met somebody called Angela that looked a lot like you.'

Rosie fumbled in her bag for a cigarette before she remembered again that she'd given them up. 'I can explain all that . . .'

'Yeh, I dare say,' said the sergeant. 'So the thing is, that fits together, in a lunatic kind of a way, with my earlier telephone conversation with Mr William Jones, Chief Executive of Streetclean Limited. He said he'd met somebody who looked a lot like you over a flat tyre. But this woman was called Veronica.'

'It was,' said Rosie, trembling, 'the first name that came into my head. Have you got a ciggie?'

'For you? No,' he said, taking one out for himself and lighting it: blowing the smoke casually across the table. 'Then there's this complaint we had a few days ago. From a Miss Elsie O'Meara. She'd been visited by yet another woman who looked a lot like you, but who didn't leave any name at all. Just drank the lady's tea and fished around her dead brother's papers and left in a bit of a hurry.'

'I didn't know what to do,' said Rosie, trying not to look at him, 'but I've written, I'm writing her a letter ...'

'So you see the work you've put me to? And where does it all leave us, eh?' The sergeant let the smoke drift up from his mouth in little rings. Rosie watched them, mesmerized. 'We have a man who, as certified, dead of a heart attack. The funeral was on Wednesday. No flowers, donations to the Labour Party. We have a man called Andrew Stephenson who seems to exist purely in your imagination. And we've got you: a shorthand-typist who claims to be a private detective and can't ever seem to give her right name to people.'

'What about the picture?' Clutching at straws, Rosie, clutching at straws; but what else was there to clutch at? She saw no sign of lifebelts. 'The picture of Bill Jones and Tommy O'Meara?'

The sergeant clicked his fingers, D C Hickey produced the picture. It lay between them on the table. 'Mr Jones,' said the sergeant, 'was seeing the leaders of the three political parties that day, to canvass support for his company. He gave them all a copy of the prospectus of Streetclean Limited. In a big brown envelope.' He tapped the big brown envelope in the photograph. 'The only mystery about all that is: why did you take the picture?'

An imaginary man called Andrew Stephenson paid me to. What was the point in saying it? What use was the truth? When this man would twist it in his hands till it took the shape of a pack of lies?

Rosie shrugged, and bit her lip.

It was another hour before she left. She spent the hour shrugging, and biting her lip, and sometimes saying 'I don't know,' as he kept asking her why she'd done this and why she'd said that. She'd given up on honesty; finally she gave up on listening.

'... so I'm letting you off with a caution this time,' he was saying, getting up to leave.

'A caution? What for?'

He leant on the table suddenly and put his face close to hers. It was a mottled, stubbly face that smelt of sour after-shave. She flinched. 'For all your various impersonations, and for wasting police time. In future,' his back to her now, on his way out, 'stick to Pitmans and forty words a minute, all right? Leave the detection to people who know what they're doing.'

Forty words a minute. Just showed what he knew, if he thought that was any sort of speed. 'Forty words a minute,' she said contemptuously, but he'd gone. D C Hickey, though, was lingering in the doorway. 'I came here,' said Rosie, feeling her jaw quiver as she spoke, 'to report my suspicions of a murder.'

The man nodded. 'Know your way out, do you?' he said, and left without waiting for a reply.

Rosie walked out in a daze. It was raining but what did that matter? Forty words a minute. She went into the nearest pub and ordered a double vodka and twenty cigarettes. Barclays Bank wouldn't like it but what did she care? She downed her drink in two swift gulps, plonked her bottom on a bar stool and ordered another with orange this time. 'They think I'm crazy,' she said to the barman. 'They think I'm a frigging loon.'

The barman looked at her. He had a nervous tic in his left eye. I think you're a frigging loon, said his look. 'Forty words a minute,' said Rosie. She pushed her glass wearily out of the way, lowered her head gently on to the polished counter of the bar, and at last allowed herself to cry.

Chapter Sixteen

'They think I'm a frigging loon, Margie.'

'Who do?'

Rosie had only just got home and was trying to pull herself together. But the telephone receiver slipped out of her grasp and she felt the panic rise in her again. 'Sorry, I just dropped the —'

'Who thinks you're a loon?'

It was too hard to explain. 'The police —'

'The police?'

'Could we go out for a bevvy tonight?' asked Rosie plaintively. 'I need to . . .'

Margie couldn't. She and her children were spending a long weekend in a friend's caravan in Formby for the start of half-term. 'Half what?' said Rosie. 'It can't be. I haven't been consulted.'

But it was half-term. So she flurried and scurried about the house, wondering what the hell she was going to do with the kids for a week or however long they'd be off school, and yes maybe Bob had mentioned half-term to her the odd nine or ten times but she'd got amnesia, hadn't she? How could she be expected to hold all these things in her teeming brain?

Then came a stroke of luck, her first since she'd won twenty-five pence on a lottery ticket last February; Bob rushed home full of how Jason's mother had said he could stay at their house on Saturday night and was that all right? 'If you really want to leave me,' said Rosie, hiding her delight behind an impassive face.

'Yes I do,' said Bob, wiping the delight away.

Soon she was busy negotiating with Carol and Margie so they'd spend the weekend together in the caravan at Formby and she could have some time to herself — free!

alone! — while fending off the children's questions about how the private detection was going. 'I'm sorry,' said Rosie, 'but I've just had a bad time with the police so I don't really want —'

'The police?' exclaimed Carol and Bob in unison.

'What did you do wrong?' asked Bob.

'Did they arrest you?' asked Carol.

'Is it a big case you're on?' asked Bob.

'Don't be sad, Mum,' said Carol.

That was the killer blow. 'That's enough of all that now,' said Rosie briskly to fend off tears rippling under her eyelids. 'Time you were packed and off, Carol.'

Then she remembered she hadn't got the car and called Jerry. It was his night for the Wavertree and District Chess Circle, but she managed to sound desperate enough for him to agree to abandon his bishops and knights just this once. 'I need you,' she said, to her own dismay, into the telephone. For it wasn't just a ride back to her own car that she wanted to beg off Jerry. She really had to tell someone about the forty words a minute and the look in the barman's eyes, and who could she tell if not him?

So with Jennifer back home losing to Bob at knock-out whist, Rosie was soon sitting opposite Jerry in the smoky pub round the corner, half-attentive while he sipped at his pint and talked to her about the news. Several thousand miles away somebody had invaded somebody and it was very important. Rosie tried to listen, but she kept hearing Bob's persistent interrogating voice over tea, saying, 'I didn't think women could be detectives,' in his uninnocent childlike way.

She lit a second cigarette from her first. 'I thought you'd given them up,' said Jerry disapprovingly, wiping beer from his mouth.

Rosie blew out smoke and agreed that she had. 'It's been bloody nerve-racking, Jerry. They think I'm crazy. Hold my hand.'

So he held her hand across the dirty table and she began at the beginning again. At first she smiled as she talked, and talked animatedly. Gradually, though, the re-

telling of the police questioning reminded her more and
more of the bare room, and her initials carved both ways
up on the table, and the brimming dirty ashtray. She
found herself feeling foolish, interspersing the story with
tears:

'... and I said to this barman, they think I'm a frigging
loon I said, and he looked at me over the Vladivar bottle,
and if you could have seen that look, I mean, he thought ...'

Rosie looked into Jerry's eyes. For a moment she saw a
glint of his fillings and his feelings. He looked quickly
away. She knew what he was thinking.

He thought she was a frigging loon.

'Don't you see?' she said into her vodka glass, unable to
look at him. 'I know Andrew Stephenson exists. Him and
Bill Jones tried to bribe the man who reminded me of my
dad: Tommy O'Meara. Tommy wasn't happy about it.
They argued even in the restaurant. On the Sunday he'd
decided he wanted no part of it and told them so. They
were desperate for the contract. They had to kill him.
Don't you see?'

'I'm sure you're right,' said Jerry. 'I expect they'll turn
out to be linked up with a call-girl racket, espionage, international drug-smuggling and organized crime. And you'll
expose the Mr Big behind the entire operation. Who do
you think the Mr Big is, Rosie?'

Ask him about tourism, Rosie. Ask him about his
terrible day at the office. You thought he was kind and
gentle till this business began. Tell him he's kind, Rosie.
Tell him he's gentle.

'How was your day at the office?' said Rosie as kindly
and gently as she could manage.

But now it was Jerry who couldn't let it rest. 'You've
got to admit,' he said, blinking at the smoke from her
cigarette, 'the attitude of the police is understandable. Try
to see it from their point of view.'

'Why? It's complicated enough, just seeing it from my
own.'

'You can't be the lone heroine,' said Jerry with excru-
ciating kindness and gentleness, putting his hand on hers.
'This is Liverpool, love. In the United Kingdom. We've

got a queen and an elected parliament and everything. People don't go around murdering one another much. They just don't.'

'Please take your hand away,' said Rosie.

'I'm only trying to help.'

'Help? Piss off!' she said, loudly enough for heads to turn including her own. Had she said that? 'You just think I'm a loon like all the rest do, right? Well I'm not. I'll prove it to you, you'll see. And you're right,' she added over her shoulder, on her way out, 'I am tired of you.'

She ran home and told Jennifer she wasn't feeling well and sat in the darkness at the dining table, counting the seconds. After six hundred and twenty-one of them she heard the scrape of Jerry's Yale key. She'd locked the mortice too, though, and he couldn't get in. He tapped at the window; he called her name. She held her breath. Six hundred and fifty-nine; six hundred and sixty; six hundred and —

The phone began to ring. She jumped with fright. Pull yourself together, Rosie. The tapping at the window; the phone ringing; she'd stopped counting but it seemed to be going on for hours.

Finally, first the ringing stopped; then, the knocking. All she could hear was the low hum of the fridge from the kitchen. Then the phone started up again. Counting the rings, she picked it up on the thirteenth:

'Aaaaaah, hurrrrrr, aaaaaaah, hurrrrrr, aaaaaaah, hurrrrrr,' said the earpiece breathily.

'I'm glad you called. I was beginning to wonder where you'd got to,' said Rosie into the receiver. 'I'm afraid you've got the wrong number, though. We make our own underwater films here. But since you've rung, let me tell you about something that happened to me today. I went to the police station to report my suspicions of . . .'

The heavy breather had rung off before she could say 'murder'. Rosie found herself laughing, laughing so it was hard to stop.

She stopped. There were footsteps in the hall.

'Mum?' said Bob. 'What's the matter? Why are you sitting in the dark? What's wrong?'

She laughed again, with relief this time, hugging him in his baggy pyjamas. 'Nothing,' she said, 'nothing.'

'I'm sorry,' he said into her shoulder.

'What for?'

'What I said. About how women couldn't be detectives. I didn't mean ...'

'That's all right,' said Rosie into his hair and the darkness, even though it wasn't all right at all. The phone began to ring again. 'We're not going to answer that and everything's going to be all right,' she said without conviction, trying to hold down the laughter that was still wriggling inside her, like a snake, bumping its body against her heart in time with the ring of the telephone.

Chapter Seventeen

'What's frigging, Mum?'

Bob had brought a glass of strange thick liquid to her bed and was sitting beside her, looking wide awake. 'What's this?' she asked blearily, playing for time, only moderately sure she wasn't dreaming.

'Orange juice. What's frigging, Mum?'

'It's a swear word.'

'But even swear words mean something. So what does it mean?'

Rosie gulped the orange and took a deep breath and faced the fact that she was awake. 'It means, it means, it's, er — playing with yourself instead of with other people. Now let me get up, eh?'

Bob lingered, smiling a complacent smile, and Rosie knew he'd already been perfectly well aware of the meaning of the word. 'Go on, off you go.'

It was her own fault for inscribing it in block capitals and leaving it by the bed. The urge to record her thoughts had come in the middle of the night when she'd feared amnesia might have struck again by the morning. But now the words that had seemed profoundly memorable at 3.00 am seemed merely ridiculous:

PROOF — I'M GOING TO HAVE TO PROVE IT. CONFESSION? FIND OUT WHO ANDREW STEPHENSON IS. MAYBE I AM A FRIGGING LOON!

Downstairs she put the phone back on the hook and made herself some sandwiches. Bob was impatient to get to Jason's and dismissive of her doubts about his welcome. 'His Mum doesn't mind, honest.' And indeed when they got there — Bob standing on the doorstep importantly with his overnight bag — Jason's mother didn't seem to mind. She stood there smiling, bathed in a disturbing aura of Good Motherliness. 'Give yourself a break,' she said, making Rosie squirm with guilt and prickle with irritation because she'd forgotten her sandwiches.

Back home Jerry was prowling outside, rapping at the window and calling her name through the letter box. As she got out of the car he spread his arms to embrace her. 'I've just come home for my packed lunch,' she said, hurrying past him into the house. 'Can't stop.'

'But I love you,' he said, pursuing her to the kitchen and out again. 'I was trying to call you but —'

'I'm just a loon, Jerry. And no, I'm not tired of you, that was just, well, let's not have a scene, okay?'

'But,' he was saying as she got back into the car. 'Where are you off to? When can we ...?'

Rosie drove away without looking back.

· For the next five hours she sat in the Mini, watching the flats by Sefton Park. People walked by and she ate her sandwiches and Andrew Stephenson didn't come or go. There was no clear plan in her mind. She vaguely thought she might sit here till he arrived, nursing her sore bum and her book about American teenage girls being possessed by devils. But what then? What if he didn't turn up for days? Would she kip down here too? And what was she going to do when he finally arrived? Make a citizen's arrest? Or just follow him again?

When the streetlamps blinked on she drove away from the unanswered questions to try and settle the Carol question at Graham's house in the suburbs. It was the first time she'd actually stepped over the threshold and she was almost as nervous as Graham seemed to be. He hummed and buzzed around her, seeking her approval. Well, Gray, you'll never guess what I do for a living now: I chase men who haven't coughed up their maintenance and I also investigate. . . .

No, she couldn't tell him. Yet with him she felt sane for the first time in a day and a half. She saw how right she was to be divorced from him. His new wife had tactfully 'gone to the shops' but not, or so it looked, before cleaning the house from top to bottom. Graham ran his fingers along a shelf here, a banister there, in a familiar gesture; he was one of those men always checking up on house-keeping standards and never helping to maintain them himself.

'Still allergic to dust, are you?' said Rosie cheerfully.

Graham smiled broadly. 'Still allergic to housework, are you?'

She didn't care any more. In fact, in small doses she rather liked it, hearing his snide remarks, for they reminded her of what she'd escaped. 'Yeh,' she said, 'I'm thinking of getting a daily in.'

'Gone up in the world, have you?'

'Working for myself, y'know.'

Investigating murders, y'know: she almost felt she could say it, careless, breezy. For Graham's smiling self-confidence was so obviously built out of lies that he made her feel an outrageously honest and straightforward person. 'Yeh, business is going really well,' he said and she knew the sales of his current line, sweets and choco-lates, were going badly. 'How's it going with Mike?' he asked with a suggestive wink and she knew he was trying to scratch a sexual itch of his own. 'Maybe I've not thought enough about Carol,' he said when they finally got round to the business of her visit, and Rosie knew, even as he was agreeing to see his daughter on her own next Friday night, that he was already working out ways to blame his wife, or his ex-wife, or even Carol herself for the fact that they didn't get on.

Rosie went back to the Sefton Park flats with a renewed sense of purpose. Darkness and an eerie mist had settled over the park but she refused to be disconcerted. No silver-grey Volvo had arrived in her absence. She locked the Mini carefully and strode over to the entrance.

The entry-phone had been mended and the door was locked. She hadn't counted on such a rare example of Corpie efficiency but refused to be thrown. She tapped out 9, 0, 6 on the raised numbers. 'Ooh ee ee?' crackled the speaker in a strangled female tone.

'I'm a detective,' said Rosie, blasé. 'I'd like to ask you a few questions.'

'O ee a-ow?' the speaker asked.

Rosie wondered what happened to the consonants in the intercom system. She imagined them all dammed up somewhere, like sperm meeting a diaphragm, while only the vowels of desire seeped through. 'Eh-o?' said the intercom and Rosie leant forward:

'Hello, yes, still here. It'd be easier to tell you what it's about when I come up.'

The door buzzed. She went in and up, and along the familiar grubby corridor, and knocked at the door Andrew Stephenson had entered seven days before.

Helen Thackray had more of a Chinese look than the name had prepared Rosie for. She wore the neutral expression of a doll: tugging at her long black hair with strange jerking gestures, creasing her caked make-up in a parody of a smile as she invited Rosie inside. 'I'm not from the police,' said Rosie, taking the seat she was offered in a deep, threadbare armchair.

'Then who ...?'

'You're Helen Thackray?'

'What's it to you?'

'I'm interested in a man called Andrew Stephenson. You know him, don't you?'

The young woman — she couldn't have been more than twenty-two or twenty-three — had remained standing, appraising Rosie, fiddling with the pockets of her jeans. Although her features were a striking mixture of Asiatic and European, her voice was pure Liverpool:

'Never heard of him. Who are you, anyway?'

'A detective. A private detective. And ...'

'Oh yeh? Come from his wife, do you?' She took a cigarette out of an Embassy packet on top of the television and lit it without offering Rosie one. 'I mean, from this feller's wife.'

The room was furnished from second-hand shops: a scratched old table, a tatty white rug, a tacky sideboard and a three-piece suite that didn't fit together. The electric gadgets gleamed among the dullness like visitors from another planet: television, stereo and . . .

'Use the home computer a lot, do you?' asked Rosie brightly.

'Belongs to my boyfriend,' said Helen Thackray, looking down at Rosie through the smoke from her cigarette. 'What's it to do with you?'

'I'm not from his wife. I think this Andrew Stephenson may be involved in something more serious than a bit of leg-over.'

The woman didn't flicker. 'Told you: never heard of him.'

'You might know him by another name.' Rosie described him, trying to imagine him sitting here, amused, condescending, among the drab furniture: the woman embracing him perhaps, him tapping at the keyboard of his home computer. Helen Thackray affected not to be interested, but Rosie saw her brows knitting with concentration as the description of him unfolded.

'Doesn't ring a bell, no,' leaning on the back of the armchair. 'And, look . . .'

'I've seen him come in here.'

'You must be mistaken,' but her hands were trembling, the ash quivered off her cigarette and on to the chair. 'You are from his wife, aren't you?'

'I think he may have been involved in a murder.'

Helen Thackray laughed, turning away to stub out her cigarette in a brimming ashtray on the table. 'I think you can go now.'

'Okay.' Rosie stood up and reached into her handbag. She placed a torn-out page of her notebook on the arm of the chair. 'I've written my name and address down here. I'll leave it with you.'

'Don't know what for, I'm sure.'

All the best detectives asked the vital question just as they were leaving: Rosie intended to be no exception. 'Think about it,' she said, going towards the door. 'Last Sunday, for instance. Think about last Sunday.'

'What about it?'

Rosie turned. 'Your friend: the one with the computer. Maybe there was something different about him when he

103

came back here that evening. Moody, upset. Something different.'

The woman had turned away for another cigarette. Her voice was fainter: 'And what if there was?'

'Maybe he'd just killed somebody,' said Rosie with apparent calmness. The woman laughed again but it sounded hollow this time. Rosie's hand was on the door handle: 'All I want is a name. An address, maybe. Think about last Sunday.'

'I think you're off your head, love,' said Helen Thackray.

But as Rosie went out into the corridor the woman was stamping out the match that had slipped from her hands, and Rosie was beginning to feel she wasn't quite such a frigging loon after all.

Chapter Eighteen

The good feeling didn't last long. Half an hour later Rosie had been stopped by a traffic policeman from following an 80 bus bearing Helen Thackray under a sign saying BUSES, LOADING AND UNLOADING ONLY. By the time she'd discussed the fact that her road tax was about to run out and the policeman's being off duty at ten o'clock, the bus was out of sight. When she caught up with it again, at the Pierhead terminus, it was parked and empty and there was no sign of Helen Thackray.

'Never mind, eh?' she murmured to the dashboard as she turned for home. At least now she could enjoy the Saturday night she'd been half hoping for all day. With the kids off her hands she was free. FREE! She could do whatever she wanted to do. She could get riotously drunk, or go out disco-dancing all night like people did — didn't they? — or pick up a sugar-daddy at some exclusive restaurant or . . .

And what did Rosie do with her freedom? She stayed at home and took the phone off the hook. With the TV for moving wallpaper she tried to put the bits of her life into some kind of order. Debts, there were so many bloody debts. She fretted over bank statements, and did elaborate calculations on the margin of an old newspaper, and finally convinced herself she could afford to eat and to put petrol in the car next week but the road tax would have to wait.

She wrote, too, a brief and simple letter of apology to Elsie O'Meara. Signing the note with her real name, she wished there was some way she could tell Elsie of her suspicions. But the dead man's sister would only think Rosie was a frigging loon too. Proof, that was what was needed. But as the note beside her bed still reminded her of that in CAPITAL LETTERS, she wondered if she could bear another precious child-free day stuck watching Helen Thackray's flat. Well, it was either that or another debt; she owed Mike one last effort to serve the writ on James MacLeish the midget boxing champion and Monday was the deadline. And then there was Jerry . . .

Chapter Nineteen

In the morning, without breakfast, she slipped on her blouse and skirt for respectable visiting and nipped round to Jerry's to kiss and make up. Lazy bugger, at ten in the morning it still took him two and a half minutes to answer the bell. He finally appeared in his plaid dressing gown that looked like it had been handed down through several generations. She reached up to kiss him on the lips.

'It's me,' she announced as a sort of apology. 'Just to show I'm not tired of you, I picked up your papers from the newsagent's.'

'Uh,' said Jerry dopily, and motioned her inside.

Rosie was planning to give birth to two birds with one egg; to reassure Jerry of the fondness of her feelings by taking him out for the day; meanwhile getting him to accompany her to James MacLeish's door, wherever that might be, if she could even track it down.

But over the toast and the *Mirror* and the coffee and the *Observer* he broke the bad news to her: 'I'm going on this local history trail. Discover Liverpool's past while taking a stroll, kind of thing.'

'Since when have you been interested in, er, local history?'

'It's this interview. The tourism job. Thought I ought to get genned up on our heritage.'

Why could he never say the right thing when she needed him? The toast in Rosie's mouth had turned to dough and she burbled at him grumpily: 'What heritage? Wife-beating and men getting drunk and women bringing up kids on not enough money? Not to mention ...'

Jerry's face suddenly looked like a rat's in a corner. He bared his teeth. 'Pardon?' he said fiercely.

Maybe she shouldn't have tried to talk through the

toast but she knew he'd got the gist. She managed to swallow the great lump of resentment in her throat. 'I've got this job, haven't I?'

'Not still on about that, are you?'

Trying to fix a cool look on her face, she lectured herself silently and sternly: Rosie, you came here to kiss and make up, not to go on about Andrew Stephenson and women's lot.

Ah, shut up, goody-goody, she replied inwardly. While out loud:

'I'm not a loon, you know,' she said sadly.

'I know you're not,' he replied with his bureaucrat's kindness and his Jerry-knows-best smile. Suddenly he seemed more like Bill Jones and Andrew Stephenson than the lover she sometimes felt sorry for; as if he belonged more to the world of her mysterious client than to her own world.

So she dropped him off on her way and arrived at the boarded-up maisonette in Speke. Nothing had changed since her last visit except the word TRACY in pink letters on the plyboard over the windows. Hi, Tracy. It had begun to rain. Rosie's malicious glee at that, thinking of Jerry's tourist trail, was tempered by the wind whipping the stuff up into her face despite the shelter of the canopy overhead. The flat blocks had been cunningly designed to catch every slight disturbance of the air and turn it into a hurricane. There was nobody about: they'd have fallen over. Rosie bent into the wind and with a deep breath knocked on the neighbouring door.

A woman in curlers restraining a snarling Jack Russell with corgi relations didn't know where James MacLeish was, but referred her across the courtyard, where a middle-aged man in overalls was mending a broken window. 'They won't come out for months, y'see: the Corpie. If you want anything doing you've gorra do it yourself. Why did you want to talk to Jimmy?'

Rosie smiled and did her best to posh up her accent. 'Jimmy's come up on the Premium Bonds. I'm trying to trace him. We have to work nights and Sundays, y'see, to catch people in.'

The address he gave her all too trustingly — what if she'd been a policewoman or something dangerous like that? — was over the water, in the Wirral, and turned out to be a startling contrast to the boarded-up maisonette. A bit down-market from the neighbourhood of the Atlantic Crossing, only half a mile down the road; but posh nevertheless, a new detached house, one of four in a cul-de-sac. Two carriage lamps hung like sentries on either side of the door. It was the sort of place Graham had promised her when they were married. Trying to remember why she'd craved such a place, Rosie took a deep breath, and rapped the brass knocker against the varnished wood of the front door.

'James MacLeish?'

He wasn't a midget boxing champion after all. He was an off-duty all-in wrestler: as broad as he was long, and giving off a strong odour of half-digested beer. 'My friends call me Jimmy. What ...?'

'This is your lucky day,' said Rosie, taking the writ out of her handbag. She profferred the papers in her left hand; 'Here you go.'

Somehow it happened very fast, yet in slow motion. 'Oh no you don't,' he was saying. And the door was closing, and Rosie was lowering her arm out of the way, and she was watching the millimetres and the microseconds race each other frame by frame, and her arm was still reaching out, and the door was closing, and there was a strange crunching noise where her left arm was, and ...

'Aargh!' said Rosie, rather loudly.

The door opened a crack; her hand dropped to her side with an unpleasant click; the door banged shut. She touched the contorted shape of her wrist.

'Ooh,' said Rosie quietly as she sat down unexpectedly on the step. She stared at her left hand, surprised it was still there, throbbing at her. The papers were no longer in it. Nor was any feeling apart from pain. 'Ooh,' she repeated unimaginatively.

The door opened a crack. 'You all right?'

'Great,' said Rosie to the blurred man.

The door closed. The world was very grey and wobbly.

Rain began to spatter on to Rosie's feet, splayed out as they were beyond the cover of the porch. Her career as a private detective was going to end here, ignominiously, in her quiet pathetic death, and nobody would ever know the truth about Tommy O'Meara: that much was clear.

A long half a minute later the door re-opened. 'Sure you're all right?'

The time for heroics was over. 'Awful,' said Rosie. 'I feel awful.'

By the time she brought the world back into focus she'd been transported to an armchair in a bare room and sweet tea was being poured between her lips by a large, hairy hand. 'Never hit a woman in my life,' his large, hairy voice was saying. 'Try and get this down, love.'

The room was very bare indeed. Only a big television, on an upturned chest, gleamed brightly in the carpetless, curtainless room. 'I'm just accident prone,' said Rosie from the only chair. 'I think I've broken my wrist. Haven't got a fag, have you?'

James MacLeish had given them up. He'd never hit a woman in his life, he emphasized, and Rosie wondered why that was so important. He proposed a deal:

'You take back the writ and promise not to serve it on me,' he said between her sips of tea, 'and I'll take you to hozzie. How's that grab you?'

Rosie allowed herself to be grabbed. Cradling her wounded left arm in her right she was guided out to the hallway. He picked up the writ between thumb and finger as if it held some filth he didn't want to be contaminated with, and dropped it into her handbag. He looked at her anxiously.

'You never touched it,' she agreed. 'Sorry about this.'

'No, no, it's my fault. You could have me up for assault, y'know,' said James MacLeish. He shook his head disbelievingly. 'Never hit a woman in my life.'

Have him up for assault? The idea of going to a police station didn't especially appeal to Rosie. On her recent record they'd probably end up charging her with breaking and not entering. So she shook her head, and said 'Oooh' again because the motion shook her wrist too, and they got into his dirty great, dirty grey Ford.

'I don't think,' said Rosie on the way to the hospital, 'I don't think I'm cut out for this line of work. You're only my second case and the first one tore his up.' Quite apart from investigating the possibility of murder . . .

'It wasn't a bad try,' said the big man kindly. He was an experienced writ-dodger, he explained as the suburbs whizzed by. His business was building houses for people, including himself — all four in the cul-de-sac, what did she think of them? — and selling them, and moving on, leaving as many debts behind him as he could, and maybe living in a Council flat if he could fiddle his way on to the waiting list while building the next one, selling, profiting, moving on, leaving the debts behind, in an endless spiral.

'But they caught up on you this time?'

'My wife walked out on me. Took all the furniture except the carriage lamps and gave the Revenue the dirt on me,' he admitted cheerfully. 'I usually dodge 'em by not being myself, y'see, in business. I'm always companies. I buy a new company every year or two. You can buy 'em off the shelf, y'know. Like cans of soup. Are you a company, love?'

Rosie said no, she was a crowd, and thanked him for the lift but there was no need to wait, she'd be all right honestly. They shook hands in the hospital forecourt and James MacLeish smiled with embarrassment and said 'Shame we had to meet like this, eh?' and got into the Ford and drove away.

Companies, thought Rosie as she waited in Casualty. The word sounded so cosy and comforting and friendly when it was just a disguise to make money and evade debts with.

Like Bill Jones's business, 'privatizing', she thought as she waited for her X-rays: that sounded like bringing something into the bosom of the family, something nice, when it was just a game to make money out of.

Companies, though, she began to think as the nurse moulded the plaster round her wrist and addressed her as if she were a little child, now that's an idea, companies . . .

Chapter Twenty

'D'you think I should become a company?' said Rosie in Mike's office the next day.

He was staring at her without seeing her, talking into the telephone about hearings and pleas and appointments. Once he'd finished this interminable conversation she was going to tell him everything about yesterday; not just about the deal with James MacLeish and the broken wrist and her idea about companies, but all the complications of persuading a reluctant Jerry, exhausted and soaked from his unaccustomed walk, to collect her car from the Wirral cul-de-sac; about Carol staying in the caravan in Formby with strangers because Margie had had to come back for her training course and Bob campaigning for a home computer of his own just like Jason's; about how the washing was behind-hand and the shopping was undone and everyone thought she was a frigging loon and did he fancy her . . .?

'D'you think I should become a company?'

He'd put the phone down and was re-assembling the chaos of his paperwork into a slightly neater version of disorder. 'Not till you want to associate with somebody, Rosie.'

His tone might have been suggestive.

It probably wasn't, though.

Still, she managed to persuade him to forgo the delights of quiche alsace and kidney bean salad just this once, and instead buy her a vodka and a stale cheese sandwich at the pub round the corner. 'It's nice to see you,' she said daringly, smiling across the rippled pseudo-brass of their corner table. 'Is it nice to see me?'

He was staring, glazed, at the businessmen and office girls grouped awkwardly at the bar like extras in a play. 'So what's all this about companies?'

Keep trying, Rosie. 'I'm not asking for myself,' she said. 'About the niceness. It's for a friend.'

'Beg your pardon?'

She didn't seem to be getting through. So she set her attempts at flirtation aside and finally got round to what (or so she told herself) she really wanted to ask:

'I want to find out about this company. It's called Streetclean Limited. So how do I go about it?'

Mike said sorry, he'd had an argument with a friend and wasn't himself today ('friend'?) and what had she just said? And then: 'Is this to do with the big case you're on, then?'

It was like talking to Jerry in one of his bureaucratic moods. Every question met a question. So she gave him an edited update of the Andrew Stephenson Affair: 'Yeh,' she said. And finally, he deigned to explain to her about company searches and how she could go down to London to do one herself at Companies House otherwise it'd cost money, normally that is but as it happened he was sending a clerk down to do one on Wednesday so if she could just give him the details ...?

'You're a pal, Mike,' said Rosie. She would have flung her arms round his neck and kissed him except she might have knocked him out with her plaster cast. Instead she offered to buy him another drink. But he had to get back to the office to meet a client. Just a quick one? No, really. But I wanted to get your advice about this —

Murder. She'd tell him about it next time, she decided, next time when he hadn't just had a tiff with a 'friend' and she didn't have to run for the bus to collect Bob from Jason's.

Murder. Mike wouldn't think she was a frigging loon, would he? No, he'd sit there quietly and soberly, taking her seriously. Oh, really? How was it done, Rosie? Well, you see, this poor man was going up the stairs for his heart pills and this Andrew Stephenson although that's not his real name ...

Next time. She'd tell him next time. Sitting with a cup of tea in the dining room later that afternoon, concentrating on not thinking about undone housework and not hearing Bob and Jason play human Space Invaders overhead, she suddenly saw Tommy O'Meara's body clearly: all twisted and misshapen at the foot of the stairs, a gash at his temple, blood smearing his grey woolly cardigan that was just like her dad used to wear, Andrew Stephenson standing white-faced over him; later, Elsie standing there in her Sunday best, just back from church, weeping.

Careful, Rosie. You're starting to see things that might not even have happened, that you didn't see happen at all. It's what comes of watching too much television.

And it turned out Bob and Jason weren't playing human Space Invaders overhead, but their very own Holmes-and-Watson adventure, the Case of the Missing Alien Spaceship. It was when she found them in her bedroom, Jason dusting the window sills for fingerprints with half a can of her talcum powder, Bob slashing with his comb at an invisible assailant disguised as her duvet, that she decided to call a halt.

'But Mum, we're only playing at being detectives.'

So am I, thought Rosie wearily. 'Come downstairs and have some orange juice.'

Jason pursued her to the kitchen. 'Is it right what Bob says? That you're a real detective?'

'It's not all it's cracked up to be,' said Rosie defensively.

While she made the tea she could hear Bob expounding in the dining room. 'I saw it in a note she wrote,' he was telling his friend in his whisper as loud as a shout, 'it's all to do with a man called Andrew Stephenson and she's got to prove something and she got her arm broken in the line of duty ...'

The boys wanted to help. Across the fish fingers and mash they plied her with questions. She found herself spinning a plausible yarn of fact plaited with fantasy — why couldn't she just tell someone the truth for once and have them believe in her? — about the anti-corruption Andrew Stephenson, who worked in a firm making computer parts, and now she had to watch this flat he might come to tonight but how could she on her own with a broken arm?

'We'll come,' said Jason eagerly.

'We'll help you,' said Bob eagerly.

A tricky moment: 'No, well, erm, I'm afraid it has to be somebody with a car, so I can follow him if he goes out, doesn't it?'

Bob pushed aside his half-eaten meal and put on his thoughtful look, conscious of his audience. His standing with Jason had clearly increased two hundred per cent now that his mother was a real live private eye. 'You need Jerry,' he pronounced. 'We'll go and get him.'

'No, look, wait, finish your tea ...'

But they were already out of the door and she'd hardly had time to clear the table one-handedly before they were back, trailing a reluctant Jerry in their wake.

'Here he is, Mum,' said Bob triumphantly, 'we've told him all about it.'

'That's, erm, very good of you,' said Rosie with an effort at conviction. Jerry shrugged at her, out of the boys' vision. 'So where are the two of you going out to now?'

'But Mum ...'

'Jerry and I have important business to discuss, don't we? Home by eight now, and if I'm not here ...'

She'd have to get Jennifer or Marie's mother to sit with Bob but for now she just wanted — seeing Jerry's frown — to get them out of the house. Thankfully, other enthusiasms were always lurking in readiness:

'Yeh, it's Hallowe'en,' said Jason. 'Let's go do trick or treat.'

'Don't get into any trouble now.'

'Or,' added Bob, 'we might get some wood for the bonnie on the holler.'

'What's all this about?' Jerry asked as the boys rushed out.

He'd had a sheltered upbringing in the suburbs and couldn't always keep up with the vernacular. 'They might get some wood for the bonfire on the derelict ground,' translated Rosie, not meaning to sound sarcastic at his ignorance.

'No, I mean, this corruption in the computer business.' He was staring, mystified, at the tea towel she'd thrust into

115

his hand. 'And how you're going to catch the villain red-handed tonight if only I'll come with you.'

'It's because of my arm, y'see, I can't drive ...'

'This detection isn't the job for you,' said Jerry severely.

The tea towel draped elegantly over his arm, he watched as she dipped the pots into the washing-up bowl one-handed. 'I should leave them to drain,' said Rosie, avoiding his stare.

Absent-mindedly he picked up a dinner plate and began drying it with a hypnotic circular motion. 'Honestly, Rosie. Getting your arm broken and conjuring up murders. Well, frankly, I'm not about to encourage you by freezing to death in the car all night.'

Maybe you should be a schoolteacher if you're so anxious for a change of career, said Rosie in her surprised imagination. 'I think you're wearing out the pattern on that plate,' she muttered out loud, piling pans precariously on top of one another.

So she phoned Margie to come and watch flat 906 with her instead but Margie was knackered tonight would tomorrow do? It'll have to, Rosie concluded, settling down for an evening in front of the telly with Jerry. He was watching an episode from a blockbuster series about the sufferings of rich people in Australia or America or somewhere equally remote like the south of England. In the boring bits he tried to engage her sympathy for the sufferings of a man on three times the money she earned a year for half the work she did — himself — but she couldn't seem to bring a tear to her eye over somebody else already being lined up for the tourism job.

Once Bob had come in — late — and been brusquely dismissed for asking her how the case was going, she sought comfort. 'Let's go to bed,' she murmured in Jerry's ear.

But even that didn't make it better. Tonight, even though he apologized for his grumpiness, he didn't seem gentle and unselfish to her. Tonight Jerry naked seemed pretty much like Jerry clothed. Tonight he seemed like a bureaucrat of the bedroom mechanically following the rules of How To Please A Woman. Tonight she didn't feel

like singing *Zip-a-dee-doo-dah*, but instead that old
Lennon-McCartney tune the kids had whistled into the
answering machine back when all this business had
begun:

> Yesterday
> Love was such an easy game to play
> Now I need a place to hide away
> Oh I believe in yesterday ...

Not that yesterday was actually anything to write home
about, she reminded herself as Jerry's sexual ardour
finally dimmed into snoring. Why was she feeling this
way? Hormones? Why wasn't her detection as Bob and
Jason imagined it to be? A few known suspects and a lot of
logical little clues and at least some agreement about a
murder having taken place so she could work it out all
neatly and rationally?

Rosie pinched Jerry's nostrils to cut down the background noise and tried to acknowledge the truth — that
she didn't know what the hell she was doing.

Come off it, Rosie. Important people — politicians, for
instance — didn't let a little thing like that stand in their
way.

Rosie was not to be comforted. As she drifted off to
sleep the words of the song were still floating through her
melancholy brain:

> Yesterday
> All my troubles seemed so far away
> Now it looks as though they're here to stay
> Oh I believe in yesterday ...

Chapter Twenty One

But the next morning Rosie woke to the sound of the man opposite failing to start his car, and rain was beating at the window, and that put her in good spirits straight off. Everyone else would be feeling gloomy today because of the weather. So why shouldn't she be cheerful instead?

So it was that the first thing she did — as regards the Case of Andrew Stephenson, that is, after breakfast for the two males and tea and a fag for the cook and a quick row with Jerry in which neither of them quite knew what it was about, and sending Bob out to call on the man in the next street, but the one who mended washing machines was in hospital having his hernia removed from the waiting list — after all that the first thing she did was to call Directory Enquiries and ask for the number of Streetclean Limited, London. No, that was all she knew of the address. Won't be a moment.

Even London was just a guess. But it seemed likely. London was where everything important happened, wasn't it? Decisions about heart transplants and which knee to kneel on before Americans and how to organize the emptying of bins?

And it was amazing how the plaster on her wrist got in the way of everything. Rosie thanked the absence-of-God for the temporary nature of her disability, as she nestled the phone awkwardly in the cradle of her shoulder like a violin and waited for a tune to come to her and — yes, Directory Enquiries had the number.

Bill Jones wasn't in. No, he wasn't expected back at all today. 'Was there any message?' asked a voice that sounded like it went with brightly-polished fingernails and clothes from trendy boutiques.

'Just say Veronica called and she'd love to see him again.'

Just at that moment the receiver squirmed out of her shoulder and jumped halfway down her back. Rosie had to twist her good arm into a newly-invented yoga position to replace it on the telephone.

Well, and Bill Jones's absence put paid to her decisive plan to go and do her own company search in London tomorrow and renew old acquaintance with the tyre-replacing tyro and ask him who was that man I saw you with last Thursday? — What, then, was she going to do with all her surplus energy and her desire to solve problems?

When Carol came dripping home an hour later, bursting with news of her weekend and how they'd had to come home this morning when the rain came in through the caravan windows, she found her one-and-a-half-handed mother sitting in the middle of the kitchen floor, surrounded by bits of a twin-tub washing machine which she seemed to be trying to turn into a jigsaw.

'What're you doing, Mum?'

'It's like a murder mystery,' said Rosie by way of explanation. 'Working out the clues. It was one of Bob's football socks that did it. Did you have a good time?'

'Yeh. What happened to your arm?'

'I was tired of the shape it was so I thought I'd have it remoulded.'

Irritatingly it was only when Bob came in from a mysterious 'out' he'd been to that the three of them together managed to reassemble all the screws, pipes, sprockets and sockets into something that, at first glance anyway, bore a remarkable resemblance to a twin-tub washing machine. The children stood watching, wearing their transfixed-by-the-television looks, while Rosie filled the machine with water and dirty clothes.

'And the amazing thing was,' Rosie told Margie that night when they were settling down in Margie's car outside the Sefton Park flats, 'it worked. We did a little jig round the kitchen to celebrate and I broke a flower-pot with a quick flip of my plaster-cast.'

'Great,' said Margie with uncharacteristic lack of enthusiasm.

'And maybe, I was thinking, maybe I should go into that line of work, eh? Washing machine maintenance. Clapped-out models a speciality. Being one myself, like.'

'Don't go into computers,' said Margie, 'whatever you do.'

There'd been a setback on Margie's training course. The whole class had gone on a visit to a real dead computer in operation. In the room where the punch-card operators worked Margie had almost passed out. 'Honest, Rosie, I felt sick. A load of battery hens hooked up to their keyboards making them cluck. It's like the typing pool but worse. Because you don't even get to type words or anything. Just a load of numbers and you don't know what they mean.'

'Thanks for coming, anyway,' said Rosie, who considered Margie the strong-woman of their friendship and wasn't sure she was up to the idea of role reversal.

But Margie had obviously been saving it up all day. 'That's the computer revolution for you,' she continued relentlessly. 'Less jobs for sellers and clerks and a few rotten jobs for women.'

'Thanks for coming out with me anyway,' said Rosie, in case her friend hadn't heard the first time.

It was cold in the car. They'd brought blankets and a thermos each but nothing seemed to take the edge off the chill. And nothing happened. A few cars and people went in; a few cars and people came out; no sign of Andrew Stephenson or Helen Thackray.

And Rosie had long run out of chit-chat about kids or computers — Bob had mystified her earlier in the day with talk about kilobytes and peripherals, as part of his campaign for his very own home computer like Jason's only better — by nine o'clock, when Margie brought out her secret weapon; a half-bottle of scotch. 'Can't really afford it but I felt like I needed some tonight. Here you go.'

Rosie didn't really like whisky. She took a scalding throat-full and then had a thought:

'You gonna be all right to drive?' With one broken

limb already, Rosie didn't relish the idea of a plaster on her other arm to match.

'I'll only have a drop. Go on.'

By nine forty five still nothing had happened and rain was rat-tat-tatting on the windscreen but Rosie was feeling warmer all over somehow and having difficulty remembering why she didn't like whisky when a man tapped on the window. 'Don't take any notice,' Margie whispered as Rosie wound her window down.

'Have you got a light, queen?'

'Oh, yeh,' said Rosie, fumbling with her good hand in her handbag and wondering what Margie was whispering about now, till the man said:

'How much?'

'The matches are free.'

'No, how much? For, er, y'know, a bit of, er ...'

'Oh,' said Rosie, seeing his point as she passed the free match through the window. 'Show us it, then.'

'You wha'?'

'Show us your doo-dah. We charge by the inch, y'see.'

It was only then that she got the strong reek of alcohol off his breath as he leered in at her, and 'Don't you ...' he was saying as he pointed a warning finger at her. But Margie had leant across to wind up the window and he stubbed his finger on the dirty glass. His mouth was opening and closing like a fish's. Then suddenly Margie had started the car and with a squeal of tyres they were away, leaving the man a fist-waving shadow at the roadside.

'Sometimes you frighten me,' said Margie as she eased the speed down.

Sometimes Rosie frightened herself. 'D'you see the look in his eyes? Why do men get that look in their eyes?'

Margie gave her a sidelong glance as the car waited at traffic lights: If you don't know by now I'm not going to tell you, said her look.

'No, I mean, why do people hurt one another? Why do they — kill one another? He looked like the sort of feller who could. Kill you. His eyes. Why do they do it?'

'Usually,' said Margie, resolutely sober, 'to keep the world safe for democracy or socialism or something.'

'No, not war. Like, people you meet, ordinary people. What makes them do it?'

She hadn't really imagined it before; the look in Andrew Stephenson's eyes as he stood over Tommy O'Meara. Now she saw it. It was the look of the drunken man at the car window; his eyes widening and at the same time glazing over, the look of someone whose anger has just passed across into another dimension where you don't exist.

The crumpled body at the foot of the stairs.

Careful, Rosie.

'Ugh,' she said, shivering. 'Someone just walked over my grave.'

Margie glanced across with an enquiring frown. 'No, I mean,' Rosie added, trying to explain, 'I mean, I walked over someone else's.'

But that didn't make it any clearer, and a tidal wave of whisky suddenly surged through the blood-vessels adjacent to her brain, and Andrew Stephenson with the look of the drunken man floated up from her imagination to hover before her eyes.

'You all right, Rosie?'

I'm frightened, Marg. Sometimes I frighten myself. 'Fine,' said Rosie, blinking the face away. 'Saw a ghost, that's all.'

'Too much whisky.'

'You're probably right,' said Rosie, thinking, if only it was as simple as that. If only her ghosts lived only in her imagination it'd be all right.

Chapter Twenty Two

When she got back home, stumbling a little over the threshold and singing 'I'm a loser' softly over her breath — thinking, Jennifer must always reckon I'm half-cut — Rosie was greeted with a strange sight and strange news. Jennifer had green hair and a man had called round. Green hair? A man? She couldn't take it in. Establishing that the visitor had neither been Jerry with a dozen red roses and an apology, nor the milkman trying to claim his last six weeks' money, she pressed the money for the night's sitting into the girl's hand, dismissed the green hair as a drunken hallucination and went straight to bed to sleep it off.

But in the morning she wondered, through her fur-lined brain: Was the green hair real? Who could the visiting man have been?

She'd promised Bob and Carol a day in town — museums and hamburgers and probably no change out of a tenner — but after breakfast she postponed their departure and went across the road to settle the mysteries. Jennifer was still in bed, and when she came down she was still green from the forehead up; the delicate shade of diluted lime juice. 'Your hair looks, er, nice,' said Rosie.

'Sorry?' said Jennifer dozily.

What the girl could remember of the man was enough: fiftyish, tall, short greyish hair, smart brown camel-hair coat and yes, come to think of it, a bit like he was talking down to you. He hadn't said what he wanted. He hadn't said he'd call again.

So Andrew Stephenson had been to see her. What could he have been after? And why couldn't he have come earlier and saved her and Margie a freezing night and the price of a half-bottle of whisky?

That night she decided to wait in, in case he came again. She got the kids off to bed and set the ironing board up in the middle of the living room, to remind her of what she should be doing. Then she switched on the television and, exhausted from a day of museums and unanswerable questions about fossils and the Beatles' early lives, put her feet up on the sofa and half-closed her eyes.

The doorbell rang.

Her heart thudded. Perhaps she shouldn't answer it. She'd asked Margie to come and sit with her but her friend couldn't make it. Okay, then. She'd just pretend she hadn't heard the bell. Don't be silly, Rosie, you've waited in for him. Waited in? What else were you going to do tonight? Waited in for *him*? You must be crazy, Rosie. Think of Tommy O'Meara and don't open your door to anyone you think might be a murderer.

On the second ring of the doorbell, resolute as ever, she went to the door.

He didn't look dangerous. In fact, he looked a bit pathetic. He'd got caught in a shower of rain between the Volvo and the doorbell, and his hair was plastered down to his skull so he looked a bit like a monk.

'Yeh?' said Rosie nonchalantly, blocking the doorway.

He stared at her, bemused. She stared back. 'Perhaps if I might ...'

'Okay,' said Rosie, turning to give him room. His smart camel-hair coat gleamed with rain. 'Make yourself at home,' she said and went to the kitchen, leaving him in the living room to stare at the telly as if it was a visitor from an alien planet. It was playing an episode about that pathologist-detective who dealt with an American Issue Of Our Time every week; now she'd never know whether he'd kept the world safe for science for another seven days.

Making the tea, she glanced surreptitiously through the crack in the sliding door. He was drying off in front of the ironing board and casting his condescending look over the children's pictures that lined the walls. She took the tray in: a tricky operation with one hand, but somehow the best tea-set made it through. Taking a cup from her, he seemed surprisingly unsure of himself. Was that a slight shaking of his hand? She settled down regally on the sofa again and waited for him to announce his business. He was still standing awkwardly by the ironing board, puffing out his chest. What was he after?

Suddenly, Rosie understood. He was trying to look imposing, with that grimace fastened on to his face, and his shoulders big and square in the padded overcoat. He'd come here to threaten her with something. 'Erm, er, do have a seat,' said Rosie conversationally, five hundred per cent cooler than she felt. 'Tuh, terrible night out.'

Yet he was nervous. His whole face jerked up and down in time with the blinking of his eyelids. Nervous of what? Of what he was about to do to her? 'Mrs Monaghan,' he said gravely.

'That's me,' said Rosie. 'Well, almost. I don't think I caught your name, though. Your real name.'

His face cracked into an imitation of a smile. A mistake; to acknowledge she didn't know his identity. He seemed to be getting her into focus for the first time. 'What happened to your arm?'

'One of the hazards of the job,' said Rosie. 'Meeting violent men.'

'I'm rarely,' with a genuine, ghastly smile now, 'rarely violent myself.'

But you'll make an exception in my case? 'Look, I don't know what —'

'You've been bothering a friend of mine.'

'She'd never heard of Andrew Stephenson.'

'Making a lot of wild accusations. Accusations which have no basis in fact, I might add. And you've been watching her flat.'

Hell. Rosie sat on the sofa and sipped at her tea, all Queen Mother and self-assured. But in her heart and her head things were getting turbulent. Hell, he'd been watching for her while she'd been watching for him. Boring days and freezing nights, and all for nothing. And now what was he after?

'I wish I could understand,' he was saying, and the blinking was easing off now as he got into his stride, 'what your motivation was in all this.'

125

'Snap,' said Rosie.

He wrinkled his forehead for a moment, as if fumbling for the meaning of the word, then smiled his smile again. 'But I do see that perhaps you weren't sufficiently rewarded for the work you did for me. Financially.'

Rosie sipped her tea and tried not to notice that it was her hand that was shaking now. She didn't dare say anything in case her voice cracked. He was staring very hard into his teacup. He was going to offer her money. Tommy O'Meara at the foot of the stairs ...

He took an envelope out of his inside pocket. 'So I'm prepared to offer you a further lump sum payment of a hundred and fifty pounds. Making two hundred pounds in all. For services rendered, shall we say?'

Cheap for turning a blind eye to murder; expensive for following a man ineptly for half a day. What was she supposed to say?

'I would, of course, expect certain guarantees; certain areas of agreement between us. Concerning your dealings with Miss Thackray.' Was her silence putting him off? She bit back the questions as his eyes flicked edgily to her face and then away. 'I'd expect you not to bother Miss Thackray any further. Nor, indeed, to spread your malicious and entirely unfounded accusations any further than, ahm, than you might already have done. Yes? Is that understood.' Suddenly he was almost shouting: 'Is that understood?'

He was sitting between her and the door; between her and the telephone. He'd slid the smile back into place. 'I'll give you a receipt,' said Rosie, loudly to cover the hoarseness of her dry throat, taking his envelope, getting up to go to her handbag in the dining room and get her thoughts straight.

'That won't be necessary.'

He reached out as if to stop her. But the ironing board was in the way, and she slipped past. 'Receipt, yes,' said Rosie, gulping, wondering if she could dial 999 before he got to her. No, Rosie, no, don't alarm him. 'In case you ever need it for the Inland Revenue, y'know,' it was just the first thing that'd come into her head that was all and now what was she going to do?

She dropped the money envelope into her bag as she took out her notebook and tore a page from it. Deep breath, Rosie. 'Another cup o'tea while you're waiting?'

'It's really not necessary.'

He was eyeing her suspiciously from across the room. She'd never felt so frightened in her life. Not even when Graham had come at her with his slipper that time.

But she was angry too. How dare he? How dare he come here to her home and threaten her? She'd show him! Rage and fear jostled inside her as she made a big show of writing out the receipt. She measured the number of strides to the door out of the corner of her eye, and turned the paper so he could read it:

Received from a fake of a man calling himself Andrew Stephenson, the sum of £150 (one hundred and fifty pounds) in consideration for keeping my gob shut about murder or foul play on his part to Miss Helen Thackray of Flat 906, Dahlia Towers, or to any other interested party. But I'll still say what I like to who I like.

'Bitch!' he said, getting up, reaching for the scrap of paper. She snatched it away. He grabbed her good wrist in his right hand, very tightly. He was blinking very fast. She raised her left arm, wincing at the weight of the plaster, shouting out with pain as she banged at his fingers wrapped around her wrist. He wouldn't let go. His eyes were looking into hers, staring like the eyes of the man at the window of Margie's car. Suddenly, with his free hand he snatched the receipt from her grasp just as:

'Mum?' said Carol from the doorway. 'Can't sleep. What's ...?'

'It's all right, Carol, it's all right.'

'Let go of my mum!'

He already had done. Now he stood, shaking, on the other side of the ironing board, massaging the back of his hand where she'd hit him. Both Rosie's wrists hurt and it took her a moment to remember which one was really broken. Carol came and put her arms round her. 'Who's that man?'

'Mr Stephenson's just going.'

He'd tossed the crumpled receipt aside. Carol went to pick it up but he kicked it angrily out of her reach and she shrank back into her mother's embrace, staring fiercely at him. 'Go away!' she said, so loudly that all three of them were rigid with surprise. Through the silence that followed her voice still seemed to echo around the walls. Then:

'Your mother was just going to give me an envelope back,' he said sharply. 'Then I'll be on my way.'

'Get me my handbag, will you, Carol?'

Carol went and fetched it from the dining-room table. Rosie placed it on the ironing board and, reaching in, tore the envelope so Carol wouldn't see the money she was shaking out of it into the depths of her bag. She handed the empty envelope to her ex-client with an effort of a smile. Was she going to get away with it? With not keeping her gob shut but being a hundred and fifty pounds the richer?

'G'night then,' she said tentatively.

He stared at her handbag for a moment, the envelope between thumb and forefinger, as if weighing up the possibilities. He looked at Carol. Carol looked back, wide-eyed. Then abruptly, without another word, he turned and went out.

Chapter Twenty Three

She should have rushed out of the door and taken his car registration number. She should have shaken her fist at his departing exhaust. She should have explained to Carol some of what was going on instead of brusquely dismissing her to bed. She should have called Jerry and made it up (whatever it was; she couldn't even remember). Then she should have had an early night instead of staying up till two in the morning worrying about whether to declare £150 to the dole, so that she could then have woken up refreshed with resolution and her nearest approximation to beauty, not with uncertainty and bags under her eyes. Then she should have —

Sometimes Rosie's life seemed full of absences, brimming with things she should have done. They nagged at her; greedy little worms in the pit of her stomach, chomping holes in her. Worms. Every time she thought about them they divided in half and multiplied and how did you kill off the things?

Yes, and over breakfast she should have been taking the opportunity of Bob's departure out — 'Out?' 'Just out.' — to tell Carol she'd be spending Friday night (which was tomorrow already) with Graham. But she couldn't seem to sort out the words to explain how Carol's request never to see her father again had transformed itself into seeing more of him. Instead she chewed unenthusiastically on a piece of toast and stared hard at the handwriting on an envelope while Carol said, 'But why were you fighting? What did he want? Who was he?'

The answer was in an anonymous note scattered among the red-shaded bills of the morning's mail. STEPHEN ANDERSON, the note read. That was all. The two words were felt-tip block capitals on a sheet of lined writing paper with a Basildon Bond watermark.

Thank you, Sherlock Monaghan.

And yes, the name fitted. STEPHEN ANDERSON, Andrew Stephenson: the swapped syllables of the shadow life of a man confident that no-one would bother to penetrate his shadow life.

There was only one possible source for the note: Helen Thackray. Why, though, had she sent it? Rosie could think of no other explanation than something *had* happened on that Sunday, the Sunday of Tommy O'Meara's death. He *had* come back to her flat that night, different in a way that had disturbed the girl.

And now something else had happened and Rosie was £150 the richer.

And now —

'I was frightened,' said Carol into her daydreams. 'What was it all about, Mum? Last night?'

'Just business,' said Rosie, more brusquely than she'd intended. But she had to get on and do things: 'Now, love, I want to make a couple of phone calls. Private phone calls.'

Carol sluggishly took the hint. Rosie waited till she heard her daughter's footfalls upstairs, then dialled Mike's number. 'Has that search on the company come through yet?'

It had and he was sorry he'd been so grouchy the other day and could he maybe make it up to her over lunch today?

'Sure, sure,' said Rosie. 'Is there a Stephen Anderson on the board of directors or whatever they're called?'

Yes there was. Rosie swallowed and Mike asked her if she was all right. Mm, fine. The man who had posed as a bureaucrat seeking out corruption by a company called Streetclean Limited was himself part of that company and yes, Rosie was fine. For things were much clearer now, weren't they?

Frankly, no.

So she hung up and cursed herself for agreeing to lunch when who was going to sit with the children and where was Bob anyway? And how could she explain to Carol that there were just some things in life you had to do even if you didn't like doing them?

Her own mother had said that to her. Rosie remembered how stupid and ridiculous it had sounded in her own childhood, and shuddered at herself.

Concentrate on The Case, Rosie. Solve The Case. Life should come second when you're a private detective in charge of solving the moral problems of the world.

Oh, should should should.

She called Streetclean and asked for Bill Jones and got the trendy London madam again. 'I'm afraid Mr Jones is in our Merseyside office till next Monday.'

Our Merseyside office? 'Could you give me the number?' she said to London, almost dropping the phone, and soon, miraculously, receiver cradled perilously in her shoulder, she was talking to the man herself. 'Veronica here.'

He couldn't place her for a moment, and then: 'Oh, yeh. Were you in trouble with the Old Bill or something?'

'I can explain all that. How d'you like to buy me lunch?'

Immediately she wanted to rewind the words and erase her fast-woman self-introduction. But he only hesitated for a fraction of a second before proposing tomorrow and naming a pub downtown and she found herself saying yes and:

'This'll probably sound a bit daft to you but does a, does a Mr Anderson work with you?'

'Yeh. You know him?'

'I'd rather you didn't tell him we were meeting. That all right?'

'Fine. Very mysterious. See you.'

Carol was standing in the doorway to the hall, smiling. How long had she been there, listening? 'I thought I told you —'

'Is that the man who was here, then? Mr Anderson?'

'Yes, he's my client, and I thought I told you —'

'Bob said his name was Stephenson. Is that the same one?'

Not now Carol, not now. 'That's my business,' said

Rosie curtly. 'Now, your father and I have agreed that you'll go and stay with him tomorrow night ...'

Carol's eyes narrowed to angry slits. 'Agreed? What about me agreeing? I never want to see him again,' said Carol, tearful, and rushed away upstairs.

Nor do I, said Rosie sadly to herself, but you've just got to do some things in this life that you don't really want to do.

Oh, stop talking like your mother, will you?

Fifteen minutes later Rosie stood in the doorway of Carol's room, willing her daughter to look up from the book she was pretending to concentrate on so fiercely. Please don't be angry with me, she wanted to say, feeling like a child herself.

Of course it didn't come out that way: 'Don't be sulky, Carol,' she said with a tired effort at sternness.

Carol looked up and smiled wanly.

'You were asking about the man who came last night ...'

'I'm not interested,' said Carol, her face set in an obstinate frown that reminded Rosie of her own face at nine years old.

'It's only for the best,' said Rosie.

Carol looked down at her book. God I do sound like my mother.

To-ing and fro-ing across the street, Rosie managed to ignore Carol's looks and persuaded her to go to lunch with her friend Marie and established that Bob was at Jason's and left a note for him to pop across to Marie's mother if he came home for lunch and slapped some warpaint on herself in honour of Mike and — only remembered when she was fumbling for her car keys at the front door that she couldn't drive the damn thing at the moment.

On the strength of last night's bonus-in-a-brown-envelope she took a cab and soon wished she hadn't. 'Seen you before, haven't I?' said the Brylcreem head behind the glass partition.

'Don't think so. I very rarely take a cab.'

She glanced up at his eyes in the rear-view mirror and

quickly looked down into her lap. She had seen him before. Once, long ago, before Eve had eaten the apple and all this had begun, he'd reminded her of Humphrey Bogart and she'd passed out on the torn black seat of his taxi.

'Did you know,' he was saying, 'did you know that there's more cabs per head of the population in Liverpool than in any other city in Britain?'

'No, I didn't know that.'

'It's a fact. Possibly more than any other city in Western Europe,' said the cabbie, and she knew from his eyes in the mirror that he remembered when he'd seen her before.

So when he dropped her by the park she smiled very sweetly as she pressed the fare into his hand. He stared at his palm disbelievingly. She hadn't tipped him. That'd teach him to remind her of Humphrey Bogart again.

At the flats there was no answer to her tapped 9, 0, 6 on the intercom, and the door was still unvandalized from last week. Standards are even slipping amongst hooligans, thought Rosie, stationing herself round the corner with a view of the entrance.

It was twenty minutes before anybody who looked like a resident approached: a tall young woman on tottering heels. Rosie was back by the intercom just before her, pretending to fumble in her handbag. 'Tuh, can't find my keys,' she said, glancing up nervously.

'Come in on mine.' There was something odd about the tone of the reply but this was no time for quibbling. Rosie followed the woman into the foyer.

They stood together in the lift. 'Haven't seen you before, have I?' said the other huskily.

'I'm new.'

'Which floor?'

'Ninth.'

'I'm sixth.'

'How d'you do?'

Rosie didn't dare say anything. The young woman's hands were very big and awkward and her chin was shadowed with black stubble and her voice reminded

Rosie of the fifty per cent of the population who didn't wear skirts and high heels as a rule.

'See you then.'

'See you.'

Why shouldn't men dress up as women?

No good reason, Rosie replied to herself, sighing with relief as the lift doors closed on the sixth floor.

Up on the ninth there was no reply at 906, nor at 905 or 904. At 907 the door opened a crack on the security chain to Rosie's knock, and an elderly woman peered out suspiciously through thick glasses. 'Mm?'

'I'm looking for Helen, Helen Thackray, in 906, it's a,' the woman's expression was as unchanging as a statue's and Rosie found herself burbling, 'I need to contact her urgently, family, personal matter, do you know where I could, have you seen her lately?'

'Not in.'

Rosie cleared her throat. 'No, but it's, well, it is rather urgent, so I wonder if you —'

'Moved out. Monday.'

Monday? So why had she only got the anonymous note this morning? Why had Stephenson/Anderson not called round till — what the hell day *had* he called round? 'You don't happen to know where she ...?'

'Never saw her. Just heard them. The removals. Noise.'

The woman closed the door with an unexpected slam. Perhaps she'd been employed in transmitting telegrams all her working life and the habit had stuck. Thanks for information. Stop. Tara. Stop.

Rosie was going to be late for Mike but, convinced that if she hailed a cab she'd get old Bogey again, she walked up the road behind the flats and caught a bus into town. How was she going to track down Helen Thackray now? And what if ...?

'Must be painful,' said the woman in the next seat to hers.

'Must be,' said Rosie. What if the request for her to stop bothering Helen Thackray was really a cover, because she wasn't around to be bothered? What if she too had been ...?

'How d'it happen, then?'

Rosie bowed to the inevitable, and found herself explaining to her neighbour how she'd hit her feller too hard but if you thought her broken wrist was bad you should see his face, and soon several lower-deck passengers were talking about violence, men and what you can achieve with a well-aimed four-pint saucepan. Rosie got so engrossed she almost forgot to get off.

At an unvandalized phone box in the shopping precinct she called 999. 'Police,' she said. What if? 'Never mind my name,' she said brusquely, 'I want to report the mysterious disappearance of Helen Thackray of flat 906, Dahlia Towers.' The man still wanted her name. 'Phyllis Marlowe,' said Rosie and hung up, pleased with herself.

Yet by the time she'd swung her handbag into Mike's favourite little bistro and had apologized for being late but no, she couldn't eat a thing (staring unenviously at his salad of raisins, carrots and various dubious leaves) — by then she was shivering. And it wasn't cold. Even her broken wrist trembled against the confines of its plaster prison. She felt like crying. Over an anonymous 999 call? She vaguely heard herself babbling inconsequentially to Mike about children, fathers and things she should have done. She was drinking the wine he'd unexpectedly bought for them like lemonade. He was staring at her oddly. 'Everybody thinks I'm a frigging loon,' she said with a crack in her voice.

Mike put his hand on hers and lightning flashed somewhere. 'I don't think you are.'

'I mean' — how soft and thin his hand was; soft and thin as a woman's; he moved it away — 'I mean, I should be worrying about all sorts of things, shouldn't I? The economic situation. Politics,' and your hand, 'and where the next meal's coming from. And here I am, thinking about' your hand and 'fathers and murderers.'

'Murderers?'

'I mean — do you fancy me?'

Two men in pinstripe suits turned simultaneously to look at her from a neighbouring table and she cleared her throat. 'I mean ...'

135

'Oh dear,' said Mike.

'I don't mean,' said Rosie plaintively. 'Have you got a copy of that company search for me?'

'Oh dear,' said Mike. 'It's not something I could ever tell Graham or any of that crowd.'

'No, of course not,' said Rosie. 'Would you like a cup of coffee?'

By the time she brought the two steaming cups back to the table she was recovered enough to wonder what Mike had meant by his last remark, and to wink at the two pinstripe eavesdroppers. Simultaneous as robots, they looked down at their plates.

'You see,' said Mike, stirring his coffee into the porcelain of the cup, as Rosie counted the revolutions of his spoon, fifty, fifty-one, fifty-two, 'I'm gay.'

Lightning withdrew into the sky somewhere. 'Oh really?'

'Really,' said Mike. 'Yes. I fancy men, as a rule. I like to have women, well, some women, as friends though. Like you, Rosie. Don't breathe a word about it to . . .'

No, no, she wouldn't, of course not.

Rosie felt as if she'd suddenly come upon the terrible secret of traffic lights; that RED meant go and GREEN meant stop and nobody else realized but her.

The what-you-should-have-dones were gnawing at her stomach again. She should have understood Mike's evasiveness. She should have learnt before now about traffic lights. And certainly she should have talked to him about murderers and Tommy O'Meara before this because now she couldn't and what on earth could she say to him at all?

'Think I'll have another coffee," said Rosie. 'Want one?'

Chapter Twenty Four

'I mean,' Jerry was saying in bed that night, 'you've got to imagine Liverpool in, say, ten years' time, the museums, the parks, the little bistros, the sparkling waterfront scene ...'

'The closed down factories,' murmured Rosie, who really wanted to talk about murderers and heavy-breathers and men who liked to have women as friends, 'the middle-aged people who've never had a job in their lives, the new slums they'll have built where the old slums used to be ...'

'Rosie!'

His protest was only partly at her words. Partly it was that her hand was tickling his serious right armpit. 'Sorry,' said Rosie, suppressing a giggle.

Jerry's interview for the tourism job was set for tomorrow. Since their mutual apologies when he'd first arrived, he'd spent the whole evening talking about how exciting and nerve-racking the prospect was, and how you had to imagine Liverpool in, say, ten years' time ...

She stepped in before he could resume: 'You don't still think I'm a frigging loon, do you?'

'Never did.'

'He came round, y'know. Round here.'

'Who did?'

'Carol saw him. The man who called himself Andrew Stephenson. The, er, murderer.'

Jerry levered himself up on to his elbow and his eyes stared into hers. She looked quickly away. 'I found out his name too,' she added nervously.

'Whose?'

'The, er, Andrew Stephenson. But it's really Stephen Anderson.'

'Oh yes?'

'It came in an anonymous letter. The name.'

Or had she hallucinated the note from Helen Thackray? None of it sounded real to her, the way she'd just explained it. It didn't sound sensible or rational or likely. Did it sound sensible or rational or likely to Jerry? She looked into his eyes. His lager-dilated pupils were gazing a message into hers; *I still think you're a frigging loon*, they were saying.

Rosie decided not to ask him if he'd ever fancied other men. She rolled over and pretended to go to sleep.

Jerry rolled over and, gallingly, soon began to snore profoundly.

He didn't appreciate her. That was the trouble. Didn't appreciate her powers of listening and uh-huhing. Didn't appreciate how long she let him snore on before pinching his nostrils between thumb and forefinger. Didn't appreciate how she'd even forborne to update him about the heavy breather — whose latest recorded message had taken a more unpleasant turn: *Oh yes I know your little habits, I know about your broken arm . . .*

Jerry, I'm frightened by what's happening to me.

He snored like an elephant. Rosie had never been in bed with an elephant, but she could imagine. She squeezed Jerry's trunk and tried to get back to sleep.

But the thoughts wouldn't stop. Her wrist itched inside the plaster. Her brain itched inside her restless body. Finally, in the middle of the night she gave up trying to sleep and went downstairs to reread the company search on Streetclean Limited, looking for clues. Solve The Case, said the itch in her brain. Okay, she replied, okay I'm trying. She copied out the Formby address of STEPHEN ANDERSON from the directors' details, noting a DOROTHY ANDERSON there of the same address, and that seemed to quieten the itch for a while.

Nobody appreciates me, she whispered silently to the snap crackle pop and sizzle of other people's breakfasts a few sleepless hours later. For here was Jerry, wanting encouragement: 'Chin up, love,' said Rosie, kissing him goodbye. Here was Carol, sunk deep into her wounded innocence: 'Cheer up, love,' said Rosie, ruffling her hair. Here was Bob, asking awkward questions about Stephen

Anderson and Andrew Stephenson: 'Shut up, love,' said Rosie, turning away.

And here was Rosie, unappreciated, baffled by her precious Case: 'Buck up, love,' said Rosie to the detective hiding inside herself somewhere.

She was trying, though. She called Bill Jones to re-arrange their lunch meeting for Formby so she could spy out the Andersons' territory. She called Martin Brown, the black member of the MCC, to buy 'Angela' a drink at her local tonight, and he accepted; maybe he'd crack The Case for her. Then, all her usual child-sitters being unavailable, she surprised herself by persuading Janice next door to give the children lunch and dodged Dave's Further Reminiscences of a Binman on the way out.

So she was trying. By the end of the day she'd know a bit more about Stephen Anderson, surely? And even if she didn't, she'd have done things. She was busy, busy as a wasp. She knew who she'd like to sting, too. *Oh yes I know your little habits, I know about your broken arm ...*

When she went out she found herself looking furtively around. Did the anonymous caller live in the street? Was he watching her, following her even now? What peculiar kick was this telephone campaign of his giving him? Would he ever reveal himself to her? On the bus she scanned the faces of her fellow-passengers for evidence of heavy breathing, but no-one seemed a likely candidate.

Never mind, Rosie. If you weren't looking out for the dirty phone caller, you'd only be thinking that Stephen Anderson was lurking round every corner, waiting to bump you off.

That's not very comforting, she replied sharply to her inner voice. Shut up, will you?

Once inside Central Station, though, she put the possibility of lurking men out of her mind. She was going on a journey; a trip out, a treat. The Southport-via-Formby train was like a — like a great grey caterpillar, yes, and maybe she'd turn into a butterfly at the other end. Soon its long grey body was slithering electrically away through the echoey tunnels and out into the air of north Liverpool. Rosie's heart fluttered with childish excitement. She stared out at the empty factories and warehouses, the gaunt flat-blocks and scraps of derelict land, and didn't care. They were just scenes along a route to somewhere else, they didn't matter. Nor did the pimply boy in the seat opposite who was picking his nose and staring at her knees: no, he wasn't even there.

As they passed the towering machinery of the container terminal, where occasional people worked like tiny dolls among the giant cranes and containers, she allowed herself one of the cigarettes she'd bought at the station kiosk. The pimply boy asked if he could buy one for six-pence; she gave him one, refusing his money, wordless. She looked determinedly out of the window, imagining him away. It was like going on holiday. She was very nearly going to the seaside. As the train hummed out through the suburbs and across fields where real cows were grazing on real grass, Rosie thought she caught a whiff of the salt sea in among the smell of cigarettes, and it was all like a TV programme put on for her benefit — unimportant and relaxing and in startling colour.

Finally she left the pimply boy behind with the gift of another cigarette and got off. At the ticket barrier Bill Jones was waiting, even smaller than she remembered, and just as pretty, and all smiles and Cockney-twanged courtesy even though she was twenty minutes late (and her watch was slow). In the station car park he held open the door of another white Cortina courtesy of Godfrey Davis, and nobody had done that for her since she was twenty-one. She gazed in wonder at the black gleam of the dashboard controls while he inquired about her broken arm and invited her to decide where they lunched. She demurred at that, and he said he knew a decent little place. His eyes glanced across at her as they drove away.

He fancies me.

Don't be daft, Rosie, he's probably just after a bit of the other.

She watched his hand on the gear lever. Surprisingly big for a little man. Smooth, so smooth. It didn't slip across on to her knee. Give him time, Rosie, give him time.

No ta. Just give him the bill for the meal.

Chapter Twenty Five

Still, Bill Jones did have a nice tight little bum on him to match his nice tight little smile, Rosie couldn't help but observe as he minced ahead of her to open the door of the restaurant. His 'decent little place' turned out to be one of those identikit steak houses where you can be sure, wherever you may be on the maps of the Mediocre Food Guide, of the same decor, identical waiters and replica stains on the menus. It reminded Rosie of the places Graham had liked to take her to when he'd been courting her; 'good value for money' and no risk of nasty foreign food. She ordered a medium rare rump steak, ready sliced please for a wounded woman, and found herself staring at Bill Jones's long eyelashes across the artificial flowers that centrepieced the table — wanting, for no good reason, to like the man.

He smiled boyishly. 'So, Veronica, what's a nice girl like you doing in a place like Liverpool?'

'Rosie,' said Rosie. 'Suppose it must seem a bit tame when you come from an important place like London.'

'Not tame,' said Bill Jones, fingering a plastic daffodil. 'Dying. Dead on its feet. All the people with talent have left — present company excepted, of course.'

She smiled unsmilingly at his capital city platitudes and wondered how to get the awkward confessions out of the way. 'I'm afraid,' plunging in, 'I was following you that day, y'know.'

His blue eyes opened mockingly wide. 'When you broke down?'

'Yeh.'

'When I stopped and fixed your tyre? You were actually . . .?'

'Following you, yeh.'

'Following me?'

Did he have to keep on about it? He was, she could see, holding back the laughter; while she struggled to control the blush that was prickling under her cheeks and neck, itching to get out into the open. 'And my name's Rosie. I'm afraid Veronica was the first name that came into my head.'

The waiter came with the steaks and the cheap red plonk; the moment of embarrassment passed. Bill Jones couldn't, though, quite damp down the grin. As he bit into a fat piece of steak the chewing warped his face into a leer of a smile. 'And why,' he pursued, 'why exactly were you following me?'

'A job. It's my job. I'm a private detective.'

'Working for ...?'

'Professional confidentiality,' said Rosie, amazed she hadn't stumbled over the syllables, wishing there wasn't that edge of scorn to his continuing smile.

'So from what he tells me, you've really got up Stephen's nose. How did you manage that, love?'

'I thought, love,' Rosie replied pointedly, 'I'd asked you not to say anything to ...'

He was watching her reaction. She took a deep breath. Stay calm, Rosie, stay calm.

But alas a fragment of french fry went down the wrong way with the deep breath and she ended up coughing violently for a minute and a half and being heartily slapped on the back by his unexpectedly powerful hand and wondering why did she always do the wrong thing? He pressed the glass of red wine to her lips; she took a sour swallow. Then he asked her again about Stephen Anderson.

'I don't know how I got up his nose,' said Rosie, staring vaguely at her half-eaten meal. 'I did a job for him, that's all. And you weren't going to mention our meeting to him.'

He shrugged. 'I don't know you, do I? And I do know him. And he told me you were a liar and a cheat and not to be trusted.'

'I won't be asking him for a reference again then,' said

Rosie mildly. It was time to wipe the mocking smile off his face: 'So who did you say to Stephen Anderson that you were seeing for lunch today?'

'Veronica, I said. The girl, I told him, the girl whose car broke down ...'

'And how did he ...?' Rosie began, but didn't finish, not sure whether to be flattered about being a 'girl' again after all these years, watching the logic of her questions tick over in his eyes. He was thinking aloud:

'He said he'd met you, and I asked him how — and the phone rang — and, you did a job for him? Did he pay you to follow me?'

'Professional confidentiality,' said Rosie calmly, trying out a smile on her features again. 'So how well d'you know him?'

'Well enough.'

'He used to work for Mersey City, didn't he? You've been using his contacts to oil the wheels of the contract there, haven't you?'

He was staring unhungrily at his food. How smooth the skin of his face was; she wanted to reach across and touch him, to see if the hands that do dishes were as soft as his face.

Hm: this is business, Rosie.

Quickly, before her fingers ran away with her, she ploughed in with her next question: 'Shame about Tommy O'Meara dying, wasn't it?'

He frowned a little boy's frown at her. 'The police asked me about that. I don't follow. Guy had a heart attack, didn't he? What's it to do with me?'

Rosie shrugged and, pushing her food away, reached into her handbag for a cigarette. 'D'you mind?'

He didn't. Indeed he pushed away his plate too and accepted one. Across the haze of smoke he told her, in the nicest possible way, that he didn't see what business it was of hers but yes, he had met Tommy O'Meara a couple of times before and yes, his death had meant that the contract went through the Council when it might not otherwise have done, but so what?

So what?

143

'So it was handy for you. Him dying like that. Wasn't it? For you and Stephen Anderson? Your friend went to see him on the day before he died, you know. And maybe on the day itself.'

She saw the flicker of interest before the cool look washed self-consciously over his features again. He didn't answer. She didn't know what else to ask. The waiter offered them the plastic cheese or the plastic icecream that came in the all-in price: they both refused, but yes, coffee please. Rosie lit another cigarette from the last one and tried to recall the excited sense of going on an outing she'd had on the train. 'Seen Helen Thackray lately, then?' she asked on the off-chance.

'Not all week,' he said, 'you been following her too, have you?'

'No, but she ...'

He nodded. 'Professional confidentiality,' he said, taking another of Rosie's cigarettes. 'Well, if you've done a job for Stephen then as his secretary Helen will of course have ...'

'What?' said Rosie, then, quickly, 'I mean, quite, it could have been that way, if, as you say, possibly — You haven't seen her all week?'

The coffee arrived. They sat in silence at the table, a pall of smoke hanging over them. Rosie stirred idly at the froth on her coffee and thought about secretaries who worked late for the boss. Sometimes, all hours.

'What exactly are you after, then?'

I wish I knew. 'Just checking if you fancied me really, y'know.'

His eyes flicked up at her; very blue, very piercing, as if trying to see her in that potentially desirable light again. She wanted to feel annoyed with him; not tired and muddled and convinced he wasn't ruthless enough for what she'd suspected him of, him and his boyish looks and his innocent eyes. She tried to talk to him about Streetclean Limited — did he really want to throw a lot of people out of work? Did he really want to stamp on anyone like Tommy O'Meara who got in his way? — but her heart wasn't in it. She only half-listened as he switched on his public relations manner in reply, lecturing her about reducing inefficiency and saving ratepayers' money and all that boloney. She doubted he really believed it himself.

Finally he dropped a VISA card on the saucer over the bill and offered her a lift back to the station. 'No ta,' said Rosie. 'I'm going to visit a friend.'

He got up to go, glancing at his watch, pretending to remember appointments. 'I'm just a businessman,' he began his exit speech, 'that's all. Shame we had to meet again like this. Don't call me again, okay?'

Okay, I'll call you Bill Jones, said Rosie to herself. Out loud she just breathed deeply and smiled. She watched his tight little bum waddle out through the swing doors and wondered what he'd say to Stephen Anderson this afternoon. Just a businessman. Lighting another cigarette, she asked herself why she liked him, why she had the feeling he was incapable of any but the most transparent lies, let alone anything — anything worse.

Maybe it was just his bum and his eyes.

She stared at the wasted steaks on their table. The kids would have loved them; and right now she fancied some of the tinned spaghetti they'd probably left on their plates round at Janice's. She was hungry, yes; hungry for good food, yes. But not here, not for this. She stubbed her cigarette out, angry with herself for smoking so much, and got ready to go, not sure if she was going to take the train straight back to town, or if she was going to have the courage to knock on Stephen and Dorothy Anderson's door.

Chapter Twenty Six

Rosie was lost. It hadn't struck her that Formby might not be on the A-to-Z; that maybe people moved to places like Formby to avoid being discoverable through A-to-Zs. Maybe they said to their passing acquaintances from Dorset or Hampshire or wherever, 'Yes, it's a terribly nice place, quite off the beaten track: it's not even on the A-to-Z, you know.'

They'd have to be acquaintances who'd never actually pass as far as Formby itself, though. Otherwise the bluff would be called. For the track to Formby had been well beaten by now. Rosie wandered through a maze of estates of detached and semi-detached houses, each with a marvellous view of other detached and semi-detached houses, each no doubt with its own individually styled Conservative head of household who came home from the office at seven minutes to six Monday-to-Friday and tried to donate his genes to a loved one three nights a week with the lights out. Rosie felt jealous of their suburban lives. Not that she wanted what they'd got. She just wished she was rich enough to be sure she didn't really want it; to be certain she wasn't disguising envy as contempt.

From a plum-voiced shop assistant in a newsagent's she got directions, but not the clip-board she needed for the cover story she'd decided on. She'd have to make do with a loose-leaf pad and a lot of unFormby bravado instead. Soon she was standing in front of the Andersons' house — des res, det, 3b 2wc, ch, Con head of hshld at off — rehearsing her lines to the cold November afternoon: Excuse me, I'm doing a . . .

Dorothy Anderson was a long time coming to the door, and when she finally made it Rosie almost turned and ran for the train home. Her ex-client's wife was a tall, imposing, grey-haired woman, wearing a purple mohair sweater and black slacks with straps under the heels that had been out of fashion since Rosie reached her teens. Imposing, yes, but the woman teetered in the doorway, the twisted weight of her body supported on two sticks. 'Yes?' she said, the way royalty did, 'Yaaaas?' Posh and disabled; Rosie couldn't imagine a more terrifying combination.

'Excuse me,' said Rosie quaveringly, 'I'm doing a pilot survey for a nationally-known company about consumer preferences —'

'I don't want to buy anything, thanks.'

The tone and the wince of pain that went with it made Rosie's stomach groan. But the door showed no sign of closing on her. 'No, I'm not selling anything. It's a question, y'see, of finding out what people really want and it'll only take a few minutes ...'

She was in. Without even a request for identification the woman turned and waved a stick at the hallway by way of invitation. Beyond, immaculate wall-to-wall carpet beckoned. Rosie hesitated: she'd only expected a glimpse of interior and a frosty 'Not today thank you'. The woman smiled. Rosie went in.

The carpet in the living room was beige and had a pile to it that tickled Rosie's ankles. The deep armchairs had springs that reached all the way down to the house's foundations: she sank into one and wondered if she'd ever be able to climb out again. The woman sat opposite in a real leather chair with its own built-in footrest that popped up at the flick of a stick. Rosie wriggled to the edge of the upholstery she was squatting in, balanced her looseleaf pad on her knee and tried to begin:

'Because this is a pilot survey,' she said, trying to remember the sorts of questions she'd asked when she'd had a four-week job asking people what they really wanted in the way of a new brand of perfume, 'it's just informal. Testing the water sort of thing.'

Mrs Anderson offered tea. It would be 'no trouble'. Rosie glanced down at the legs propped up on the footrest and said she'd just had one, thanks. If she could just get down the details of age, household and so on? Entirely confidentially, of course.

'It's the hip, you see,' said Mrs Anderson.

It was one of those things; the more Rosie told herself not to look at the evidence of the woman's disability, the more she kept glancing at it. 'I'm sorry, I didn't mean ...'

'Don't worry. Arthritis. I'm waiting for the operation. Marvellous what they can do nowadays. Then I went and sprained the ankle of the good leg.' A ghost of a smile; a glimpse, unless Rosie was being fanciful, of a lost girl, defying her age and her crumbling joints.

'Yes, well, Mrs,' referring to the blank sheet at the front of the looseleaf pad in dumb show, 'Mrs Anderson, your name and address have been picked at random from the electoral register, and what I want to ask you about is ...

Getting the family details down, encouraging the woman to ramble on while she worked out what questions to ask next, Rosie found herself instead speculating on their lives: Stephen and Dorothy Anderson and their two grown-up boys, 'one at London University', a proud smile, a nod to the picture on the sideboard of a bland youth wearing a bland expression; one 'fending for himself', uncertain, a little frown, no pictures in sight. And did all the past decades seem worthwhile now to Dorothy Anderson? To end up here, arthritic amid deep-pile carpet and expensive furniture, lonely enough to rattle on about your children to a complete stranger who you never even asked for identification or a name? And what did she think of ...?

'Your husband, let me see, he works as a ...? For classification purposes, you understand.'

'Company director.' A deeper frown even than the one for the errant son. And what would she say if Rosie suggested she might be a murderer? For a moment she felt the words on her lips, I have reason to believe your husband ... For a moment she imagined the woman merely nodding politely, as if that was the sort of thing company directors did. Murder? — Oh, I expect so. 'Of course,' the woman was saying, 'he was a local government officer for some years. Till the private sector beckoned,' yes, his phrase no doubt, echoing in her gentler, less arrogant tones, a phrase coined for his cronies at the golf club and for his wife after the 19th hole or late on Sunday evening after playing with his computer and his mistress at 906 Dahlia Towers ...

God only knew what other questions she put to Dorothy Anderson. She forgot them as soon as she asked them, wanting to escape. On the train home, reading through her shorthand notes, the fragments of answers she'd recorded gave her little clue as to what she'd inquired about:

'... I'm inclined to prefer that, yes, although in some circumstances ...'

'No, I wouldn't say money was a problem in that sense. I expect it's rather hard to fit my answers into the little boxes ...'

'... I'm sorry, I need to take a pain-killer now ...'

Looking out at the grey silhouette skyline of north Liverpool, the train stuck at a signal, the lights of tower blocks blinking on, Rosie saw superimposed on the dirt-streaked window Dorothy Anderson's face: a big mournful oval, the lips set tight together, the pencil lines that had once been eyebrows jiggling up and down as she shifted from frown to frown. What good would it do? Rosie silently asked the face. Even if she weren't a frigging loon after all and she somehow exposed Stephen Anderson as a fraud and a murderer, what good would it do anyone? How would it benefit Dorothy Anderson? Or her sons? Or Helen Thackray wherever she was? Or the binmen of Mersey City? Or the late Tommy O'Meara? Or tearful Elsie? Or even Rosie herself?

It would solve a problem. It would stop that problem nagging at her and enable her to get on with the business of her life — whatever that might be: serving writs, children and so forth.

Was that all?

It didn't seem enough.

The train crested a slight gradient and hissed down into the tunnels of the city centre, and Rosie's thoughts plunged from her high-flown speculations about life and death to what was in the fridge for tea and how she'd have

149

to call Graham to come and would Carol go quietly? And who was going to sit with Bob? And she was neglecting her children for the sake of his bloody problems and later —

Later there'd be a drink with Martin Brown at 'Angela's local'. Maybe he could help her understand what was going on and convince her it was all worthwhile.

Or maybe he could just help get her well bevvied and oblivious to it all.

Chapter Twenty Seven

It was only when Rosie was sitting in the Earl Grey, wondering what had made her drinking partner so late and how come so many pubs were officially named after royals or nobles or generals — it was only then that she had a terrible thought and rushed out of the bar.

The phone was in the corridor outside the Gents — a good place to get leered at, so she didn't like to linger. But she gave Martin Brown's phone fifteen chances to ring and be answered before she reluctantly hung up.

Back in the lounge bar she nursed her half of lager and wondered if he'd track the place down. For Rosie's local was only called the Earl Grey by readers of the phone book or of the sign outside. By anybody who was anybody it was known as Tommy's. That was the name she'd given Martin on the phone earlier. But he wasn't anybody who was anybody. He was somebody, a stranger, who might not know that pubs round here were known by the name of the last publican but one; who was probably, even now, hunting for pubs with 'Tommy's' on the sign outside.

Still, there was nothing she could do about it. So she sat in her ill-lit corner, pretending not to have noticed Billy the mechanic and his mates propping up the bar with their paunches, and she brooded. It was a way of passing the time — brooding. She brooded on Graham, who'd at first refused to pick up Carol and had implied that Rosie's broken arm was part of a conspiracy to make him revisit the scene of his broken marriage, before suggesting outright that he was doing her some kind of a favour by looking after their daughter for the night. She brooded on Carol, who was brooding. She brooded on Jerry, who'd come round expecting lager and sympathy after his (disastrous, it sounded like) interview for the tourism job and had soon gone off in a huff to his

151

Friday night chess circle. She brooded on Bob, whom she'd trusted to look after himself alone for the first time tonight and what cunning way would he discover of burning the house down while she was out? Brooded, too, on herself, who'd been as bloody incompetent as usual in all this and now probably Martin wouldn't come ...

Just then, of course, he arrived. Heads turned as he came over to her table. His was the only black face in the bar. Two old women on the bench seat next to Rosie's table shuffled along conspicuously to make room for the other ten black people who might follow any minute. Rosie gave them a big smile for their warm-hearted cosmopolitan tolerance, and they grimaced down into their Mackesons.

Soon he was settling down opposite her with two pints of bitter in front of him and a pint of lager for her when she'd asked for a half. Demurely she filled her half-pint glass from the pint and raised her glass to his. He winked at her, and returned the gaze of the two old women with a big smile. One of them smiled awkwardly back, the other gave her a fierce reprimanding nudge.

'So I had a call from our friendly neighbourhood police about you, Angela,' he said cheerfully.

'It was all a misunderstanding. And the name's Rosie.'

How many times in the past week had she had to correct people's impressions of her name? Maybe she should just wear a placard round her neck: MY REAL NAME IS ROSIE MONAGHAN SORRY FOR ANY CONFUSION.

'... the bizzies let me off with a caution this time too,' he was saying through the beer foam round his lips. And then, with a kind of pride: 'My seventeenth caution. Still, at least I'd been doing something for once. Breaching the peace, like. The other sixteen times I was just driving my car or walking down the street. Or, once I was stopping two white guys knock hell out of each other. So the boys in blue send the honkies home to cool off, and take the Good Samaritan here down to the station to see if his fingerprints fit. Did you know the Good Samaritan was a black man, Rosie?'

'Haven't read the Bible for years, la'.'

Bravado and nervous energy — he had plenty of both, with a big show of street-wisdom to match. How, for

152

instance, had he found the pub when she'd given him the wrong name? 'No sweat, Rosie, no sweat. I just asked around.'

And he'd taken some care with his appearance. Rosie felt dowdy, in her same old blouse-and-skirt, against his blue shirt open to a glimpse of wiry chest hair, slimline purple trousers, a grey jacket that had zips in extraordinary places, and expansive gestures as he talked. Yes, he was telling her, the campaign against Streetclean was really gaining mooow-mentum, and how come she'd been talking to the bizzies about him? 'You wha'? A private detective?'

'Yeh, and the official guardians of law and disorder aren't too keen on us irregulars, y'see,' she explained from the depths of her inexperience.

'You, Rosie, are private enterprise. I can see their point of view.'

'So can everybody.'

She'd only sipped at her lager and he was already halfway down his second pint. Maybe, she thought, she'd better get the business questions out of the way while he was still coherent:

'You saw Tommy O'Meara,' she said just as she'd rehearsed, 'on the day he died. The Sunday. So who exactly was he expecting?'

'Thought I said. The other side, that's all we knew. Meaning, somebody from the company, I s'pose. Or the local Tories, which amounts to the same thing. So what's your handle on this, Rosie?'

He was one of those people who kept using your name and touching you on the arm to persuade you they were a friend of yours. 'Just a case I'm on,' she said, getting up. 'Same again?'

He was also one of those men who didn't believe in women buying drinks. Normally Rosie didn't have enough cash in hand to let that worry her, but right now most of Stephen Anderson's hundred and fifty quid was burning a guilty hole in the bottom of her handbag, so she insisted. A double order for him, a half for her, and a hello for Billy the mechanic, who glanced meaningfully at her table then back at her while returning the greeting.

153

After a deep gulp of his third pint Martin Brown got inquisitive; what was it like to be a private detective and who was paying her and did she get the broken arm in the line of duty? Wanting to tell him the muddled truth, wanting there to be someone she could confess to that she didn't really know what the hell she was doing, nevertheless she somehow couldn't do it. Maybe his bluff and bravado was catching. Maybe she just didn't want to risk being regarded as a frigging loon by any more of the human race. Or maybe bad jokes were part of her nature, genetic along with her bumpy nose and her disorderly brain.

'I've always had the arm,' she found herself saying, 'but I did get it broken in the line of duty, yeh,' and she was smiling too much and too artificially and talking too loudly; the two old women were stealing glances at her over their Mackesons. She lowered her voice.

'That feller, sort of thin, posh, in the Council meeting, leader of the Sames you called him....'

'Andrew McLachlan?'

'That's him. What's his wife's name, d'you know?'

'We're not, like, mates that meet over cocktails, him and me.'

'Just wondered.' Rosie dug out the company search from her handbag. 'Does he live at ...?' She showed him the address against the name of DEBORAH McLACHLAN.

'Think that's it, yeh. A deputation of us went to see him there. Well, waylay him more like. Yeh, that's right. So what's this?'

'It's a list of the board of directors of Streetclean Limited. His wife's one of the directors.'

'So he's got a financial interest in ...?'

Martin Brown was impressed. He whistled to show just how impressed he was. Then he leant across the table, elbows in beer puddles, suddenly conspiratorial. 'So,' he said out of the corner of his mouth, 'you're digging up all this dirt. Are you, er, a left winger?'

'Never played football,' said Rosie tiredly, reaching into her handbag.

'No, y'know, politics.'

'Why d'you and the bizzies think I must be in it for the sake of the frigging revolution?'

'Why else?'

'For the money. It's a job,' said Rosie, lighting the cigarette she'd forbidden herself to have, noticing the lager was slipping down her glass more quickly as the evening wore on. For the money? A hundred and fifty quid obtained under false pretences. It's a job? Who for? 'D'you know,' she asked, wondering if the drink was making her maudlin, 'd'you know a feller called Stephen Anderson?'

'He's a bastard,' said Martin, nodding to his pint glass as if it might confirm the observation. 'I'm a sort of left winger myself, you see.'

'No, Stephen Anderson, do you know him?'

'Smooth. Slippery. Like a corrupt pebble. Used to be boss of our depot. The white collar brigade. Brigadier. Bastard. On the make. But the trouble is, about politics I mean ...'

Men always want to lecture you about the state of the world, thought Rosie. She didn't mind. She felt excited by the information about Stephen Anderson; she let Martin's profound analysis of the decline of capitalism wash over her. Smooth. Slippery. Like a corrupt pebble. Bastard. Funny word. Bastard. Why was it an insult to have no father? Some children might even be pleased. Like Carol. Some mothers of children might even be pleased. Like yours tr—

She inhaled deeply on her cigarette and looked round the now crowded bar. For a moment she hallucinated Jerry, not six feet away, watching her out of the corner of his eye. She blinked and looked again. The hallucination was still there.

'... even have some respect for Labour Party hacks like Tommy O'Meara,' Martin was saying. 'But when you consider the devastation of Merseyside and how little they've done —'

'Won't be a minute,' said Rosie and went over to the hallucination. Close up it still looked remarkably like Jerry. It had his sad eyes, boring dolefully into hers. She listened and stared. I thought you were out drinking with a friend. Martin is a friend. I didn't know you meant that kind of friend. What kind is that? No, I don't mean black, I mean — male, you mean —

155

None of this was spoken. It was all in the eyes, trying to outstare their silent messages into one another.

Or maybe Rosie was just a bit drunk and this really was Jerry in front of her. She touched him; his eyes glanced away. I won, I won. 'Chess circle finished early tonight, did it?'

'My mind just wasn't on it,' said Jerry. 'What with ...'

She managed to kiss him on the cheek even though he ducked away at the last moment. 'This is just business. See you in the morning,' she said, and, wickedly pleased he was jealous, went to buy her and Martin another round.

Half a pint later a black hand had encircled her pink one, and she had to say 'Excuse me' to get it back to lift her drink to her lips while he was saying:

'I'm a sort of communist, you see. A communist without a party. Do I want to be ruled by Russians? Nah. But I think, what I believe, sincerely Rosie, is that we're all in this together. Working people together ...'

'Let's have your glasses now please!' said the publican fortissimo in Rosie's ear, and all the working people together seemed to have left the pub for the late-night movie on television — even the Mackeson women were putting on their coats.

'It's been very nice but,' said Rosie, clasping her handbag to her.

'Back to your place?'

'Another time, maybe,' said Rosie, feeling mean but sure she wouldn't be able to deal with beery embraces over the black coffee. 'It's been very nice, though,' she said, kissing him quickly on the forehead. 'G'night now.'

She left him looking for the Gents. Outside she breathed in the dirty Liverpool air, and hurried across the road to pass on the other side of two men fighting while a woman in fluffy slippers bawled obscenities at them. She hoped the Good Samaritan wouldn't feel inclined to test out his virtue tonight and land an eighteenth caution. She hoped there wouldn't be fire engines parked outside the house when she rounded the corner. And she hoped it'd be clear what she ought to do about Stephen Anderson in the morning.

Chapter Twenty Eight

It's now or never.

No it isn't. It's now or some time.

Two or three cooks make a better broth.

Down these not-so-mean streets a woman doesn't have to go.

A walking dustbin of warped clichés, Rosie put her arm in Margie's; fifty yards ahead was Jerry, with Carol and Bob and Margie's three. Their breath steamed into the cold night. There was the smell of gunpowder and woodsmoke in the air. While Margie rattled on about computers and the antics of her children, Rosie was silently arguing with herself. Do it, Rosie. Why bother? No, get it over with. Give me one good reason.

She'd woken that morning absolutely resolved. It's now or never, she'd said to herself. So she'd called Stephen Anderson in Formby and arranged to meet him. Get it over with. 7.30 pm, flat 906. Sorry, can't discuss it now.

Later she'd answered the heavy breather with a few choice obscenities and slammed the phone down. She'd apologized to Jerry, told Graham off, hugged Carol on her return; all with brisk yet caring efficiency. It was now-or-never day.

But she could still avoid going through with it. It was seven fifteen and Bonfire Night, and they were strolling down to the Sefton Park fireworks through streets called Arundel and Cheltenham and Buckingham, names that were tokens of a different England from the one Rosie lived in, streets where social workers and architects and schoolteachers peered out from behind their Habitat curtains at no-marks like Rosie going by — and she could still avoid going through with it. It could still be now or some time. She hadn't, after all, told anyone else. Okay, so she'd written out a history of THE CASE OF STEPHEN ANDERSON and left it in a big brown envelope on her bed marked, with a great flourish, TO MARGIE IN THE EVENT OF SOMETHING HAPPENING TO ME. But she could still tear that up when she got home.

They were in sight of Dahlia Towers now. It was almost beautiful: a big cake glittering with lights; and above, the sky over the flat block was very clear. The moon hung, a slice of lemon, over nowhere in particular. Ahead she heard the raucous laugh Carol had, sadly, inherited from her mother. The kids were waving sparklers at one another and laughing gaily even though Bob had insisted to her earlier that sparklers were sissy and had demanded bangers.

Rosie detained Margie with her good hand: 'I've got to see this feller.'

'You should be so lucky. What about?'

What about? Stephen Anderson had asked her the same thing on the phone. Everything, she'd said to him, not really knowing the answer herself. 'Now, I've got to see him now. And if anything should — look, I'll just slip away.'

Many a slip twixt something and something else. Not the cradle and the, er, grave, was it?

Rosie stopped and lit herself a cigarette. Her father had always said to her: ladies don't smoke on the street. Sorry, Dad. Sorry, bushy eyebrows. I'm just not a lady. 'All very mysterious,' said Margie.

'Tell you about it later. And if anything should happen … You'll know what to do. Don't mind, do you? Tell the kids I've had to go and do a job, eh? See you at our house.'

The children were excited; at the fireworks, at the staying up late, at the fact that Margie's children were sleeping at Rosie's house tonight. Rosie was excited too. It was now or never. She ducked through a gap in the wall and didn't look back.

But then she had to walk past the entrance to the flats three times, circling the block, trying to get her bearings. She couldn't remember the number of Helen Thackray's flat. Amnesia again? From a garden nearby a rocket whizzed up into the blackness. 906, that was it. There was no spoken reply when she tapped the numbers on the intercom: just the buzz of the door opening. She threw away her cigarette and went in. A jumping bean had lodged itself inside the pulse at her neck: all the way up in the lift and along the corridor it bumped and bounced inside her, trying to get out.

The door to the flat was already open. Stephen Anderson was hunched next to the TV screen, playing a computer game. 'Won't be a minute,' he said gruffly, not looking up. She sat in a threadbare armchair and breathed deeply to quieten down the jumping bean and admired the view. The place was as she remembered it — but dirtier. A film of dust had settled over everything; newspapers lay scattered around; there was an ashtray full of little cigar butts on the little table next to the man. He was smoking now as his fingers played over the typewriter keys. Bips and beeps and explosions interspersed the screen's incomprehensible whirr of shapes and colours.

Finally, he looked up. GAME OVER said the screen. He was, like the room, as she remembered him — but dirtier. A day's stubble on his chin; his shirt crumpled, open at the neck; shadows under his eyes.

Or maybe that was just her imagination. Maybe he looked as self-assured as ever and she was indulging in wishful thinking. She'd already lit herself a cigarette and was telling herself to keep her hand steady and wondering whether to leave her coat on for a quick getaway. 'I think I should warn you,' she announced with an effort at sternness, 'that a friend of mine knows where I am and what I'm here for. So if anything happens ...'

'Very dramatic,' said Stephen Anderson. His upper lip curled sardonically. 'Relax, for God's sake. Now, are you here to return my money? Or have you, since your recent discussions with my business associate, come to make more wild accusations?'

He hadn't drawn the curtains. Outside the fireworks had begun: a rocket exploded in a trail of green and yellow stars. Ooooh! and Aaaah! Bob and Carol would be saying, with an edge of irony, they'd seen it all before and thought they ought to pretend to be blasé about such things nowadays.

'Are you a good father, then?'

It wasn't at all what she'd meant to say. 'None of your bloody business, frankly,' said the haze of cigar smoke.

'My ex-husband,' she continued coolly, surprised at herself, 'my ex-husband struck my daughter today. She told him she never wanted to see him again. He's not an unkind — well, not a mean man. He just does that when he can't control people, and they're physically weaker than him. He hits them. Are you like that?'

'Jesus,' said Stephen Anderson, stabbing his cigar out fiercely, getting up. 'Some people are natural victims too, you know. Let's have a bloody drink, shall we?'

From a cupboard in the sideboard — the cheap plywood-and-glue affair that Rosie remembered, still adorned with Helen Thackray's bric-a-brac — he took out a half-full bottle of Johnny Walker's and two blue tumblers. He poured them both a generous measure. 'Water in mine,' said Rosie, startled by the explosion of another rocket at the window. Why had Helen Thackray left so suddenly? Leaving behind her sideboard bedecked with cuddly toys and glass paperweights and the picture of herself in a bikini, embracing some smiling Latin in some sunny holiday place?

He clinked glasses with her and gulped at his scotch. What had he said to Helen Thackray? Or done? 'Come on then,' he said brusquely. 'What have you got to say for yourself?'

'I saw your wife.'

'Thought it must have been you. Prying. You don't want to take any notice of her, you know. Change of life.'

Might Dorothy Anderson, then, have been indiscreet? What about? He'd underestimated his wife's loyalty. And women's bodies were always easy to blame, weren't they? *Change of life?*

Pull yourself together, Rosie. Drink your whisky and tell him what you think of him.

Ooof. The whisky hit the back of her throat and she gasped out loud. Concentrate, Rosie. Tell him what you wrote in the letter to Margie you hope she'll never have to read. Tell him.

She cleared her throat, and began her speech:

'To begin at the beginning. In that pub, the Atlantic Crossing. You'd checked up on me. All you'd found out was, there was nothing to find out about me. You looked me up and down and decided I'd fall for a line about a bureaucrat concerned about corruption. And there were, you said, advantages to my inexperience. What might those be? Naïvety? An unenquiring mind? Some tart whose mistakes couldn't possibly be traced back to a smooth professional man like you?

'And you gave me a great pile of photographs. But that was a blind, wasn't it? From the start it was Tommy O'Meara you were after. You and Bill Jones work together; Helen Thackray probably makes his appointments for him in Liverpool; so you must have known he was meeting Tommy O'Meara that day ...'

She wasn't even sure how much she was saying out loud. He just sat there, wordless, sipping his drink, puffing at his fancy little cigar, and she might as well not be there. Fireworks over the park kept startling her in mid-sentence. And on the screen that bloody computer game was still bipping and beeping and pchow!ing away, playing itself when no humans joined in — like the whole frigging world, she thought, a gigantic game that carried on whether you want to play or not, a game where the Stephen Andersons are winning and the Rosie Monaghans don't even understand the rules but somebody somewhere is clocking up the score ...

Steady, Rosie. It's not like the whole frigging world at all. It's simply a machine with an on-off switch. 'D'you think we could manage without that thing?'

'What?'

'That machine. D'you think we could have it switched off?'

He flicked a button on the TV. The screen died to a pinpoint. Where the hell was she up to?

'Bill Jones's appointments,' he prompted her drily.

So she was talking out loud. That was a start, anyway.

161

'It's expensive,' she resumed, 'keeping up two house-holds, isn't it? A wife and a mistress? So you needed the Mersey City contract pretty badly. Of course, you'd already fixed the Sames ...'

'The what?'

'With Andrew McLachlan's wife being on the board of directors.'

'You have been busy. But you're out of date, Rose.' He almost managed a smile over his whisky glass. 'She's resigned.'

'Oh yeh? In favour of her second cousin twice removed, I 'xpect?'

'Can I help it if she wants to sell her shares to her sister? Not illegal, is it?'

She'd let herself be sidetracked. Renewed confidence was oozing across the room at her. She tried to make herself look at him. Yes, he was smiling. Smooth. Slippery. Like a corrupt pebble. Bastard.

'Be that as it may,' said Rosie determinedly, 'you still didn't have a majority for the contract. The decision could turn on one vote. Tommy O'Meara's was the one you picked on. Maybe Bill Jones knew nothing of what you were planning. Maybe he just handed over the envelope for his own reasons, and I photographed him doing it for yours. And maybe in the first place you'd tried a simple bribe on Tommy O'Meara.

'But he was a man of principle. So you had to black-mail him. Show him evidence that looked as if he'd taken a bribe anyway. That was what I provided. Maybe, too, you threw back at him some of the dirt you'd picked up about him while you worked for Mersey City. And still he wouldn't go along with you. You were desperate. You thought about your debts, about the career you'd aban-doned when "the private sector beckoned"; he was in your way. You're probably not a mean man. You just couldn't control him and his pathetic little ideas about right and wrong. So you struck him. And he died.'

Elsie's face: podgy and blotched with tears, as they stood at the foot of the stairs, the stairs where —

'Is that it, then?' he asked quietly.

He'd refilled his glass. Rosie's was hardly touched. She didn't want whisky. She wanted nothing more than a cup of tea and to be in her own home and for somebody to hold her hand and tell her everything was all right. But she had to go through with it now:

'No, that's not quite it. Helen Thackray knew something. What I said to her confirmed her suspicions. She wrote to me — it must have been her — to tell me your name. Maybe she told you she'd done that. Maybe she wanted to show you that you couldn't control her either. So suddenly she disappeared. Leaving — only me.'

He was standing by the curtain now, idly picking at the peeling paintwork of the window sill, looking out. Beyond him the green lights of lasers speared among the fireworks, like another version of his computer game, playing on the screen of the sky framed by the window. He didn't turn to her. When he began to speak he seemed to be chatting quietly to the night, or maybe to his own reflection:

'You've got it all wrong, of course. And then, in some crazy way, right. In spite of yourself, right. But why me?'

He turned to her. His fingers were gripping the whisky tumbler very tightly. Suddenly he was shouting: 'Why pick on me? I gave you a tinpot little job. And out there are muggers and terrorists and knee-cappers and you have to pick on me! Why?'

He was putting on the anger, his very own firework display. Rosie shook her head. Muggers and terrorists and knee-cappers were handy if you wanted your own crimes to look like little misdemeanours by comparison. 'You picked me,' she said, lighting another cigarette, the smoke rasping against her dry throat.

He'd subsided into his chair. 'I picked you,' he said 'because you'd be cheap. And an amateur. Because I'm an amateur too. A blundering bloody amateur. All this doesn't come naturally to me, whatever you think: bribery, blackmail, having people followed. I'm just a businessman. I thought an amateur wouldn't ask too many awkward questions.'

Just a businessman. Maybe he wasn't pretending.

Maybe the little-boy whine in his voice was genuine; the genuine pathetic whine of a man who felt trapped and had had too much to drink, for his words were slurred, and Rosie was beginning to think the whisky bottle had been a full one not many hours before, as he went on:

'I'm a blundering amateur. I needed the money, true. I was desperate. Already in debt. And Dorothy, my wife, she has to have an operation. Privately. If I don't pay she'll have to wait for years. She can't bear the pain. I can't bear to see her pain. Whatever you might think.

'And Helen. She's been blackmailing me. Demanding more and more, threatening to tell my wife about us. It'd kill Dorothy if she knew. About me and Helen. About all this.'

He gestured at Rosie and the tawdry furnishings and rubbed at his reddened eyes. He didn't know how to tell the truth, even to himself. Rosie realized that, as she listened to the sincere tone he was using to tell what, from the words, sounded like feeble melodramatic lies. She wasn't frightened any more. She was even having to stop herself feeling sorry for the man.

'So I made a pathetic effort at bribery. Of Tommy O'Meara, yes. You took the photograph. Bill thought he was just trying to change the man's mind. He didn't know about you — at the time. And by then I'd paid a little money into O'Meara's bank account without his knowing. Plus, yes, I threw some old dirt at him.

'And after that, did he have any objections? To the idea of being bribed? Your fine old-fashioned socialist? Did he hell. Right and wrong? Your precious man of principle said it'd cost more, much more. And I didn't have it to offer him. More, he said. It'll cost you more than that. So I . . .

'And Helen skipped. Skedaddled. All of a sudden. Asked me what I'd been doing that Sunday. Working, I said. Next day she disappeared. Not that she disbelieved me. She hadn't swallowed your murder story. She thought you were from my wife. She thought my wife had found out about us. So she hopped off the gravy train because the gravy was about to get thin.'

'But your name,' Rosie cut in, surprised at the melancholy in her own voice, 'she sent me your name.'

'Her parting shot. She thought you weren't quite sure that I was the adulterer you were looking for. But you'd find out soon enough, and she'd give you a little help. To make things difficult for me. Her parting shot.

'And as for you; I picked you because you were cheap. I didn't think you'd be so bloody poor you couldn't be bought cheaply. So there you are.'

He was, he really was crying. And she did, in spite of his tired phrases and his contempt for the man who'd reminded her of her father and had died; nevertheless she really did want to go across and comfort him.

Instead she lit another cigarette from the last one and, licking her lips, said to him, 'I don't believe you.'

'No!'

He banged his hand down on the computer keyboard. The ashtray tumbled off the table, a scatter of butts and ash across the carpet. Neither of them moved to pick up the debris. The jumping bean had come back to life in Rosie's neck. 'No,' said the man. 'You want it all in black and white, don't you? Heroines and villains, and in the middle are put-upon men of principle and innocent young secretaries seduced by their bosses and, and oh, it's not like that.'

She fished in her handbag and pulled out his money. She rose to go. 'I've spent a few quid of it, but here's the rest.'

'I don't want the bloody money!'

He threw it back at her. Fivers spilled over her skirt and on to the floor. 'You're right. Don't you see? I just went up the stairs after him, to reason with him that's all, I put a hand on his arm, I was so angry. I've never been so angry, and he fell down, I ran back to the bottom of the stairs but he was ...'

Rosie closed her eyes. She was clearly dreaming. She counted to five, very slowly. One; two; three; four; five. She opened her eyes. She was still in flat 906. Stephen Anderson was still sitting at his computer keyboard, head in hands, having just confessed to a murder.

'The administration of shit,' said Rosie, enunciating

the words very clearly. 'You told me at the start that was your business.'

He didn't move. She picked up the fivers and tapped them on the table to make a neat pile. Dirty money, she wanted to be rid of it. Dirty room, she wanted to be out of it. Dirty, she felt dirty herself, she wanted to run home and throw off her clothes and soak her body in the bath until she felt washed clean again.

'It's this place,' he said, rubbing away his tears, pouring himself more whisky to drown in. 'Liverpool. It's a corrupt place. It corrupts you.'

'Nothing to do with the place,' said Rosie with a briskness she didn't feel. 'So you'll tell the police ...?'

'In the morning.' His eyes glinted sharply at her. 'I want to tell Dorothy first. Police, yes. But in the morning.'

How long had she been there? The fireworks seemed to have ended. Down below people were straggling home, shadows emerging from the park into the harsh street-light. Rosie turned and tossed the money on to the table. 'G'night, then,' she said, feeling very tired. 'And if you don't tell the police ...'

'I will. I will. In the morning.'

His chin cupped in his hands, he stared into nothing. His eyes were still brimming with tears — and lies? Why had he looked at her so keenly, for a moment, when she'd mentioned the police? Did his story really make any more sense than her own?

There was nothing more she could do to get it any clearer in her mind. She left him to his melodramatics and his games, and went out into the night.

Chapter Twenty Nine

They went to a late night drinking club. Margie had taken
one look at Rosie when she'd come in, and had immediately sat her down, and made her drink sweet tea, and
forced her to eat an extraordinary meal of two biscuits, a
slice of toast and a banana. Then in some mysterious way
she'd persuaded — instructed? — Jerry to mind the house
and families while the two women went out on the town.

'I don't want to talk about it,' said Rosie, desperate to
talk about it but not knowing where to begin.

'Of course you don't,' said Margie smoothly, clinking
their glasses of vodka and orange. 'No, d'you remember
when we came in here last year and those two fellers chat-
ted us up and said they were from Granada Television?
Well, I saw the big one in town the other week and ...'

The club was crowded. They sat at a side table
surrounded by a wall of bodies and voices. Rosie tried to
concentrate on the story of the big man who really did
work for Granada Television after all. But she found her
comprehension ebbing and flowing with the swell of
conversation in the smoky basement. It was as if some
invisible sound-controller kept turning the volume on
Margie's voice up and down; Rosie couldn't follow it.

Then, through a tangle of arms and heads and glasses,
she glimpsed Mike's balding head across the room with
his arm round someone. 'Just got to go to the Ladies, Marg.'

She had to force her way through. Scouse voices, posh
voices; black faces, white faces; a fair-haired man who put
his arm around her and was rewarded with a sharp cuff on
the chin from her plaster cast.

Mike's arm was round his 'friend': a startlingly young
man, just a boy really, blond with a pink streak in his hair

and blue eye make-up. Mike was all smiles. 'Rosie, hello, I'd like you to meet....'

The boy held a tiny box, the size of his palm, out to her. 'Snuff?' he said with a teasing smile, taking a pinch from it, snorting it up his nose, giggling.

Rosie had a funny feeling the white powder wasn't really snuff and that this should all be part of a dream that had begun in flat 906, Dahlia Towers. She tried to recall Mike in his pinstripe suit, at his disordered desk: 'Look, Mike...'

'I'm a new man, Rosie,' said Mike. He was grinning inanely. 'It was after we talked, you and me. I decided. I'm coming out.'

In spots? she wanted to ask, relieved to hear a glimmer of humour returning to her inner voice. 'Nice for you,' she said, hypnotized by the enamel box in the boy's hand, the hand with pink painted fingernails. 'Look, Mike I'm with a friend. Can't stop. I just wanted to tell somebody — tell you. I'm not a frigging loon, you see.'

'But who on earth'd say that? You're —'

Somebody jostled her in the back but she mimed a backheel and felt the satisfying collision of shoe and shin. She felt breathless, as if it might be the last coherent thing she said:

'No, you see, I did it. I really did it. I don't care what anybody says. I solved a murder!'

Chapter Thirty

Rosie dreamt of happy endings. She dreamt of clear-cut stories, in which she was the leading character, with beginnings, middles and happy endings.

And here, at last, was one such story, with many happy endings trailing in its wake.

For in the morning Stephen Anderson went to the Mersey City police and confessed everything to Detective Sergeant Murdoch.

Later in the week a police inspector caused a stir in the street by arriving at Rosie's front door in his souped up Ford Escort to deliver in person his apology on behalf of the force for her previous treatment, and his thanks for her help in uncovering a murder and a murderer.

And that was only the start of it. The trial, once it wriggled into life through the pupae of remands and social and medical reports and legal bureaucracy, got her name in the papers. PETTICOAT PRIVATE EYE CORNERS KILLER said one of the tabloids after the Guilty verdict. Even though Rosie hadn't worn a petticoat since she was fourteen and a half she felt pleased. The fee for her story, 'as told to our reporter', was a handsome one; and private eye business began to roll in. Within a month of the publicity she'd set herself up in an office in town with a sign that said ROSE MONAGHAN INQUIRY AGENT on the glass panel of the door, behind which a secretary and ex-DC Hickey for her assistant beavered away at detecting things. Before long she was having to ask Mike if he knew the name of a good accountant, and soon she was much in demand as a guest speaker to Soroptimists and Rotary Club lunches.

And somehow the magic of her success rubbed off on her family, both past and present. Graham's sales took an upturn; he and Carol were happily reconciled to one another; Rosie and Graham were able jointly to buy Bob his very own personal computer for his birthday, one far superior to his friend Jason's.

And the ripples of Rosie's little miracle, dropped into the still waters of her life, spread out to lap against all she knew. So it was that Jerry got the tourist job, and loved it; that Margie's special aptitude for computers was noticed by one of her teachers, who persuaded her to take up programming and later secured her a job with IBM; that Mike became a partner in his solicitors' firm and, having ditched the boy sniffer, met the man of his dreams on a winter holiday in Inverness; that even Dave next door got a job; that Elsie O'Meara wrote to thank Rosie for uncovering her brother's murderer and, six months later, featured in the Marriages column of the *Liverpool Echo* in association with an old Labour Party stalwart; that Helen Thackray sent her a postcard from Miami, Florida where she was working as a nursery nurse; that Martin Brown led the Mersey binmen in a famously successful strike against the privatization of the cleansing and refuse services.

And, as if these individual successes and transformations weren't enough, there was more. Rosie would lie in her bed, staring at the newly-hung woodchip paper on the ceiling, thrilled and awed by it all: by how the ripple of miracles had turned into a flood, all stemming from her one tiny success; how the whole world suddenly changed course, how the revitalization of Liverpool gathered momentum, with new factories pumping out new products; how unemployment plummeted as even the rich and the self-made better-off began to see the errors of their ways and agreed to pay higher taxes to help others; how the spirit of togetherness that old people recalled from the wartime was at last rediscovered in peace, how men began to treat women honestly and decently and joined in what later became known as the Great Campaign for Sexual Equality, how everything began to get better and better ...

— Or —

Chapter Thirty One

Rosie dreamt of happy endings.

Rosie's dreams never came true. She kept waking up in the morning, in the midst of another muddle she didn't quite understand.

On the Saturday night after Stephen Anderson had confessed to her she lay sleepless, dreaming of happy endings.

On the Sunday nothing happened.

On the Monday the kids went back to school and Rosie scanned the columns of the *Echo* eagerly but nothing seemed to have happened.

On the Tuesday at eleven o'clock in the morning Rosie was having a sit down, while the children's clothes exchanged dirt with one another in the washing machine that was on the blink again, when a taxi deposited an arthritic middle-aged woman at her door. Dorothy Anderson announced, as she hobbled inside, that she'd instructed the taxi to come back in half an hour so she didn't have much time and no, she wouldn't have any tea thank you, she'd just come to give Rosie a piece of her mind.

Rosie had an uneasy feeling it was going to be the piece that was married to Stephen Anderson.

Rosie was right. 'In the early hours of Sunday morning,' said the woman, refusing to sit down, standing over Rosie, her weight balanced awkwardly on her sticks, 'on Sunday morning my husband attempted — there were — well, he consumed sufficient sleeping pills and whisky to ensure that he never woke up again and then lay down beside me to, to, to . . .'

I'm sorry, Rosie wanted to say. Not for Stephen Anderson; for his wife, surely duped again. For now he was recovering in hospital, and Rosie felt nausea mingling with her sympathy at the suicide attempt that sounded like a gesture intended not to succeed: what with the note he'd left and the knowledge that his insomniac wife would soon wake beside him.

'And now,' the woman resumed, her voice cracking with emotion, 'now he's told me everything.'

'Everything?'

'Everything. His pathetic secret life. And how you've been hounding him, you and that Helen Thackray woman,' said Dorothy Anderson, perched on a dining chair now, her mouth quivering as she lectured Rosie like a school-mistress. 'Blackmailing him or you'd tell me about his affair with her. As if I'd care; the silly man. And then, how on earth you had the effrontery to come to my house ...'

Rosie was hunting frantically in her bag for a cigarette. She seemed to have run out. She couldn't look the woman in the eye. 'But he admitted to me that he'd killed a man.'

'He told me you were concocting some story like that. Some extraordinary yarn about a man who died of a heart attack but whom, you say, Stephen pushed down some stairs. And have you a scrap of evidence to back up this preposterous claim?'

'Well,' said Rosie. Her mouth worked up and down but no more words came out.

'You have not. Frankly I'm appalled at your conduct. If it weren't for the need to avoid any strain on my husband, I should have gone to the police already to have you prosecuted for driving him to this. And I must warn you that if you repeat your allegations I shall have no choice but to lay the true facts before the police in order to protect my husband's reputation.'

But, Rosie tried to say, but her vocal chords wouldn't obey her. She stared in awe at Dorothy Anderson.

Thus, on the Tuesday, she learnt a little of the power of human love, loyalty and deception.

On the Wednesday the heavy breather left a brief message on the answering machine while Rosie was out shopping; and in the evening Jerry came round to tell her he hadn't got the tourism job.

On the Thursday Rosie told Mike the whole story of the Case of Stephen Anderson. He was very sympathetic. Of course he'd come to see the police with her. But he had to say, in all fairness, that if the man denied his confession there really wasn't any evidence to nail him on. Oh and by the way he'd ditched that dreadful boy, and perhaps this wasn't the time to tell her but he'd been offered a partnership in the firm he worked for ...

On the Friday Rosie went with Mike to the Mersey City police station. She came away knowing they didn't believe her story, and with a warning that they were considering preferring charges against her for demanding money with menaces.

On the Saturday Rosie took Bob, alone, to see Graham, and told her ex-husband he'd never see his daughter again after the outrageous way he'd treated her the week before. Graham said he'd see her in court.

On the way home she stopped off at Khan's newsagent and general store. She had them take out of the window the card advertising her services as an inquiry agent. In its place she put a card which read:

ROSE MONAGHAN
TYPING SERVICES

Reasonable rates. All typing work done.
Theses a speciality. Ring 471-5243 now!

She stood outside the shop, in the rain, staring at the card, thinking: Down these main streets a woman doesn't have to go. What a relief it would be to get back to typing men's dull thoughts on to clean white paper and waiting for her giro from the DHSS.

Why, then, was there a lump in her throat as she contemplated the future?

Chapter Thirty Two

Finally Rosie failed even to keep to her one resolution about the private eye business; she ended up attempting to resort to physical violence — with her handbag.

It was the day after she'd been to get her plaster removed and had seen Helen Thackray approaching her down a long grey hospital corridor. The girl had dodged into a lift as soon as she saw Rosie. She'd been coming out of the ante-natal clinic.

It was a day in December, a day that froze your finger-ends — especially Rosie's through her holey gloves. She was hurrying home from delivering a writ for Mike (the typing work being thin on the ground so far) across the scrubby parkland that locals called the Mystery for mysterious reasons while maps called it Wavertree Playground. She was reduced to Shanks's pony; even though she could drive again, she couldn't afford the petrol. Twilight; grey and orange layers of gloom in the sky, people and trees shadowy and sinister in the half-light.

A man in a shabby raincoat sat on the vandalized remnants of a park bench. He stood up as Rosie approached. Clean-shaven; heavy-jowled; grinning foolishly. He stood in her path and parted his raincoat. His fly was open.

It was a pathetic little thing really: a shrivelled baby elephant's trunk, a dangling worm. Yet he was pointing it at her as a sort of weapon. She looked up at his face. He was still grinning. His skin was a blotchy red-blue. His breath was coming in short gasps, like a man in a diving suit under water, like the voice of a man on the telephone. Down below the worm was growing.

Her handbag was laden with the rubbish of the six months since she'd last cleaned it out — and with the self-defence aerosol Margie had recommended so long before, but which she'd never had to use. Should she spray him with polish then wipe the smile off his face?

No. She didn't really have to think about what to do. She'd swing back the bag; its own arc would carry it inevitably forward into the man's crotch ...

Except that he moved. It was like a bullfighter's flourish — with a dirty mac for a cape — and a jig from a dance all at once. Then there he was, standing on one leg on the verge beside the path, while Rosie was just stopping herself from falling, propelled past him by the weight of her handbag.

But at least he'd stopped smiling. His features were twitching like a child's fearing punishment. He was holding his coat closed. Was he going to cry? Rosie felt a great wave of pity, in spite of herself, wash away her anger.

'Just stop phoning me, will you?' she said tiredly.

'Not me, girlie, not me, not me, not me, not me ...'

He was still chanting it. 'Not me, not me,' as he ran off with amazing speed, his coat flapping in the wind as if he were trying to fly away, and Rosie knew she'd never heard a thick Welsh accent like his coming out of her black telephone.

Later, in bed after an evening's television, Jerry and she 'made love' — that was what people called it, didn't they? Oh, and Rosie sighed with pleasure, and Jerry grunted happily. But then she remembered the dangling worm of the man on the Mystery, and all at once her pleasure seemed just pretence.

And in the middle of the night the wallpaper over the bed finally fell down. Rosie woke to the drip of plaster on her face. Beside her Jerry stirred vaguely. A piece of wallpaper crowned his head, a bizarre hat. The plaster-dust streamed into her eyes, like sand leaking from an hourglass. She turned over and closed her eyes. She'd clean it up in the morning. Sometimes it seemed as if there was always some kind of a mess to clean up in the mornings. It ought to be depressing.

But Rosie couldn't help it. Maybe she'd just been born that way. She laughed. Jerry, the wallpaper tangled in his hair, rolled over to embrace her. Soon he was sleeping again. Her face had relaxed into a crescent moon of a smile as she sang her favourite song to herself: 'Zip-A-Dee-Doo-Dah' and then she suddenly realised she was singing the song herself, for herself; not because Jerry had made her want to sing it. As the tune lulled her to sleep, she was dreaming of a woman called Rosie Monaghan who worked for herself now. This woman was tearing up a card that advertised her typing services and replacing it, in the window of Khan's Newsagent, with one that offered the services of an experienced enquiry agent: murders a speciality ...

ROSIE AMONG THORNS

Chapter One

If only Rosie had switched the answerphone on that Thursday night, maybe none of it would have happened.

The trouble was, she was waiting for a call from her friend Margie about the LBHA business. Since Monday Rosie had, during working hours, been following a grey Nissan pick-up with LBHA written on the side in red letters. The initials stood, in theory, for Liverpool Better Homes Association. The association's auditors were, however, of the opinion that the driver of this particular grey pick-up believed the letters were an abbreviation for Loadsa Bread for Harry Allsopp. The young accountant with receding hair and a stripy tie briefing Rosie for the job had paused for a long time after telling her this. He'd stared at her expectantly, the contact lenses glinting in his eyes.

'Ha ha,' Rosie had erupted spontaneously, once she'd finally caught on.

'It's the driver's name, you see, Harry Allsopp.'

'You never? Ha ha,' Rosie had re-erupted, hoping it was coming out right.

She always thought jokes were so much funnier when they were thoroughly explained to her.

Still, following a van for a week made a nice change for ROSIE MONAGHAN INQUIRY AGENT from the usual round of writs, repossessions and missing persons who preferred to stay missing. The pick-up had already led her on some beautiful excursions through the surrounding countryside. En route Harry Allsopp had delivered building materials to a wide range of unusual sites, including the cellar of a derelict house in Southport, a back garden in New Brighton and, in Meols, the back of another grey pick-up with WIMPEY written on the side.

Unfortunately Rosie didn't know where today's deliveries had illicitly gone. Steaming along the M62 in pursuit of Harry Allsopp, her old blue Mini had itself erupted spontaneously — with steam. So now she was waiting for Margie to call back and tell her she could borrow her van tomorrow. Margie was out with the latest man who wasn't going to fall passionately in love with her, reveal he was a millionaire disguised as just an ordinary feller and ask her to marry him. It was ten-thirty. Sometimes it took Margie as late as that to discover the sadly pertinent details.

Rosie had been watching a discussion programme on the BBC. But after a while it had progressed from her favourite subject, law and order, to the moral value of family life. And that reminded her too much of what Jerry had kept lecturing her about lately. So she switched off the TV, hesitated, fatally, over the answerphone and went up to her bedroom.

Which was also, in its spare time, her office. Bills in various shades of red were scattered across the double bed she shared with Jerry sometimes, when they hadn't been rowing about the moral value of family life. She piled the papers into a tidy-looking heap on the desk by the window in the hope that they'd forget they were there. Finally, she was halfway through undressing, and had just tracked down her nightie under a folder of old invoices from which she really ought to be reconstructing a year or two's accounts, when the extension-phone rang.

'Margie, at last,' said Rosie, trying to wriggle into the nightdress while holding the phone with one hand. 'What?' she was asking, bemused but clothed, a moment later.

'It's me,' said Jerry. 'Look, about earlier . . . '

Rosie sighed and settled down into the revolving chair at her desk for a long listen. Spring was rat-tat-tatting April hail-showers at the window and Jerry was rat-tat-tatting his apologies in her ear. 'You see, the thing is . . .' he was saying.

It's spring, Rosie wanted to say to him, come on Jerry it's spring so why isn't your sap rising?

Jerry's rising had been decidedly sapped of late. Once upon a time he had clasped Rosie warmly to him on cold nights and had made her want to sing 'Zip-a-dee-doo-dah' at midnight. Nowadays, alas, a paunch had swollen his belly into mock pregnancy so that Rosie was barely capable of embracing him at all. And 'Zip-a-dee-doo-dah' was no longer the carefree sort of tune he had in mind. More, a little number by Mendelssohn: that ditty about funerals or weddings or something equally gloomy. She could faintly hear it playing now, yes, about weddings it was, playing in her imagination as he rat-tat-tatted: 'You see, the main thing is . . . '

The main thing was, Jerry wanted to be a father. Rosie had a faint suspicion this fathering was going to involve her in some minor way: like, mothering, for instance. 'It's just the spring,' she interrupted brightly.

'What is?'

This delusion of the joys of family life, of course. It's the sap getting diverted. 'I'm sorry,' said Rosie, 'what were you saying?'

He was saying, he said, that he wanted to help make the future. Charles Darwin, he was adding furthermore, had shown that the ultimate purpose in life was to reproduce itself.

Go ahead then, reproduce yourself.

Rosie leafed through her notes about the LBHA case and didn't remind Jerry she'd only ever taken him on as her bit on the side. On the side of what? On the side of the important things in her life: her children, her home, her work, her sense of humour. How unfunny Jerry had become since he'd got reproduction on the brain. Keeping half an ear open in case he said anything he hadn't said to her a dozen times before, Rosie thought about the important things: the fragments of future she'd helped to make. There was, for instance, her darling little son Bob, who liked to shoot weapons or goals or, now he was thirteen,

7

sticky dampness that left stains on the bedclothes which Graham had said he was going to talk to the boy about but Rosie would have to wouldn't she? (Could ex-husbands be relied on for anything, such as maintenance or talks on the meaning of masturbation? No, they could not.) Or, to take another example entirely at random, there was her charming daughter Carol who had taken against her father and red meat at more or less the same time, causing chaos on fortnightly access-weekends and at every meal-time.

No, if Rosie made the future any more it was going to be for herself. This womb is not for rent.

'Can't this wait?' she found herself saying gruffly into the telephone the moment after she'd resolved not to be gruff with him. 'Y'see, I'm waiting for a call.'

'If that's the way you feel,' said Jerry, putting the receiver down just before she could reply.

Refusing to feel guilty about that, Rosie had just settled down with a good book when the phone rang again. 'Where've you been?' she asked impatiently, at 11:28 by her digital watch that wasn't really hers but her son Bob's and she really must give it back to him. 'Not with that Yank again?'

'It's Paddy,' said the phone.

'Oh,' said Rosie, doing her best not to hide her disappointment. 'I'm afraid I'm expecting a business call.'

'No, but,' said Paddy, 'I need your help, Ro.'

There were only two ways her brother ever needed her help. 'I'm skint, I'm afraid,' said Rosie. 'But if she's chucked y'out again . . . '

'Y'see,' said the voice at the other end as if she hadn't spoken, 'me partner's walked out on me with a load of me cash, and . . . '

'Tell me about it tomorrow, eh?'

' . . . and Debbie's had the baby but it's driven her potty and anyway the baby's not . . . '

'I'm expecting a business call. Didn't you hear me? Look, I'll meet you tomorrow lunchtime. The Crooked

Man,' said Rosie, and put the still-chattering receiver back in its cradle.

The Crooked Man: that was her brother alright. Still, his problems wouldn't be anything a few stolen grand wouldn't put right. Never had been before, anyway.

'Shut up, spring,' said Rosie fiercely at the showers still battering on the window. Clearly, however, the season had decided to imitate her children and take no notice of her. Like Margie who still hadn't rung back and was probably having a sickeningly good time. Rosie wedged herself into the tiny part of the bed that Jerry would have left for her if he'd been there, embraced the empty space where his body would have been, and spoke aloud. 'Go to sleep, Rosie,' she sighed.

Rosie was as bad as the season and her children: she didn't take enough notice of herself. She resolutely refused even to close her eyes. After all, Margie might still ring. Meanwhile, she might as well try her book again. Usually stories such as this, about a pipe-smoking, poetry-quoting detective somewhere in the south of England, comforted her. Nicely unpleasant middle-class characters lived nicely unpleasant middle-class lives and it all came out right in the end. Usually. Tonight, though, she found herself comparing the man's simple murder-solving life with her own. Why couldn't she be like him? Damn it, she'd only ever solved one murder and then nobody had believed her. Since then it'd mostly been writs and repos and wronged wives for whom nothing could be done. Frankly, the highlights of her detection career had been the odd week following a grey pick-up or the occasional stimulating video repossession like the one she and Margie had done the night before last. Four teenagers had lain around the floor of this grotty flat, glazed amid glue fumes, watching a horror video with the sound off. And . . .

And, hey, that was another good argument to save up for Jerry, wasn't it? What if the wonderful future he so desperately wanted to make turned out like them?

And why could she never think up any of these power-

9

ful rejoinders when actually facing the man?

Fortunately the phone rang again before that could make her feel too annoyed with herself. She stumbled across the room on automatic pilot and fumbled for the receiver. 'It's the middle of the night, Marg, where . . .?'

'Mike here,' said the phone.

Mike who? After all her solicitor-friend Mike never rang her in the middle of the night. 'Mike?'

'I've got a case for you,' said her solicitor-friend Mike, sounding like it was the most normal thing in the world to say that to her at . . .

'It's one in the morning,' said Rosie.

'It's only eight at night in New York.'

'Uh?' said Rosie brightly.

'For example, I meant. New York. Can you get here right away? It's important. This is the address.'

'Wait, wait,' and Rosie searched among the bills for her pad and on the floor for her pen. A case? What repossession could be that urgent at this time of night? And how did New York fit in?

Chapter Two

New York didn't fit in anywhere. It was just an example of where people would still be awake. Unlike Rosie, who only discovered how dopey she was feeling when she remembered she couldn't go out because Jerry wasn't there to mind the kids; remembered, just as Mike put the receiver down.

Fortunately Margie was awake when she rang. It turned out Rosie's friend had been at home since ten-thirty after all, only her teenage son had forgotten to give her the message. And no, the night's meal-ticket hadn't been a secret millionaire with a yacht in the Mediter-ranean. And yes, it only took a small bribe to persuade Margie to come round.

Anyway, Rosie didn't have to think about that any more. Now she could settle back comfortably in the back of the cab, and clear her head ready for the job ahead, whatever that might be.

Now that she needed to clear her head, naturally it filled up with inconsequential trivia: like, why am I here?

You are here, Rosie, said a voice in her ear, because you love the thrill and excitement of private detection — down these mean streets a woman must go — murders solved, racketeers exposed — good triumphing over evil ...

Don't give me that, said Rosie to Rosie. Both of them knew she'd only fallen into the work by mistake after market forces had put paid to her last job on the processed-foods production line. She'd just happened to be reading about Philip Marlowe at the time, that was all, and knew she could do better. Plus, it paid as well as typing or being a waitress but you weren't beholden to anyone, were you?

Except to whatever crooked client Mike's dug out of the

woodwork this time, Rosie reminded herself, staring out of the window. The address Mike had given her was in the suburbs. So it couldn't be far now. They were gliding along tree-lined avenues where the bay windows glimmered in the moonlight. And yes, this was where she should have been living, if her upbringing and her ex-husband Graham had had their way: gardens for the kids to play in, stuck-up neighbours for her not to get on with while Graham played golf with their husbands on Sunday mornings.

Graham had spent several years blaming Rosie for the fact that they couldn't afford to live in an area like this. Finally he'd taken to blaming her with his fists, because that was the only way she couldn't give him back more blame than he could deliver. And now she was scraping her living from the processed-crime production line, while he was bluffing his way to a living with his salesman's patter that had once persuaded her to say 'I will,' and now, yes, he had even bought just such a suburban house for his new wife and what he liked to call 'his' new baby. And was he happy? The house he'd always wanted was, he told her when she enquired impolitely why the maintenance was late, a fucking millstone round his fucking neck.

Which was all a cunning device to prevent Rosie from noticing that the cab had stopped and the cabby was mentioning a sum of money to her in gruff, I'm-on-nights-and-I-hate-it tones and blow me if she didn't have the cash to pay the fare.

Finally she deigned to notice him. 'Won't be a minute,' she said brightly, stepping out into the night; adding, to herself: 'I'll be two.'

Well, she liked to keep herself amused.

And this was a house beyond even Graham's early dreams: a little detached palace, glowing in the moonlight. In the fierce glare of a light pointing straight into Rosie's eyes from above the garage somewhere — one of those lights rich people kindly installed so that burglars could see their way more easily — Mike was already waiting for her, standing in the gravel drive between a Volvo and an Aston Martin. 'Come on in,' he said, but to her surprise she kissed him on the cheek and, taking him by the arm and leading him back towards the cab, said:

'Saw you on the telly tonight. I've always wanted to know famous people.'

Mike groaned. 'Don't talk about it.'

He'd been on the regional news, being a spokesperson in front of a lot of chanting demonstrators about gay rights. 'But I thought you were great.'

'The boss didn't,' said Mike, nodding inside towards the boss. 'Rosie we're walking in the wrong direction.'

So Rosie explained about the Mini being on the blink and the government's quantity of money theory affecting her very directly at the minute. And then an entirely unplanned question leapt out of her: 'What,' she asked, 'what do gay men do if they want to be a father?'

Even at half-one in the morning, paying off her cab, Mike was one of those irritating men who was not only homosexual and fanciable as hell, but could find a smart remark to cap your own. 'They don't. They want to be mothers. Well, that's my experience,' said Mike. 'So they find a man that needs mothering.'

'That shouldn't be hard.'

Finally the cabbie was paid off and she let herself be steered back towards the glow of the light while Mike told her about the case. 'His daughter's done a bunk. Fourteen. He's a prat but he's a friend of Langton's. One of the partners. On the nineteenth hole, y'know. Down at the gun club. So be nice to him, eh? He wants a woman.'

'I haven't stooped that low,' said Rosie and Mike gave her a look:

'A woman detective,' he explained, as if she didn't know. And before she even had time to comb her hair he'd steered her into a room you could have fitted every room of Rosie's terraced house into — and the backyard — full of a load of people who wouldn't be seen dead in

13

Rosie's terraced house. Well, there were only two men there, but they'd have filled up Rosie's house between them. David Langton (as Mike did the introductions) was about fifty, and almost as much round the girth. He smiled in a sneering sort of way down his half-spectacles when Mike said he was the senior partner, then introduced 'our client', Luke Greenfield: same girth and age, but with a suntanned smile he managed to switch on briefly for Rosie's benefit before reaching for the almost-empty whisky bottle on the glass-topped table.

'Ms Monaghan,' Mike was saying, 'is our most experienced female operative.'

Rosie smoothed down the folds of her experienced smile. 'Just a small one,' she replied demurely to the offer of a whisky, sitting where David Langton indicated: in one of those leather armchairs whose cost would have kept Rosie's kids in fishfingers for a year. And it creaked every time you moved. Don't move, Rosie.

'Perhaps,' taking the small Scotch that made her glad she hadn't asked for a large one, 'perhaps you could fill me in on the case, Mr, er, Greenfield?'

'Call me Luke,' said Luke, waving his whisky glass so the liquid almost swished out, 'you see my Ruth, she's never been away so long, my Ruth . . .'

Rosie nodded encouragingly, trying hard to look serious and interested. She sat back, relaxing briefly — no it's not a fart Rosie, it's the chair creaking — as Langton, with occasional interruptions from 'our client', told the story. Ruth Greenfield, he explained, was fourteen years old, had never been home later than ten o'clock and now it was whatever-it-was (1:44 said Bob's digital watch) and Mrs Greenfield was in bed with several sleeping pills inside her and actually Ruth had never come home from school and . . .

'And which of these is she?' asked Rosie, creaking into an upright position to examine a photograph on the mantelpiece. In the gilt frame Call Me Luke smiled out of a suntan, his arms round two teenage girls that a father might have called pretty. A dowdy woman who was presumably Mrs Luke grimaced from the edge of the picture.

'Ruth's the blonde one. But here, David, you've got a picture,' and 'David' produced one from his inside pocket. It was of a girl with very long fair hair, wearing a blouse and skirt that would have looked old-fashioned on a thirty-mumble-year-old like Rosie, a girl half-child but with more than a half-adult look in her smile. 'Beautiful, eh?'

Rosie smiled in friendly disagreement: 'And the police . . .?'

Luke gazed straight into Rosie's eyes so that she had to look away from the bloodshot intensity of it: 'I haven't told her mother. She took most of her clothes y'see. But no suitcase. Her mother's not been well, y'see. With her nerves. Mrs Greenfield. So I haven't told her. About the clothes. And the suitcase . . .'

Now that she'd stood up and didn't want to sit down and make the leather chair fart all over again, Rosie bypassed the questions about finding it hard to believe the mother didn't know about the suitcase and repeated: 'I don't understand why the police . . .'

'No p'lice. No p'lice,' Luke slurred. A wry look passed between Langton and Mike, who'd been sitting back from the group, saying nothing. Luke caught the look too: 'I know what you think but, Rosie, come here will you love,' and he grabbed hold of her podgy fist in two extraordinarily big hands and she immediately re-christened him Damp Hand Luke in her imagination, 'I've got enemas, y'see. Enemas. Mies. I can see them looking, I know what they think,' and Rosie happened to catch Mike's eye and began to find breathing difficult, 'but my little girl wouldn't go away on her own. No. I'm waiting for a phone call 'cause she's been kidnapped. By my . . .'

'By your enemies,' said Rosie quickly, patting the two hands that still soggily gripped hers. He looked down at his knuckles, as if just remembering they were his, and let go. She went on: 'But, er, you're sure she hasn't just gone out on the town with a mate?'

'She's only fourteen, y'know.' Luke was shocked. Appalled at the very idea. 'Out on the town? Not my Ruth. No, somebody brought her back from school, I mean, if she'd just gone on the town why take her clothes? If she went of her own acc, acc, accord why no suitcase? No, somebody brought her, and then . . . '

Rosie had had enough of this. She got out her note-book, and sat firmly down in the leather armchair, and said: 'Perhaps I could get a few details. When she was last seen. Description of the clothes . . . ?'

That had a decisive effect on Damp Hand Luke all right. He became even more incoherent. 'Not my Ruth,' he was wailing, 'not my Ruth . . . '

Langton took the whisky-glass from Luke's hand as he was about to take another drink. 'I tell you what, Luke,' he said. 'Why don't you get some sleep while my assistant fills Ms Monaghan in on the details?'

'Can't sleep,' said Luke, as Langton helped him to his feet, 'how can I sleep when my Ruth . . . ?'

Actually he looked in acute danger of passing into unconsciousness right where he was. Langton glanced meaningfully at Mike, smiled benignly and meaninglessly at Rosie, and steered Luke out.

Rosie stared at Mike.

Mike stared at Rosie.

She would have been all right if she'd just kept silent. Instead she had to speak, didn't she?

'Have you got enemas?' she said.

And then both of them were laughing, tastelessly, help-lessly, and so loudly that Langton came back into the room to ask with his eyes what the hell was going on. And somehow that shut Mike up but made another gale of laughter whoosh up from inside Rosie somewhere, only dimming as she heard Langton say:

'Are you sure Miss Monaghan's the right person for the job?'

16

Chapter Three

'Of course you're the right woman for the job,' said Margie on the phone.

'Thanks, Marg.'

It was seven-thirty in the morning. After a cramped night on the sofa, waiting for kidnappers who hadn't called, Rosie was now squatting in the Greenfields' hall. Beneath her the carpet was as soft and deep as Jerry's feelings. She'd told Margie the story in hushed tones; now she had to endure Margie's barbed endorsement of her worth.

'I mean,' her friend was saying, 'what other silly cow'd drop everything for a job at one in the morning?'

'Thanks, Marg,' murmured Rosie, with more feeling this time. 'But, look . . .'

'Quite apart,' Margie continued relentlessly, 'quite apart from happening to have a best mate who's soft in the head enough to come and babysit for her. At the aforesaid one in the morning. Who else? You're unique.'

'Thanks, Marg,' said Rosie sharply. 'Look, what I want you to do is . . .'

Rosie refused to be disconcerted by the apparition of a middle-aged woman in a very short white nightdress staring at her from the top of the stairs. Calmly she explained to Margie that Carol had to take her swimming things today even if she pretended to have a cold, and that it was Bob's day for football, and about the LBHA job that Margie would have to do for her now, and (quickly) how much money that was worth before Margie said no.

'Lolly! Lolly!' said the woman, slowly coming down the stairs towards her.

'That's quite all right,' said Rosie into the phone when Margie thanked her for the generous notice she'd given her of all this. 'I'm sorry?' she said to the woman with young suntanned legs and an ageing face who was teetering towards her rather quickly and was, Rosie now saw, brandishing a toilet brush.

'Lolly! Lolly!' — Yes, for whatever reasons of her own that was what the woman was saying, as she banged the stiff bristles firmly down on to Rosie's skull.

'Rosie,' said Rosie, holding her hands over her head by way of introduction, 'Rosie Monaghan. I'm here to — agh! — help you look for your daughter,' and at last her pyjama'd client had arrived on the stairs and was saying 'Barbara! Barbara!' in a resigned sort of a voice.

The woman retreated suddenly across the hall. She clasped the toilet brush to her, her arms across her breasts like a sulky child. 'I didn't do anything wrong,' she was saying,'I didn't do anything wrong . . .'

'Of course you didn't,' said Rosie, approaching, eyeing the toilet brush warily,'I'm here to help you . . .'

Then a dishevelled Luke Greenfield was between them and had his arm around his wife. 'Did I take my pill?' she was saying confusedly, looking up into his pale face for guidance. 'Oh, Lolly, what's Josephine been doing now?'

He was guiding his wife into the living-room and saying, 'It's Ruth that's gone, Ruth, you remember.' At the doorway he turned to Rosie. 'Tea. In the kitchen,' reinforced with a nod of the head. 'You can use that phone anywhere,' he added finally, indicating the receiver that Rosie suddenly realised was still in her hand.

The kitchen might have been lifted direct from the pages of *Good Housekeeping* and transformed into three dimensions — except that it looked even more unused than the ones in the magazine pictures. Rosie stood by the door, pretending to herself that she was examining the beauty of the room. Really, though — no, you can't fool yourself Rosie, not often anyway — she was trying to overhear the conversation in the living room. But they were keeping their voices down. Maybe she could hear a woman's tearful voice; maybe she was just imagining it.

So she found the kettle and the teabags and some cups and saucers and said 'Hi, Martin,' cheerfully into the fancy phone. 'Got a little job for you.'

Martin Brown was a dangerous revolutionary — well, a dangerously good-looking man — that Rosie had met on her first case. Since then she and the Department of Social Security had accepted joint responsibility for his income, though Rosie was more ruthless about making him work for his money.

'D'you know what time it is?' said his bleary voice at the other end.

Thanks to Bob's watch she did indeed know that. She informed Martin precisely what time it was. He didn't seem to be terribly interested, even though he'd asked. So she told him what she wanted him to do, then said no sorry capitalism hadn't collapsed since yesterday, then repeated it all again. And all the while she kept busy making the tea so that she didn't have to acknowledge to herself that Martin's voice on the telephone, even at this time in the morning, made her heart flutter as Jerry's voice once had done.

'Got all that?' she asked brightly, the tea-tray ready before her.

'Could you just say it once more?'

'What?'

'Joke,' said Martin.

Rosie honestly didn't feel like even a token spontaneous eruption of 'Ha ha' right now. She flipped the button on the phone from Talk to Standby without another word.

In the living room there was no sign of Mrs Greenfield: only Damp Hand Luke slumped in one of the leather chairs, his hands over his face, amid the stale smell of last night's cigar smoke. Rosie cleared a space among the debris on the glass-topped table and set down the tea-tray. Her client stared up at her from bloodshot eyes. 'My wife,' he said, 'has gone to lie down. She's overwrought.'

Only then did he actually get round to blinking. 'It

might be helpful if I could talk to her later about . . . ' said Rosie.

'She won't have anything to add. But I'd be grateful if you'd stay and keep an eye on her this morning.'

'No way,' said Rosie. He gave her the look of a man who wasn't used to people saying 'No way' to him but she wasn't to be diverted: 'I've got to get out and about. Talk to your daughter's friends. Check up on your enemas, mies.' And she just managed to swallow the laugh before continuing: 'And I've summoned one of my operatives to monitor the phone. But I don't handle agency nurses.'

His hangover squinted at her for a few minutes while the rest of him absorbed a swallow of tea. Then, with a creak of his stubble, he smiled. Oh, no, thought Rosie, I've gone and done the right thing, he's going to say . . .

'I like you, Rosie.' Which he did say. 'You've got spirit,' he added, 'I admire that.'

Rosie had met men who'd admired her spirit before. Lord save us, she'd even married one. Alas, what they usually admired about her spirit was that they thought they could break it — so they could then complain that she wasn't as spirited as she used to be. 'Maybe,' she said, 'maybe your other daughter — Josephine, is it? — could come and . . . '

'I'm afraid Josephine and I are not on speaking terms. No, I'll call up my sister. If you're quite sure,' cranking the smile back into action again, 'if you're quite sure you've finished talking to your, er, operatives on my phone.'

Not that he was all that pleased when Martin turned up on the doorstep with Rosie's answerphone and her standard contract for Greenfield to sign. Nor did Martin get much of a greeting from Greenfield's square-jawed sister Alice, who'd arrived in the meantime to keep an eye on her sister-in-law's pills. Why were they shocked? Just because she had a man in her employ? Maybe it was because of his big smile and his T-shirt that said BORN TO BE WILD: GREENPEACE?

One thing she was sure of: they couldn't possibly be shocked merely because the colour of his skin was black, could they?

Martin settled down with his smile and a load of papers that he'd always tell people like the Greenfields were racing form. Actually they were for an Open University course he'd decided to do to improve himself, once he'd realised the world wasn't going to improve unless he did. Rosie felt like kissing him lightly on the forehead but somehow suppressed the urge. 'I'll call y'every hour,' she said instead, brisk, business-like, taking Damp Hand Luke's arm and leading him out to his BMW. 'Now,' she said, 'why don't you just sign my contract for me? Then you can tell me why you don't want to call the police. And all about these, er, enemies of yours.'

But he didn't seem to want to explain about them at all. At first all he wanted to do was apologise for his wife: 'Barbara, you'll have to excuse her. Nowadays she ... but in her younger days — well, she could have been a beauty queen. Miss New Brighton. If she'd been taller.'

That must be a great comfort to her. 'Now, look,' said Rosie decisively, 'tell me again about these enemies of yours. And why you don't want to call the police in. If Ruth was a daughter of mine ... '

He acted as if he hadn't heard. Instead he sat, fat and important at the flight-deck of his BMW, the gleaming car-phone waiting for radio contact with Ground Traffic Control, the car's controls like an extension of his body, so smooth were his movements, and farted surreptitiously into the air-conditioned atmosphere. He drove as frighteningly as her brother Paddy did in his souped-up Cortina (and oh my God, she had to see him for lunch) but shouted at the other road-users twice as much. And in between all that he just wanted, now that his wife was explained away, to give Rosie a lecture on scroungers and self-made men. No prizes for which he was:

'Lot of fellers, y'see Rosie, they got their redundancy, from the docks, and what did they do? Spent half on birds and bevvies and gee-gees; the other half on pacifying the wife by buying the house off the Council. Then what are they left with? Scrounging off the State, that's what. Whereas me . . . '

'Yes, but,' said Rosie vaguely, staring gloomily at the rain through the wipers and trying to recall the lines of that cheerful song about April showers, unable to stop his flow:

'Me I saw the opportunity,' he went on, turning alarmingly to nod at her in emphasis before his eyes went back to the road again and his hand went to the horn: 'Stupid bastard. Did you see that? — No, me, I said to meself, say there's ten thousand dockers getting twenty thousand each. Pay-off, like. That's two hundred million quid looking for a home, that. Just from the docks. Not counting all the other businesses that're closing down: fat redundancy cheques everywhere. I said to meself: there's money to be made out of unemployment. So what did I do? Sit back on my arse?' — as he farted again and Rosie coughed indiscreetly, but to no effect — 'Wait for some bureaucrat to tell me there wasn't no jobs? No, I got up off my backside and set up in business. Greenfield Investment Services. Advised me old mates where to stick their redundancy: five per cent for me: everybody's happy.'

Except for your wife, said Rosie to the mesmeric wipers. And your daughters? 'Oh yeh,' she said out loud, 'it's a wonderful thing, redundancy. Especially for the old and needy.'

'No . . .'

'No,' said Rosie sweetly, 'it's what first got me into detection, y'know: being made redundant. A wonderful thing. So,' with a smooth change of gear to match the car's, 'so if everybody's happy — who are your enemies?'

He turned to smile at her then. Luckily they were stopped at some traffic lights at the time, while his smile said: 'People resent success, Rosie. You musta noticed that yourself. So . . .'

Rosie, whose redundancy only ran into five figures if

22

you added in the two after the decimal point, thought about all the people who resented her success at private detection. She could count them easily: on the fingers of no hands: unless you included Jerry. But even she didn't think he'd stoop to kidnapping Carol.

And already they were at Ruth's school and he was telling her there wasn't any point in going there. No, she should be waiting by the phone instead of that, er, operative of hers.

Rosie smiled sweetly and, giving up on his enemies, asked him instead about Ruth's friends.

'She didn't have none, any,' said Luke Greenfield.

He was avoiding looking at her; revving the engine as if impatient to be off to fleece some more scroungers. 'She must have some,' protested Rosie, whose house was constantly full of young people whose names she half-knew but who always assured her, if asked, that they were friends of Bob or Carol.

'Home-loving girl, Ruth. And, well, frankly — she had a bit of difficulty adjusting when we moved from the Council estate. A few years back. I don't think she's brought a friend home for, oh, two years now. But,' looking dangerously as if he was working himself up to say something frank, honest and fearless to her, 'but don't get me wrong Rosie. Ruth's always been happy with her family.'

'Unlike Josephine?' Rosie asked sweetly, and he glanced sharply across at her:

'D'you ever get the feeling,' and yes here was frank, honest fearlessness, plus a blast of last night's whisky full in her face for good measure, 'the feeling you've watched your children grow, you remember the first time they fell off their bike and suddenly — you don't know them? D'you ever get that feeling?'

Damp patches on the bed and vegetarianism, yes I know the feeling. But he didn't give her the chance to reply: 'I'm sure,' he went on, staring out at the rain, 'sure as I'm sitting here that my Ruth wouldn't go away on her

23

own. Now, if you'll excuse me . . .'

Rev rev. The rain hadn't stopped but Rosie didn't feel like talking any more. 'Call your home if you want any news,' she said, 'Martin will be . . .'

But she didn't get a chance to say what he'd be: Luke Greenfield had pressed a button to wind up the window and was up and away in a trail of spray.

She looked up through the rain at the long low concrete-and-glass of the school and shivered. There was something about schools that reminded her of, she wasn't sure whether it was prison or just factory work. Telling herself she just wanted a bar of chocolate to keep her going, she sidled down the street to the welcoming glow of the little shop on the corner.

You don't want cigarettes, you've given them up, said Rosie.

'A packet of, er,' said Rosie, pointing to what she wanted and smiling at the tired eyes of the Asian woman behind the counter. Then she caught sight of her own eyes in the mirror behind the shopkeeper. My God, thought Rosie, the state of that face. *She* should be smiling comfortingly at me. Why am I doing this?

Out in the street she was just sucking in the smoke and remembering she was doing this for the money and the sheer wild enjoyment of it all when she noticed the BMW at the kerbside. A silver-grey BMW, with the engine running and a man bearing a remarkable resemblance to her new client leaning out of the window into the rain. And was that a tear in his eye? Or just the rain caught on his lashes? 'I'm sorry,' he said in a plausibly sincere tone. 'Sorry if I was brusque with you, Rosie. I love my Ruth,' and was that a catch in his voice now? Or had she just blown smoke at him? 'Find her. Please. Just find my daughter for me.'

Chapter Four

'No, I can't honestly say she did have any friends that I knew of,' said Mrs Hepworth.

No wonder the three R's were suffering. Mrs Hepworth was Ruth's form-teacher and most of her time, Rosie assumed, must be spent teaching children how to find their way round the blasted school. It had taken Rosie half an hour to track her down among a maze of corridors and inaccurate directions provided by various local representatives of the future. Now the two women were standing in a sort of clothes cubicle outside the staff-room because there wasn't anywhere private to talk. Rosie sipped instant tea from a plastic cup and asked incredulously: 'No friends at all?'

'Why exactly are you asking these questions?'

Mrs Hepworth had a small bird-like frame and a tiny mouse-like voice. But her eyes were wide and didn't look like they missed anything. So Rosie wore her most convincingly earnest look as she explained again about being a friend of the family who was trying to help them find out why Ruth hadn't come home since yesterday. At that Mrs Hepworth expressed squeaky surprise . . .

. . . pausing only to remonstrate with two frighteningly mature-looking boys for running down the corridor, then pretending not to notice when they squeaked at her once they were safely behind her back . . .

'A strange child. Ruth. Very withdrawn. Sometimes she can be as sulky as an eight-year-old. Sometimes she tries to pretend she's about to start the menopause.' Mrs Hepworth briefly and surprisingly frowned, though it might have been at the tea. 'A friend of the family, you say?'

'They're both too upset to come,' said Rosie with what she hoped was an appearance of profound sympathy. 'There doesn't seem to be any trouble at home.'

'Hm,' said the teacher, and that was more or less Rosie's opinion really:

'But if you're aware of anything . . .'

'No, no,' said Mrs Hepworth, looking away so that Rosie knew the woman had her suspicions. And why, you fool, would a so-called family friend have said that? But the teacher didn't seem to have spotted her mistake: 'Bit of a loner, that's all,' she went on. 'Not a mixer. Thinks school's a waste of time. But then, so do most of them. They all want to be off on some tremendously stimulating and exciting youth training scheme instead. Still, she's almost the last girl I'd have thought . . .'

'Would have gone off somewhere?' said Rosie when the thoughtful silence was lengthening towards lunchtime.

'Hm,' was all she got in reply before a deafening bell sounded just above them and suddenly Mrs Hepworth was up up and away: 'My God, I've got to be in the Annexe in five seconds.'

And Rosie, in pursuit, was asking for a rethink on the question of whether Ruth had any friends. Well, wheezing rather than asking, for the schoolteacher moved surprisingly quickly for such a small woman. Rosie had to ask her to repeat whatever she'd just mumbled to the staircase ahead, and the teacher stopped:

'She picks up strays sometimes. There was a cat she brought into class once. Flea-bitten thing. And Susie Gould. She's Ruth's latest stray.'

'Could I see her? I'm sorry,' because Mrs Hepworth was looking at her watch and they were on the move again and Rosie had never realised how much physical fitness was involved in teaching:

'I'd better take you,' said the other woman over her shoulder as they headed out into the rain.

*

26

Rosie waited outside the classroom, shaking the water from her hair and the bad memories of her own schooldays from her brain, as Mrs Hepworth negotiated with the schoolteacher in room 347. There was a lot of gesticulation and a look in Rosie's direction — smile, Rosie, smile — before a remarkably fat girl waddled to the front and followed Mrs Hepworth out.

'I'll leave you to it,' squeaked the teacher. In an instant she was breathlessly away and Rosie was saying, 'Susie, Mrs Hepworth was telling me,' before the girl turned to look up at her full face. Rosie couldn't help it. Whatever words she'd been about to say vanished into thin air when she saw the strawberry birthmark that, except for a little patch under the ear, covered the entire right half of the girl's face.

Susie looked at her coldly. An I'm-used-to-your-reaction look glinted in her eyes. 'So am I really off for the whole class?'

'Er, yeah,' replied Rosie, realising too late she'd been conned when the girl set off up the corridor saying:

'We could go the shop then. For some chocolate.'

And soon Rosie was in earnest moral debate with herself about whether being born with a vivid birthmark — there were strange bumps and pocks all over it, like a contour map, she couldn't help looking at — whether being born so blemished justified a fundamental nastiness of spirit as Susie said:

'You're a bit of a mess. You got pretty wet, didn't you?' — and —

'My mum gives me fifty pence a day to spend on sweets. How much are you gonna give me?'

— and, looking at Rosie sidelong (in the shop now) from the right side of her face, as if forcing Rosie to look at the birthmark and nothing else —

'You're not a friend of Ruth's family, or I'd have heard of you. What d'you want to know and how much are you gonna pay me for it? Better double the number you first thought of, 'cause these Pakis rob y' blind.'

27

— turning to bare her teeth at the Asian woman behind the counter who pretended not to understand, then quietly slipping a tube of tomato paste into the pocket of her blue jacket and winking in complicity at Rosie before finally letting Our Heroine get a word in edgeways.

'I wanted to ask . . .'

'Go on, then, whaddya wanna know? We can stay in here out the rain, can't we?'

The Asian woman smiled again as if uncomprehending, and ignored Rosie's apologetic look. And Susie was already eyeing the chocolate counter gluttonously so Rosie, suddenly not knowing what to ask but anxious to avoid being an accessory to any more shoplifting, said, 'Tell me about Ruth, then.'

Susie smiled. Then she was showing Rosie her remarkably large open palm. Two thin silver rings were already trapped by fat in the flesh of the index and little fingers. Rosie stared at her for a moment; the hand shook in a deliberate motion; the smile wavered.

Rosie fumbled in her handbag and found fifty pence, wondering how she was going to account for this on expenses — 'Bribes to corrupt minors, 50p'? — but the hand remained outstretched. Two pound coins had to be placed there, it turned out, before the girl would start:

'She's a scaredy-cat. Some days she wouldn't come to school if I didn't bring her. And she never has any money, I have to pay her share an' all to the, er . . .'

Oh gosh what have I said, said the girl's movements, hand to mouth, eyes wide. Was she overplaying it a bit, though? 'Pay her share to who?'

'The, er,' looking round to see that nobody's listening, 'Nazis. They're a gang. It's like protection. Protection from them, y'know. But I don't mind. I'm tough. I'll be one when I'm bigger. A Nazi. Not like soppy Ruth.'

'And have the, er,' hushing her voice as the girl had done, conscious of the Asian woman still blandly smiling, within hearing-distance, 'have the Nazis been frightening her lately?'

'No more than usual. 'cept I was off sick this week. Food poisoning. So I never saw her, although maybe when she was on her own they might have. Nothing's happened to her, has it?'

'Not that I know of,' said Rosie, wondering how to handle the next thing she wanted to say. A plump middle-aged woman was scanning the shelves beside them and appeared to be whistling rather conspicuously. 'Between you and me, though, she's not been home for a day or two. That's a secret, though.'

The hand was outstretched again. 'Come on,' said Rosie. The hand stayed where it was.

'Secrets cost money,' said the girl.

Rosie sighed. 'Well you'll have to give me the quids back, I've got no more change.'

Then, when the fiver had changed hands: 'She's not,' asked the girl, now with a less aggressive look in her eye, 'had no trouble at home, has she?'

'Might she have?'

'Nah,' with a shrug that might have meant anything. 'Are you looking for her then?'

'Yeh.' The truth seemed simplest; this girl was more worldly-wise than her teachers. 'I had to say I was a friend of the family's though, to get to see you.'

'I'm with that.'

'Any boyfriend trouble?'

'Any boyfriends, more like. She reckons she's got one. A secret one. But I don't believe her.' Suddenly Susie was tapping the scarred side of her face. 'See this. Boys really go for this. Like a magnet. That repels, right? Fieldsie, they call me. From Strawberry Fields, y'know. Funny, eh? Ha fuckin' ha. But Ruthie's got one an' all. An invisible one. Boys can see it, somehow. Are you with me?' Susie was shaking her head, really upset? 'Poor old Ruthie. Find her, won't you?'

Really upset: yes. For out of the blue, to the amazement of Rosie and, indeed, of the woman along the shelves who suddenly stopped whistling, the tough girl

29

with the strawberry birthmark and the cold eyes burst into tears. Rosie reached out to touch her shoulder.

'Sod off,' said the girl, shaking her curly hair violently as if in reply to some unspoken question. 'Poor Ruthie.'

And then she was gone. Leaving Rosie to stare at the rusty cans of soup and baked beans and to say to the Asian woman, 'How much for a tube of tomato paste?'

'You do not have,' said the woman, frowning gravely.

'No, but how much?' Rosie insisted, and counted out the money on the counter.

'But . . .'

But nothing, said Rosie to the damp air she walked out into, reaching for her cigarettes, wondering what it was about Ruth Greenfield that made her pushy father and her thick-skinned friend weep for her.

Chapter Five

Rosie went home and paused for thought. Rosie leant back so the dining-chair was balanced on two legs like she'd told the kids not to do a thousand times and thought: Why do the girl's father and her best friend have to invent ghostly kidnappers and non-existent Nazis to explain her disappearance? What's wrong with the notion that she might just have headed off on her own? Don't they think she has any willpower?

Nonsense, thought Rosie, nobody's that wet: especially not a loner with an invisible birthmark. She reminded herself not to lean back in the chair any more and sipped at her tea. Okay, at this moment she should have been sitting on a bar-stool sipping at a half of bitter with her brother Paddy. So what? Just for once he could wait for her. Sometimes it felt as if Rosie had spent her entire life being kept waiting by her brother: from waiting, in childhood, for him to finish in the bathroom, through an adolescence spent waiting for him to ask her to do his homework while he slipped out to play with his mates, all the way down to an adulthood of waiting for him, the great white hope of the family, to make good.

Rosie was still waiting.

Rosie sipped at her tea and refused to look at the wall-clock. She thought about a fourteen-year-old girl who'd left home. Only this girl was called Rosie Monaghan and she had a spoilt brother called Paddy. Every Friday night this girl, back in prehistory, sneaked out in her make-up and her finery to go and have a wild time drinking Espressos in the Carousel coffee bar. She and her friend Angela McGovern gazed adoringly at the young hairy-armed Italian behind the counter while enduring the boring conversation of Tony Halliday and whatever Angela's was called.

One Friday night this Monaghan girl was tiptoeing up the stairs at eleven o'clock as usual — to meet, at the top, her father: a habitually gentle man who only flew into rages once every three years. Fourteen-year-old Rosie looked up into his face and realised three years must have passed since the last one.

Fourteen-year-old Rosie discovered, the next day, that her brother Paddy had split on her in revenge for her refusal to write his essay on A Day In The Life Of A Roman for him.

And so, after the tears and the confinement to her room and the Friday night curfew, Rosie and Angela plotted their escape. One morning they set off innocently for school, never to be seen again. They took the train to London to seek their fame and fortune, far away from idiot teachers and intolerant parents and traitorous brothers who always kept them waiting, far away from Tony Halliday and whatever Angela's was called, soon to be cradled, they imagined, in the hairy arms of handsome Italians . . .

And yes, wasn't this what was likely to have happened to Damp Hand's precious Ruth too? Didn't the father himself suspect it? Why else would he have told her not to call the police? Why else wasn't he personally leading the house-to-house search? Yes, poor Ruth would have spent a sodden night under a railway arch in Willesden or somewhere. Soon, as the sun rose on her damp spirits, she'd finally obey the urge to call her parents that had been nagging away at her all night. On the telephone she'd tearfully ask forgiveness and how to pay the fare home because she didn't have enough money left. Just like Angela McGovern and that pure innocent Rosie of long ago.

Yes, that's how it'll be, thought impure and guilty-as-hell Rosie. That settled, she finally allowed herself to look up at the wall-clock. Gosh, you're late, she said to herself, smiling, languidly reaching for the telephone to call a cab.

*

It was only when she was sitting at the bar of The Crooked Man, trying to stop herself apologising to Paddy for keeping him waiting, that Rosie remembered she should have called Martin by now. But the phone along the bar was busy taking illegal bets from a thin man in a hat. So she sipped at the half of bitter Paddy had bought her when she'd asked for a pint and tried to concentrate on what he'd been saying.

'So you see how bad things are, Sis,' he was saying. 'So if you could . . .'

'That's a shame,' said Rosie brightly. 'I'm on a major kidnapping at the moment.'

'Bad with you, huh?' said Paddy. 'No, but if you . . .'

'So,' said Rosie, trying to sift through which of her brother's problems he wanted her help with now, 'so you want me to track down this ex-partner o' yours who's in Ireland somewhere and get back the money he owes you and . . .'

'Get off,' said Paddy, shifting his beery bulk to look her in the eyes. 'Not still dreaming about being a private eye, are you? Nah,' waving his empty glass at the barmaid, 'I want you to come and look after the kids. While Debbie's in hozzie with the new babby. And help me get the accounts straight. The VATman's after me, isn't he?'

There was something in Rosie that still made her want to defer to him. Some voice inside her, sounding remarkably like her mother's, was saying, Don't upset our Patrick, it's just a phase he's going through.

There was, on the other hand, something in Rosie nowadays that could strangle her darling brother with its bare hands. At this moment, for instance. 'If,' she said, almost angrily, 'if I had any beer in my glass I'd empty it over you. Instead, you can get us a refill while I make a phone call.'

'You wha'?'

The thin man had only gone to the Gents so she

33

hurried along the bar to the phone. Dialling the Green-fields' number, she smiled grimly at her speechless brother and mimed drinking to him — he seemed to have re-ordered for himself but not for her — as Martin answered:

'There's a panic on,' said Martin. 'Call his nibs at work. Mister Greenfield.'

Rosie was still trying not to remember all the times Paddy had assumed that the fifty per cent of the human race who could bear children were there simply to serve him. So she didn't really take in the edge in Martin's voice. It came, therefore, as a shock to her when she got through to Luke Greenfield and he was angry:

'I don't know where the hell you've been but I want you over here now. I've just had a call from the kid-nappers.'

Kidnappers? Don't be ridiculous. I've just worked it all out. She's been sleeping under a railway arch in Willesden just like I did when I was fourteen and . . . .

'Kidnappers?' said Rosie, taking it in.

'Kidnappers,' said the phone, then brrrrrred in her ear.

Rosie found herself staring at the scratched board behind the phone. LUSCIOUS LINDA's number and measurements were there, among the graffiti and taxi numbers and a message to Harry Hartley. 'Kidnappers,' she said out loud again, shaking her head. Then, calling to Paddy across the bar. 'Make that a double vodka, a'right?'

Chapter Six

The long hair of the girl at the reception desk was as pink as Rosie's face was from hurrying through the April shower. The girl interrupted her telephone apologies for something or other to inform Rosie that Luke Greenfield had 'just stepped out for a minute'. 'Ffffff,' Rosie could hear herself beginning to say. But the girl's smile stopped Rosie's anger at source.

Anyway, it gave Rosie time to collect herself. She went back down the stairs and out into the air. The cold sun was glittering on the brass plate that said GREENFIELD INVESTMENT SERVICES. The fresh smell of the recent rain rose from the stone pavement. There were a couple of yachts in the basin of the Albert Dock, their sails very white in the suddenly bright sun. Nice place for an office. Nice expensive place. Rosie leant over the railings and stared into the water and got her breath back.

'Kidnappers,' said a voice from the lapping water as Rosie sucked on another mint to disguise the alcohol. 'Kidnappers,' the voice repeated but Rosie decided to ignore it and admire the view. She had to admit it was beautiful: the refurbished docks where once ships had loaded and unloaded, where once the likes of Paddy and Luke Greenfield had worked . . .

'Kidnappers,' said a voice in her inner ear.

And okay, Rosie reflected, determined not to hear the voice, okay it had been hard and casual labour on the docks in those days but wouldn't it have been better in some way than Paddy's grubbing around the edges of crime and Greenfield grubbing around the edges of other people's money? Wouldn't some good honest dirt and cargoes swinging on to the decks and swearing and laughter ('Kidnappers') be somehow better than all these over-priced people slouching in and out of over-priced shops, then ('Kidnappers') dropping ten pence in the cap of the busker singing old Beatles songs before going on to the Maritime Museum and the Tate Gallery of the North?

'Kidnappers,' This time the voice was a man's. Rosie was just going to ignore it again when there was a tap on her shoulder and there was Luke Greenfield saying to her: 'Kidnappers: this morning you didn't, really believe in them, did you?'

Rosie felt nervous, at a disadvantage, till she noticed his pursed mouth. He was sucking mints too. Just stepped out for a minute, eh? 'I never discount any theory. However far-fetched.'

But he wasn't listening. She followed him up the stairs to his office. 'So while you've been gadding about getting wet,' he was saying, 'they've been on the phone to me, haven't they? Some Scouse feller.'

Rosie tugged at a strand of hair self-consciously. He wasn't saying 'kidnappers' out loud now because they were crossing the carpeted wastes of the foyer. The girl with pink hair had suddenly picked up the phone they'd heard ringing all the way up stairs. 'Did anybody else,' Rosie asked with a nod and a wink to the girl, 'hear his voice?'

'Did they hell!' He stopped at the door to his office to make a point in a loud voice: 'I've got two girls out here and they know only one of 'em can go to lunch at once and I end up answering me own calls.'

'But you said,' the receptionist was saying.

But he'd already swept Rosie into his office. Her heart sank — really, she could feel it bumping down near her liver somewhere — as she saw the two leather farting-chairs that were all there was for visitors to sit on. He gestured to one of them. Rosie tried to smile and crossed instead to the window: a placid view of water and the red brick of converted warehouses, playing against a sound-track of 'All You Need Is Love' from the busker below. Luke

36

Greenfield sat behind his big leather-inlaid desk and tapped a little cigar out of a mock-marble box. Then he picked up his phone executively to say 'No calls' into it, for all the world as if he hadn't just walked past the girl he was speaking to. 'Have a seat,' he said expansively. Rosie eyed the leather chairs warily and remained standing:

'Did you record the call?'

'I didn't know it was gonna be them, did I?'

In a flash of inspiration Rosie took one of his little cigars and watched his surprise — don't the women you know smoke these? — as she bent to the light he profferred from the heavy silver desk-lighter. 'I think the police should be called in.'

'They expressly said not.'

'What did they say then? Expressly?' She had her little notebook out now and stood at the desk, the model of efficiency and taller than him for a moment even though she felt a bit of a divvy for not sitting down. And then, as if he didn't want her to look down on him, he stood up himself and went to the window, wrinkling his brow in recall:

'He was very brief. Asked who I was. "Mister Greenfield?" And I said, who is this and he said, "It doesn't matter who I am. We've got your daughter."'

Which somehow, with the deep voice he put on for the kidnapper and everything, made Rosie want to laugh. Fortunately she managed to turn it into a little cough with the cigar-smoke, and okay, why not? Why shouldn't kidnappers talk in real life the way they did on telly police series? And what was the tune she was humming to herself when she should be asking him the next question? Ah yes: 'I feel fine' from the Beatles medley down below. 'And then . . .'

'Then, well, frankly I swore at him a bit, y'know, don't you harm a hair on her head you bastard kind of thing, and he said, the way I remember it he said: "Give us a hundred thousand and she'll come to no harm."'

The script wasn't getting any more original. 'Can you really lay your hands on that sort o' money? A hundred grand?'

'Not without liquidating a few assets, queen. And that's it. He said he'd call me tomorrow about the arrangements.'

'Saturday. Tomorrow's Saturday.' Then, at his interrogative look: 'Could be used to stall them.'

He seemed to be distracted; though whether it was by the busker beyond the window (The best things in life are free / But you can give that to the birds and bees) or by something going on behind his eyes, Rosie couldn't tell. Then suddenly he was at his desk and shuffling papers into a briefcase: 'I've gotta meet a man.'

'Yeh, but . . .'

'I'll be back in half an hour.'

'No, wait.' Rosie placed a hand on his arm. Come on, you like a woman with spirit so de-jut your jaw can't you? 'I won't be here in half an hour.'

And his jaw did relax, and he did listen to her while she said he really ought to call the police (I told you, they said not) and he should be ready to record calls coming into the office now (all right, all right, can I go now?) and David Langton should be told about this (I'm not paying you to be my guard-dog so I can bark meself) and he'd better be thinking about liquidating some of those assets as soon as poss (I'm seeing the bank manager at three, I'm not an idiot y'know) and, as he was at the door and about to go, because Rosie knew from a childhood of Perry Mason back when she wanted to be Della Street not Perry himself that you always asked the vital question last:

'When did they say not to call the police?'

'When they called, I told you . . .'

'No, I mean, when, precisely? Before you swore at him, or after he said to give him a hundred thousand, or when?'

His jaw was jutting again. 'For God's sake, it all happened very fast and this is my Ruthie we're talking about. Have a heart, woman.'

'I'm sorry,' said Rosie, who wasn't feeling sorry at all. 'But when exactly was it?'

He shook his head but it was a gesture of resignation.

'After he asked for the hundred thousand. "And she'll come to no harm", he was saying. "As long as you don't do nothing stupid like calling the police in." Okay? Have I got your permission to leave my own office now?'

Rosie smiled graciously, stubbing out her cigar on the mock-marble ashtray. She made a sort of bow and he was gone.

She sat down in his high-backed chair and gazed after him and thought maybe she should have a chair like this too. It made you feel important, just sitting in it and reaching out for the push-buttons on the phone.

Unfortunately Rosie couldn't work out which button to press to actually call anybody so she had to go out to the foyer. Pink Hair was apologising into the phone for something being late again. She'd been joined now by her equal but opposite: another teenager, but with short undyed hair and a neat white blouse and sensible brown skirt and the name of Margo. 'I'm doing a spot of, er, detective work for Mr Greenfield, the name's Rosie,' said Rosie with a flash of her Association of British Investigators card that sometimes impressed impressionable people, 'tell me, er . . .'

'Janine,' said Pink Hair with a ready smile.

'. . . Janine, when I came in with Mr Greenfield and he was complaining about both of you being out at once . . .'

'He never,' said neat Margo.

'He did,' said Janine with her eyes raised to heaven.

'After he said I could nip down the dentist even though you were on lunch?' Margo asked in amazement.

'Yeah,' said Janine, then collected herself and turned to Rosie. 'Er, what was it you wanted to know?'

'That's all right,' said Rosie, 'just put a line through to Mr Greenfield's office, will you?'

My God, Rosie, sometimes you give every appearance of knowing what the hell you're doing.

I know, it's remarkable isn't it?

So she sat in the important and powerful chair and rang Mike to tell him about developments and get some background on Luke Greenfield but he wasn't in. So she rang Margie to see if she wanted to come out for a bevvy tonight but Margie wasn't in because, Rosie remembered on the fifth ring, she was out on a job for Rosie Monaghan Inquiry Agent. The only other person she could think of to ring was Martin. But he'd only ask her when he was going to be relieved. So Rosie gave up her delusions of being important and powerful and strolled back into the foyer. Janine was entering figures in an account-book; Margo, filing papers in a filing cabinet. They'd both, clearly, been working since at least a micro-second before Rosie came out of the office. 'So tell me,' said Rosie, sitting herself up on the reception desk, doing her best to mix woman-of-the-world with we're-all-girls-together, 'Mr Greenfield's having a spot of trouble at the moment and I wondered, have you two noticed anything wrong?'

'What sort of trouble?' asked Janine, whose pink hair obviously wasn't a compensation for shyness.

'I'm afraid I'm not at liberty to disclose that,' said Rosie importantly, 'but it would be helpful if . . .'

If you want to know what's really going on in a place, ask the people at the bottom of the pile, thought Rosie twenty minutes later. She was treating herself to a wildly expensive cup of capuccino by the dockside and trying not to hear the drunk who'd replaced the Beatles busker. Janine, barely restrained by the warning glances of sensible Margo, had given her a good run-down, had, indeed, thoroughly run down an investment business that ran on (a) girls like them on government training schemes and (b) doubtful investment bonds with companies no-one had ever heard of before that were always late on their repayments and people were always complaining. But no, Mr Greenfield had always been very polite and friendly with them, said Margo. Except when we want a rise, said Janine, running matching pink fingernails through her hair. And no, there hadn't been any trouble, no letter or phone calls or anything — not unless you counted — she doesn't want to hear about that, said Margo — not unless

40

you counted Jack Fountain, he used to work here you know, awful trouble that, mm . . .

Well, it was a lead of sorts: a disgruntled ex-employee who'd come in and physically threatened Mr Greenfield one day, oh I don't think we could tell you where he lived, Marine something up Waterloo way, isn't it? Janine asked mock-innocently.

Mm, thought Rosie, stirring the milky remnants in her cup, might be the kidnapper. If there really is a kidnapper. It's the same the whole world over, the drunk was singing, it's the poor what gets the blame. Mm, agreed Rosie, it's the rich what gets the pleasure. Mm, must be a coincidence, thought Rosie, that the so-called kidnapper happened to phone when Luke Greenfield had allowed both girls out of the office yet had wanted to deny it. Mm.

Still, said Rosie to herself, still I think I'll just try and catch his wife on her own and see what she has to say . . .

Chapter Seven

Mrs Greenfield was cleaning. After a brief greeting at the front door and an 'Any news?' which was the first sign Rosie had seen of any solicitude for her missing daughter, the older woman waved the J-cloth in her hand and said 'Excuse me if I get on, won't you?'

Rosie raised an eyebrow at Martin, appearing at the living-room door. He shrugged: 'I reckon,' he murmured softly, 'she'd like to clean me up an' all. Make me whiter than white, y'know.'

'Anything but that,' said Rosie, who found Martin's blackness a welcome change from Jerry's pale blushes; just as Martin's edge of danger tweaked her nerve-ends, in contrast to Jerry's kind, safe certainties.

But Rosie was on duty and resolved to stop thinking about such things. She struck a deal with Martin. If he babysat tonight while she and Margie went out for a drink she'd cover for him now. The fact that nobody had to cover for anybody, since the kidnappers weren't due to call again till morning, somehow slipped her mind.

With the guilty stoop of the ruthless executive, Rosie went through into the kitchen. Mrs Greenfield was still cleaning. In a flower-printed dress that was absurdly young for her and a plastic apron saying SUPER-WOMAN which Rosie suspected of being one of those child's presents an adult felt they ought to wear — like that awful brooch Bob had given her, last birthday — the wife of Rosie's client was on her hands and knees, cleaning the oven. Their early-morning fracas in the hall seemed to be forgotten in the joy of dealing with dirt:

'I like,' she was saying, 'I know Mrs McHale comes in and does but I like, after I've done a casserole the night

before I like, to make sure, to my own satisfaction, don't
say anything to Alice will you, she's just popped out to the
shops for me, well I said, I know I haven't got my purse
but really I could have gone myself, it's very kind of her to
take the day off work but I could have . . .'

'Scuse me a minute,' said Rosie, almost running out
into the living-room, gulping in air. 'Fffff,' she hissed at
the walls, shaking an imaginary Mrs Greenfield by the
shoulders and telling her to sit down and relax and stop
cleaning.

And what is she going to do with herself instead, Rosie?
Sit there and worry about how dirty the place is ?

Rosie decided to stop trying to impose her own lack of
housekeeping standards on Mrs Greenfield. She took the
family photograph from the mantelpiece and looked at it
more closely. The proud father, open-necked shirt showing off his suntan and his chest hair, his arms round the
two girls in T-shirts and bikini bottoms: Ruth, yes, the fair
one, how thin she was, her face half in profile, glancing up
towards her father; and Josephine, taller, darker, staring
straight at the camera, dark circles under her eyes.

And to Josephine's left, in another unsuitable flowered
dress, her hands clasped together across her belly
nervously, smaller than the rest, almost seeming to apologise for being in the picture at all, stood the dowdy grey-
haired woman who looked as if she was smiling through
pain.

Rosie went to the door and listened. The smiling-
through-pain woman was still scrubbing away in the
kitchen. Rosie tried the dining room. It was a dining
room. There was dining room furniture in it that was so
clean it was hard to believe anyone had ever eaten there.
She tried the other room off the hall: locked.

'Locked,' said the smiling-through-pain woman, nearly
giving Rosie a heart attack as she passed with mop and
bucket. 'Lolly's den. He's got the key. Well, he keeps his
guns in there, doesn't he?'

Rosie flinched at the mention of 'guns' and, perhaps, at

the memory of being assaulted by an almost equally deadly weapon — a sharp toilet brush — on this precise spot. 'Y'see, Mrs Greenfield,' but the woman was gone. Rosie took the stairs two at a time but her client's wife had already disappeared into the bathroom. There was a glimpse of avocado units and cork tiles and no, Mrs Greenfield wasn't going for her favourite weapon again. She was kneeling as if in prayer to the toilet-bowl and saying, 'Shan't be a minute, dear.' Then, seeing Rosie looking at her, she got up and closed the door. The lock turned on her private ritual.

'It's just, I wanted to talk to you about Ruth,' said Rosie to the scrubbed pine door.

'Shan't be a minute, dear.'

The sound of water running. Leave her to it, Rosie.

She looked around. Even up here, where no visitor could be expected to tread, everything was immaculate. Deep-pile carpet as fresh as the day it was first trodden on; an Ali Baba laundry basket, empty; prints of matchstick people on wooden blocks along the walls. And this must be — nosey bugger, Rosie — ah, a lucky strike, Ruth's bedroom. Rosie smiled at a brief flashback of her own Carol's bedroom — clothes everywhere, the bed perpetually unmade even when Rosie had begrudgingly made it for her an hour before, blue-tac marks on the walls where idols had fallen from their poster pedestals, the posters now of Terrance Trent d'Arby and Prince and a sickening picture of a slaughtered pig's carcass with THERE'S BLOOD ON YOUR HANDS scrawled in vivid red across it.

And here: order, order everywhere. The pinks and mauves and greys of the furniture and decor echoed every other room in the house. The bed was made; every piece of furniture stood neatly at right-angles to everything else. There was no glimpse of a personality at all except in the photograph beside the bed of Ruth, two or three years ago probably, in school uniform, not so thin, not so anxious as in the mantelpiece family-picture, flanked by her parents;

and in the row of cuddly toys along the desk by the window, teddy bears and a My Little Pony doll and a big sentimental pink dog and . . .

Hm, thought Rosie, turning quickly and guiltily back into the hallway as she heard the bathroom door opening: what girl would voluntarily leave all her cuddly toys behind?

Thank you, ace detective. 'Lovely house,' said Rosie, seeming to admire the matchstick men in the pictures, 'You must, er . . .' — you must have to work hard to keep it so nice, she didn't say, being interrupted by:

'Excuse me won't you, but I thought I heard you go. You know: *go*. You didn't go did you? But I thought you had. I do like the, you know, it, I like it to be spotless.'

After every flush? Real or imagined? Rosie followed Mrs Greenfield back down the stairs as the monologue got back into gear again: 'Alice says I'm silly, even Lolly says I'm silly but he's the first to complain if, agh, how awful of me, I haven't even offered you a cup of tea have I?'

'No, that's all . . .'

'Honestly I'd forget my head if it wasn't screwed on. What must you think of me, not even offering you anything?' — in the kitchen now, the mop and bucket put away, the perpetually busy hands already filling the kettle, setting a tea-tray — 'Tea or coffee will it be? I'm sorry, memory like a sieve, I've even forgotten . . .'

'Rosie. As in Rosie Lee,' said Rosie. No reaction. Oh well: 'Tea would be lovely. Then perhaps we can sit down and have a chat about . . .'

But it wasn't easy: sitting down and having a chat about. About anything at all. By the time the tea was poured they were on to:

'. . . well I'm not from round here, oh you can probably tell, no, I'm from Bury St Edmunds actually, so I've no one close and Alice is very nice but, Rosie isn't it? There's nobody like your own family is there?'

She didn't want to talk about Ruth at all. It wasn't her fault: that, as her hands wrapped and unwrapped them-

45

selves around each other, was her chief preoccupation. And that Alice had gone shopping for her and while that was very kind she could have gone herself, just because she'd lost her purse, well they take cheques don't they? Pardon? Trouble at school? No, they'd always had such good reports from there. What, rows at home? No they never had rows with Ruth, such a home-loving girl, her father dotes on her you know, no no trouble. Of course she was upset that night, yes *the* night, the night before she, no don't know what it was all about, but no no trouble isn't Ruthie. 'And Josephine? asked Rosie, more in sorrow than in hope.

Sorrow was what she got. Mrs Greenfield — who'd said to call her Barbara but the name didn't seem to fit her somehow — burst into tears. 'Oh, what must you think of me? But last Sunday, was it last Sunday or, I lose track you know, when she said those things to Father, to my Lolly . . .'

'What things?'

Suddenly Rosie thought she glimpsed a sharp, a frightened but nevertheless a sharp look, the look of a cornered yet cunning animal, before the woman went on in the same tone: 'Unrepeatable things, unrepeatable words, oh what am I saying? It never happened, I get confused you know, Lolly said . . .'

Did it never happen? Did 'Lolly' say it never happened? On some Sunday or other? 'I'd like to talk to Josephine,' said Rosie, her hand on the other's tiny, surprisingly hot hand.

Tears again: 'That's just it, I don't know where she is, my own daughter and she won't tell me, oh I shouldn't be telling you all this, a perfect stranger, oh dear, Alice.'

And Rosie thought that was another delusion until she turned and saw the square-jawed sister-in-law, arms full of Sainsbury's bags, at the doorway. 'I'm sorry,' Rosie began, but Alice was already at Barbara's — no, the name still didn't fit somehow — shoulder, a sturdy arm on the other's thin frame:

'You come with me, Barbie, time for your lie-down isn't it? Come on now,' guiding her skilfully out. And then, at the doorway, she turned to Rosie sternly: 'I'll have a word when we come down.'

Rosie sat and waited. And worried. Alice reminded her of her fierce Auntie Dora who used to tell her to be a good girl or the bogeyman'd get her, grasping her thin (those were the days) arm in a witch's claw, smelling of sweat and age and the musty rooms she lived in. A clock was ticking that Rosie hadn't noticed before: a brass carriage-clock on the dustless windowsill. Tick tock. Rosie waited. Tick tock.

'I'm sorry,' said Rosie, standing up as the fearsome woman came back in, 'I didn't mean to ...'

'Don't worry, love,' said Alice gruffly but disarmingly. 'She gets upset if someone dies on *Coronation Street*.'

'Yes, but ... ' said Rosie, wanting to echo Mrs Green-field: It's not my fault.

The other woman had planted herself firmly down opposite Rosie. Her strong hands were clasped together on the table. Beneath a conspicuous and greying moust-ache her lips were set. 'Now,' she said, 'you seem a sensi-ble young woman. Oh God I suppose I can only talk while I unpack the groceries. She'll report everything back to that brother of mine.'

Rosie's question must have begun with the look in her eyes, for the older woman, now up and busy with the carrier bags, had raised a deprecating hand before any words came out: 'Now, I don't know what's going on. He tells me nothing. Except that he needs me. Well I only work part-time but I can't just take days off like that can I? He seems to think I can, mind. Then tells me nothing. Except that Ruthie's gone missing. Vamoosed. Like her sister. That one tells me nothing either. But she trusts me.' Then, at Rosie's blank look: 'Josephine. Ruthie's sister.'

'You know where Josephine is?'

'I expect Ruthie's gone to her, don't you? I'd find out for myself but I've got my hands full here, I'm afraid. Now

47

take this address down — but you can't tell her I told it you, mind. You'll have to have found it out from somewhere else . . .'

So the square-jawed sister-in-law who for some reason hadn't been told that her niece had been kidnapped rattled off Flat 9, 23 Birkenhead Street, Liverpool. Meanwhile, the last of the cheese and marg went into the fridge and the woman's moustache quivered with — emotion? And then it was 'You can let yourself out, can't you? I've got to see to madam.' And she was gone, leaving Rosie dazzled by her own brilliant assessment of character — for she'd known for sure she'd get nothing out of that old battle-axe, hadn't she? — and wondering how the hell she could have found out Josephine's address from anywhere else.

Chapter Eight

But that would have to wait. First there was some unfinished business to attend to. Which was why Rosie was standing at the gates to Ruth Greenfield's school, while dark clouds hurried across the sky in that scudding April way they have, looking for a girl with a strawberry birthmark.

This was one job Rosie had definitely told herself she had to have Martin or Margie along for, to be her strong-arm person. So, with her usual logic, here she was, alone. And yes, there was Susie now, alone, seeming to try to merge with the graffiti'd wall amid the crowds of school-children, her birthmark as hidden as it could be by a grey scarf. And no, Rosie, don't get involved in anything foolish like asking her to show you . . .

'Hi, Susie,' said Rosie.

The girl's shoulders bounced beneath her navy-blue jacket. She glanced nervously towards the voice. Then, seeing Rosie, her expression very nearly transformed into cocksure bravado. Only the instinctive twist of her profile so that her scarred cheek was in shadow gave her away. She was chewing on a sweet; she pushed it, with what seemed deliberate ugliness, to one side of her mouth. 'It's the friend of the family. What can I do for you?'

No, Rosie, don't ask her to show you — 'I thought you could, er, maybe, show me the Nazis.'

A flicker of worry crossed the good side of the girl's face. 'You don't want to go being a friend of the family with them.'

'Are any of them about?' Rosie gestured to the river of children floating around and past them.

'Don't be daft. On a Friday? None of them's at school on a Friday.'

'But then how do they find you, to get their, er, protection money?'

Susie pursed her mouth in derision. 'They don't find you. *You* have to find *them*. Or they'll come looking. You don't really want to see them, do you?'

Now Susie was chewing her lip. Was the girl winding her up? About the 'Nazis'? They were only talking about a bunch of schoolkids, after all. 'Show me.'

'You won't say I showed you?'

Rosie crossed her heart, doing her best to look ironic and devil-may-care. Then they were hurrying down an alley, across a field and up a faded suburban avenue: an older suburb than the Greenfields', lined by rendered houses and drives with battered old cars in them and a smell of respectability masking imminent decay. There was no conversation any more. The girl hurried ahead as fast as her fat legs would take her, periodically stuffing sweets from her pocket into her mouth and not offering Rosie one. Finally they stopped at a corner: 'It's that bommie down there. That burnt-out semi. That's where they hang out. You won't tell 'em it was me, willya?'

'Of course I won't. Look, Susie . . .'

But Susie was already hurrying back the way they had come without another word — without, Rosie suddenly realised, demanding the payment she'd been expecting, had had ready in the pocket of her coat. She was on the fringes of an old Council estate. Georgian doors and windows marked occasional owner-occupiers. But the roadway itself was pocked with holes and there was no one about and the boarded-up burnt-out house didn't look inviting. Don't go over there on your own, Rosie . . .

Rosie strode over to the house. They're only a bunch of schoolkids, she was saying to herself — should've had a fag shouldn't I? — no, she didn't need her nerves calming. It was going to be all right. There was no sound from within. Obviously nobody there. Rosie could try the front door and the back to go through the motions, then go home reassuring herself that she had at least tried . . .

50

The front door gave to her push. Simultaneously, somewhere in the darkness beyond, an animal squealed. Rosie wandered into the ruin of a house. Sitting on the rubble where the wall between the hall and the living room had been, a teenage girl was polishing her nails on an emery board. She had long dyed-blonde hair and a navy-blue pleated school skirt that had been cut almost impossibly short. The poor girl must be freezing. 'Adolf,' she called back over her shoulder, not looking up, and the distant squealing stopped. Rosie smiled and the girl, with a disdainful look borrowed from some American soap opera, went back to her nails.

Clambering over the rubble into the wreckage of the living room, Rosie saw that it had been a very particular kind of animal, squealing: a human animal — a black boy of thirteen or fourteen who now rested on his knees, as if praying to the god that had once inhabited the fireplace, crying. Three white boys of fifteen or so with cropped hair and camouflage jackets stood in a triangle, around but a little away from him. Rosie thought it might be a good idea to say she must be in the wrong house and turn right round and go straight back to shorthand-typing for a living. 'What the hell's going on?' she found herself asking.

'Who the fuck are you?' said the boy nearest to her. Then, turning to the shorter of the others: 'D'you know this one, Heinrich?'

Heinrich? Adolf? Who did they think they were: reincarnations from the Berlin bunker? The boy nearest to her was a little taller than the others: maybe nine foot where the others were only eight foot six. Rosie didn't feel a flicker of fear. No, just heartburn.

She looked the nearest boy squarely in the neck. 'You're Adolf, are you?' The boy gave her a look that might have been affirmative. 'What're you doing to him?'

'What're you doing here?' said Adolf, smiling at one side of his mouth. She heard the other two laugh as she approached the black boy, wishing she wasn't in her for-

51

important-clients gear amid all this dirt and rubble. It'd make a terrible mess of her tights if she had to get out of here in a hurry.

And one of these three might, she thought, make a terrible mess of her if she failed to get out of here in a hurry.

Rosie touched the black boy on the shoulder. 'Come on, love, come with me,' she said softly. Tears stained his face, soaked her hands as she touched his cheek; but he wasn't sure he wanted her to rescue him. 'Come on, love,' no need to be macho and brave now, 'come on.'

By the time Rosie had cajoled the boy into standing, her arm round him, the way out was blocked. The triumvirate were a parody of soldiers: at attention, almost identical. It was so quiet that she could hear, from beyond them, the slight scrape of the girl polishing her nails. 'I asked you a question, missus,' said Adolf. 'I didn't quite catch your answer.'

Rosie and the black boy took a step forward. The others didn't move: forward, or back. Don't bite your lip, Rosie. Look Adolf in the eye and don't ask him where his moustache is. No, don't stick your right arm up in the air for goodness' sake. 'I came here to ask you about Ruth Greenfield. But I found some other business that took priority. Come on, love.'

But now they physically stopped her. The one Adolf had called Heinrich put a hand on her shoulder. She looked at his hand; then at him. Spotty faced kid. They may be able to look down at you as if they're on stilts but really they're only children, Rosie. That's only half a pint of sweat dripping out of each armpit: you're not really scared.

Surprisingly it was the girl who spoke: 'What happened to Ruthie, well, she only . . .'

'She only what?'

'She only did to herself, like.'

'And what's that supposed to mean?'

'What business is it of yours?' said Adolf, playing the

leader, not glancing at the others but performing for them, his admiring audience. Above her, Rosie identified the faint shaft of light where she'd stepped. Grey sky filtered through the hole in the ceiling and the bare rafters of the roof. Enemy bombing's been bad, has it? — That's it, Rosie, joke to yourself, just don't try cracking any to the Führer and his mob and you'll be all right.

'Ruthie's disappeared,' said Rosie with astonishing calm, even though she didn't believe a word of the reassurances she'd been giving herself. 'I'm looking for her. I'm a detective.'

That worried them for a moment. 'She's never a copper?' said the one with no name, and she felt the black boy shiver in the crook of her arm. 'Nah,' said Heinrich, 'she'd have said.'

'What did Ruthie have coming to her?' Rosie asked firmly, hearing her voice rattle around the derelict house.

'Nothing,' said Adolf. 'Nothing.'

Strangely, he seemed to be shrinking in front of her. Yes, he was only seven foot tall after all. You're only a child, she wanted to say to him. Bet you're good at basketball. Let's stop playing silly games. Sieg Hiel.

'You didn't, like, decide to teach her a lesson and then the lesson got out of hand and — and do anything to her?'

'No,' said the one with no name, 'we never, we only . . .'

'Shut it,' said Adolf. 'Out, a'right? But leave him behind.'

Rosie didn't answer. She gripped the black boy more tightly — feeling him quiver again, feeling the sweat on her hand — and stepped forward against the pressure of Heinrich's outstretched hand. She fixed her eyes on the girl and walked, and as the restraining hand gave way she kept walking, and didn't stop. And they didn't stop her.

She'd reached the girl by now. Keep walking Rosie, don't say . . .

'You're Eva, I suppose?'

'How did you guess?' with an aren't-you-clever screwing-up of her face.

'Nice friends you've got.' A shrug. 'So what did Ruthie have coming to her?'

'Eh!' Adolf was saying from behind her, but Rosie grasped the girl's wrist lightly with her free hand, stopping her nail-polishing. 'Nothing serious,' said the girl. 'Honest. Nothing serious. I dunno where she is.'

'Come on, love,' said Rosie again to the quivering jelly on legs beside her, feeling the boy begin to sag. Come on, love, only another couple of steps to the doorway now. Just walk, don't listen. See, I'm not hearing what they're shouting now about slags and cunts and older women and tits and nigger-lovers because I've learnt — this is something for you to learn, love — you've only got to try and look brave and people think you are brave, even if you're terrified inside. See, we're in the daylight and it's raining, doesn't that rain feel good for once? No, not yet — squeezing his arm, feeling him about to run too soon, when they'd still be watching. 'Just walk till we're out of sight,' she said softly, 'just a few more steps. And tell me: why were they hurting you?'

But he broke free and ran. Rosie's heartburn worsened for a moment but it was all right, they were far enough away after all. 'That's all they're good for is running, coons,' and more of the same, expletives undeleted, rang out across the street. But the boy was round the corner and out of sight and Rosie was still walking, steadily, her back ramrod-straight. No, she wouldn't reach for a cigarette yet. She'd show them how icy-calm she was. Ah, but weren't her shoulders shaking slightly; mightn't those be tears streaming down her face?

No, it was only the rain. She leant her head back. For once it felt good, bouncing hard off her cheeks, washing her clean, rinsing the memories away.

Chapter Nine

Something had gone badly wrong with Rosie's upbringing of her children. Not only did they not want to become Nazis but also, instead of remaining helpless dependants on her whim they had become appallingly adult and reasonable.

'Look, Mum,' said Bob patiently over tea in answer to her questions, 'I'm not in a gang 'cause I don't like 'em 'cause I've been brought up by a wonderfully liberal mother. And by the way, I hate burnt sausages.'

'And,' added Carol, in response to a short lecture about the importance of Auschwitz and Buchenwald, 'we're both reasonably well informed about what the nasty Germans did in the war, even though they're our allies now. And by the way, I hate burnt broccoli.'

Rosie hated her burnt toasted sandwich as well so she didn't see why they felt so underprivileged. 'If you're both so damned grown-up, you can start cooking the tea instead of complaining about me burning it, a'right?'

Bob and Carol exchanged a look. 'Come on, Mum,' said Carol, a sympathetic hand on Rosie's arm. 'Tell us about whatever exciting case you're working on, eh?'

'Actually, it's a kidnapping. For a hundred thousand quid,' said Rosie. 'But it's very hush-hush.'

Bob and Carol exchanged another look. As one they rose to clear away the pots, every glance and gesture conveying one simple message to their mother: Why do you have to nurse such pathetic delusions when we love you as you are?

*

Feeling guilty about her brusque departure from The Crooked Man at lunchtime Rosie went round after tea to see how Paddy was and whether he'd been in a gang. Before she realised what she was doing, she found herself transforming the chaos of his house into two daughters tucked up in bed and washing-up done. And she only narrowly escaped becoming his babysitter for the night: arriving downstairs to find him jacketed and reeking of after-shave and saying, 'I'm real glad you came, Sis. You see I've gotta see this feller and anyway I can't cope on my own . . .'

Rosie had to physically restrain herself from forcing him to sit down at the table bespattered with the mess that had once been his children's tea.

Then she abandoned all restraint and physically forced him to sit down anyway. 'Cleaning and housekeeping', she said briskly, 'require minimal training. A child of six could do it. If they hadn't been brought up to think it was their big sister's job.' But he carried on looking at her like little boy lost so she cranked up the decibels: 'Look, Paddy, I'll look in when I can and I'll help you with your accounts when this job's over and LISTEN TO ME WILL YOU! If you can find out anything sordid about a feller called Luke Greenfield — here I've written his name down for you, ARE YOU LISTENING? — there's money in it.'

Paddy was a self-avowed socialist whose eyes always lit up at the mention of money. She left him staring at the name on the sheet of paper she'd given him: trying, she guessed, to remember what she'd just been saying.

And no, she couldn't hear him saying to her, as she strode resolutely out of the front door, 'Help. Help.'

*

She'd forgotten to ask him about gangs, of course. But that was soon forgotten.

It should have been forgotten because she was too busy worrying about kidnapping and Nazis and Paddy's voice saying 'help' and persuading Margie to come with her to Josephine Greenfield's tonight and getting the car mended. If it hadn't been for Jerry and Martin.

Jerry, in his sudden obsession with the arguments for fathering, had decided to forego pawn to king four tonight, his Chess Club night, in favour of knight takes queen — i.e. he had swooped unannounced to say he was taking her out for a meal. Jerry had insisted there wasn't a problem with sitters because he'd even taken the precaution of asking Janey from up the road. Jerry had looked a bit puzzled at Rosie's uncharacteristic silence and the children's smothered laughter. Jerry's face had turned to purple when the next knock at the door had been Martin's.

Which was why she now found herself hiding in the bathroom.

Was this what Ruth Greenfield was doing somewhere? Hiding from the implications of her own actions in her equivalent of Rosie's bathroom?

'Mum. Mum,' said Carol, knocking at the bathroom door.

Rosie flushed the toilet noisily and wished she could flush away the memory of standing in the living-room, her arms waving about like a traffic policeman's, saying, 'Martin, this is Jerry. Jerry, this is Martin.' Followed by an immediate and undignified exit.

'Mum. Mum.'

'Jerry,' said Rosie, washing her hands, 'I have enjoyed having you as my bit on the side — on the side of the important things in my life — but now you are looking for wombs to went, er, rent, it really is time you rent, er, went.'

Rosie did not say this aloud to the bathroom mirror.

'Martin,' said Rosie, washing her hands again, 'I have this absurd resistance to juggling with more than one man at a time — Margie calls it my morals, not that she knows the meaning of the word — but once I've plucked up the courage to give Jerry the heave-ho you're welcome to become my bit on the side.'

Rosie did not say this aloud either.

Or did she? 'Mum, Mum,' said Carol, 'who are you talking to?'

'No one,' said Rosie briskly, unlocking the bathroom door, admitting Carol but excluding a smiling Bob in her wake. She re-locked the door and demanded a full report on what had happened since she'd fled here.

'Well they didn't say much at first,' said Carol breathlessly, 'nobody said Do you come here often? or anything . . .'

'Cut the jokes,' said Rosie, staring at her crow's feet in the mirror.

'. . . then Jerry asked Martin what he did for a living and Martin said Not a lot, and after a bit of a pause Martin said And you? and Jerry got going on his favourite speech about how tourism's the industry of tomorrow and then Margie came and . . .'

And Carol suddenly became helpless with laughter. 'This is not funny, Carol,' said Rosie, 'I should be out solving a kidnapping.'

Finally Carol gulped in enough air to continue. 'That's all that happened. Margie came. She stood at the doorway for a minute. Hello Hello, she said. That was all she said. Looking at each of them in turn, like. Hello. Hello. Then she laughed. And laughed. And Jerry went. I felt sorry for him. Can I try some of this?'

'You're too young for it,' said Rosie, snatching back the eye-shadow to add to her war-paint, for she felt sorely in need of a disguise tonight.

Chapter Ten

'I was wondering,' said Rosie.

'No, but I couldn't help it,' said Margie, still laughing at the memory. She was driving her noisy old Escort van in her usual unnervingly jerky fashion, and Rosie was trying in vain to butt in with a mention of visiting Josephine Greenfield before their night on the town. 'I just couldn't help it,' said Margie. 'Jerry was sat there, looking so, so, I dunno.'

'Earnest,' said Rosie.

'Pathetic,' corrected Margie. 'I just doubled up. I couldn't help it. And when I looked up he was gone. I don't know how you do it, Rosie. Keep two of 'em on a string. I can't seem to hang on to one long enough to get the noose round his neck.'

It was, in its way, baffling: why Margie, who could still go bra-less without sagging and trousered without inviting remarks about big ends, whose crow's feet managed to make her eyes look sexy, whose low-pitched croak of a voice still made men's heads turn, should have any difficulty with the opposite sex. Or maybe she secretly preferred it that way? Brief encounters that left her free to complain about the briefness of her encounters?

'I was wondering,' said Rosie.

'How I got on with following the pick-up?' said Margie smoothly, steering the van on to the road for town with an exaggerated flick of the wrist. 'Thought you'd never ask.'

'No, Marg,' said Rosie, 'I was wondering if, before we . . .'

'Yeah, where are we gonna get paralytic tonight then?'

'Whether we,' said Rosie, 'you see it's this case I'm on.'

But Margie readily — too readily — agreed to call in

on this Greenfinch girl on the way and didn't stop to be corrected or enlightened because she really wanted to tell Rosie about her day with Harry Allsopp.

'With?' asked Rosie suspiciously.

'Yeh, well, he stopped at this alehouse for lunch, y'see, and I hadn't had time to make meself any sarnies, so I goes in, and the next thing I know he's buying me a drink . . .'

Rosie pinched the bridge of her nose between thumb and forefinger. She'd seen people do it on TV when they despaired of their colleagues. It didn't seem to help though.

'. . . so we didn't get out of there till half three but there's no need to worry he didn't find out who I was and I got loads of gen off him.'

'You were supposed to be following him. Not letting him buy you drinks all day. You go right, here.'

Margie took one hand off the steering-wheel to squeeze Rosie's arm in the midst of the right-turn. The van lurched alarmingly. 'You worry too much, Rosie. Now tell us who I'm going to see.'

So Rosie told her all about the case of Ruth Greenfield. The more she told it, the more complicated it seemed. Naturally, therefore, Margie immediately said:

'It's simple, isn't it?'

'How d'you mean?'

'I mean,' Margie went on, 'either these Nazis or this Fountain feller with a grievance that you haven't got round to finding out about yet, one of them's kidnapped the girl and you've just gotta wait for the next phone call then hide me in the boot when you deliver the money and I leap out at the right moment with me machine-gun and mow down the lot of them, or him as the case may be, and there you go. Simple.'

Sometimes Rosie thought Margie let her love and admiration for Clint Eastwood go too far. 'But . . . ' said Rosie. But why doesn't a perfectly ordinary girl like Ruth have any friends except a girl with a strawberry birthmark? Why, if she was kidnapped, did the kidnappers leave all her cuddly toys behind? Why, on the other hand, if she left of her own free will, did she leave all her cuddly toys behind? Why wasn't her father patrolling the streets in search of her? Why couldn't he remember the details of the kidnappers' phone call properly? Why did Rosie get the feeling he was lying every time he opened his mouth? Why . . .'

'So why do we have to see this sister?' asked Margie, peering out into the night to look for street-signs.

Why? Just because. Because this square-jawed woman who reminded Rosie of her Aunty Dora thought it was a good idea. Because it was funny that the girl's mother didn't even know where the girl lived when square-jawed Aunty Alice did. Because it was odd that Josephine hadn't had anything to do with her parents for two years but had been round to see them only three days before her younger sister disappeared. Because, 'because I've got a feeling about it,' said Rosie, 'that's all.'

'Maybe we should stop off for a drink,' said Margie, 'that's a good cure for feelings.'

'No,' said Rosie with unexpected decisiveness. 'Here we are.'

Here they were: 23 Birkenhead Street: a big old Georgian terrace with more bell-lights on the wall by the door than there were windows to its four storeys. A coat of paint had been slapped over the woodwork and the walls, but the way it had been peeling before was beginning to show through again. Rosie made to press the bell marked with the number 9 but Margie reached out a restraining hand then showed her why: the front door gave to her touch.

The lights for the hall and stairs, when Margie had groped her way to them, were on those push-button time-switches that didn't give you quite enough time to get to the next one before the lights went out again unless you were in training for the Mersey Marathon. But Margie was puffing more than Rosie by the time they got to the second floor, the pair of them baffled by a numbering system that leapt into the teens on the first floor then back to number four on the second. At last they were both exercising their lungs in front of the door of number nine. Now it was Rosie's turn to stretch out a restraining hand: 'Let's make it look official to get in, a'right? Have you got that old bus pass?'

'You're corrupt, you are,' said Margie, fishing the pass out of her handbag as Rosie held her Association of British Investigators card at the ready. 'Okay,' she nodded, and Rosie knocked in an official sort of way and only slightly scraped the skin off her knuckles.

Of course the light went out behind them just as the door opened a crack on a security chain and a timid voice said 'Who is it?'

'Lights, Margie,' said Rosie imperiously, and flashed her card up for a brief inspection when they came on again. 'Josephine Greenfield?' Then, at a slight nod from the thin face in the crack she took a deep breath and found the deeper registers of her voice: 'We're detectives investigating your sister's disappearance and we'd like to come in.'

'Oh, sorry, right, just a minute,' said the timid voice, already making Rosie feel guilty. After a fumbling at the chain, the door opened tentatively to let them inside.

Into — Rosie's first impression — complete chaos. Clothes, plates of half-eaten food, bottles of cider, old magazines were scattered everywhere, amid a powerful smell that reminded her of Jerry's flat only more so: unwashed socks and rancid food. In one dim corner lurked a baby Belling cooker with dirty plates and an encrusted milk-pan stacked on it. The girl, wearing a thin pink housecoat over a nightdress, was collecting discarded tights and copies of *True Romance* off a threadbare sofa. 'I'm sorry,' she was babbling in her timid way, 'I usually have a bit of a clean on a Sunday, somebody visits me on a Sunday y'see, so that's when I usually have a bit of a clean, sit down won't you, I'm sorry.'

Her voice had the same sad whine as her mother's. Rosie and Margie, glancing at each other blankly, sat uneasily together on the sofa. Josephine settled opposite them, on the edge of the unmade bed, clasping and unclasping her hands. She looked thinner, paler, and somehow smaller than the dark-haired girl in the photograph on the Greenfield's mantlepiece. It was hard to imagine her on that beach in Spain. Hard to imagine her at the Greenfield's, either: the squalor was an almost unbearable contrast to the orderliness of her parents' home.

'Is this it, then?' Margie was asking. 'Where you live?'

'I share a bathroom. On the landing.'

Rosie felt in need of the facilities already but her nostrils could imagine what the toilet was like. Hold yourself in, Rosie, cross your legs or something.

'D'you wanna drink?' the girl was asking, 'I've only got cider, I'm afraid.'

Rosie, flinching involuntarily as the girl took a drink from the neck of the cider-bottle, had finally recovered her powers of speech. 'You don't seem very surprised,' she said, trying to stay stern and steely when she felt like cradling the poor girl in her arms and taking her home. 'That your sister's gone missing.'

Josephine waved the bottle. So what? said her grim little smile. Then she seemed to notice the bottle in her hand, and drank from it again. 'Nothing surprises me much. Good luck to her.'

'You went to see your family last Sunday, right?'

'What kinda detectives are you, anyway?'

The girl seemed to be gaining confidence with every swig of the cider bottle; in proportion, it looked to Rosie, to how much their faces went out of focus. 'Private detectives. Your father . . .'

She visibly shrank into her scanty clothing, tucking her legs beneath her, hugging her knees. 'I don't want him here. I know it's a mess, I usually have a clean on a Sunday, somebody comes on a, I don't want him here though, I'm sorry — how,' looking up at them suddenly, the rising panic abruptly subsiding: 'how did you find me then?'

'I won't tell your dad where you are. If you don't want me to. I know I'm working for him but I've got a girl of me own, I just want to be sure Ruthie's all right. Not been — kidnapped, or something. Look, love,' and Rosie couldn't be doing with the distance between them any more — especially with Margie squirming next to her on the sofa as if the sour smell of the place was soaking up into her bum through the upholstery — so she went across and sat next to the girl, trying to take her hand:

'Get away from me! I don't want him here! Get away from me!'

The girl dodged away from her. Gripping her bottle tightly she scurried away in her pink-bobbled slippers to the opposite corner of the room. She sat behind a little dining table scarred with the ringed stains of mugs and glasses, peering at them defiantly from the security of her defences. Rosie and Margie looked at one another; exchanged a shrug and a slight shake of the head. Then Margie was up, saying 'Why don't I clean up a bit while you two have a little chat?' Ignoring the girl's protests, she was soon busy at the sink cursing the lack of hot water and Rosie was at the table, gesturing to the bottle and saying 'Maybe I will have a drop o' that,' God knows what I'll catch off it but it seems like the sociable thing to do. Bottoms up.

The cider was sweet and the bottle-top tasted of whatever Josephine had had in lieu of a meal tonight. Banana and onion crisps? Rosie made herself swallow the taste, and smile, and say, 'I just want to know if you've seen her. And if what happened on Sunday had anything to do with her leaving. Last Sunday. When you went round there.'

Josephine began to talk then; not that it helped much. For she didn't know where Ruthie was, and good luck frankly, she'd got the hell out of it so why not Ruthie? And she'd just gone back on Sunday, she said, to try and make it all up with her dad but he didn't want his little girls to grow up that was all, and Ruthie wasn't even there he'd sent her to her room when the row started, and 'I don't want to talk about this any more. I don't want him here, you won't tell him where I am will you? I don't want you cleaning any more, okay? Just leave me alone!'

Margie had been trailing an old U-bank over the worn carpet by the bed. She shrugged at Rosie; went back to the sink. The girl was shaking her head and screwing up her eyes as if about to cry. Rosie reached out a hand but the one with bitten nails withdrew itself quickly to the shelter of the girl's lap. Her voice sounded so like her. mother's. Yet she'd never mentioned her. Rosie was trying to decide how to worm more information out of the girl and not think about her increasingly acute need for a pee when the girl's whine began again: 'I usually give it a clean on Sunday. Somebody comes to see me on Sunday you see, so I . . .'

'Your Aunty Alice?'

'You wouldn't think they were brother and sister would you? Well of course they were brought up in different places so it's only to be expected . . .'

And that was almost the last, surprising information Rosie could extract from her: that Luke Greenfield and his sister had spent their childhood apart, he in children's homes and she adopted, and had only found one another in their early twenties, and that was why he had such a thing about families. 'Honest, he wanted us to be like Peter Pan, me and Ruthie, I mean, it can't be done, can it? I can't help it, can I? No, it's not my fault!' — and she was almost shouting, a pitiful reminder of her mother — 'it's not my fault, I don't want him here . . .'

'Come on, love,' said Rosie.

This time the girl allowed herself to be touched. Rosie clutched the thin wrist and guided her over to the bed. 'I don't want to,' she was murmuring. But Margie lifted the girl gently on to the bed, and Rosie tucked the dirty bedspread up to her chin. She was about to leave Josephine to sleep it off when Margie spoke:

'Rosie was telling me your sister didn't have no friends. Is that right, then?'

'Dunno,' said a sleepy voice. Rosie tugged at Margie's sleeve but her friend persisted:

'Not even any boyfriends?'

They had to bend close to hear the girl's childish whisper.

'There used to be a feller. Older, much older. Came to the house a lot. To talk — business. Ruthie . . .'

The girl's thumb was in her mouth and her voice trailed away to nothing. As the nothing faded into snores, Rosie gently prised the cider-bottle out of the girl's grasp, and looked round for somewhere to put it. There wasn't anywhere. The place was transformed: well, as transformed as a grotty bedsit could be by half an hour's elbow grease. 'You've done a good job, Marg,' said Rosie, dumping the bottle in the overflowing plastic bin. 'Let's get off now, eh? The girl's tired out and I'm busting for a pee.'

'Can't you smell the loo from here?' They were on the landing now, closing the door of the bedsit behind them. And yes, perhaps there was a bit of a whiff in the air. 'Hang on till we get to the pub, can't you?'

No, she couldn't. She was too relieved to be out of the bedsit and too nervous of the possible consequences of bumping around in Margie's van. So a minute later she was squatting in a back alley like a kid in potty-training with Margie on watch in the street. But she wasn't going to get upset about that. No, those weren't tears pricking at her eyes at all. No, it didn't matter a bit, the embarrass-ment of peeing in an alley, or the sadness of a teenage girl drinking cider in a grotty bedsit, or the mystery of a kidnapped fourteen-year-old girl who maybe had a busi-ness friend of her father's for a boyfriend.

'Come on,' she said to Margie, respectable again, 'let's go and get really bladdered, eh?'

Chapter Eleven

'I had thought,' Luke Greenfield's rasping voice was saying the next morning down the phone, 'I had thought I might have heard from you last night, Mrs Monaghan,' oh, not *Rosie* now, eh, we are in trouble, 'since after all the kidnappers are due to call again today.'

Rosie wasn't dressed yet. Rosie wasn't really awake yet. Only her hangover was conscious. Its rumblings in her stomach were enough to wake the dead in the next street; while its pounding in her head was enough to kill them all over again.

'Haven't you got anything to say?'

Concentrate, woman. 'I had my handbag nicked last night,' no this isn't what you should be saying Rosie, 'down a club, well it was found in the Gents five minutes later minus my purse and then when I was in bed I kept dreaming about losing things like you do and I was thinking — When did your wife lose her purse?'

Luke Greenfield hardly saw that was relevant. But if it was any of Rosie's business, his wife hadn't lost her purse at all. It was just one of her little obsessions and hardly a priority in the light of . . .

Okay, have it your way. 'When can you get the money, then?'

'Monday afternoon. But I am hoping you will have got off your arse and found the bastards by then.'

Well you'll have to tell me a bit more about your famous enemas then, won't you? Rosie rubbed her thumping forehead in the hope that a genie would appear and tell her what to say next. But no, she had to work it out for herself: 'Okay, tell 'em Tuesday to be on the safe side. Make sure you record all your calls. And I'll get Martin round there pronto.'

'I really think it would be more appropriate if you . . .' Luke Greenfield began.

'I'll be there at lunchtime,' she said gruffly, banging the receiver down.

She wasn't in the mood for that stuff today. People not having anything against black people but. People banging telephone receivers down. People — eleven-year-old female people, for instance — just waiting till she'd banged the telephone receiver down to start jabbering at her again:

'It doesn't mean I don't respect Dad,' Carol was saying to her. 'I mean, I respect Jerry and Martin even though I call them Jerry and Martin, and whoever else you're gonna bring home in the future, I'll call them by their first name . . .'

I'm not bringing home any more of them, Rosie said to no one. Things are quite complicated enough as it is. 'I'll be down in a minute, love,' said Rosie. 'Just leave us to get dressed, eh?'

Carol had very kindly woken her at eight this Saturday morning, her fortnightly day out with her father, to announce: 'I'm not going to make an issue of it. I just don't want to call him Daddy any more. I think Graham's a very nice name.'

Rosie had groaned. Then jumped in alarm: for in reply, a large growling bear in the bed had stirred.

Underneath the bedclothes the bear had turned out to be Jerry, dribbling handsomely on to the pillow. How had that happened? Surely last night, the last thing she remembered . . .?

Rosie groaned. She ransacked the chest of drawers for a clean pair of tights and groaned again. The last thing she remembered, before Carol and the bear, it was midnight in the dining-room and she was asking Martin if she was mutton, dressed as lamb. And staring hypnotised at her pink hand on Martin's black one. And wondering why a night of vodkas had failed to wash the taste of banana and onion and sweet cider from her mouth. And listening to

Martin having a severe attack of honour and decency about it not being fair to see her behind Jerry's back.

Why, then, was it Jerry's back that had ended up in her bed?

Rosie hauled some clothes on and decided to call Martin from downstairs in case Jerry's snores were just a cover. Over breakfast Bob was holding forth to Carol: a dad was always a dad, he was saying, just like a mum was always a mum and it was silly to pretend any different by calling them by different names. Rosie closed her ears and resolved again to talk to him about the damp patches in the bed. She called Martin. 'About last night . . .'

Martin didn't want to talk about it.

My God, what had she done?

No time to worry about that. Could he perhaps while not wanting to talk about 'it' whizz round to the Greenfields' again? Martin grunted in what might have passed for an affirmative — if sulky — tone and was replaced by the sound of the dialling tone and of Rosie's stomach. Not to mention the continuing argument. 'You can't wish away fathers just by calling them something else.' Bob was pontificating in a remarkably accurate parody of his father, 'Everybody's got one whether they like it or not.'

'Not,' said Carol, who was getting sulky. Rosie thought she'd better call a halt to all this and sent them off to Dennis's up the road to see if he'd mended the Mini. She gave her hangover a coffee to be going on with and made another call. 'Look, Mike,' she said urgently into the receiver, riding roughshod over his greeting in return, 'just because you're a star of stage and screen now doesn't mean you shouldn't be digging up the dirt on Mister Greenfield for us. I need to know.'

'Hi,' said a hunky American voice that didn't remind her of Mike at all. 'I guess you want Michael. I'll get him.'

'Is that your new one?' she said to her sleepy solicitor a few moments later.

'Mm hm.'

'I need to know about this Greenfield's business mates.

I've been trying to call you. Where've you been?'

'Considering my future.'

So would I if I had the time. 'No, look, I need names, addresses, lowdown.'

And no, when Mike went all I'm-a-partner-in-the-firm-now on her she said Monday wouldn't do. She heard his brain whirr reluctantly into action: 'Works on his own really. There used to be a bloke called Fountain' — yes yes I know about him even though I've still got to cross-check the phone-book with the A-to-Z to track him down — 'and let me think, there was another client put some money into the business. Italian name. Patresi, 'spelling it out for her. 'I'd have to check the address.'

And Rosie'd have to call him back. For Bob was at her shoulder telling her they were going to be late — as if it was a son's duty to tell his mother what she already knew. And Dennis was at the door, his round cheerful face obviously looking forward to giving her some really bad news about the car. 'Have a crisp,' he said jauntily, shaking a giant packet at her that he'd just taken from the bib of his giant overalls and reached into with his giant greasy fingers.

'Er, thanks all the same,' said Rosie. At least her car was outside so it must be mobile. She went and patted it affectionately: 'What d'you think, then?'

Between mouthfuls, Dennis launched himself into a complicated technical explanation that'd have to wait because Bob was already getting into the back seat ready to go:

'But is it driveable?' she asked plaintively.

Dennis shrugged. 'As long as you don't mind the clutch slipping and the engine pinking and the front suspension being a bit dicey and the two back tyres being bald as Kojak — yeah, it's driveable.'

So Rosie pretended he hadn't added 'to the end of the road and back' and said she'd pay him when she could get to the bank. 'Come on, Mum,' Bob was saying and 'Carol!' Rosie was calling. The brief sunlight had disappeared and it was raining again. So Rosie had to go back in to hunt for her mac, and there was Carol on the stairs, hugging her knees and saying, 'You see, Mum . . .'

'Please, love.'

'Come on!' Bob was calling.

'You see,' said Carol, 'he keeps calling me Daddy's little girl and wants me to wear those stupid dresses he's always buying for my birthday and . . .'

'Please, love.'

'Come on!'

'. . . and I think,' Carol went on, reluctantly being pulled up and out, 'if he can just see that I'm a human being that doesn't eat meat and doesn't wear dresses we'd get on better . . .'

And if if if, agreed Rosie, if the two of you could just erase from your conscious or unconscious memories that Dad hit Mum once and Carol tried to stop him and got one in the eye for her pains, then everything would be better yes, and if a name will help then okay, what's in a name? — So Rosie thought, all the while fervently praying that when they finally got into the car Bob wasn't going to say —

'We're really late now. Dad'll be mad as anything.'

— okay, I can take that, maybe I deserve it, just as long as prayers will stop Carol piping up from the back seat as soon as we start off —

'Well, I'm going to call him Graham, anyway. Or I never want to see him again, that's all.'

— So much, thought Rosie as she turned to give Carol a brief lecture then thought better of it; so much for the power of prayer.

It was only when they were halfway to the meeting-place with Graham and five minutes past the allotted meeting-time that Rosie remembered Jerry, asleep in her bed. She slowed the car for a moment.

'Hurry up, Mum,' said Bob.

Poor Jerry. She still couldn't remember how he'd come to be there. And she did wish, as she stepped on the accelerator again, that he hadn't turned into such a forgettable man.

71

Chapter Twelve

What was Rosie hoping to find out, she asked herself foggily, from the renegade investment consultant Jack Fountain? Whether he was enema, er, enemy enough of Luke Greenfield's to kidnap his daughter? Or poor enough to need the money? Or whatever-it-was enough to fit Josephine's description of her sister's 'boyfriend'?

Rosie parked a hundred yards from the address — what she deduced, from Janine Pink Hair's clues and the phone book, was the address — and strolled over the grassy dunes towards the beach. She needed to clear her brain. Of its hangover. Of the memory of Graham's face crumpling up as he drove away from their usual meeting-place while Carol's voice from the back of his car was saying, 'It's not that I don't respect you, Graham. . . .'

Across the mouth of the Mersey, emerging from a slowly clearing morning mist, she made out the distant pinpricks of seaside villas and empty amusement arcades of New Brighton: where Mrs Greenfield might have been a beauty queen once if only she'd been taller; where Rosie had played on the sands and been happy once — before the Mersey mud had silted up the beach and the mud of years had silted up Rosie's capacity for happiness.

— No, I'm happy sometimes.

No, Rosie was happy sometimes. Now, for instance. Below her, in the marina, little dinghies raced along in the freshening wind that only smelt faintly of sewage; wind-surfers were hauling themselves damply out of the bright blue water; a loving young couple walked along the path hand in hand. See, Rosie, there is happiness out there: you could almost reach out and touch it.

Rosie stretched out her hand to catch a discarded

Kentucky Fried Chicken wrapper that was floating on the breeze. As the loving couple passed, she heard the bitter tones of their argument; the girl was crying. Turning back towards the shore, Rosie chucked the paper into an overflowing litter-bin and headed for her next unhappy moments.

*

Jack Fountain's house, on the sea-front, was under repair. In the middle of the long front garden were heaps of sand and cement, surrounded by a scattering of broken roof-slates. The paintwork of the house itself was peeling except where, at first floor level, it had been burned away. And instead of the french windows leading on to the lawn, there hung a heavy black tarpaulin. Rosie picked her way carefully up the muddy path and pulled at the old-fashioned doorbell.

After half a minute she decided the doorbell was under repair like everything else in sight and banged at the door.

After another half a minute she'd just decided the residents must be under repair as well or being rehabilitated elsewhere when. . . .

A tall man with dirty clothes and crinkly eyes — eyes of the same vintage as Rosie's, she guessed — opened the door to her. 'Mr Fountain? I'm, er,' oh sod it her card had got nicked in her purse last night, 'I'm Rosie Monaghan. I'm a private detective.' A quick flash of Adulterer's Alarm crinkled even more lines at the corners of his eyes until she added: 'I'd like to ask you about Luke Greenfield, if I may?'

'Somebody's on to him at last, eh?' he said in that same poshed-up Scouse as his former boss. He waved her inside. She stepped gingerly over the occasional floor-boards that lay in the hall, a random path over joists and earth, and followed him into the back room. 'Just doing the place up,' said Jack Fountain, a bit superfluously Rosie thought, 'but at least we've got the dining room done.'

'Ah yes,' said Rosie, bewildered, looking around. It was impossible to see the floor, walls or windows except for occasional square-inch glimpses among the furniture that was piled almost to the ceiling.

'It's just that we've, er, had to move most of the gear in here from the other rooms while we're doing them, like.' Jack Fountain lifted a wooden chair off a pile in the corner, gave it a cursory dust with his hand and sat her down in it.

'Who is zat, darlink?' said a Welsh dresser with a Scandinavian accent. Rosie had never hallucinated with a hangover before. Not now, either, for a body emerged from the furniture to go with the voice: a big woman of thirty or so, with big bones in her face and shoulders with built-in pads. She offered a smile and a big floury hand half-wiped on her blue jeans: 'I don't sink ve've been interrodouced.'

So they were interrodouced, and this was Sigrun — Siggy — Jack Fountain's, er, 'companion', the woman supplied herself. 'We're waiting for the divorce to come through, y'see,' the man added awkwardly. Rosie was offered coffee and Siggy disappeared into the furniture again. Soon the drone of coffee beans in a grinder punctuated their conversation and Jack Fountain was pulling up his chair so that their knees almost touched:

'Luke Greenfield,' he said importantly. 'Not that his name's really Luke, y'know. Lawrence Kenneth. But Luke sounds a bit more, well, doesn't it? Down at the nineteenth hole? Among the huntin' shootin' fishin' set? — We go back years, him and me. On the docks. In the offices, like. So what's he been up to?'

'I hope you'll understand that I can't discuss in detail why I'm investigating Mr Greenfield. But any information you can give me about his financial activities,' get your notebook out Rosie, make it look official, 'would be extremely helpful.'

Jack Fountain leant even closer in his chair: 'Would it surprise you to know,' he said earnestly, 'that I suspect

74

Mafia money is involved?'

Rosie was staring wide-eyed at the word 'Mafia' she'd just written down, and coughing. 'I'm sorry, it's the ciggies,' she croaked. For some reason that made him offer her one, finding a butt-filled ashtray from somewhere. As he lit her fag he took the opportunity to murmur to her:

'My wife's in a mental hospital, y'see. I can't divorce her when she's like that, can I? Even though me and Siggy are — ah, the coffee,' suddenly smiling and expansive as his, er, companion arrived with the pot and three little one-gulp-and-it's-gone cups like you were supposed to drink coffee out of.

Siggy smiled her full-lipped smile as she handed out the coffee and told Rosie she vas a Norvegian and a designer, if Rosie vanted any cards, letter-headings, votever. But also, of course, she had vorked for Meester Greenfield, 'no not designer, you know, temping.'

'Really?'

'He like me because I have no vork permit. So he can pay me as a monkey.'

'Peanuts,' Jack Fountain supplied helpfully.

'Vair ve meet. Greenfields. Jack and me.' The two of them held hands for a moment.

'So, about the Mafia?' Rosie enquired, clearing her throat, pretending to examine her cigarette curiously, 'gosh these are strong aren't they?'

Jack Fountain raised his eyebrows — so what if it said Extra Mild on the packet? — but he let it pass. He was anxious to launch into his account of the rise and fall of Greenfield Investment Services. Although, if he was to be believed, the whole thing should have been called Fountain & Greenfield from the outset. Everything that had gone right for the operation had been down to him; everything that had gone wrong was the fault of (as he insisted on calling Rosie's client) Lawrie Greenfield.

Rosie, intent, forgot about the tininess of the cups and knocked back her bitter coffee in one gulp and wrote it all down.

'It was while we were working in Wages in the Mersey Docks and Harbour Board, you see, that I had this idea. Well, I've always been a bit unworldly, I paint y'know, that's what I'd really like to have done: painted.' How about starting with the front of the house, then? Rosie didn't say, as he went on: 'But I had this idea. So, like an idiot, I told Lawrie all about it. How between the Commies on the shop-floor and the idiots in the management, jobs were gonna start falling like nine-pins and there was gonna be money in it. So there's me, having the idea then forgetting all about it. And the next thing I know, he's borrowed the money off his sister to set up in business and got himself a few dubious contacts in the money game and he's asking me to work for him. On me own idea! But me, I'm not a proud man. Swallow your pride, I said to meself: do it.'

Plus, I bet you were being made redundant yourself at the time, thought Rosie. She tried to listen but kept being distracted by Siggy's hands. They were big yet beautifully proportioned. And they kept stroking Jack Fountain: on his bare arms, on the nape of his neck, along the line of his shoulders. Rosie kept scribbling, but every time she looked up there they were, the hands, stroking.

'. . . something special,' the man was saying, not seeming to notice the hands, 'Lawrie said we needed something special to get the punters through the door. A big investment. High rate of return. That's where Ricky Patresi' — spelling it out for her — 'came in. Italian Scotsman. Mafia man.'

Maybe she shouldn't have coughed. Over the Mafia. After all, she knew from Mike that Patresi really did exist.

And then she suddenly thought: this'd be a good house to hide a child in — behind a stacked bed or two — what was that noise?

It was only a cat mewing but Rosie felt chilled somehow. 'Hang on,' said Rosie, staring at a muddle of notes about Lawrie=Luke and Mafia=Patresi, 'I don't quite understand . . .'

'No, of course. I've tried to explain it all to Siggy a few times, but it goes in one ear and out the other. Doesn't it, my little chuck?'

His little chuck smiled a big, false smile as he ruffled her hair. Like a dog. Woof woof, smiled Rosie in a puppy-ish sort of way, no of course, woof, us little, er, bitches don't understand the big man's world of high finance. 'Woof,' said Rosie, 'would find it helpful if . . .'

'If I explained it all again,' said Jack Fountain help-fully. He was even scratching Siggy behind the ear now but Rosie told herself not to bark but to listen. Greenfield and this Patresi had, it seemed, set up various companies to turn other people's redundancy money into profits for themselves. One such company, CP Investments, had gone broke and defaulted on its repayments. But Green-field had promised all his old mates for whom the repay-ments were their income for life that they'd be repaid by M-Int — Money International— which was just another paper company set up in the Isle of Man. . . .

'I once went there for a holiday,' said Rosie to keep up dumb puppy appearances. 'Rained all week. In the Isle of Man. So the upshot of all this is . . .'

'The upshot is,' said Jack Fountain, 'I thought it stank. To high heaven. People who don't hassle about their yearly interest don't get paid. I complained. I got paid off. And Lawrie and this Patresi bought bigger houses and told bigger lies and as far as I know they're still doing it. Juggling with other people's money. It stinks.'

At that point the story seemed to have ended. Rosie was just beginning to wonder how she could conduct a discreet search of the whole house calling 'Ruth! Ruth!' — whose name she had mentioned, but without discern-ing any flicker of worry or concern from Jack Fountain and Siggy — when big-boned Siggy all of a sudden stood up and said, 'Let me show you our lovely house.'

Rosie allowed herself to be guided up a banister-less staircase; through dusty floorboarded bedrooms and one little haven where, it seemed, they slept; even peeking into the bathroom and seeing no hiding place for a fourteen-year-old kidnapped girl; finally being steered by the sturdy hand on her arm up to the attic.

Here April sunlight, flooding the room from the dormer window, illuminated a different kind of disorder. Everywhere she looked were paintings, and palates, and half-finished Letraset on a drawing board, and jam-jars and brushes and pencils, all scattered in that organised chaos Rosie recognised from her bedroom/office: it looked a mess but you knew where everything was.

Suddenly as Rosie peered round for nooks and crannies and secret cupboards, seeing none, Siggy took both Rosie's hands in her own and led her to the window: 'Beautiful, isn't it?'

And yes, it was a slight improvement on the view from Rosie's house: green grass, and mist over the water beyond where a boat was steaming out to sea. 'Quite nice,' said Rosie effusively.

'You must, 'said Siggy, not quite looking at Rosie though her face was close to hers, 'You must forgive Jack. He is bitter. About Greenfield. Not everysing he says is, vot? ze objective truce. You understand?'

'I understand,' said Rosie, relieved.

No she didn't understand. She thought, briefly, that she understood but she didn't. The woman's arm was still around Rosie's shoulder as they gazed out at the view. The soft yet guttural Norwegian voice was mumbling what might have been a question.

'You wha'?'

Siggy's voice was suddenly so quiet that Rosie had to strain to hear: 'You and your man. You have a man? Do you, er, sving?'

'If y'mean me husband,' said Rosie, beginning to get the drift as the hand on her shoulder began to flex its fingers lightly over her collar-bone, 'there's times I wouldn't have minded seeing him swinging, yeh. From a gibbet, like.'

'Jib it,' said Siggy softly. Her eyes flicked nervously

78

away from Rosie's. 'I hope you do not mind. Zat I ask?'

'Mind? No, no, it's just that — I've gotta be getting back,' said Rosie, heading for the stairs, 'thanks all the same.'

'I am sorry if . . .' the woman was saying behind her but Rosie didn't take it in. Forgetting even to check whether there was a cellar and if so how many fourteen-year-old-girls could comfortably be held hostage in it, she thanked Jack Fountain for his time and his valuable help and shook his hand and even that brief goodbye meant she had to negotiate a way round Siggy on her way out. 'Only from trees,' she said as the woman squeezed her hand, and then she was out into the air.

Of course the sun had gone in now but Rosie didn't mind. She ran to the car — why had she parked it so far away? — and sat there for a few minutes, reading her notes and telling her teeth to stop chattering. Perhaps it was something about the sea air that made Siggy the way she was.

Rosie told herself to stop shaking. The important question was: what way was Jack Fountain made? Kidnapper? Child-molester? Or just a harmless sensualist with a mad wife and a strange tale about the Mafia? Stop shaking and think, will you?

Rosie stopped shaking.

She started shivering instead.

Chapter Thirteen

Rosie had calmed down. She had strolled along the promenade, and called Mike from a phone-box, and strolled back to the car, and she'd calmed down. Really.

Rosie's fingers drummed on the dashboard. She was running late if she was going to get back to Greenfields' for the promised 'lunchtime', but she wanted to get a look at the man Fountain had maintained was Greenfield's partner, the Mafia man. So she left the decision to Fate, otherwise known as her ancient Mini. If the car started first time it was Patresi: between second time and never, it was back to Luke Greenfield.

Frodsham, being the address for Patresi that Mike had given her, and what Fate had decreed via the miracle of the Mini starting, was bathed in sunshine. That was the sort of thing Frodsham people expected as their right. For they were the sort of people blessed by Fate: footballers and night-club owners and Stock Exchange gamblers and all those other people who never had to worry about whether their car would start first time or where the next job was coming from: for they were the ones deciding where the next job came from. Their houses sat cosy and alone, in grounds that gardeners cultivated, protected by electric fences and burglar alarms. Even a hundred thousand pounds from a kidnapping wouldn't buy much more than a garage and greenhouse out here.

Birds were twittering among the trees as Rosie got out and approached the wrought-iron gates. BELLA and VISTA were moulded there in curly script, each word shaped within a separate gate. Neither opened to Rosie's touch. A button and intercom were set into the stone gate-post. Rosie wiped the sweat from her hand and pressed the button. Okay, this'd be a good place to hide a four-teen-year-old girl; it was possibly as hard to get out as it was to get in. But then, there'd have to be more than money involved. An argument between business partners?

'Hlocnahelpee?' said a woman's voice from the inter-com speaker.

'You wha'?' said Rosie in her best accent.

The woman was Scots and spelt it out this time: 'Hello, can I help you?'

'Mrs Patresi?'

'That's me, hen. Who are you?'

'Er, you don't know me, but . . .'

'If I don't know y',' said the voice briskly, 'y'll have to ring me f'r an appointment.'

Rosie shook her head in a surprise assault on her hangover. 'I'm working for Luke Greenfield,' she said with a sudden attack of resolution. 'It's urgent. The name's Rosie Monaghan.'

There was a short pause; a buzzer opened the gates. Rosie's heels crunched up the gravel past the trim flower-beds. Croquet hoops were set up on the perfectly striped lawn. She stopped for a moment to admire the big stone bungalow. There were flowers in window-boxes; a Virgi-nia creeper twined around the doorway. To the side a long picture window looked out over the Dee to North Wales. Rosie tried hard to imagine the miseries of the rich that made living in a place like this a terrible burden.

Finally, though, she had to admit to herself: the damn place was perfect. Well, it just went to show what a good thing redundancy was, didn't it? For wasn't that what had paid for all this? Patresi's percentage of the money Green-field had persuaded his old mates on the docks to let him look after?

'Coo-eee,' said a woman at the front door. 'Come on in, love. Rosie, did y'say? How are y'? I'm Sally Patresi. Come on through.'

Her handshake was firm and cool. She wasn't wearing very much: just a white bikini and a white towelling robe, unbelted to show off her suntan. Taking Rosie's mac, she saw her looking: 'I grab what sunshine I can,' she said, 'don't you? Come wi' me. M'husband 'll be wi'us in a jiffy.'

She might have been Rosie's age but looked ten years younger. Her lips were very pink and her eyelids a vivid blue: a painted doll? No, there was a sharpness in her superficially casual look as she sat Rosie down in a lounger on the little patio at the back. 'Working for Lawrie, y'say? Luke,' by way of explanation; and, perhaps, defining that Lawrie was what his friends called him.

Rosie's hangover had come back. Or maybe she was just in shock and that was why she was gazing spellbound into the clear water of the swimming pool and not answering Mrs Patresi's offer of 'a wee Martini'. Half an hour from Liverpool, she was thinking, there are houses with croquet hoops on the lawn and swimming pools and suntanned women who drink martinis at eleven-thirty in the morning.

Had she given the instinctive alcoholic nod to the offer of a drink? It had, at any rate, arrived in front of her, in a tall glass with crushed ice in it. Rosie took a grateful sip and smiled at Mrs Patresi. An expansive, very false smile looked back at her.

Then a tall pale girl appeared at the door into the house, a yelling baby in her arms, a toddler straining at her arm. 'I have luncheon in oven,' said the girl in a French accent. 'We go walk now. We rrreturrrn in one hourrr.'

'A'right Anne-Marie,' said the lady of the house. She opened her arms to the toddler: 'Come and say goodbye to mama, eh?' The toddler looked at her mother suspiciously; clung to the French girl's skirt. 'Bugger off then,' said Mrs Patresi maternally, turning to Rosie with her false smile still in place. 'Kids, eh? Wanna fag?'

The cigarette was very long and said 'International' on it. Rosie took another sip of her drink, and inhaled the smoke deeply. Mrs Patresi seemed to have given up her efforts at conversation; her red-nailed hands were flipping idly through a *Cosmopolitan*. Rosie leant back and closed her eyes for a moment. This was the life.

Had she actually dozed off? No, the cigarette between her fingers was scarcely burnt down. But when she looked up the sun had gone in, and standing at the door to the house was a thick-set man in dark glasses. Mrs Patresi immediately went over to him and touched his face. The gesture reminded Rosie of Siggy and Jack Fountain.

'Ricky, this is . . .'

'Aye, I've just been speaking to Lawrie.' Damn. She hadn't caught him on the hop. He'd have his line as prepared as his superior smile. As he advanced towards Rosie, his arm outstretched in welcome, Mrs Patresi hastily moved ahead of him to push a chair out of his way.

'Don't fuss, woman. Rosie, isn't it? Call me Ricky.'

Ricky might have a little of his wife's Scots accent, and a little of the fake informality of his friend Greenfield. But Rosie looked up at his eyes masked by the glasses and realised there was something fundamentally different about him.

Ricky Patresi was blind.

And, after the introductions, very relaxed. He lolled back in the lounger next to Rosie's and pushed away the drink his wife clasped his hands around for him and said to Rosie casually. 'I've just been talking to Lawrie. He says his sweet little Ruth's done a bunk. But how can I help?'

Good question. Rosie took another sip of Martini and thought of a terrifically intelligent reply: 'In need of a hundred grand, are you?'

An expansive gesture around his property: 'As y'can see, I'm desperate for that kinda small change. But what's that to do with sweet little Ruth?'

So he didn't know about the kidnapping call. Or didn't act as if he knew. So? 'So there's just a faint chance,' said Rosie, 'I mean she's probably trying out the good life away from home for a few days but there's just a chance she didn't choose to go. That somebody else persuaded her to. Somebody who maybe had it in for Greenfield.'

Ricky Patresi's features creased into a smile. Then, a laugh. 'Like me, y'mean? You hear that, Sally?' Who wasn't listening, but looked up and smiled, as if that was what he would want her to do, if he could see her. Ricky went on: 'Did he tell you how much he's into me for? Greenfield? — I'll tell you: a fuck of a lot. A lot more than some schoolgirl on the loose is worth. You find the kid, I'll be glad. Might get his mind to concentrate on what he owes me. What he's into me for.'

'And what is he into you for?'

'Ah,' said Ricky, 'I'm with you. Play chess, do you?' At Rosie's shake of the head: 'Just thought you might. I can play it blind, y'know. Well I would, wouldn't I? In my head. Imagining the moves. The next move as well as the last. Like, that you're thinking, Greenfield owes this man and can't pay him back. And this blind feller here knows what'd hit a nerve with old Greenfield so he puts a finger on that nerve — I've got your daughter. Pay me and you'll get her back. Isn't that what you were thinking?'

'No,' said Rosie, because that was exactly what she'd been thinking and she was a stickler for the truth.

'I don't mind admitting, Rosie,' the smile again, 'there was a time I was that kind of businessman. Entrepreneur of the streets, sorta thing. Send the heavies round. But nowadays my heavies are solicitors and accountants. I don't get my hands dirty. I'm not into that no more.'

He sounded almost regretful. Sally, half-unthinking as she leafed through her magazine, had reached across to stroke his leg. On a sudden impulse, Rosie touched him on the arm: 'And what are you into, eh? Besides chess?'

'Money, Rosie, I'm into money. I can't see it no more but I can still touch it and smell it and count it. And I like that. Know what I mean?'

No, said Rosie to the cooling air. No, I only want money for what it can buy for me and my kids and the people I know. 'No,' said Rosie, not meaning to say it out loud.

He smiled again; taking his Martini glass and suddenly draining it. 'D'you know how much money I've got, Rosie? I've got fuck-off money. Know what I mean?'

Rosie sipped at her own glass and said 'No' again because it seemed to be expected.

'I've got,' said the blind man, nodding to himself, 'I've got enough money to tell anybody I like to fuck off. Right? So fuck off, Rosie. This interview is terminated. Now.'

Chapter Fourteen

The car wouldn't start.

Rosie banged her fist against the steering-wheel angrily.

She immediately apologised. For it wasn't the damn car she was angry with, was it? It was Ricky Patresi and his self-satisfied dismissal of her.

And it was herself, for blushing and going quietly and not saying anything.

None of which was going to make the car start.

Rosie propped the bonnet open and bent over it with a rag in her hand, her skirt blowing in the breeze. Usually that was effective in getting knights in shining armour to dismount their 2.4 litre steeds and ask her what the trouble was.

Not today, though. Five minutes over the bonnet and all she'd got was a cold bum from the draught. Not a single car passed.

Well, she was parked in a cul-de-sac.

So she used the rag to give a quick wipe of the plugs and decided to give the car one last chance before she hit it again. And it started. 'Thank you, car,' said Rosie.

On the way over to Liverpool she went through all the witty replies to 'Fuck off' that she could think of. There weren't any. A taxi darted out of nowhere in front of the Mini at the tunnel exit and she waved her fist and shouted two words at the cabby in her anger and frustration:

'Thank you!' she shouted.

That made her feel better. And the Martini had done wonders for her hangover so ....

'Thank you,' she said brightly when Martin answered the Greenfield's door before she'd even knocked. 'Taken you on as a footman, have they?' Martin squeezed together the lines on his forehead. 'Is that a warning look?' she whispered.

'The kidnappers have called,' he whispered back. 'And there's something . . .'

'Wondered when you'd pop in,' called Luke or whatever his name was, from the living room. 'Come on through.'

The earnest faces of David Langton and Damp Hand Luke stared at her coolly as she went in. The whisky was on its way out of another bottle into his glass, she just had time to notice, before the recriminations began:

'I realise you must have a lot of domestic duties, Mrs Monaghan,' said her client. She hadn't seen him in this mood before: angry, upset, sarcastic. She hadn't seen him so bleached white in the face before either, so that his eyes seemed to stand out from his face as he pursued her: 'But while you've been doing whatever you've been doing . . .'

'Tracking down your enemies,' said Rosie, not sitting down. She was trying to catch Martin's eye but he was avoiding looking at her.

'Whatever you may claim to have been up to,' he went on, gulping at his whisky, 'the kidnappers have called, while you were visiting my friends' — with emphasis — 'and it seems . . .'

'Did you record it?'

'Of course.'

'I'd best listen to it then. In the kitchen, eh?'

She strode out, winking at a cheerless Martin, unplugged the answerphone and took it into the kitchen that was as sparkling as ever. Martin, following, pushed a rough transcription of the conversation in front of her and began to say, 'Rosie, there's something funny,' but she waved him away to read and listen. The kidnapper's voice was a woman's this time: either foreign, or pretending to be, and very deep:

WOMAN: Mr Greenfield?

MARTIN:	I'll see if he's available. Who shall I say . . .?
WOMAN:	Eez about heez daughter.
	(PAUSE AND CRACKLES ON THE LINE)
GREENFIELD:	(BREATHLESS) Can I help you?
WOMAN:	Zat man, he eez not police, no?
GREENFIELD:	No, no, he's just a, he's workin' for me. So what's this about my . . .?
WOMAN:	Ve haff Ruthie. She is okay. Ve vant feefty thousand on Monday afternoon.
GREENFIELD:	Fifty? But that's, er, I can't lay me hands on that much, and deffo not by Monday afternoon, look . . .
WOMAN:	Eef not, your Ruthie gets hurt, okay. Ve call again Monday noon . . .
GREENFIELD:	No, no, wait, how do I even know you've got her?
WOMAN:	You veesh speak vith her? (MUFFLED) Bring her over here. (MUTTERS) Nossing foolish now . . .
RUTH:	(SOBS)
GREENFIELD:	Ruthie. . . .
RUTH:	(THROUGH SOBS) Please Daddy do what they say or . . .
WOMAN:	Eez enough.
	(SOUNDS OF RUTH SOBBING, GOING AWAY)
GREENFIELD:	Look, love, if you hurt my Ruthie. . . .
	(DIALLING TONE. GREENFIELD SOBS)

'He did seem,' Martin was saying at the doorway as Rosie went back through, 'he really did seem. . . .'

Langton and Greenfield were talking in low voices that hushed as soon as Rosie went in. Rosie wished Alice was in on this conference: she trusted the woman somehow. She didn't really know Mike's senior partner behind the half-glasses well enough to understand what he was about. And there was an uncomfortable smell of hostility mingling with the whisky in the air: a wall around the two men that excluded her. 'So I'd better,' she began.

'So you'd better get back here on Monday,' said Luke Greenfield. 'That'll be all for now, eh?'

'You wha'?' said Rosie, sitting down in the farting-chair in her surprise before she remembered about it.

'If you'll excuse us,' he went on. 'Me and Mr Langton have things to discuss. And take your, er, coloured friend with you, eh?'

'Hang about,' said Rosie, leaning forward, deciding not to care about the chair. 'You don't think I should be looking for whoever this caller is, for instance? Unless you've finally decided to call the cops in?'

Langton looked down his specs at her benignly and spoke with a snooty effort to be friendly that came out like a sneer. 'Mr Greenfield will give you a call later on. When we've discussed things. All right?'

You've been dismissed, Rosie. Don't outstay your welcome. 'I don't understand,' said Rosie. 'I mean, I've got some leads on who this might be, on the 'phone — Lawrie,' she said with emphasis, and the pale man looked up at her sharply for a moment before signalling to Langton to get rid of her. 'It could be the kids at school who've been bullying your Ruthie. Or Jack Fountain and his bit of Norwegian wood. Or Ricky Patresi. Or maybe even your older daughter . . .'

'Do not insult my children or,' said Greenfield.

'Look,' Langton interjected quickly, 'you heard the voice.'

'Easy to pretend to be foreign,' said Rosie. Then, at Langton's approach: 'A'right, I know when I'm not wanted. But I'm just telling you, I've got plenty of info here. And every moment you don't call me is a wasted moment. Tara now.'

It would have been nice to make a big dramatic exit. But the two men had already turned to one another, as if she wasn't there. There was something else to say but she couldn't think what it was. 'Now,' said Langton to Greenfield, looking sideways at her: Why are you still here?

'I'm glad,' said Rosie on her way out, as square-jawed Alice came through the door, quivering eyebrows reminding her of her fierce Auntie Dora again, 'glad you're here anyway' — but suddenly Rosie was a non-person to Greenfield's sister too. The older woman wordlessly swept past her into the living room and slammed the door shut behind her.

Martin followed her out to the car: 'Eh, Rosie, I cabbed it here, me bike's on the blink y'see. . . . '

At least she existed to somebody: even if they only wanted something from her. 'I'll give y'a lift. You got that transcript of the tape?'

'I got the tape an' all.' Martin patted his pocket and climbed into the passenger seat.

Rosie could have told him that might well be a waste of time.

Fifteen seconds later he got out again and leant against the back of the Mini. 'Are you pushing yet?' asked Rosie.

'Have you taken the hand-brake off yet?' asked Martin.

But soon they'd sorted out that little dispute to the dissatisfaction of both parties and were on their way back into Liverpool. Martin, in between wincing unjustly at Rosie's immaculate driving, was explaining what he'd been trying to say in the Greenfields' house except Rosie wouldn't let him get a word in edgeways. 'There's something funny going on,' he said with his hands over his eyes.

'Ho ho,' said Rosie, who saw the red light now.

'No, funny peculiar,' Martin went on, peeking out through his parted fingers, 'didn't you notice? He never mentioned the other kidnappers' call yesterday. And the woman didn't either. The foreign one. Did it really happen, Rosie?'

'Of course it did,' said Rosie, patting Martin's knee comfortingly as she accelerated round a stalled learner.

'Well, he told me it did.'

Martin was looking out of the side window now. 'And he was shocked. Like, real shocked. When she called. Like, white people aren't often actually white, are you? More pink, as a rule. But he went white, real white. Dulux Brilliant. I could get a bus from here,' he added hopefully.

'I can't have my operatives taking buses.'

'I think I'm gonna be sick,' said Martin but Rosie knew he was just kidding. 'Eh, and I don't wanna go there again. To Greenfield's.'

'Even if I promise never to give y'a lift again?'

It wasn't that. He wouldn't say why at first. Well, he went on about being a socialist and how self-made men got up his nose, but Rosie knew there was more to it than just that kind of politics. 'Plus,' he said finally when they were parked outside his flat and he was breathing more evenly again, 'plus, as a minor contributory factor, I may not have felt entirely happy when he was talking to that snooty solicitor feller. And I was trying to chip in my pennyworth, like. And he said, your Mr Greenfield, he said: Someone tell that coon to shut up. That may have a little bit to do with it.'

'I'm sorry Martin,' said Rosie sadly, putting her hand on his knee again. He looked at her hand, as if it was a strange animal that had landed there and he didn't know whether to stroke it or shoo it away. 'About last night . . .'

'Another time,' he said, squeezing the strange five-fingered animal on his knee then giving it back to her. As he started to get out she hung on to his hand:

'I just wanna know what happened.'

Sometimes people found the truth too hard to contemplate. 'You know what happened,' he said grimly. 'Here, you'd better have these,' he added, handing her the tape and his transcript.

'What do I want the sodding things for?' demanded Rosie, feeling a dangerous dampness pressing at her eyes as she hurled them back at him.

He picked them up, dripping, from a handy puddle

91

that had been specially placed in this precise gutter on this precise road at this precise time just in case Rosie happened to throw anything over it. 'You'll want them so you can crack the case,' he said, tossing the soggy tape and papers on to the passenger-seat. He slammed the door shut, smiled wanly and waved.

He's had a bad morning, Rosie. Don't be hard on him.

So she only hit the steering-wheel with her fist a couple of times before she remembered she wasn't really angry with the car.

Then she remembered she wasn't really angry with Martin either. Maybe she should follow him up to his flat and. . . .

No. What, after all, did the little matter of her love-life and a blank in her memory matter compared to The Case of Ruth Greenfield?

It mattered, said Rosie, because it was the difference between pleasure and work.

'Oh, Martin,' she said to the windscreen, treating herself to one more blow of fist upon wheel before turning the car into the traffic.

Chapter Fifteen

Rosie was trying to draft the report on the LBHA pick-up driver because it had to be on the auditor's desk by Monday lunchtime. But she kept getting distracted from that by yet another thought about Ruth Greenfield. Who had been kidnapped; or not, as the case may be. Her father said she'd been kidnapped by his, er, enemies; but he didn't want to talk about them. The girl didn't have any friends she might have gone to; or perhaps only one friend, with a birthmark more visible than her own; or perhaps another, an older man that her father did business with but who probably wasn't blind Ricky Patresi or stroke-me Jack Fountain. The person who claimed to be the kidnapper and certainly had the missing girl in the room with her had a foreign voice: both of the potential enemies/older men had foreign women who might make a call for them.

There, that's got that all straight, Rosie lied to herself, picking up the thriller she hadn't had time for since this business began. She only managed one page. She found herself thinking: what would *he* do? The pipe-smoking poetry-quoting detective? Commissioner of Police Buckingham or Bedford or Berk or whatever his name was: what is your opinion, sir?

The trouble was, his crime would have happened in a village or at most a small town, and anyway he'd have lots of minions rushing around the place being less posh or subtle than him but doing the basic legwork and filling out the index cards.

And he wouldn't have just been as-good-as-sacked by his client, would he?

Oh, stop being sorry for yourself, woman.

Rosie's hangover was grumbling at her from inside her stomach as she flicked through the channels — snooker, racing, wrestling — hunting for something intellectually demanding enough to fill up her brain. Finally she settled on an old edition of Star Trek. That should be pretty gripping. She'd only seen it half a dozen times before.

The next thing Rosie knew, she was asleep. She knew because she was smiling for no reason at a clock. And she kept trying to wake up when she saw how late it was, but a hypnotic voice assured her that Bob and Carol were safe with Graham. So she could safely carry on sleeping and smiling, couldn't she?

Safe? With Graham? You must be mad, Rosie, she said to herself, waking up properly this time.

Oh my God I should have collected the kids five minutes ago and why doesn't Greenfield ring up, damn him? Though, because I'm in a hurry, preferably not . . .

. . . now, as the phone rang and Rosie began to wonder about the transmission of thought across distances. . . .

'Look, Luke,' she said, 'I'm afraid I've got to . . .'

'Where the fuck are you?' Graham's mellifluous voice enquired sweetly.

Rosie held her nose between thumb and forefinger. 'This is a recorded message,' she nasalled. 'Rosie Monaghan is not available right now because she is on her way to collect her children from her charming ex-husband. If, however, you would like to leave a message. . . .'

But he'd rung off before she could pretend to be the beeps. Concluding she might as well be very late as quite late, she rang Luke Greenfield in case he'd lost her number or something. On the fifth ring the phone answered: 'I'm afraid Luke Greenfield is not available at the moment,' it said in nervous tones. 'If, however, you would like to leave a message. . . .'

Sod it. Hoist by her own petard. For wasn't that Rosie's bloody answerphone Luke Greenfield was avoiding her on?

Coming Graham I'm coming, she said to a voice in her ear, just like she used to lie to him at midnight during the halcyon days of their marriage: coming, Graham, I'm coming. . . .'

*

Rosie kept expecting the world to conform to known laws. She didn't know what to do when it confounded her expectations. As it regularly did. 'Whaddya mean, you had a row?' she asked Bob again on the way home.

She'd known something was wrong when she'd arrived at their neutral meeting-place up by Newsham Park and Graham was walking around his car, holding his screaming new baby in his arms, smiling and goo-gooing to the infant. Now Carol, who didn't get on with her father under any circumstances, confirmed that the world had turned upside down and really they were living in Australia: 'He said it was a really good idea. Me calling him Graham. Said it was very mature of me. He wanted Bob to do it too. Bob wouldn't. Bob cried.'

'I never,' said red-eyed Bob, who got on with his father under any circumstances. Usually. 'He's gone all soppy, that's all.'

Carol couldn't help overdoing it when she'd got the upper hand. Not that she'd picked up that habit off her mother, of course. 'Graham,' with emphasis, 'just likes babies,' she smirked at her hangdog brother.

'Likes babies?' asked Rosie incredulously. The steering wobbled in sympathetic amazement as she turned into their street. Briefly she remembered all the nights Graham had refused to get up to feed a crying Bob; all the days he hadn't deigned to dirty his hands with a soiled nappy. Then, slamming on the brakes: 'What the fu, er, what's that?'

Bob informed her quietly that it was a flashing blue light usually to be seen on top of police cars. Rosie thanked him for the information while Carol kindly, though with a tinge of excitement in her voice, pointed out that it seemed to be outside their house.

'So it does,' said Rosie, engaging reverse and zooming back round the corner while Bob, rather unnecessarily she thought, asked her what she was doing. 'Making my get-away, of course.'

'What've you done, Mum?'

That was the question. What had she done? Okay so the car-tax was overdue but didn't they usually just send you a summons through the post for that? And even if the Inland Revenue had found out about all those receipts she'd lost, would they really have arranged to send a patrol car round?

'If anybody asks you, this is yours, right?' she said, taking her notebook from her handbag and stuffing it into the satchel of homework and other games the children always took to Graham's and back without ever opening.

'What is it?' asked Carol.

'It's your notebook,' said Rosie, driving round the corner again at a sedate speed.

'But what've you done, Mum?' Bob still wanted to know (not to mention his mother) as the neighbours looked out from behind their nets and Rosie considered waving then thought better of it.

'So what've I done?' Rosie asked the uniformed police-man at the door as she stood there with her key out, all brisk and unconcerned.

He didn't like to say. He and his female oppo and the plain-clothes woman detective who was getting out of the back of the patrol car just wanted her to accompany them to the station to assist them with certain enquiries. Hm, thought Rosie, bundling the kids inside, giving in to the temptation to wave to Mrs Bundy from Number 17, police are just like kidnappers: they watch too much television. Ruins their natural use of language. 'No, but . . .' said Rosie.

'DC Collins,' said the plain-clothes woman. She had a

long thin lantern sort of a face with spots around her mouth and hollows under her eyes. A wide-eyed Carol was whispering to Rosie that she should demand to see the woman's identification but Rosie wanted to know:

'What sort of certain enquiries?'

'They'll tell you all that down at the station,' said DC Collins, somehow overhearing Carol's modestly loud whisper and flashing an ID card at Rosie.

Which made relief course through Rosie. 'Oh yeh,' she said brightly, 'I've been meaning to report it, my purse being nicked I mean, so somebody's handed in my ID card have they . . .?'

'It's not about any ID card,' said Lantern Face, who obviously had a way with children; a way of turning away from them when they stared at her curiously. 'It's about a missing girl, you with me? So, if it's convenient . . . ?'

So Rosie, the relief all coursed out of her again, went through the motions of asking what'd happen if it wasn't convenient (that wouldn't be helpful) and what was she going to do about the kids' tea (she was going to leave them with somebody) and was she being accused of something because if so she'd like to know what (just a question of assisting with enquiries, said DC LF Collins lugubriously). 'So what've I done?' Rosie asked again, but even she was bored with that question now.

So finally she was calling Margie up and explaining how she was just being arrested (not arrested said the policewoman's shake of the head). 'So what've you done?' Margie asked unoriginally.

'Just get round here, a'right?' said Rosie charmingly.

Then they were all sitting there, not saying anything for a while: DC Collins and her, and Bob and Carol whom she'd told to shut up in her kind motherly way when they started to ask questions. A uniform inhabited a body at the door and looked dangerously as if it might flex its knees and say 'Evenin' all.' No you're imagining it Rosie come on now don't get hysterical.

And finally Margie arrived and Rosie explained to her

friend unhysterically how the police were wanting to know about her two villas in Spain and her dangerous under-world friends — 'Oh, y'mean your brother,' said Margie helpfully.

Rosie shot her a look. Margie winced. 'Tell Mike,' Rosie muttered in an urgent undertone. And no, she didn't feel angry or frightened or anything. No she didn't. But it was somehow a relief, when she was about to accept DC Collins's invitation to accompany her out of the door, that the phone rang and it was Paddy saying, 'Look, Sis, I know you're busy but I've got a hell of a problem with the kids so I wondered if. . . .'

'Can't stop,' said Rosie into the phone with a sudden attack of giddiness. 'I'm being kidnapped. By some people pretending to be bizzies. So I won't be able to babysit for five years or so. Tara Paddy.'

Chapter Sixteen

Having, at last, cut a near-perfect circular section from the rim of a polystyrene cup that had once, a few centuries ago, contained tea, Rosie felt tired of grappling with the Forces of Nature and decided to reinvent the art of conversation.

'Did y'ever watch Star Trek?' Rosie asked.

The uniformed policewoman at the door of the interview room shook her head.

'Beam me up, Scottie', said Rosie. She smiled at the stony-faced policewoman. 'That's what Captain Kirk used to say, y'see. When he'd had enough of life on a hostile planet. So he could be magically transported back to the Starship Enterprise Culture.'

The policewoman at the door coughed slightly, not looking at Rosie.

'Beam me up, Scottie,' said Rosie, meaning it this time. 'I have had enough of life on this hostile planet.'

Scottie didn't seem to be listening.

Neither did the policewoman at the door. She seemed to have decided to turn into a statue.

'Been a copper long?' said Rosie affably.

The statue briefly came to life, shrugged, became statuesque again.

Oh well. Back to the polystyrene cup.

*

Eventually the door opened and DC Collins came in and sat down opposite Rosie and took out a little black notebook. 'Right,' she said briskly, 'if we can just . . .'

'Sorry to keep you waiting,' said Rosie.

'If we can just,' refusing to be knocked out of her stride, 'go through all your dealings with Mr Greenfield since the early hours of Friday morning . . .'

It was the waiting, Rosie decided later. That had addled her brain. That made her start on about how she'd visited Luke Greenfield on this alien planet called Suburbia. Only, she went on, he was disguised as a whisky bottle and had this pet vacuum cleaner on a lead that he called Mrs Greenfield.

This is not helping, Rosie.

'This is not helping, Mrs Monaghan,' said DC Collins in a pleading sort of a way.

'I'm sorry. It's the waiting,' said Rosie. 'It's the staring at the blank walls,' and the statue at the door but I'm not going to mention her. 'Not to mention the statue . . .'

Mercifully, she was interrupted. 'If we could just go back . . .'

My God, it had only been forty hours or so ago, Rosie realised as she forced herself to recount the sober details: forty hours since all this began. Forty hours in which, as she told DC Collins slowly and patiently and cutting out the jokes, she had met Luke Greenfield; encountered Susie and the Nazis; learned of the kidnappers' first and second calls; discovered. . . .

Well, that was all they needed to know, wasn't it? Why should she tell them about a thin girl drinking cider and eating banana-and-onion crisps in a tatty bedsit? Or Jack Fountain and Siggy with the hands? Or the blind man with fuck-you money?

— Because that's what they want to know, Rosie.

Rosie felt sure a good reason for her silence on certain matters would come to her sooner or later.

It didn't. A few more millennia passed and Rosie was failing to sleep on the crook of her arm when DC Collins returned with a bulbous-nosed middle-aged man who, with a brusque nod of the head, dismissed the police-woman at the door. He introduced himself: 'Norfolk,' he said. 'Detective Inspector Norfolk.'

It was like Margie seeing Jerry and Martin together. Rosie just couldn't help it. She thought of that avuncular detective named after some county or other that she'd been trying to conjure up this afternoon and she couldn't help it — she laughed.

'Y'mean, like the county?'

'If y'like.'

'You,' said Rosie, wheezing, 'are the man of my dreams. Sure you're not Commissioner of Police?'

He looked down his bulbous nose at her. He didn't smile. She'd said the wrong thing. Maybe he thought he would have been Commissioner if only he'd joined the Masons or something. He settled himself down opposite Rosie, and told 'Tracy' at the door to sit down for goodness' sake, and said, 'I've been talking to your Luke Greenfield.'

'Lawrence Kenneth. That's his real name.'

'Whoever,' said the inspector, with the air of a man who'd prefer not to be interrupted from now on, if Rosie didn't mind. I don't mind, she said silently, breathing normally again now. 'I'll be frank with you, Royzin, don't mind if I call you Royzin do you . . .'

Nobody's called me that since the vicar at my wedding, and he mispronounced it just like you, but all right, go on. . . .

'. . . this Luke, Lawrence Kenneth, Lord-Knows-What Greenfield has made certain accusations. In the light of which, I was wondering whether you'd like to change what you told Detective Constable Collins in any way before we turn it into a formal statement.'

In the light of which. A bare formal bulb hung overhead, in the light of which Rosie wondered what the hell he meant by certain accusations. 'No ta,' said Rosie, not feeling like laughing any more, 'thanks all the same.'

'Fine,' and he was getting up already. She recognised the formal moves of a practised game; in the light of which, she knew her part:

'No, hang on,' she said, 'can't you tell me what these'

101

certain accusations are?'

'If you want to leave your statement as it is,' he was saying, banging his papers together on the table so they formed a neat rectangle.

'Yeh, but,' said Rosie, cunning, like, 'I might've got some of the details wrong, mightn't I? I mean, my memory's not what it was. Sometimes it needs refreshing. Go on, tell us what he says.'

He sat down again. Rosie promised herself not to interrupt him. Not even with a thought: knowing how her thoughts sometimes turned into conversation when she least expected them to. 'Right,' he said, and read from the statement on top of his bundle of papers. 'I, Luke Greenfield . . .'

'Changed his name by deed-poll then, has he?'

Don't interrupt, said his eyebrows. Don't interrupt, said Rosie.

He, Luke Greenfield, had, it seemed, on the advice of his solicitor David Langton, decided to utilise the services of a private investigator with whom the solicitor's junior partner was acquainted, a woman named Royzin Monaghan known as Rosie. Mr Greenfield's fourteen-year-old daughter Ruth had left home the day before of her own free will . . .

'Uh?' said Rosie, not interrupting.

. . . as attested by the note she had left her father, a copy of which was attached to his statement. Being, however . . .

'Aaargh?' said Rosie, not interrupting.

The policeman wordlessly passed Rosie the note. It read:

Daddy

I've got to get away for a few days. Please don't worry about me. I'll be safe with a friend. I just want to be on my own for a while. I'll ring you up in a few days.

Ruthie

'Urgh,' said Rosie, passing back the note, rubbing the gloss from the photocopy off her finger unthoughtfully.

Luke Greenfield, being, despite the note, naturally concerned about his daughter's welfare, engaged Mrs Monaghan to attempt to establish the whereabouts of his daughter. Mrs Monaghan — perhaps taking her cue from a wild theory Mr Greenfield had himself formulated under the influence of shock and alcohol in the emotion of the moment, but had subsequently come to dismiss — Mrs Monaghan rapidly became curiously obsessed with the idea that Ruth Greenfield had been kidnapped . . .

'Eeeooo,' said Rosie, dangerously close to interrupting.

. . . and insisted on installing a telephone answering machine at the Greenfield home to record any calls made by the purported kidnappers. Throughout the following day no calls were received from these alleged kidnappers . . .

'Bollocks,' said Rosie, interrupting. 'Knickers,' she interrupted more mildly.

Nobody took any notice. Either time.

. . . and throughout Friday Mrs Monaghan made no apparent progress in locating Mr Greenfield's daughter. On Saturday morning, however, at approximately 12.30 pm, a call was received from a foreign-sounding woman, demanding the sum of £50,000 for the return of Ruth to her parents. At this time, it transpires, Mrs Monaghan was en route from the home of a business associate of Mr Greenfield's called Ricardo Patresi, who had been forced to ask Mrs Monaghan to leave when she made offensive remarks about the supposed client. Mr Greenfield's suspicions as to the true identity of the foreign-sounding woman received strong corroboration when Mrs Monaghan, on arriving at his home, proceeded to remove the cassette tape on which the call had been . . .

'I've got it, I've got that tape,' said Rosie brightly.

'Good,' said Detective Inspector Lincoln, sorry, Suffolk.

'But,' added Rosie darkly, 'I did drop it in a puddle.'

'Bad,' said whatsisname.

'It's been raining,' said Rosie. 'I'd like to see. . . .'

But would she? Like to see her solicitor? When his senior partner must be in on this too?

Ah, come on, that's your old mate Mike you're talking about.

Your old mate Mike the junior partner who's been curiously unhelpful so far and who's out of a job if his senior partner says so.

'You'd like to see . . .?'

'Forget it,' said Rosie. 'Just tell me this, though. Who called you in?'

'I don't really see how that's relevant.'

'Was it him? Or his solicitor? Or, 'pause for effect,'his sister?'

The flicker in the inspector's eyes before he went on about relevance again suggested to Rosie she might have guessed right. Maybe Alice had called in the police; even though her name hadn't come up till now. Suddenly Rosie felt a bit light-headed. 'So how,' she asked, smiling, 'so how exactly have I done this, er, sort of non-kidnapping?'

Mr Greenfield's allegations, the inspector continued smoothly, quickly wiping the smile off Rosie's face, centred on two possibilities. One, that Mrs Monaghan has indeed located his daughter and may or may not be exploiting this opportunity by detaining her against her will. Alternatively, two, that Mrs Monaghan has failed to locate Ruth Greenfield but has instead spent most of the last forty hours hatching this conspiracy to deprive Mr Greenfield of his hard-earned money.

'Hard-earned?' interrupted Rosie. Why had she felt briefly euphoric at the thought that Alice might have called the police? It wasn't going to get her out of here, was it? 'Look, I want to see . . .'

'You want to see . . . ?'

No, not see: be. Be somewhere else. Be someone else. Be someone else somewhere else. In Norfolk, for instance. That was it, Norfolk. 'No, not see: pee,' said Rosie, leaning across the table intimately. 'I've got this trouble, y'see. Down below. I've got to. I've really got to. I'm sorry.'

Norfolk leant back. He nodded resignedly. Well, it gave him a chance for a quick one from his hip-flask, didn't it? While Rosie, escorted down the corridor by Tracy's lantern frown, had a chance for a quick think about how she was going to get out of this one.

*

Rosie sat in the cubicle, listening to DC Collins breathing loudly outside. What could she do? Discounting suicide in such a small bowl; rejecting the idea of continuing to tell the truth since that wasn't getting her anywhere; Rosie finally arrived at the only rational answer. Escape. But she'd never battle her way out as she was. No. She'd have to turn into something. Yes, that was it. She'd simply — turn into a fly. Yes. Her legs would become thin stalks, and as she shrank two more legs would grow from her hips. And already her ears were turning into feelers. And what were these flimsy things growing from her shoulder blades? Why, wings of course.

Bzzz, went Rosie as she flew under the cubicle door. Pausing only to land briefly on DC Collins's neck — leaping off into the unknown again the instant before the slap of the hand — she flew out through the crack in the door and down along the hospital-green corridor. 'Bit early for flies, isn't it?' said one policeman to another as she passed, onward ever onward, stopping briefly at the enquiry desk for a crumb or two of stale jam sandwich. Then she was off again — out into the world — free — wheeeeeeeeee!

But she wasn't. Free. For, waiting for her outside was a great web that trapped her in its sticky strands. As her six legs struggled feebly for purchase, she looked around her. And there were all the other members of the Greenfield family — Ruthie, Josephine, his wife, even his sister Alice — all flies, struggling in the web. She peered down to where the hairy spider was waiting for her. And yes, it had the face of . . .

'Are you all right in there?'

. . . the face of Luke Greenfield. So how was she going to get out of this one?

'Mrs Monaghan?'

'Don't worry. I'm fine. Bzzzz,' said Rosie. 'Everything's fine.'

*

Rosie made her statement to DC Collins. Rosie gave up on metamorphosis and told the truth. She knew this wasn't the sort of thing people did nowadays, but some flaw in her character made her feel there was no alternative.

Several centuries passed in the company of the statue at the door and a fresh polystyrene cup to strike up a relationship with.

The next thing she knew she was being shaken awake and a bulbous nose and the hot smell of recently drunk whisky were extremely adjacent to her. 'A word in your ear,' the man was saying.

Rosie shook her head so the words would go in one ear without coming out of the other. 'Yeh?' she mumbled brightly.

'About your line of work. While Tracy's typing up the statement.' He'd sat down on the edge of the table, swinging his legs to and fro. 'Y'see, I'm just hanging on till me pension's assured. So I was thinking, if somebody with hardly any experience like you can get by on it, sounds like the thing for me. Think I'd make a reasonable living?'

Rosie was tired. Rosie didn't understand what this had to do with anything. Rosie said as much to the inspector, and added that it was a living but it wasn't very reasonable. This was, she explained, because most of the work she did was immoral but perfectly legal, like most major crimes. And anyway, she concluded, the money wasn't that good.

'So you wouldn't say no to fifty grand, eh? If you saw the opportunity.'

So that was where all this was leading. 'If I came up on the pools, maybe. But not . . .'

'Ah, come on.'

'Look,' said Rosie, 'I don't know if you can under-stand this, what with all the perks in your job, but I'm the sort of person that pays their income tax on time and doesn't say a slap-up meal I had with a mate was for busi-ness purposes. I'm not proud of it but that's what I'm like. Honest. Ridiculous, isn't it? Should land me with a few years inside, d'you reckon?'

The inspector jumped down from the table. He smiled. 'Right,' he said. He pressed flat a statement that Tracy hadn't still been typing at all. 'Sign here. Then you can go.'

Rosie stared blearily at the statement; at the open door-way. 'No but . . .' she found herself saying. 'But . . .'

'But what?'

But there's a spider waiting for me out there. 'No, but why? Why aren't I being arrested and clapped in the cells for the night?'

He sat himself down in the chair opposite her and leant back. 'Because,' he replied, 'I haven't got enough evidence to hold you on.'

'Oh great,' said Rosie, signing every page with an angry flourish then getting up to go. 'Ta very much. For the declaration of innocence, like.'

His hand detained her. 'Because,' he went on, not look-ing at her, 'because I've been talking to you and your, er, client and trying to decide which of you's honest. Being an honest man meself, like.'

'Oh yeh?' said Rosie on the rampage. 'Y'see, I was brought up on *Dixon of Dock Green*. I thought all police were honest and good and kind. Aren't they?'

'Most of them would like to be. Honest. Yes they would,' at her look. 'Okay, true, sometimes I think I'm in the wrong job an' all. But that's me: honest. I don't take

107

kick-backs and I don't raise me trouser-leg to get promotion and I've been in this job nearly twenty years so I've got a nose for people. And I don't think you're a liar. But your friend is.'

'Fffff,' said Rosie, at the door and wanting to be home now. 'He's no friend of mine. Greenfield.'

The policeman jumped up from his seat to accompany her down the corridor. 'Not Greenfield, no. If it was just you and Greenfield I'd've had to hold you. Whatever me nose said. No, you've got a friend, you have. Lying for you. I'll be seeing you.'

She needn't have worried about Mike, then. She should have insisted on speaking to her solicitor after all. For even though his senior partner was up to his neck with Greenfield, Mike must have got her out somehow, mustn't he? Must've said how Greenfield had been going on about kidnapping that first night and — and lied for her? Wasn't that what the copper was saying?

So at least there was some kind of rough justice in the world, thought Rosie, suppressing the urge to run as she passed the counter where, as a fly, she'd scooped up a few crumbs earlier. So what if there was a spider waiting for her out there? She could dodge or outwit it, couldn't she? She hurried out, past the Watch Your Handbag notices and the pale man with a cut across his cheek sitting there waiting for tomorrow or the desk sergeant whichever came sooner, out into the night. So what if it was cold and raining? Rosie didn't care. 'Though April showers,' she was singing, 'may come your way' — whatever the world was up to, she was free. So maybe there was justice in the world.

And maybe that tooting horn was for her. Parked on a double yellow line opposite the police station, yes, it was Margie's van with that irritating jingle advertising carpets blaring out of its radio and who was looking after the kids then if Margie . . .?

'Great to see you,' said Martin through the open window from the driver's seat. 'Hop in.'

I could kiss you. But it wouldn't be wise and anyway you might not welcome it after all that hassle with Jerry and whatever happened last night. So I'll just quietly get in the car and tell you all about it.

— Such were Rosie's thoughts as she bent to kiss him. She pressed her cheek against his and felt the tears running down on to his rough skin and failed to find anything to say.

Chapter Seventeen

Rosie was babbling about letters and spiders and fuck-you money. 'Wait till you've got a drink down you,' said Margie, sitting her down, telling Martin to hurry up with the home-made wine.

'You shouldn't have waited up.'

'How could I sleep, knowing you were down the cop-shop? I mean, they say it's almost as dangerous in Beirut as being in the hands of the bizzies.'

'I met an honest policeman.'

'Have a drink,' said Margie, giving her a glass, 'it's very good for hallucinations like that.'

'Replacing them with hallucinations of your own?' said Rosie, remembering the last time she'd had any of Margie's home brew. She took a big swig all the same and felt better already.

'So what's all this about letters and spiders?' said Margie.

'It was terrible,' said Rosie, taking another swig. 'This Luke bloody Greenfield, he's only had a letter on him all the time. From this Ruth. Saying she feels like a bit of a holiday.'

'Don't we all?' said Margie. 'But what were the police after?'

Martin was strangely quiet. Rosie glanced at him. He was smiling, in a neutral kind of way. 'They gave me the third degree. They thought I'd kidnapped this girl meself 'cause private detection's such a rotten earner.'

'Never,' said Margie.

Martin, though, didn't look too surprised. 'Naturally,' Rosie went on, watching him, 'my reputation for honest dealing eventually ensured my release.'

'Naturally,' agreed Margie, topping up their glasses.

'Plus,' said Rosie, looking at the black face she'd so recently kissed and now suddenly found inscrutable again, 'I thought Mike must have got me out.'

'How's that?'

'I've got a friend. That's what this copper reckoned. A friend who'd lied for me.'

'Who could that be, though?' asked Martin, smiling.

'I was wondering,' said Rosie, knowing she should be grateful yet feeling a little pulse of anger bumping at her temple.

'Well,' said Martin, pleased with himself, 'I thought it was funny. Funny peculiar, y'know. When Greenfield didn't mention the first kidnap call. At the house today. So when Margie called me and said you were in the bridewell, I went down there meself. And while I was in there I sort of suddenly remembered, in passing like, that he'd told me about them calling yesterday.'

'He didn't, though, did he? *He* never told you. *I* did. Isn't that right?'

Rosie found her voice had gone all foggy somehow. And she was gripping her wine glass very tightly. 'I forget,' said Martin.

'I don't want anybody to lie for me. Not anybody,' said Rosie.

'Eh now,' said Margie.

'I thought you'd be . . .' Martin began.

'Grateful? Pleased? Well I'm not,' said Rosie, refilling her own glass this time. The pulse at her temple said: You're spoiling the party, Rosie, shut up now. 'Shut up, Rosie,' said Rosie out loud, hoping that'd have some effect on her.

'Let's get you off to bed, eh?' said Margie soothingly.

And she was guiding Rosie up and out and upstairs and telling Martin she'd give him a lift in a minute and not to worry, it was the shock after all that Rosie had been through. But Rosie didn't want to go. She resisted as Margie hauled her along. She wasn't tired any more, no.

111

She just wanted to let loose all the anger and fear she'd been bottling up all night — and all day before that — so she knew what she had to explain to Martin before Margie could drag her to bed. 'Sometimes,' she said, surprisingly loudly, 'd'you know what, Martin? Sometimes I call for Scottie. And he's not there! And d'you know what else?'

'The kids are asleep,' Margie was saying in a whisper.

But Martin was still stood at the bottom of the stairs, the wine glass in his hand and bewilderment spread across his features. So Rosie knew she just had to tell him the most important thing on her mind: 'Sometimes, d'you know — sometimes I even wish I was a frigging fly!'

Chapter Eighteen

Today Rosie wasn't a fly. Today Rosie was a — well, a human being. An angry human being. A very angry human being.

Today Rosie was tired of solving cases. Today she thought she might try and become a case instead.

By murdering somebody, for instance.

Jerry, for instance.

At home there was a note from Jerry. Well, the first draft of an essay from Jerry. *I'm sure you will understand that . . . from the very outset of our relationship . . . at this crucial point in my own development. . . .*

Jerry, you sound sickeningly like a police statement rather than a man in love. Why don't you say what you mean? That if my womb isn't available for rent you'd like to go fathering elsewhere? Then I could tell you to f---- off? That's 'f' for 'father'.

'What are you doing, Mum?' asked Carol, who was in one of her clingy moods: meaning, she'd refused to be packed off to one of her friends while Bob was at his Sunday morning football match.

'I'm tearing up a note from Jerry,' Rosie replied gleefully. And, at Carol's look: 'Well, it's better than murdering him. So are you ready?'

'Dennis hasn't brought the car back yet.'

Carol looked up at her nervously as the two of them marched up the street. Dennis emerged from the Mini's bonnet. He glanced at Rosie's face and quickly offered Carol a savoury snack shaped like a starfish. Carol took the packet and inspected the list of contents carefully. 'So have you got it going then?' Rosie snapped.

Dennis slapped the Mini's roof like it was an old and

113

unvalued friend. If he so much as made a crack about her car then he might not live to regret it. . . .

'I could sell it off for you. That's all it's worth really: selling off for the spare parts.'

'Sometimes,' said Rosie, her fists tightly clenched, 'I feel the same about me. But I'm all I've got. So will it go?'

Yes it'd go, said Dennis, beating a retreat into his house as Rosie unclenched her fists and Carol began to give him a lecture on all the additives he was eating. A girl after my own heart, thought Rosie proudly, even though, on the way back down the street, she felt obliged to say: 'There is something to be said, love, for letting people go to the devil in their own way.'

'People need their consciousness raising about food,' said Carol in her modestly fanatical way.

Rosie, feeling modestly fanatical herself, decided to give the man she was really planning to murder one last request. So she dialled Luke Greenfield's number but after five rings the phone beeped and clicked in a familiar way. The man himself spoke: 'I'm afraid, er, nobody is available to take your call at the present time . . .'

'Frigging hell,' said Rosie. 'Delete frigging,' she said to Carol quickly.

'What's up, Mum?'

'That's my own fr, flipping answerphone that's talking to me again.'

But Rosie wasn't going to let a little thing like that get in her way. He might still be in and just using the answer-phone to fend off callers and potential killers. 'Come on then, if you're coming.'

Carol, breathless, joined her in the car. 'Where are we off anyway?'

'We're gonna beard the lion in his den.'

'What's that mean, Mum? Bearding the lion?'

Rosie wasn't going to get annoyed by a little habit like Carol's of asking what everything meant. Not today, when there were so many other things to get annoyed about. 'It's shaving a big four-legged animal with a mane that eats meat,' said Rosie entirely without irritation.

Well, maybe just the faintest trace.

No, without. Today she could safely ignore Carol saying 'That's no answer' and simply enjoy the fact that today was a lovely day. Out in the suburbs the sun glittered on tree blossom, gleamed on the windows of newly cleaned cars; there were daffodils and tulips enjoying the sunlight and men and some women digging their gardens; children did wheelies and played cricket and football in the streets; dogs and cats slept and ran and crapped happily along the kerbs.

Yes, today the suburbs were beautiful; so beautiful Rosie could happily bomb the lot to smithereens.

Alas, the planned seat of the explosion was unoccupied. Maybe Luke Greenfield had suspected that he might not be her favourite person today. Rosie kicked at a stupid little plant by the front door in frustration. Carol was busy patrolling the grounds and peering in at the windows and saying loving little things like 'I wished we lived in a place like this, Mum.' Rosie pretended to be busy bearding the lion's head door-knocker — well, hammering at it — but there was still no reply and she had to acknowledge that she could really hear Carol chuntering on: 'Can we? When we win the pools? Live in a place like this?'

I bet they share a gardener with Ricky Patresi, thought Rosie, looking at the perfectly weeded flower-beds and the trim rockery. She had already picked up a nice sharp boulder to hurl through the window when she thought about the kind of example she was setting Carol. Okay, she'd just have to come back in the dead of night and do it. Or maybe plough up the lawn. Mm, a sort of spider's web pattern might be nice.

'It's great, isn't it? said Carol, skipping up the lawn.

'It's revolting,' Rosie replied between her teeth.

'There's so much space,' said Carol, skipping back down the lawn.

Rosie didn't consider throwing the rock at Carol. No, not even for an instant. Instead she quietly replaced the weapon in the rockery. Taking a quick last look for evidence of recently disturbed soil that might be the shallow grave of a fourteen-year-old, she gave up on the Greenfields. 'Space? Come on, I'll show you space. Back in the car, you.'

*

'Yeh, but this doesn't belong to us, does it?'

'Yes it does. It belongs to all of us,' gesturing at the greenery and litter as far as the eye could see.

'Yeh, but not to us, just us: y'know, you and me and Bob and whatever man you've got on the go at the moment.'

Rosie squinted down at her daughter and bit back the angry reply. They were walking in Calderstones Park and she'd decided to buy Carol an ice-cream for a treat because she quite fancied one herself. She soon regretted her moment of altruism. Carol held up a queue of a dozen hungry children in order to interrogate Luigi from Kirkby about exactly what went into his ice-cream.

Which wouldn't have been so bad, if she hadn't continued her tirade as Rosie strolled in the sunshine, licking her cornet. 'It's not just the additives, Mum,' she was saying, 'they pump air into it y'know, just so you think you're getting more than you are, and . . .'

Rosie took hold of her daughter by the shoulders. 'CAROL!' she shouted. 'I HAVE BEEN THINKING ABOUT KILLING SOMEONE ALL MORNING AND IT MAY VERY WELL BE YOU!'

Carol looked up at her, astonished. And then, from the mouth upwards and the eyes downwards, her face began to crumple. 'I hate you!' she managed to gasp, before she turned, howling, and ran away across the park.

*

It was just a tiny bit embarrassing, being employed to find someone else's daughter then losing your own. It took Rosie half an hour to find the girl and felt like half of her life. 'Carol!' she kept shouting out.

'You bloody fool!' she kept shouting, silently, within.

She finally found Carol back where they'd started: on a bench near the ice-cream van. Familiar territory. Rosie's daughter was holding her head in her hands and pretending not to look out for her mother through parted fingers.

'I'm sorry love,' said Rosie, putting her arms around her daughter.

Carol clearly hadn't been crying for a while until that moment, but now her wailing began again.

'I'm not gonna kill anybody, love. Least of all, you. I'm sorry. Really.' Which wasn't enough. Rosie had to emphasise how really sorry she was, and Carol had to replay the scene several times over, before they could get back on an even keel.

'Really,' said Rosie, 'really, I am sorry.'

'Show me,' said Carol, still trying hard to look sulky.

'Tell you what. I'll buy y'an ice-cream.'

'Ugh. No thanks,' said Carol, who'd been glancing towards Luigi's van longingly for the past five minutes.

Rosie sighed. What had ever made her think there might be a murderer in her? In her penitent heart of hearts she knew now that all she wanted — apart from retrieving the affection of her daughter — was to find Ruth and her 'kidnappers', not to extinguish her client. She was the sort of person who finds what's lost, not the sort that makes them lost in the first place.

Familiar territory, she suddenly thought. That's what Carol had looked for, wasn't it? 'I want you,' she said seriously to Carol, 'to imagine something.'

'Like what?' grumped Carol. But she was having trouble keeping up the sourness now: 'Does it include having a big house with lots of space?'

'No, I mean, yes. Yes it does. Imagine you're three years older than you are . . .'

'That's old,' said Carol, who was still pretending not to look at Luigi's ice-cream van longingly.

'Sure you don't want a cornet?'

'Ugh. No ta.'

'So you're fourteen,' said Rosie, 'and you've had enough of me at home . . .'

'Because you've threatened to kill me or something?'

There was almost a smile on Carol's face. Rosie almost smiled too: 'Yeh. And home is a big house with lots of space like the one we've just been to see, and Bob is your sister not your brother and he's moved out, and you've only got one friend at school, and you've decided to leave home. Where would you go?'

'Maybe if you had one I could have a lick,' said Carol.

'Have you been listening to what I've been saying?'

'Of course I have. But I wouldn't leave home. Not when I've got a wonderful mum like you,' said Carol with a glitter of cunning in her eye.

Rosie got up. 'Come on then. I didn't get to eat much of that last one anyway.'

Carol suddenly became anxious as Rosie handed over the money: 'You won't tell Mo, willya? I'd never live it down.'

'Lick,' said Rosie, resigned to working out where Ruth Greenfield had got to on her own. The one lick was an enormous bite that puffed Carol's mouth out. 'Here, you hold it for me.'

And then she'd had another idea and was propelling Carol quickly back towards the car. 'Mum,' said Carol with difficulty, 'where's the fire?'

It was obvious, wasn't it? Rosie smiled down at her red-eyed daughter: 'In a flat in Birkenhead Street, of course.'

Chapter Nineteen

'But what are we gonna do when we get to this Birkenhead Street?' Carol wanted to know.

'I told you,' snapped Rosie, then remembered she was being nice to Carol. 'Didn't I say, love? We're going to do a survey.'

They'd stopped off at home for Rosie to type up a few spurious survey forms. She'd taken the opportunity to try and cajole Carol round to see Mo, her partner in the Wavertree Junior Animal Liberation Front. But Carol had refused, on the grounds that her friend would know intuitively if she'd had two, er, licks of additive-filled ice-cream. Now, though, in the car, Rosie could see her fidgety daughter already wishing she was at her friend's.

'But what kind of survey?'

'We're doing,' explained Rosie patiently, 'a survey of changing attitudes in modern Britain. With a side order of finding pseudo-kidnap victims. To take away.'

'Fine,' said Carol, enlightened.

'Her sister lives there, y'see,' said Rosie, taking a right turn a bit quickly. 'Ruth Greenfield's sister. At flat number nine. So we're gonna knock at every door except number nine till we find her. Ruth that is, not her sister.'

'Fine,' said Carol, even more enlightened. 'By the way, Mum. See that car in the mirror?'

'Don't be silly,' said Rosie, 'there's no room in a mirror for a car.'

Which she thought was quite witty. And resolutely didn't look in the mirror. Until Carol gave her a look.

'That blue one?' asked Rosie as she was parking the car.

'Yeh. Japanese or something. Whaddya reckon? Is it following us?'

'I reckon,' said Rosie, 'there isn't a blue car behind us at all.'

So Carol looked, and there wasn't. She was just trying,

Rosie knew, to add a little excitement to the outing. But after a night almost in the cells and a morning spent thinking she was a murderer, Rosie had had quite enough excitement to be going on with, thanks.

23 Birkenhead Street looked even more run-down by day than it had by night. There were slates off the roof and a lot of drawn curtains in the middle of the day and a broken window on the second floor. And next-door was a boarded-up shell: the plywood sheeting had been torn away from a ground-floor window to reveal the wreck of a house behind, open to the elements. Rosie shivered, remembering the Nazis, then clutched her official-looking clipboard to her, tried the door — it gave to the touch again — and they were inside.

And maybe it was a good idea after all to have Carol along. Since her purse had got nicked, Rosie didn't have anything that might look like an identity card. Her daughter became, therefore, her passport to credibility and information. 'Smile, whatever they say love,' she murmured to Carol. As the first door opened she launched into the standard spiel she'd thought up on the way there: 'Excuse me but I'm conducting a survey of changing attitudes in modern Britain. I'm not asking for your name or anything: just the ages and sexes of everybody who lives here,' pause for answer and write it down, 'and do you own any of the following? (a) a video; (b) a car; (c) shares in a publicly quoted company' — pause and ditto — 'oh and by the way, I couldn't get a reply next door, could you tell me how many people live there, roughly what age, just for me statistics, y'know . . .'

Well they only got one outright refusal — from a bald man with very bushy black eyebrows and L,O,V,E tattooed on both sets of knuckles — and some remarkable results. For a start, no one in the whole house owned a video, a car or shares in a publicly quoted company. This came as a devastating shock to Rosie, who'd read in the papers that at least every other person you might meet these days drove home from the video shop where they'd rented *The Battleship Potemkin Chain-Saw Massacre* paid for out of the profits from their shareholdings.

The second remarkable result was that, among the absent-but-described, and the old drunken couple who invited them in for a drink, and the three students who made bad jokes, and the girl with black spiky hair who had to ask her out-of-sight male partner for the answers all the time, and an old woman with steely grey hair and a posh voice who asked Rosie where her ID card was but seemed satisfied when Rosie made a big show of not finding it in her handbag, and the two Asian men and ... well, among all the residents of 23 Birkenhead Street there was no one resembling thin, fair, kidnapped-or-escapee Ruth Greenfield.

There was, however — coming down the stairs when Rosie and Carol had just made their last call — a woman bearing a remarkable resemblance to Ruth's Aunt Alice. 'Going to see Josephine?' the woman boomed in that challenging way that was only slightly belied by the glimmer in her eyes.

'Not exactly, er, this is Carol my daughter, Alice, er, I'm sorry I don't know your proper name.'

'Alice Corrigan. My adoptive parents' name. I never married.'

'We've been doing a survey,' said Carol with an innocent air.

'Oh really? What into?' asked Alice with that grave air of seriousness that children themselves had sometimes. And Rosie could see, suddenly, why Alice might get on with her neices.

Rosie could also see that it might be wise to change the subject. Immediately. 'Well y'see,' Carol was saying, 'we've been asking people ...'

'I'll see you back in the car in a minute, love,' said Rosie, giving Carol a little nudge in the back to help her on her way.

And then, neatly left alone with Alice Corrigan, Rosie suddenly didn't know what to say. So they mumbled to one another about Josephine's state of health and there being no sign of Ruth. It quickly became apparent that Alice didn't know Rosie was off the case. So ask her, Rosie, go on.

They were out in the street, Greenfield's sister struggling to put on her silk headscarf in the wind, and Rosie still hadn't found a way of putting it:

'Here, let me help you,' Rosie offered, tucking the scarf under the bristles on the woman's chin. 'I, er, hope you won't take this, er, amiss, but your brother's not been very, er, forthcoming with me.'

'Snap,' said Alice.

The scarf was firmly fixed now. Framed by it, the woman's face looked strangely girlish all of a sudden: a schoolchild's mock-severity trapped in middle-age. 'You don't happen to know,' Rosie burbled, 'if he had any woman-friends, do you? You get my meaning?' *Foreign-sounding women*, she couldn't quite bring herself to add.

'I get your meaning.' Suddenly Alice reminded Rosie of her Auntie Dora again: severe and disapproving. 'I think my brother is capable of most vices, Rosie. But I don't know of him indulging in that one. Why exactly . . . ?

And no, this still wasn't precisely what she meant. 'You, er,' said Rosie, seeing Carol signalling to her from the car, 'you called the police, eh?'

'How did you know?'

No that's what I do: answer a question with a question. 'But you didn't think I'd, er, done it? Taken Ruthie?'

'I really don't know why he didn't want to call them in. Ridiculous. And you? Whoever suggested that you might have . . . ?'

'Oh, nobody. My daughter'll be fretting. Be seeing you . . . .'

Carol was indeed mouthing 'Come on': impatient, no doubt, to be home and discussing vegetarianism. But Rosie quickly forgot to pretend to be hurrying, as she thought: Why hadn't Luke Greenfield wanted to call in the police? And where the hell was his daughter?

Chapter Twenty

It was when I was in the park with Carol, Rosie was explaining to her invisible partner, that it all became clear to me. *Familiar territory*, that was where the lost Carol was found. That was where Ruth, if she really had gone missing of her own accord, would be found. If not in Josephine's house, then with her only girlfriend.

Rosie sat in the car outside Susie Gould's house and wished she had a real visible partner to talk to. But Margie had been brusque on the phone. She was, she said, busy writing this report about a day spent following a man called Harry Allsopp for some private detective or other. And Martin was. . . .

Rosie had timed her visit to Martin's perfectly. His three small children were hurling cushions at one another across his living-room. His ex-wife Des had arrived on the doorstep to collect them just before Rosie herself had turned up. Then Des was shouting at the children to stop, and telling Martin it was always the same when the kids came to see him, it took her days to settle them down again, and looking Rosie up and down doubtfully.

'I just wanted to say I'm sorry, for Saturday and, and . . . .' — and for whatever did or didn't happen on Friday night, Rosie had given up trying to say. 'I'm sorry,' Rosie remembered shouting at Martin, 'it's a bad time.'

'I'm sorry, it's a bad time,' Martin had shouted to her above the cacophony of his ex-wife and children all yelling at him at once.

Family life, Rosie said ruefully to her invisible partner. Another good example. For here she'd been, about to tell Martin he could be her bit on the side once she'd got Jerry sorted out, and what had she seen? She'd seen Martin looking suspiciously like just another father who insisted on his rights and tried to wriggle out of his duties. Was he, then, just another man who cast off his children and then went looking for another family to make a mess of? Was love just a vast and complex game of pass the man-parcel? With each woman unwrapping hers and saying 'Ooh, just what I always wanted,' little knowing the quiet venom with which it had been so recently tied up and sent off into the unknown by the last woman along?

Rosie's invisible Watson didn't reply. Rosie tried to put all that out of her mind. She strode up the path to the little Council semi, trailing her fingers through the grass that hadn't been cut since the summer before last. At the standard Corporation green door she hesitated briefly; knocked. At first there was no sound from within. Then:

'Oh, it's you,' said Susie at the door, as if she'd been expecting her. 'Whaddya want?'

'About Ruth. . . .'

'You'd better come in.'

What? Was Ruth going to appear from the back kitchen? Or . . . ?

A fat sickly-looking woman sat in an armchair by the coal fire, cradling in her arms a young child that was too old for the dummy it had in its mouth. There was a black-ened kettle in the hearth, and a musty smell in the air. 'Is Ruth, er?' asked Rosie.

'She's not here. I don't know where she is. Siddown,' said Susie tiredly.

'But I thought,' said Rosie, nervous of the dirty shawl-like thing draped over the settee where she was being invited to sit, 'why did you . . .?'

'I just thought you'd come, that's all,' said Susie. Strangely her birthmark was less conspicuous here, where everything was in shadow. The air was dark with soot and dust. Susie stood, careless of which profile she was show-ing, waving her hand vaguely at the chair by the fire: 'This is my mum. This is my half-brother. This is my home. Siddown.'

Neither mother nor half-brother showed much sign of acknowledging their visitor. So at first Rosie didn't realise, when the prematurely greying woman started talking into the fire, that the words were meant for her: 'I know I said in the note she was sick, but in actual fact, well you can see for yourself, I mean I'm not well am I? So she had to look after me. Didn't you, love?'

'Mam,' said Susie in the tired voice that was in such contrast to her school-time animation, 'she's not from the welfare. They don't work on Sundays. This is Sunday. She's looking for a mate o'mine. Want a cup o'tea?'

'I'll come and help you,' said Rosie, following Susie and the kettle out to the kitchen.

'It's no good following me. It has to be boiled on the fire,' said Susie at the sink. 'We've had the gas cut off y'see. And the leckie kettle's bust.'

Susie went back with the filled kettle into the living-room, but Rosie stayed where she was. She stared out of the window at the waving grass in the back garden, and the view beyond of other houses; a block of flats; a few splinters of grey sky. She was wishing she hadn't come. She had the sinking feeling that if she searched this house, all she was going to find was poverty and dirt and neglect. Perhaps, she thought, she could nip out of the back door now . . .

. . . when Susie came back to join her. 'But,' Rosie said, gesturing around her, 'you said your mum gave you however much for sweets every day and. . . .'

'Gotta keep up appearances, haven't I? I mean, really I help down Ali's shop, don't I? He pays me. And I nick a bit. I'm sure he knows but he doesn't seem to mind.'

'And when you said,' Rosie went on, half of her not wanting to, 'when you said Ruth was soppy and you were tough — like with the Nazis — was that keeping up appearances?'

Susie didn't reply. She stared out of the window, her back to Rosie.

Rosie wished she'd brought some sweets with her and

125

said: 'Forget the tea. You sure you don't know where she is?'

'Timbuktu,' said Susie, still staring out of the window, blowing her nose. 'Where I should be. But you'd better have a look around. To make sure I'm not hiding her nowhere.'

'No, no,' Rosie was saying.

But Susie had already preceded her into the living-room. Rosie smiled nervously at the woman by the fire, and followed the girl upstairs. She glanced desultorily into unkempt bedrooms. The house was indeed full of poverty and dirt and neglect — except for the chaotic but clean bathroom that Susie insisted on showing her.

'See?' said the girl defiantly.

She seemed to be trying to show Rosie something more than just the absence of Ruth Greenfield; as if she had to demonstrate just why she had bluffed Rosie at school about the money and the courage and everything. 'I'm sorry,' Rosie found herself saying at the front door, thinking, I must stop apologising to people, 'but if you could just. . . .'

The sun had come out. Susie Gould blinked, her birth-mark suddenly vivid in the light. Her hand was on Rosie's arm: 'Me and Ruth, we're bezzy mates y'know. Two of a kind. I miss her something awful. I do. You will find her, won't you?'

And when the girl blinked again tears leaked from beneath her lashes. She flinched, though, when Rosie tried to return the squeeze of the arm. 'You don't think the Nazis . . . ?'

'Maybe,' Susie was suddenly animated again. 'If you got Davy on her own, y'know, the girl, hang on, I'll find her address. . . .'

So Ruth Greenfield, Rosie said to her invisible partner when they were back in the Mini together, isn't on any familiar territory that I know of. Where the hell's she got to, then? When I was fourteen, Rosie went on, my 'bezzy mate' was Angela McGovern and we had no secrets from

126

each other. When we ran away, we ran away together. I wouldn't have run away without telling her what I was doing. Ruth would have told Susie. She didn't. So she must have been really kidnapped, mustn't she?

But what about, the invisible partner suddenly piped up, what about the note Greenfield showed to the police?

'Forged,' said Rosie.

Why, then, did Ruth's father want to pretend she hadn't been kidnapped?

'The kidnappers called again and told him to deny everything,' said Rosie to Rosie with a sudden flash of insight. 'It's taken you a frigging long time to work that out,' she snapped at herself.

A face appeared at the Goulds' window. How long had she been sitting here, talking to herself? She turned the key in the ignition and, pausing only to thank the car for starting first time, drove off in search of kidnappers.

Chapter Twenty-One

The Davies family lived on the other side of the tracks from the Goulds: in a respectable semi on a respectable street in a respectable neighbourhood. Eleanor Davies, also known to Rosie as Eva Braun — but known at school, according to Susie, as Davy — wasn't at home. Rosie was greeted at the door by a man with a military moustache and an air of astonishment that anyone in her right mind would be wanting to see his stepdaughter.

So Rosie drove nervously back to the Council estate, to where Susie had correctly forecast that Rosie would find the girl: sitting on a wall by a run-down shopping parade, drinking beer out of cans with the lads. Except that, to Rosie's relief, of the boys from the bunker only Heinrich was there, and they were drinking OneCal not beer. She marched straight up to the pair of them, remembering how her ring of confidence had stood her in good stead in the derelict house. Without a tremor of nervousness — well, maybe half a tremor — 'Davy, they call you Davy, right?' she said to the girl. 'I want a word with you.'

'Knickers,' said the girl, whose leather-look skirt was short enough almost to show hers. 'That's a word, isn't it?'

Heinrich laughed.

'Don't wet yours,' said Rosie to the boy. She turned to smile coolly at Davy. 'It's about Ruth. It's important.'

The girl cocked her head to one side like a cat. Black make-up was scrawled across her eyelids: she opened her eyes very wide, to show off the blue in them.

And then, to Rosie's amazement, she went over to the Mini and got into the passenger seat.

So Rosie drove. To the accompaniment of — silence, for a while. When did you last see Ruth? Do you ever talk in a pretend German accent while demanding fifty thousand pounds in ransom? — Subtle questions like these provoked no response.

Rosie drove.

Finally, for no apparent reason, Davy began talking. 'Ruthie's really gone missing, has she? Flown the coop? Hopped out o' the nest?'

'Looks that way.'

'Good luck to her. You're a terrible driver, y'know.'

Rosie decided to ignore that, in view of her wider objectives, and contented herself with noting the girl's voice: an odd mixture of a girlish sing-song, with the occasional drawl that she probably thought was sophisticated. 'So, Ruth,' Rosie began.

'I like her, y'know. Ruthie. Mostly I don't like girls. They're just stupid. All giggles and "ooh d'you fancy him?" I like boys better. But I like Ruthie. She's kinda — like a flat — y'know, self-contained. All locked up and she won't let no one in. I like that. I kinda wish I was like that.'

'Instead of,' Rosie tried, she did try, but she just couldn't keep the censorious note out of her voice, 'instead of hanging out with the Gestapo.'

'Ve have vays,' said the girl with an unexpected contribution to Rosie's researches, 'of having a good time. But we didn't do nothing to Ruthie. Honest. The gang, they're all bluff y'know. Adolf and them. And d'you know what? D'you know why I like Ruthie? She stood up to 'em. Yeh.'

The girl stopped; stared out of the window. 'What happened to Ruthie,' said Rosie, 'she only did to herself. That's what you told me.'

'That's what I mean, yeh. Why I, like, admire her. 'Cause she didn't pay up once. Her protection. So she gets called to the house. The bommie where you came. And Adolf's got this thing, he lights a fag, he waves it in front of 'em, the ones as don't pay, as if he's gonna burn 'em with it, like. And they pay up. I've never seen him really do it. Burn anyone. It's all bluff.'

Rosie made herself drive steadily. There was nothing to

get upset about, was there? It was perfectly normal to get kids to part with their pocket-money by threatening to torture them, wasn't it? Happens every day. Anyway it's only bluff, so that makes it all right. 'I don't see,' said Rosie as evenly as she could manage, 'what this has to do with Ruthie.'

'So Adolf,' said Eva/Davy, warming to her everyday tale of torturing folk, 'he waves this fag in front of her. And Ruthie, she just snatches it out of his hand. And stubs it out on the palm of her hand. Without a flicker. And says, "Now what're you gonna do to me?" "Take zees girl avay," says Adolf. 'Cause he don't know what to do. So what else d'you wanna know?'

I want to know about love, joy, peace, prosperity — and whether that's the best German accent you can manage. None of which Rosie said. Instead she stopped the car at the shopping parade and didn't say anything at all; just reached across the girl wordlessly and opened the passenger door.

*

It has been a big mistake: taking Carol with her this morning. Now Bob and his friend Jason were demanding to 'help' her on her next assignment and brimming with questions. Like, 'What the hell's that noise?'

Rosie was playing the be puddled tap of the kidnapper on Bob's cassette-recorder. 'It's a foreign woman.'

'Sounds like she's underwater.'

Bob's friend Jason laughed.

Rosie turned to him sternly and said, 'It did fall in a puddle', to him and for some reason that didn't make him stop laughing.

He was right, though. Only occasional syllables poked through the gibberish that her moment of anger had made of the recording. She consulted Martin's transcript of the call and reached back into her memory of what the voice had sounded like. Her recall was perfect: perfectly

130

blank. How, then, could she be scientific about seeking out her suspects and tricking them into using the same phrases as the kidnapper had used?

'Can we come too?' Bob was demanding. At last she relented and agreed Bob and Jason could come and play on the sands while she 'made a business call'.

'Play on the sands? No way,' said Bob, wearing his don't-you-know-how-old-I-am? look.

Rosie had to face facts. There was only one moral way to get the boys off her back: bribe them. So she parted with three quid for bus fares and burgers, and, once they were safely out of the way, fixed up another appointment for later:

''Allo,' she said into the phone, 'I wish parler with Anne-Marie.'

It was almost too easy. Yes, the Patresis' *au pair* would love to talk about the Anglo-French Friendship Society. Yes, she could meet tonight after the children were in bed. Yes, she would be at the gate at eight-thirty. 'But how do you get my nombre?'

'Pard-on,' said Rosie hurriedly, 'I must partir now for Waterloo. At eight-thirty, then.'

*

It was almost too easy in Waterloo as well. The big-boned Norwegian woman arrived, flushed, at the door: 'Sorry, I vas in ze attic.'

Rosie, nervous of more intimate forms of contact, reached out her hand and shook the other's heartily. The palm was sticky; paint-bespattered; crimson red. 'Ha, I paint,' said Siggy. 'Ha ha. I am sorry, Jack is not home. You vish speak vith him?' — And the last sentence came so quickly, while Rosie was still staring at her reddened hand, that she almost forgot to notice it was very nearly one of the sentences the kidnapper had used.

'No, no, it's all right,' Rosie was babbling. She'd followed the woman through into the furniture-stacked back room and Siggy wasn't offering her a seat off the pile to sit down on. 'Y'see, I wasn't quite honest yesterday about Luke, about Lawrie, about Mr Greenfield. Y'see, the main thing is . . .'

'Eez about heez daughter,' said Siggy.

Rosie gulped. She gulped because she didn't see how Siggy could know what it was about.

She also gulped because Siggy had used another of the kidnapper's sentences.

'How did you, er . . .?'

'Zis man comes . . .'

'Police?'

'Zat man, he eez not police, no,' and didn't the woman realise she was supposed to wait to be tricked into using the kidnappers' phrases instead of scattering them spontaneously through her conversation? It was as if she was reading from Rosie's transcript. 'But thees man, he say he come from Meester Greenfield. He ask about you.'

'About me?'

'He speak Jack. I paint then. I paint now.'

Combined with the gesture of the head towards the door, Rosie had the faint feeling that Siggy's words constituted a signal to depart. But I've only just got here. What ever happened to, er, 'swinging'? But, 'But who was he? What did he look like?'

Now the big hands came into action. Oh-oh: an arm round Rosie's shoulders.

Then she rapidly realised it wasn't affection. She was very firmly and definitely being propelled out. 'Jack say not speak vith you if you come. Eez enough.'

Rosie was already tottering on the randomly spaced floorboards of the hall and thinking 'Eez enough' was the last straw, the phrase that confirmed Siggy knew precisely what the kidnappers had said and was deliberately taunting her. 'This Patresi feller, Greenfield's partner,' she said, resisting the hand, 'can you tell me anything about him?'

'Jack say not speak vith you,' said Siggy, in a different, sadder tone. Rosie looked up quickly. Now that her heart had stopped fluttering like a trapped butterfly, it struck her that Siggy was subdued today; avoiding Rosie's gaze; her face unanimated, the big lips hanging loose, not yesterday's flashing-toothed smile; her whole body drooping somehow. So what if she'd used the kidnapper's phrases? The accent was wrong, wasn't it? She couldn't speak English well enough to imitate another accent, could she?

'If Jack say not,' Rosie gulped, 'if he told you not to speak with me because of, because of what you said to me about me, er, how you feel about, er, women then, er, please don't worry about that.'

Even the woman's eyelids were huge; closing as they did now, like a lizard's, over leaking tears. Her hand was very clammy as it clasped Rosie's. 'Jack, he frightens me sometimes. And he does not understand. How a voman feels. Even if she loves her man. You? You understand?'

Lie, Rosie, lie. It's in a good cause.

'I understand,' said Rosie steadfastly, squeezing the woman's hand. 'Look, I've got to go now,' and I'll never come within a quarter of a mile of here again, 'but . . .'

'Mr Patresi,' said Siggy, behind her now. 'He is not good man. Zis you should know. But you vill come again?'

'I vill, will, sure,' said Rosie, fingers of both hands crossed, not looking back.

*

At eight thirty-five Rosie was staring out through a fresh shower of rain at the gates of BELLA VISTA and wondering if Anne-Marie was coming.

She was also worrying if the car would start again in the dampness.

At eight thirty-six she stuck her arm out of the window to try and wash some more of the redness off it. 'No of course it's not paint,' she'd told an inquisitive Bob, 'it's blood from where I had to staunch the bullet-wound, isn't it? That I got by leaping in front of the intended victim?'

At eight thirty-seven Rosie was worrying about Jerry. He'd turned up at home just when she'd got the baby-sitter safely tucked up on the sofa while the children watched TV and raided the fridge. Jerry had wanted to talk about the future. She'd replied that her future, immediately, consisted of loving him and leaving him.

At eight thirty-eight, as a girl in a bright yellow mac peered nervously towards her, Rosie wondered whether she'd been entirely truthful with Jerry — about the 'loving him' bit.

'D'you know any good pubs round here then?'

Anne-Marie was redistributing the raindrops from her hair over Rosie and the Mini's interior. 'The Atlantic Crrrossing?' she offered nervously. Rosie smiled and, yes, the car started, and 'But you are not Frrench?' said the girl.

'Non,' said Rosie in her cosmopolitan way.

'You are not, errr, kidnapperrr?'

The girl looked pale and alarmed. Rosie patted her on the elbow and smiled: 'I was just going to ask you the same question. Don't worry. All will be revealed.'

A few minutes later they were sitting in a squashed corner of a bar filled with posh voices. Pictures of ocean liners covered the walls. Rosie had looked around and decided to be subtle and tell the truth, so she said to the pale face: 'I've been here once before. To meet my first client. He wanted to be, like, one of this lot. All Porsches and Down with Arthur Scargill.' The girl was staring at her uncomprehendingly. Rosie had a flash of inspiration: 'Nouveaux riches,' she said, pleased with herself. 'Like your Mr Patresi.'

'But the Anglo-Frrrench Frrriendship Society . . .?'

'Just a front. Really I'm a private detective and I want to ask you a few questions. About your boss.'

Rosie was sticking to orange juice tonight but the girl seemed to have a taste for strong lager. On her second Pils and with a tenner from Rosie tucked in her handbag, Anne-Marie began to forget her fear of kidnapping and open up. Well, it sounded like the poor lamb didn't have anyone to talk to. There was a German au pair along the street but she was called Helga, which apparantly meant they didn't have much in common. Which was in turn why Anne-Marie had been so pleased to hear about the Anglo-French Friendship Society. It had been a how-you-say of sunlight. . . .

Rosie didn't know whether to feel guilty at raising the girl's hopes or pleased with herself for finding the right lie. The Patresis, near the bottom of Anne-Marie's second Pils, were not good people. Madame hated her children. Monsieur hated Madame but expected her to wait on him arm and leg.

'Hand and foot,' said Rosie, glad she'd resolved to stay sober. 'Fancy another?'

Perhaps these were terrible things to say, said Anne-Marie over her third glass. After all the man was blind. Perhaps that had helped to make him what he was: ruthless, with a liking for words that weren't in the dictionary. And when you guided him somewhere he was free with his hands.

Rosie plucked the picture from her handbag: 'This is Ruth Greenfield. Have you ever seen her?'

Maybe she'd left it too late; Anne-Marie seemed to be having trouble focusing. But no, it was just that she had to put her glasses on. She stared at the picture for a long time. 'No, I do not know this one. No. I do not know her,' said Anne-Marie decisively. 'But Grreenfield, yes? I know the man of this name. Her papa?' Rosie nodded encouragingly as the girl took another swig of her drink. 'He comes often. They talk money. Today he comes. They shout. They say bad names. Why do I come to such people?'

There was no more information to be had. 'Why do I come to such people?' became a refrain, as Anne-Marie wept mascara into her beer, and told Rosie all about her beautiful mother and wonderful father all those miles away in Aix-en-Provence, leaving Rosie to her own un-rosier dreams of family life.

It was almost midnight before Rosie finished the report on LBHA and allowed herself to think about Ruth Greenfield again.

Then she decided she wouldn't think about it again because it was all too complicated. So she got into bed and couldn't stop thinking about it. Had Ruth Greenfield been kidnapped or not? Did she have an older man-friend or not? If she had been kidnapped, who was the foreign woman on the phone? Feeling that the day's work must constitute some progress on the last count, if only she thought about it, Rosie got out her notebook and wrote down a list of suspected voices:

1. Siggy — Used kidnapper's phrases. But definitely a different accent from the kidnappers', and not sufficient command of English to imitate another accent?
2. Susie — Not in character.
3. Eva Braun/Davy — Oddly honest and the girlishness of her voice comes through in everything she says.
4. Josephine — Ruth not with her. Can't imagine her having enough brains or initiative to think it up alone.
5. Patresi — Rich? No need to kidnap? Hard to imagine Mrs disguising her Scottishness. Anne-Marie too French for phone voice.
6. Unknown woman-friend of Luke's — Dismissed by Alice.

Rosie stared at her sheet of paper and came to the unavoidable conclusion that the kidnapper on the phone very probably wasn't one of these women. Who else could it be, though?

The solution was obvious. Who else had the motive, the opportunity and the skill? She wrote down the name of the only woman who could possibly have done the deed:

7. Rosie Monaghan.

Okay, she'd give herself up to that nice honest policeman. In the morning; for now she needed some sleep. Everything was bound to be clearer to her in the morning.

Chapter Twenty-Two

Rosie hadn't expected everything to become clearer quite so *early* in the morning.

Convinced it was past breakfast-time and there was no time to lose, she'd already shaken herself awake and had half her clothes on when the lack of daylight, and the strange quietness of the house, street and the rest of the world, made her recheck her watch. Sorry, Bob's watch. 3:14, it blinked at her. Must have misread the 3 for an 8, thought Rosie, not swearing all that profanely under the circumstances. Must give Bob his watch back. Must get back to sleep.

No chance. Now she was wide awake.

She tried counting sheep but after three tatty-fleeced ewes had leapt over a stile in her imagination she found herself wondering why you were supposed to count sheep anyway which only helped to wake her up.

Still, there were advantages to the peace and quiet of the middle of the night. Everything *was* becoming clearer, for a start. Rosie decided to write letters to everybody to show them just *how* clear. Dear Jerry, she wrote on the front of her brain, if you still want to make the future, you could start by clearing my name and finding a kidnapper, and then maybe we could talk about babies. . . .

Rapidly erasing that on the grounds that she didn't want to talk about babies under any circumstances, she started again. Dear Martin, she began. I came round today, no yesterday, to apologise because I didn't want you to think I wasn't grateful to you for lying for me. But when I came and saw Des and her children which maybe you think of as your children, then I found myself thinking about pass the parcel, no, thinking about whether you were Graham to her, that is. . . .

It was strange how the clarity of everything seemed to find it hard to turn itself into words.

Dear Paddy. Have I been neglecting you? Dear Bob and Carol. Have I been neglecting you? Dear Mike. Why have you been neglecting me?

Simplicity was better. But probably not worth sending. Getting back to sleep would be even better still.

Rosie tried that murder story which had made her laugh at Detective Inspector Norfolk's name, but the book didn't grip her. It was all too neat and orderly somehow. She wanted to read about lives as messy as her own.

Finally she got up and really wrote, on real paper with real ink, the letter she'd wanted to write all along:

Dear Luke Greenfield

I do not know why you have chosen to lie to the police about me and the first call the kidnappers made to you on Friday, but I would like to remind you that I was employed by you to look for your daughter Ruth and you now owe me the sum of £300, being the fee for my services and the services of my associate Mr Brown for two working days. There will also be a sum in respect of expenses, details of which will be furnished to you in due course.

Rosie stopped for a moment and pondered on furnishing in due course in respect of. Where did this strange language of police statements and Jerry's bureaucratic reports and love letters come from? Some alien planet? Was Scottie there? If so, why would he never beam her up? — Oh, just spell it out for him, Rosie, she resolved as she took up her pen again:

I have considered the suspects for your daughter's kidnapping and have to agree that I am the most likely of any of them. The only problem is: I didn't do it. I don't know who did, though I have my suspicions.

Some of these suspicions I have not told the police about, out of some maybe mistaken principle.

Rosie stopped and had a cup of tea because the next words that came to her were *This may be a dirty word to you, 'principle'* and she knew that was going too far on this spell-ing-it-out lark. She continued:

I mean, that there are some things a detective should tell her client not the police. And some things a detec-tive won't even tell her client because they can't be bought for money.
 If you would like to discuss any of the above, please tell me in the letter you will no doubt be sending me along with your cheque.
 Yours sincerely

It was 5.12 when Rosie crept out of the house and into the Mini. Mercifully the car started first time. She prayed the house wouldn't burn down in her absence, and, reminding herself that she'd given up praying, drove off in the marvellously blurry dawn light to the Greenfield's house. What are you doing out at this time in the morn-ing, madam? enquired the shadowy figure whom Carol said was following her (the road clear ahead and behind, just the newsagent unloading papers at the street-corner shop and Rosie doubted he doubled as a snooper in his spare time). Me? Rosie replied, flashing her most charm-ing smile at the copper or competing detective or alien robot or whatever Carol thought he was: me, I just thought, isn't 5:18 (as it now was) a wonderful time to post a letter?

139

Chapter Twenty-Three

Rosie had given up the case of Ruth Greenfield. Her client didn't want her on the case; her inner voice didn't want her on the case. So she was leaving the detecting business to DI Norfolk and going back to normal life.

Indeed she could tell life was getting back to normal because Paddy rang her just as she was going out of the door. And when she tried to put him off he said, 'It's important, Sis.'

'It always is, Paddy, look, I've got to . . .'

'No,' he insisted with his usual urgency, 'I want you to meet this feller.'

So she agreed to see him in The Crooked Man for lunch. Because that was what normal life meant. Listening to Paddy's latest complaints about the cruel blows of fate. Half-tuning in to Margie's disgruntlement while they drove to the repossession job she'd forgotten about till Margie had called to remind her:

'I dunno who's running this detective business, you or me. I mean, Rosie, I'm only supposed to be helping you out, it's your frigging business . . .'

'My contribution to the Enterprise Culture,' said Rosie brightly.

'. . . and,' Margie went on, disregarding that, 'and my love-life's in ruins what with you inconveniently getting yourself locked up in jail . . .'

'I'll try not to let it happen again,' said Rosie meekly.

'. . . and,' disregarding that too, 'there's my Alan up before the beak on Wednesday for receiving stolen goods, to wit and viz two cassette tapes worth £1.99, well he'd stolen the ghetto blaster the tapes were in but they couldn't prove that . . .'

'Here we are,' said Rosie.

Here they were: back to normal.

Here they were, too, at the address. Thomas Cullinan, basement flat, St Jude's Street. He was already outside, as if ready to meet them. 'Come on in,' he said cheerily.

They picked their way gingerly down the rickety metal steps to where he sat in his basement living room: two armchairs, a pot of tea and two mugs on a little table beside him, telly stacked on the video on top of a hard chair six feet away from him. Normal life. What, after all, could be more normal than that?

The only trouble was that his furniture, his 'room' was set up in the yard outside his flat. Last night's rain dripped from the gutter far overhead on to the tea-pot. The carpet was moss-green paving stones. 'Nice day for it,' he said. 'Cup of tea?'

'Pass,' said Rosie.

'We've come for the telly and the video,' said Margie. 'On behalf of . . .'

'Take 'em away,' said Thomas Cullinan with an expansive gesture. 'They don't work anyway.'

This problem could be related, Rosie idly speculated as she examined the television, to the fact that the set was an empty shell. From it the man had removed the tube, the circuit boards and anything else that might have remotely resembled the inner workings of the greatest form of communication known to modern Man or Person. Rosie lifted the set to show Margie its disembowelled state. 'Okay, wise guy,' said Margie, 'where's the rest of it?'

'Inside,' he said smiling.

'There is nothing,' Margie said through teeth so clenched she was almost inaudible — well, she'd trapped her heel in a metal grating he probably regarded as a rug — 'there is nothing inside the damn thing as you perfectly well know . . . .'

'Inside the flat,' he pronounced carefully, as if talking to an imbecile. 'D'you want it?'

Margie's look told him it was faintly possible that that

was what she wanted. So he went inside and Rosie went over and only slightly broke the heel of Margie's shoe in extracting her from her predicament. 'Thanks, Rosie,' snarled her friend, examining her shoe with a grateful frown.

'So this is normal life,' said Rosie to no one in particular.

Margie said nothing. The sun shone. Two young black men looked down incuriously at them from street-level as they passed.

Finally Thomas Cullinan emerged from his flat hauling a black rubbish bag behind him. 'It's all in here,' he said, handing Rosie the bag with a clank of metal against metal. 'I just wanted to see how it worked.'

*

Yes, and that was how Rosie felt about people and her cases: she just wanted to find out how they worked. And, like Thomas Cullinan, she sometimes took them apart and couldn't put them back together again.

But she wasn't going to worry about that kind of thing today. If she'd taken anyone to bits lately they'd just have to carry on being fragments. For today was going to be the sort of routine day when, for instance, she'd deliver the LBHA report to the prematurely balding auditor and he'd say, 'Loadsa bread for Harry Allsopp' to her as if he'd just thought of it.

Yes, he did say that. Rosie refused to laugh; they weren't paying for her time any more. 'It wasn't that funny the first time, Kojak,' she said, with a lilt to her voice, on her way out.

Then Margie dropped her off in town because Rosie fancied a bit of window-shopping and maybe a spot of lunch with Mike. And yes, this was normality too: landing herself in town without the car then discovering Mike was off sick so if she wanted to see him she'd have to get to his flat somehow.

Rosie had decided cabs were off-limits unless she was on expenses so she only had to wait half an hour for the two buses to arrive in tandem. Not that she minded really. It must be lonely being a bus driver. You could understand them wanting a bit of company. Like her and private detection really: she needed Margie or Martin at her side, whingeing at her, before she could enjoy it properly.

Mike's flat was on the first floor of a refurbished block of flats, protected by trees from the prying eyes of passersby who couldn't afford the deposit, overlooking, at the back, a scrubby patch of parkland. Desirable residences. But when Mike answered the door he didn't look very desirable. He was pale and hollow-cheeked and there was a more than momentary delay before the smile and the 'Rosie, nice to see you, come in.'

She was introduced to the American friend: a handsome curly-haired man lolling in a wicker chair, who flashed her a quick hostile look while Mike said his name was Petey. Rosie sat demurely on the uncomfortable Habitat canvas chair and refused tea, remembering the bizarre flavours she'd forced herself to gulp down on previous visits. Mike was making himself busy pretending to be watering the forest of plants that would prevent anyone using the window as an emergency exit. He glanced up at her nervously. 'I'm sorry about not getting you out of the nick. The police station,' he explained to Petey, even though the curly-haired man was buried in the *Herald Tribune* and didn't seem to be listening. Mike put down the watering can and squatted on a bean bag beside Rosie. 'Not that I'm actually sick, of course. Whatever they told you at the office. I'm considering my future.'

'As long as you're not planning to make it,' said Rosie. 'The future. Eh, you wanna get some decent furniture in here.'

'I've been *asked* to consider my future. By Langton. Whether I might not be — what was his phrase? — more at home in my own practice.'

'Eh, you've never uncovered major corruption on a scale previously unrecognised,' Rosie asked eagerly, 'in which your principles conflict with your loyalty to your fellows?'

Petey snorted and Mike gave him a look: she's often like this, said his eyes, it's probably biochemical. 'D'you know,' said Mike sadly, 'what I do when I see corruption? I fearlessly look the other way. No,' and now he seemed to be looking to the American for sympathy — if so he wasn't getting any — 'it's because I was on the telly. Representing, ah, "homosexuals". As my senior partner would say. It's not that he's prejudiced, you understand. Very happy to have a, er, homosexual on the team. But setting up on my own might well be, as he put it, the right career move at this juncture. If I'm planning to become a public spokesman for, er, homosexuals. And perhaps I'd like to take some sick leave while I think about it.'

'I'm sorry, Mike,' said Rosie, taking his hand and wondering whether she fancied him just because she knew it was safe. 'Still, I can recommend the Enterprise Culture. I mean, look at all it's done for me.'

Rosie got up to go. She felt embarrassed that she'd been going to tear him off a strip for leaving her to the tender mercies of the police force when she should have been feeling sorry for him all the time. She pretended to herself that she wasn't leaving because the quiet presence of the American was nagging at her, and felt a great burden lighten as soon as she was out in the hall.

Mike had folowed her out. 'You wanted to know about Greenfield,' he was saying. No, I've given that up, thanks all the same. 'Greenfield,' Mike went on, 'quite apart from being permanently on the edge of bankruptcy, is the sort of man who makes up the truth as he goes along. If you know what I mean.'

I don't need to know this any more, Rosie was unable to say because Mike was in full flow:

'Him and Patresi have got a few dummy companies

together. But Patresi's the real thing. Chairman of the local Conservatives. Owns a couple of homes for geriatrics. Developing a theme park in Cheshire based on an old Roman salt-mine. Forward-thinking, y'know.'

'Not in the Mafia, I s'pose?'

'Only the Tory version,' said Mike. 'Look . . .'

'Nor short of fifty grand?'

'Not that I know of. Look . . .'

'Anyway, I'm off that case,' said Rosie at last. 'Enjoy your sick leave, eh. Say tara to the chatty one for me.'

＊

It was just a short stroll across the park and up Park Road to The Crooked Man. Or so Rosie half-remembered. Wrongly. She hadn't walked so far in years. She had to stop for a fag halfway, to counteract the healthiness of it.

Still, it gave her time to think. About normal life. And Paddy. He'd been ringing her up for days, but this was the first time she'd had the space in her brain to take in what he'd been saying to her in all these phone calls. His partner had walked out on him. Something like that. And his wife Debbie had had the baby but it had driven her — mad? Was that what he'd said? Why, then, hadn't his big sister dropped everything to help him?

Never mind. She'd make up for it now. She leant briefly against the pub doorway to get her breath back then went inside. Paddy was sat hunched over the bar again. She went straight over, and put her arms around him. 'Paddy, I'm sorry,' she said, ruffling his hair like she used to do when they were little.

'What're you doing, Sis?' asked Paddy, for some reason pushing her away.

Clearly he was so unused to kindness from her — because she had let herself become so used to ignoring him — that it would take a while to recover lost ground. She clasped his wrist and kissed him on the cheek. 'I just want you to know, I'm always there if you need me.'

'Great. Thanks,' said Paddy, effusively turning away from her. 'This is Albert, the seller I wanted you to meet.'

'No, but,' said Rosie in hushed confidential tones, still clutching his wrist, 'I'm only just taking it in. What you've been trying to tell me. About your partner, and Debbie, and . . .'

Paddy prised her fingers off his wrist and signalled to the barman. 'Not here,' he whispered fiercely. 'Not in front of me mates. Vodka for the, er, lady!' he called to the barman, with a last warning look for his sister in case she hadn't got the message.

The, er, lady had got the message. She'd have to choose a better time and place. Paddy was performing the introductions again and for the first time she took in the little man at the barstool beside her brother. His little legs hung far from the ground; his small hand was very damp as he shook hands with Rosie; and he was a warty man. The warts seemed disproportionately large for the rest of him: the sort of warts that belonged on a full-grown man. If they belonged anywhere, that is. One dangled from his left eyelid; a patch of them scattered his forehead, like a relief map of the Lake District; as he tugged nervously at the wart on his nose she noticed one in the V of his hand between thumb and forefinger. 'I've tried everything for 'em,' said Albert. 'Even witchcraft.'

'I didn't mean . . . ,' said Rosie, lying.

'Albert runs the action group. The Greenfield Unsatisfied Lenders Action Group.'

'Of course, we're not really lenders,' said Albert whose warts Rosie was resolutely avoiding looking at. 'We're investors. But it wouldn't have spelt GULAG then, would it? I mean, GUIAG, it's not the same, is it?'

Rosie wanted to resume normal life. So how come, as soon as she'd resolved that, how come everybody wanted to help her crack the case all of a sudden?

'. . . so I bumped into Albert yesterday and he was saying, like, there's loads of these dissatisfied investors. I thought you'd be interested,' Paddy was saying. It was the end of a long speech about his business difficulties that she'd missed:

'I'm leaving that to Norfolk,' she replied. 'An honest man.' Adding, by way of explanation: 'Near Suffolk.'

Paddy stared at her for a moment.

'I'm perfectly all right,' said Rosie unconvincingly.

Paddy turned to the warted, no she wasn't going to get a thing about that, turned to the small man beside him: 'Go on,' he said, 'tell her all about it.'

Listen, Rosie, listen.

She knocked back her vodka and listened.

So there were dozens, according to Albert, literally dozens of ex-dockers like him who'd accepted their redundancy . . .

'Sold their fuckin' jobs for a mess o' pottage,' said the socialist bit of her brother quietly in her ear.

. . . and had invested the proceeds with Lawrie Greenfield: a man they'd known for years. 'You'd trust him with your wife, you would,' said Albert, and Rosie bit back the urge to mention that she hadn't got one of them to entrust to anyone. So a year and half after they'd all been made redundant, they got the news that this firm CP Investments had gone down the tubes. Even so, at first they'd felt sorry for old Lawrie. The man was weeping, distraught that he'd let all his old mates down by advising them wrongly. But then he'd picked himself up and promised that nobody would lose — in the long run. For if they put some of the rest of their money into M-Int he'd see they were all paid back in five years. Promised. 'On his mother's grave, like.'

'He never knew his mother.' said Rosie, feeling faintly Victorian as she said it, especially when she was talking to someone called . . .

. . . Albert, who said 'Quite,' warming to his theme and to the seemingly ever-full pint of bitter Paddy kept him supplied with. The proof of the pudding, Albert said, licking his chops, was still to be eaten. But lately rumours had started circulating. Rumours that people weren't getting their yearly income, even from the respectable part of their investments that weren't in M-Int, unless they pressed for it. Rumours that Lawrie — 'I know he calls himself Luke these days but I can't get used to it, I mean, it just reminds me of Matthew, Mark, Luke and John, hold my horse till I get on, know what I mean?' — that Lawrie was himself tied up with this CP Investments and M-Int in some way. Rumours that he was living above his means and not too worried about making his ends meet.

'And did y'ever,' asked Rosie, whose vodka seemed to be getting replenished as often as Albert's beer, 'did y'ever hear of a feller called Patresi?'

'Pat who?'

When he blinked and looked at her the wart over his eye — no, Rosie, you've not been noticing them for ages, don't start now. The wart does not look like it's about to plop into his pupil, no. Speak, woman: 'Scotsman. Patresi.'

'Didn't he used to play right back for Celtic?' Paddy asked brightly.

'Never heard of him,' said Albert. 'So what we're planning to do, is. . . .'

*

They weren't planning to do anything really. That was probably why they were called an Action Group, Rosie speculated later, back at home. It was always a good idea to give yourself an impressive-sounding name; it gave you an excuse for not trying too hard to live up to it. Like 'private detective': you could get away with detecting sod-all if you had that title on a bit of card with your name on. Like 'Action Group': you could have lots of group meet-ings and make believe you were acting on something.

Like, she was beginning to think, 'investment consult-ant': maybe you could dodge actually having to invest in anything much with that for a job description.

Nevertheless, she wasn't really going to think about all

that, was she? She was going to think about . . .

. . . the important things in life? Yes. For a start, she was going to make the kids a decent tea for once. Vegetable curry and chips cooked in vegetable oil and maybe a side order of vegetables followed by fruit salad and she could imagine their happy smiling faces now.

Mercifully, at that moment, the phone began to ring.

Rosie often thought that her most beautiful moments were like that — like the Action Group's, maybe — planning things, getting them straight in her mind, imagining the happy consequences of what she was planning to do.

It was always a relief to be interrupted just before she actually had to start doing them, though.

Almost always a relief. 'Luke Greenfield, here,' said the phone.

'You got my letter then?'

'Your letter? Oh, your letter, um, look, I've got to see you.'

'You can easily,' said Rosie, aloof, thumbing casually through the recipe book, 'send my cheque through the post.'

'No,' said the urgent voice at the other end, 'really, I've got to see you. Tonight.'

'To hand me over to the bizzies, d'you mean?'

'No look, please,' and he really did sound upset but Rosie didn't trust that, look what had happened when he'd gone really pale before. 'I'll explain all that. I will. Not here, though. At the Khyber Pass Restaurant, d'you know it? Seven thirty. And,' as she was about to demur, 'money's no object.'

As if the mere idea of money would tempt Rosie away from the kitchen stove. 'What time were you thinking of?' she asked inadvertently. And then, reminding herself not to be so bloody mercenary (why not, Rosie, why not?): 'Eh, no, but how come it's so bloody urgent all of a sudden?'

'The kidnappers have been on again. Twice. And, 'and yes, that really was a sob in his voice before he added: 'And they'll only deal with you.'

Chapter Twenty-Four

Rosie paid off the cab outside the Khyber Pass and took a few deep breaths and remembered why, bored with normal life, she'd taken up private detection. Because it made this thing in the left side of her chest bounce up and down a lot. With fear.

What person in their right mind would deliberately seek out fear?

Rosie looked in the shop window next to the restaurant entrance and couldn't see anyone in their right mind reflected there.

So she took another few deep breaths and went up the Khyber Pass — well, up the stairs lined with red velvet curtains towards the smell of curry and lager — and of course, Greenfield wasn't there. Which meant there was plenty of time to sit in a comfy chair by the bar and prepare herself by thinking about kidnappers and spiders and family life.

So Rosie didn't think about them at all. She thought about the two strange girls she'd found round at Mo's house when she'd gone to tell Carol her tea was getting cold. They were draped in sheets and wore tribal markings on their faces. 'We were just, er,' said one of them in a close approximation to Carol's voice.

This was what happened as soon as you abandoned normal life again. Your own daughter turned into a stranger. And, later, your friend Martin would turn up to apologise about something-or-other that you didn't have time to remember and insist on baby-sitting for you.

'Where's the babies, then?' said Bob in Rosie's memory.

'Ah there you are,' said Greenfield, more recently than

that. Now, in fact. Ah there you are. As if she was the late one. Him and his smart suit and his ingratiating smile. But no, Rosie, don't get off on the wrong foot with him tonight, call him Luke and don't ask him for ...

'I'll have a cut-the-crap and tonic please,' she said with a fierce little smile. 'Y'know, the stuff the Russians make. Large.'

That nicely established the tone of the small-talk over the menus. And there was something about him that reminded her of the day he'd driven her to Ruth's school: yes, that he'd farted, silent but deadly. So she said she'd have a Chicken Madras and he felt he should warn her, that was a hot one. 'Some like it hot,' said Rosie, feeling at her most witty and original tonight. He's trying to be nice and charming with you Rosie. He can't help his bodily functions after all. So ease back on the throttle, all right?

Finally a dark and obsequious waiter came to take their order. 'No tomato, under-stand, no tom-ma-to?' Luke Greenfield was soon enunciating for the benefit of the hard-of-hearing. And the waiter was bowing and smiling, and Rosie wanted to ask him if he wouldn't prefer to be nice and rude and unfriendly like they were in Chinese restaurants. Maybe, though, she tried to comfort herself, maybe when they're talking in Hindi or Urdu they're secretly saying, See that prat over there with the smart suit, isn't he a divvy?

Then another waiter in a long maroon jacket was leading them to a cubicle. In the centre of the table a candle burned inside glass. A bunch of plastic flowers glowed beside it. Rosie settled herself down and reached for a spicy poppadom. But Luke was more interested in business than in eating: 'They called at noon, y'see. Like they said they would.'

'And vas it me again? Disguisink mein voice?'

This is not funny, said his narrowing eyes. My dear, his sneer added. 'It *was* the foreign woman again. Whoever she is.'

Rosie dipped a poppadum in some mango chutney

and waved it at him: 'So you still think it was me, eh?'

He smiled confidently: 'Not on the phone, no. When the call was made you were walking across Princes Park, weren't you?' Fifteen-love, his look said as she dropped her poppadom in her vodka glass in surprise: 'The police had put a tail on you. As you may have realised.'

Oh of course, indeed, I mean I never poured scorn on anyone resembling my daughter who might have suggested that to me. 'But they called twice today, you said. The kidnappers. Why twice?'

He leant across the table and lowered his voice. 'The police don't know about the second call. And I don't intend to tell 'em. So if they get to hear about it, I'll know who from, okay?'

Should she pick the poppadom out of her glass? Or just take another piece and pretend it hadn't happened? Dithering, she fell back on conversation: 'I've had enough of phone calls that never happened, thanks,' wait for it, 'Lawrie.'

'Luke,' said Luke, 'if you don't mind.'

'Sorry — Luke,' said Rosie, fishing the soggy poppadom out of her vodka. Now what could she do with it, though? Make a nice still life of it in the ashtray next to her stubbed-out fag? No, resolutely she dropped it in her mouth and discovered she'd invented a new and untempting delicacy. She swallowed it quickly and took a bite out of the starter that had arrived in the meantime. 'Y'see,' she said through her sheek kebab, 'the trouble is, I get this weird sort of anger building up in me. When I'm having dinner with somebody whose lies could land me in jail for a few years. I know I should get over it, but. . . . '

He wasn't touching his prawn cocktail. Just downing his large Scotch and ordering another. 'Lager,' said Rosie quickly. 'Y'see,' she went on, 'I've got this theory.'

Luke — yes, not Lawrie, Luke — didn't seem to be listening. He'd taken a little jeweller's box from his pocket. Oh, Luke, you shouldn't have. Anyway, don't distract me:

'This theory,' she went on, 'is to do with CP Investments and Money International. Or M-Int, as it's known'
— which got a flicker of a reaction, as he fingered whatever was in the jeweller's box — 'to all those old mates o'
yours who've invested in it on your say-so. Now these two
companies seem to be having a bit of difficulty paying
what they owe. And they seem to have some sort of
connection with you. And you seem to be living pretty
well. But kinda worried — on the edge of bankruptcy,
some say. Falling out with your partner Patresi, some say.
So this theory says that maybe your Ruthie's left you of
her own accord, or maybe you've even bumped her off' —
a sharp look, don't stop now Rosie — 'whatever, 'cause
the important thing is, she hasn't really been kidnapped.
According to this theory. But as long as she stays wherever
she is for a day or two more, you're quids in. Your foreign
woman that's probably your bit on the side, she keeps
making with the threats. You draw the money out. You
pay up. Ruthie comes back or she doesn't. You go bust
and everybody's sorry for you: Ah, poor old, er, Lukie, he
did it for his daughter. You go bust and you've salted
away fifty grand ready for when you go bust. Of course,
there was a bit of bother . . .'

'Look . . .'

'Just let me say my piece,' said Rosie, a piece of kebab
still on her fork, waiting for a break in the conversation.
'You had a problem on Saturday. When your sister Alice
barged in demanding to know why you hadn't called the
police in. Calling them herself. But you're quick on your
feet, you. Even turned that to your advantage. Got the
finger of suspicion pointing at Muggins here. Police on my
tail. You in the clear again, ready to pay yourself some
money. So, er, how's that for a theory, eh?'

'Not bad,' he said, grim-faced. 'Plausible, even.
Except. . . .'

A hell of a speech anyway, thought Rosie, downing a
big gulp of lager and finally biting into her kebab. He was
still not eating; just fiddling with that damned box. Event-

ually he took a tatty note from the thing and passed it to her. His tone was serious: 'The second time they called me today was at the office. This avvy. And while they were phoning up, this got delivered there.'

She scanned the note: block capitals, lined paper that can be bought at any stationers (thank you Sherlock):

We know the police are at your house. They'd better not see this. Tell Rosie to be ready for a call at 9 am tomorrow. And remember: no police. Just Rosie. And the £50.000.

Rosie shrugged. It was curiously intimate of the kidnappers: 'Just Rosie'. She had a flicker of worry that this was somebody who knew her well. Martin? Margie? Paddy who was desperate for money? — No, no, no, stick to your theory Rosie, don't let him sow seeds of doubt with his glum look and his even glummer voice:

'And that's not all they sent. Y'see, I'd taken the bizzies' advice and stalled them, first time around. Couldn't get the money for days, that sort o'thing. So with the note they sent this.'

He passed the jeweller's box to her. Inside it, wrapped in cotton wool, was a plain silver ring. The ring nestled on top of a blob of pink and blotchy red: a thin circular blob of softness with, on closer inspection, a strange whorled pattern on top of it that reminded Rosie of something. 'There's plenty more where that came from, they said to me. On the phone. I heard her screaming.' His eyes were misty and afraid. 'I gave her that ring.'

'But what is it?'

'Can't you see?' said Luke Greenfield, tears running down his red cheeks. 'It's her fucking fingertip!'

Rosie stared at the blob in the box. Then she stared at the sheek kebab on her plate which, now she came to look at it, was faintly, er, finger-shaped. And, now she came to think of it, she was feeling faintly, er, faint. With great aplomb, she put down her napkin, said 'Excuse me,' in her poshest voice, and groped through the fog to the Ladies.

*

'You think I'd do a thing like that?' asked Rosie.

'Do I?'

'You were watching me. To see how I'd react.'

'Was I?'

'Yes you bloody were.'

They'd both regained a kind of composure now. Rosie felt pale and hot all at the same time somehow. She'd pushed away her food without touching it. But Greenfield — no first names now, matey, not after the wonderful surprise in the jeweller's box — Greenfield was tucking into his tandoori as if nothing untoward had happened.

'Passed the test then, did I?'

'What test?'

'Don't mess me about,' said Rosie, wondering why she hadn't walked out by now.

'Let's eat.'

'Sod you,' said Rosie, cool and rational to the last.

She would have got up to go if a big hand hadn't suddenly appeared from nowhere and gripped her wrist. Somewhat to her surprise, when she looked down she found it was Greenfield's hand. 'The kidnappers want you,' he said gruffly.

Well the feeling's not mutual, Rosie didn't say, responding in her usual foolhardily brave way to the threat of physical violence: she sat down and smiled. She added a strong moral argument: 'It'll cost.'

He pushed his food away. 'I'm going to tell you,' he said, wiping his mouth, 'a little story. Something that I'll deny if you ever claim I said it. Right?'

Wrong, actually. Dishonest, unprincipled, immoral. 'Go ahead.'

'We had a row. Me and Ruthie. About — well it seemed like nothing at the time. Y'know, those rows y'have with kids that seem to be about one thing but really they're about them growin' up. . . . '

No I never have them, do I, Carol? Do I, Bob?

' . . . and the next day, I get home from work and she's gone. And her suitcase. And her bike. And the note's there. That I never showed you. And Barbara doesn't know what fu, what day it is, does she? So I can't get any sense out of her. So the idea starts to come to me that night, with you and Langton and everybody there. Your theory. Pay a ransom to meself. Go bust. Like you said. It's Patresi's line actually: Every businessman worth his salt goes broke at least twice.'

The waiter came to take the food away. It was only when he had Rosie's Chicken Madras and chapatis in his hand and was asking if there was something wrong that she realised how hungry she was. 'Eh, I'm sorry, could you warm it up for us? And d'you know what else I fancy — whaddya call it, bhindi stuff?'

'Lady's fingers,' said the waiter, smiling as he backed away.

Lady's fingers, I knew it had a nice attractive-sounding name to it, Rosie recalled. 'No, perhaps I won't, er,' her voice began and trailed off; the waiter had gone. She reached into her handbag for another cigarette. 'Go on,' she said, 'go on, every businessman worth his salt. . . .'

'So, the next day, I invents this phone call. While the girls are out of the office. Well, later I thanks God I only told you and, er, only told you . . .'

'And Langton?'

' . . . 'cause I still hadn't quite made up me mind. I mean, y'may not believe this. . . .'

Meaning, I won't.

' . . . but I really don't want to let me old mates down. I don't. But me and, okay, Patresi, we were putting it into currency. Dollars. To make big money. For me old mates. Really,' to her sceptical look. 'Okay, plus a little for me on the side. 'Cause the dollar was rising like the clappers. And then — then it started falling. And then . . .'

'Then you started thinking, how can I cheat my old mates out of their redundancy?'

'You really don't understand, do you?' He'd been fiddling with a big cigar for several minutes; now he bit off the end and lit it, blowing out a great gust of smoke with something like relief. 'I care. I do. But I'm in it up to here with Patresi. And he doesn't give a, he doesn't, the bastard simply doesn't care.'

Rosie's curry returned at last. She glanced nervously at the bowl of bhindi, the perfectly formed little shoots of, er, forget them Rosie. Force some food down yourself, after all he's paying, shame to waste it. Go on, tuck in and keep him to the point: 'So you thanked God you'd only told me and, er, because ... ?'

He took another draw on his cigar and looked at her hard. 'Because on Saturday morning I really did get a call. The call you heard. From the foreign woman. I nearly died. Honest, she's nothing to do with me, I swear to God. I swear it.'

And Rosie remembered Martin saying how genuinely shocked, how unusually white this white man had become when that call came through, and she thought, at least this bit of the story's credible but how much of the rest can I believe? He wasn't saying anything, just looking at her. 'Do I have to swear an' all? I had nothing to do with that call either.'

'Well, my problem is,' and somehow another double scotch had arrived at his side of the table and he was swigging it down almost in one and Rosie was finding it hard to swallow both his story and her food, 'my problem is, Rosie, I don't trust you. But I'm landed with you. Aren't I? After the — after the fingertip. I don't want my Ruthie hurt. I want my Ruthie back. And okay, I never wanted the coppers in on this. You never know what they might stir up. So it looks like I'll have to deal with you.'

Rosie had vague memories of more gracious proposals of work. So why should she reply graciously? 'A grand,' she said tersely.

'Done.'

'They won't call you at home. Not now they know the line's on intercept. It'll be either at your office or . . .'

'Or where?'

'I'll call y'in the morning.'

Suddenly Rosie was getting up to go and it was his turn to be saying 'No, but . . .' But she'd seen a shambling figure approach their table from the bar.

'I'll call you. Not a word to him,' said Rosie quietly. Then, turning to the approaching man: 'It's an honest cop if ever I saw one. What a coincidence. I was just leaving.'

'What a shame,' said Inspector Norfolk, wearing a trench-coat and his nearest approximation to a smile. 'Thought I might join the party.'

'Didn't have you down for a politician,' said Rosie. 'Actually this is a spiders' convention. Spun any good webs lately?'

The men were staring at her blankly. She had to sympathise; in their place she'd be doing the same. What she needed was a triumphant exit-line. She thought hard for a moment. 'Tara now,' she said, and exited triumphantly.

Chapter Twenty-Five

Maybe it was all an elaborate trap.

When she woke at six and remembered yesterday should have been washing day and tried to decide whether to tiptoe downstairs with the laundry basket, Rosie couldn't remember her dreams. But she thought she should have been dreaming of being pursued down the streets and alleys of Wavertree and the suburban avenues and back gardens of Luke Greenfield's suburb, never sure, whenever she met a friend — Margie? Jerry? Paddy? Inspector Norfolk? Martin? — whether they mightn't turn any moment into a hideous monster that she'd have to flee from because they were all in this conspiracy together and what they really wanted to do was land Rosie in jail without passing Go or collecting fifty thousand pounds.

At 6:10 by Bob's watch she tiptoed downstairs with the laundry basket and nearly passed out at the sight of a shadow on the couch.

Then she remembered.

Half of the time on the journey home from seeing Greenfield last night she'd been saying to herself, you can't ask Martin to stay the night, Rosie, what kind of example is that to set your children when morality's in decline the way people are always saying it is?

Half of the journey, she'd that to herself. The other half, she'd said to the invisible Martin: Stay with me, I'm lonely and I'm scared.

So of course when she'd got home there he was, the visible version, asleep on the couch, unconscious under the influence of an Open University textbook and six cans of lager that were neatly arranged beside him. So, there he was now, at 6:13: the ultimate in imperfect compromises: with all the embarrassment of his having stayed the night without any of the comfort or, er, pleasure. Clearly normal life was still in operation after all. She kissed him on his squashed and sleeping nose and went to put the washing in the machine.

*

'Maybe it's all a trap,' said Margie on the phone an hour and a half later, after the ritual grumbles about what time Rosie called this, and so forth.

'That's why I want you to come in the back way,' said Rosie. 'Park the van a coupla streets away, a'right?'

'What for?'

'I'll explain later,' said Rosie patiently, for Martin was stirring on his sofa. 'Tara now.'

*

'Maybe it's all an elaborate trap,' said Martin after the first cup of coffee had got his circulation moving and his brain tentatively into gear.

'That's why I want you to keep me in sight,' said Rosie. 'You're sure the bike's all right?'

'Stripped it down yesterday,' said Martin. 'At first I thought it must be the drive pinion, but then when I replaced that it still wasn't firing properly, so I thought, maybe it's the . . . '

'As long as it goes vroom vroom,' said Rosie technically. 'I'd grab the bathroom if I was you. Before Bob gets in it.'

*

Carol and Bob weren't taken into her confidence about the day ahead. Even if she'd wanted to, they wouldn't

160

have let her get a word in edgeways. 'Er, about Martin,' she began nervously over breakfast, while he was still in the bathroom and taking an extraordinarily long time about it.

'Yeh, did he tell you?' asked Bob, spilling cereal over the table in his enthusiasm.

'Tell me what?'

'About Jerry coming round,' explained Carol, tidying up Bob's spillage with a patient look. 'I thought you'd given them up, Mum.'

Rosie was having a quiet fag away from the table and refused to try and explain away her bad habits to her daughter. 'What happened?'

'They played chess,' said Bob.

'They drank lager,' said Carol.

'But what did they talk about?' — not that I can be bothered with that today, I've got an important kidnapping to sort out but I can't tell you about it. . . .

'You don't think we would?' said Bob.

'Listen on the stairs?' said Carol.

'No,' said Rosie. 'I *know* you would.'

'They talked about you,' said Bob.

'What a wonderful woman you were,' said Carol.

'How that showed in how wonderful your two children were,' added Bob.

'Especially your daughter,' added Carol.

'You couldn't hear, eh?' said Rosie.

They nodded sadly.

Clearly they didn't have the basic espionage skills to follow their mother into the detection business.

*

'Maybe it's all an elaborate trap,' said Luke Greenfield on the phone.

That's my line: and you're doing the trapping. 'Whaddya mean?'

'I dunno. Maybe they've got me at the office so they

161

can rob my house or something. I dunno.'

'Just wait,' said Rosie. 'You didn't tell Norfolk, didya? The copper?'

'I said I was paying y'off. I'm nervous, that's all.'

'It'll be all right,' said Rosie, thinking, yes, dammit, she should have got him to make out a cheque there and then — and wondering why she had to be Mother Comfort even to crooks who might well be taking her for a ride.

*

Margie's arrival up the alley and through the back door, just before leaving-for-school time (i.e. five minutes after the latest possible time they should have left so as not to miss Assembly) aroused Carol and Bob's suspicions. 'What're you all up to?' asked Bob, laying down his bag inscribed with the names of all the squad members of LIVERPOOL FC.

'Nothing,' said Rosie, 'off you go.'

'Something's going on,' said Carol, reluctantly accepting from her mother her bag inscribed with the names of all the members of various rock groups.

'Your mum didn't like to tell you,' said Margie in low tones, 'but we're off to a funeral.'

Which got Bob heading out the door, but didn't quench Carol's morbid interest: 'Whose?'

'Yours,' said Rosie, 'if you don't get off now and stop taking any notice of your Auntie Margie. Run, go on.'

'Now what?' Margie asked once Carol had run back in for her gym things and the house was finally quietly filled with three adults drinking tea.

'We wait,' said Rosie.

*

'Rosie Moneygone?' asked the foreign-sounding woman out of the telephone.

'Near enough,' said Rosie, gesturing to the other two to come and listen. 'Who's that?'

'You know me. Be at ze phone-box . . .'

'He's not picking up the money till eleven.'

'. . . ze phone-box,' said the imperturbable voice, 'on ze Otterzpull Promenade road at precisely eleven sirty. No police, no strangers. Only you.'

'It's nice to be wanted,' said Rosie.

'And ze money,' said the foreign woman, 'eez to be in two rucksacks. Got zat?'

'And when does Ruthie get handed over?'

'Got zat?' the voice repeated.

'Yeh, but, er, no, but . . .' said Rosie decisively.

No, but they'd rung off.

'I haven't got two rucksacks,' said Rosie.

'I'll get 'em from home,' said Martin.

'What now?' said Margie.

'Put my coat on,' said Rosie, 'and my headscarf . . .'

'You never wear a headscarf.'

'Well, stoop, and look like me somehow, and drive off in my car nowhere near Otterspool Prom or Barclays Bank in Dale Street.'

'I'm not with you,' said Margie.

'That's the idea,' said Rosie, 'I'm being followed and I don't wanna be. Go on, get moving, willya?'

*

Rosie's plan was only slightly complicated by the fact that Margie drove off with the keys to her van, which Rosie had been going to drive. Just when she was panicking about that and thinking she might have to learn to ride a motor-bike in a hurry, Margie rang to say, 'Nobody followed me.'

'Are you sure?'

'Positive.'

'Get back here, then,' said Rosie, 'pronto.'

At eleven o'clock Rosie was in a room in Barclays Bank in Dale Street with two rather smelly old rucksacks, a surprisingly female but still pin-striped bank employee, Luke Greenfield and a blind man who lived in a house called BELLA VISTA. 'So nice to meet you again,' said Rosie, all la-di-da and proffering her hand.

Patresi grimaced at her. What was he doing here? Her look must have been asking the question too for Greenfield took her to one side and murmured:

'I couldn't raise the money. Without him.'

'No, but ... ,' said Rosie.

'It's all right, he doesn't know the details,' said Greenfield, giving her one of his straight-in-the-eye looks which had thus far always convinced Rosie that he must be lying.

Still, Rosie wasn't worried. Outside the bank were her trusty henchfolk M and M, in Mini and motor-bike, ready to divert pursuing police and diligent detectives. So there was nothing to worry about, was there?

Rosie looked at the blind man and Luke Greenfield and the two rucksacks with £25,000 each in them in five-pound notes and she couldn't avoid acknowledging it — she was beginning to worry.

Oh, come on Rosie, you'll only be carrying fifty thousand pounds through the crime capital of western Europe. What is there to worry about?

'Is there, er,' Rosie asked the pin-striped woman out of the corner of her mouth, 'is there a loo anywhere?'

Chapter Twenty-Six

The money was remarkably heavy actually. Rosie stooped on the marble steps of the bank, blinking in the sunlight. She felt as if she stood on the edge of a new world: Christine Columbus on the shores of America. For one marvellous, magnificently mad moment she imagined something remarkable was going to happen: that she was going to do the sensible, rational thing and turn, at last, dishonest.

Then she thought: why the hell not? Why can't a lifetime be made out of marvellous, magnificently mad moments? She slung the two rucksacks into the back of Margie's van with a feeling very like joy. She would have liked to have torn up the parking ticket tucked under the wipers too. But this probably wasn't the time to engage in minor illegalities. Not when she was planning to. . . .

It was simplicity itself. Margie and Martin followed their brief to perfection: the Mini stalling in front of the unmarked police car, just as the lights changed; Martin's motor-bike 'accidentally' crashing into the side of what must be some private detective's flash motor.

Free of pursuers, Rosie headed towards home, carefully within the speed limit. She took a right, a left, another left and back on to the main road: nobody following.

At first she refused to explain to Bob and Carol what was happening. She just told their teachers that 'an urgent family problem' had come up and whisked the pair of them out of school. Of course, riding in the back of the van, they wanted to know what was in the rucksacks.

'Just some stuff we're taking on holiday with us,' said Rosie calmly, still checking the mirrors.

'Holiday? When are we going on holiday?'

'Now,' said Rosie. 'And for evermore. Amen.'

Soon the two children had filled a suitcase each full of spare clothes and Rosie had stuffed a pair of jeans or two and her bikini into the rucksacks and they were out on the motorway.

'Can't you tell us where we're going, Mum?' Bob demanded.

'Spain,' said Rosie.

'But why do we have to go now?' Carol wanted to know. 'I've got double Art this avvy. I like double Art. Why now?'

'It's now or never,' said Rosie, following the signs to Manchester Airport. She'd never felt so free in her life: marvellously, gloriously free. Of course, fifty grand wouldn't last them for ever. But it'd tide them over till she could plan her next big job. There were lots of unemployed villains with time on their hands over on the Costa del Crime, she'd read. Why, she began to ask herself, why had she spent all these years struggling to make ends meet? Stuggling to be honest and decent and nice to her menfolk when deep down inside she'd wanted to lie and be evil and tell them where to get off?

Now all that was going to change. The terminal building was coming into view. She was, quite simply and straightforwardly, going to dump the van in the car park, and march up to the British Airways counter and buy their tickets on the spot for the first available flight — Greece, that'd be okay as an alternative, somewhere to establish a new expatriate criminal community. Maybe she'd invite Margie over, once she'd got herself settled in a nice little villa. She could just see the two of them, sipping vodkas on the patio in the sunshine — while Bob and Carol splashed in the private pool — speculating about the pair of gigolos who were due at eight to take them out on the town for the night. Meanwhile, though, the two women could lean back on their sun-loungers, stoking up their suntans, reminiscing maybe about the day it all began, that day when Rosie walked out of Barclays Bank with a heavy rucksack over each shoulder and. . . .

Chapter Twenty-Seven

The money was remarkably heavy actually. Rosie stopped on the marble steps of the bank, blinking in the sunlight. She felt as if she stood on the edge of a new world: Christine Columbus on the shores of America. For one marvellous, magnificently mad moment she imagined something remarkable was going to happen: that she was going to do the sensible, rational thing and turn, at last, dishonest.

Then she thought: I can't do it. You can't make a lifetime out of marvellous, magnificently mad moments. You might get found out, for a start. You might, for a follow-up, be deluded about the marvellousness of the mad magnificence of the New World. Christopher Columbus thought he was discovering something; Christine would have had the lurking feeling somebody had been there before.

And besides, back in her Old World Rosie still had this lurking feeling of her own that it would be morally wrong to steal fifty thousand pounds that she had been entrusted with by a fellow human being to exchange for his daughter's safety.

No wonder, she concluded sadly, no wonder she was so low in the pecking order on the Starship Enterprise Culture.

She slung the two rucksacks into the back of Margie's van wearily. She leant across the windscreen and tore up the parking ticket tucked under the wipers. Then she sat herself behind the wheel and gave herself one last chance. Spain or the phone box on Otterspool Promenade.

If she'd had a coin on her, she'd have tossed up. But unfortunately she didn't have any loose change: just fifty grand in the back in fivers. So she reached into a rucksack for one of the notes and threw that up in the air. Duke of Wellington, Spain; Queen, Otterspool.

She'd forgotten to wind up the window, though, and the note blew out. She just caught sight of it — Elizabeth R uppermost — before it blew away down Dale Street. Reluctantly she started the van and hoped the kidnappers wouldn't mind about there only being £49,995.

*

The plan was — not that it had any chance of working, of course, but — the plan was that she'd drive through the Queensway Tunnel to Wallasey, then leave at the first exit, round the roundabout and straight back through the tunnel to Liverpool. On the way Margie and Martin would identify any pursuers and find some way of diverting them.

Much to Rosie's amazement, the plan that had no chance of working worked. Even more extraordinarily, it worked in the same way it had on that other planet where she'd fled to the Mediterranean with the money. At the Wallasey roundabout she saw Margie in the mirror seem to stall the Mini, then, in her apparent confusion, reverse into the (police?) car behind her. Then, as Rosie emerged in the van from the darkness of the tunnel back into the Liverpool sunlight, Martin's motor-bike, that had been weaving in and out of the traffic behind her alarmingly, suddenly bumped the wing of a blue Vauxhall Cavalier.

Rosie felt the urge to go back and thank her friends for their help.

Perhaps, though, that'd rather spoil the object of the exercise. Put your foot down, Rosie.

She was only a couple of minutes late at the phone-box and wasn't at all worried that it wasn't ringing.

What if it was out of order?

No, it wouldn't be out of order, they'd have checked that, no need to worry Rosie, no.

There was next to nobody about: a middle-aged

woman walking her dog; a young couple and then a lone
girl on bicycles; the occasional car loaded with rubbish in
the back for the refuse dump a few hundred yards beyond.

There was next to nothing to worry about, either. Even
if they'd rung and got no answer they'd call again,
wouldn't they? Honestly, two minutes' fantasising about
Spain outside the bloody bank wasn't going to be the
difference between life and death, was it?

Rosie finally faced up to the facts: she was worried sick
and desperate for a pee and wishing she'd brought that
nice thriller along to read to take her mind off things.

The middle-aged woman was on the return journey,
five yards from the van with her Alsatian, when the phone
began to ring. Rosie rushed out of the van in alarm as the
woman stopped, staring at the phone, clearly wondering. . . .

'It's all right,' said Rosie, 'it's for me.'

'Vair haff you been?' said the voice on the phone.

The woman hadn't moved. Her Alsatian was barking
at Rosie, baring its teeth affectionately. 'Spain,' said Rosie
into the phone. 'Explain,' she added quickly, 'it's difficult
to explain, there's somebody here, hang on a minute.' She
put her hand over the mouthpiece: 'We haven't got a
phone at home, y'see,' she said to the woman.

The woman looked her up and down. 'Come on, J R,'
she said to her still-barking dog. 'Home boy.'

'Vot ze hell is goink on?' said the foreign-sounding
woman.

'Nossink,' said Rosie, 'I mean, nothing. What now?'

*

It did seem to Rosie that if people like police and kidnappers and so on were going to insist on imitating their
TV and movie counterparts, they should take some
account of the eccentricities of real life too. For the next
phone-box she'd been directed to was occupied. And in
front of Rosie in the queue were a small greasy-haired

169

man with the racing page folded open and the large mother of push-chaired twins who already had her ten pence ready for a call. A self-respecting kidnapper might, Rosie thought, have observed that the call-box was situated by a busy shopping parade if they'd done the minimum of research.

It was, in addition, only two streets away from the Greenfields' house. Maybe that seemed like something of a challenge if you'd kidnapped the Greenfields' younger daughter. To the delivery-woman, though, it felt dangerously like tempting fate.

'You haff been engaged,' said the phone accusingly when Rosie's turn finally came around.

'I have been waiting in a queue,' said Rosie with infinite patience, forebearing to mention that she'd had to wait an embarrassing fifty-three seconds and counting (with a fierce elderly woman glaring at her from outside) before the thing finally rang. 'I don't have to go and buy a parachute now, do I?'

'Sorry?'

I just saw it on the telly once, they dropped this ransom out of a plane. 'Where now?'

*

In the car park was a warning sign: LOSE IT OR LOCK IT — CAR THEFTS HAVE BEEN REPORTED IN THIS AREA. Yet it was hard to believe in the looming thieves. There was no one about, and hardly a building for miles except for the smart little village of Hale, half a mile behind. The only other vehicle in the car park was a battered old black VW with a NUCLEAR POWER: NO THANKS sticker so she felt safe enough. Or maybe the Friends of the Earth were moving into kidnapping as a way of raising funds nowadays?

Rosie strolled down the path towards the Mersey, breathing in deep to enjoy the fresh air then breathing in shallowly because of the pollution floating into her lungs from Widnes, just up-river. She tried to enjoy herself; to savour the space and the freedom of being alone in the country. Unfortunately she had two rucksacks full of money on her back and a continuing need for a pee and a faint fear in her heart that a sniper was lurking out there in the undergrowth somewhere, ready to kill for £49,995.

Nobody shot at Rosie. She peered over the hedgerows on either side of the path: nothing but fields and birds. And, reaching the fence that bordered the mud and shingle of the river bank, the old lighthouse a little ahead, there, sure enough, as the foreign woman had predicted, was a small heap of stones piled up around a wooden fence-post. She unloaded the rucksacks — for which her shoulders immediately expressed profound relief — and quickly re-arranged the stones over them.

There, it was done. The sniper could shoot now if he or she wanted: she didn't have any money to be robbed of. She had an impulse to sit down on the little wooden stile, and stare out across the mud-flats at the scenic view of the ICI works and Ellesmere Port power station on the opposite bank, and watch the birds dive and soar from the water while she helped the pollution along a little with a quiet cigarette.

'No vaitink about,' though — that's what the woman had said. So, pausing only to hop behind a hedge for a little light relief, Rosie reluctantly retraced her steps to the van. She ought to have been skipping — joyous — glad to be alive! Now that the weight of the money was off her shoulders; now she didn't have to worry any more; now that she didn't even have to pretend to herself not to be worrying any more.

Now, though, a different weight settled on her aching back. It was the weight of a feeling she'd had all day but hadn't been prepared to admit to herself till now: like the smell of rubber in the air that you could pretend for a while wasn't there, until you admitted to yourself that you could smell it.

Why admit to it, though? Why not just go back to Jerry

and Martin and Bob and Carol and Paddy and normal life?

Maybe it was just curiosity; maybe, the need to know whether or not she was right; maybe, too, some relic of her Catholic childhood again, some flotsam of a feeling that she ought to do the right, moral thing. Wherever it came from, Rosie had this strong feeling that she knew who the kidnappers were; that she knew where to find them; that she should go and, er, beard them in their den.

She also had this strong feeling that that would be a mad, foolhardy, completely irrational thing to do. And those are only three of the arguments in favour of it, she said to herself, smiling, as she lit a fag and pointed the van towards Liverpool.

Chapter Twenty-Eight

Rosie had run out of fags but she didn't dare move.

She'd been propositioned by four men in passing cars and one pedestrian of uncertain sex but she didn't dare move.

She'd been sitting on this stone step for so long, since dumping the van at Margie's and posting the keys through the letter-box and taking a cab down here, that she'd lost all feeling in her legs and bum so she didn't dare move.

A police car crawled by and the uniformed cardboard cut-out in the passenger seat seemed to stare at her for a long time and she didn't dare move.

Had an APB been out for her ever since she'd phoned the office of Greenfield Investment Services and said 'Mission accomplished' to her startled client and immediately cradled the phone?

The police car crawled on and she finally dared to move.

Her legs tingled with pins and needles.

In Denmark or somewhere they'd found the people stopped speeding and disobeying traffic lights at the sight of a cardboard cut-out policeman.

These were the sorts of thought you were reduced to if you'd been sitting on a step for two hours while the sun went briefly behind a cloud and forgot to come out again.

At last, two girls on bicycles rode down the street. As they dismounted she saw that one was tall, thin, her long dark hair streaming out behind her; the other, smaller, even thinner, scratching at her black spiky hair, wobbling on a man's bike that was so much too big for her, it must be borrowed. They lugged their machines, which seemed to be heavy with some considerable weight in the back panniers, up the steps of 23 Birkenhead Street, and into the house.

Rosie hauled herself up by the railings at the entrance to number 26 opposite. She jumped up and down for a minute or two until the pins-and-needles in her legs turned slowly to agony. That was Rosie's life: when agony began, she knew things would be getting better at any moment.

Finally, armed to the teeth with nothing but her wits and her misplaced sense of morality, she strode across the street.

*

With typical brilliance Rosie guessed at flat nine. There was no reply; not even any secret sounds from within. Cursing herself for trying there first — it was one floor higher than she'd needed to walk and her lungs and legs weren't what they had once been, even without all that sitting on stone steps and running out of cigarettes — she strolled down to flat three, which was, on the perverse numbering system that applied in the house, on the first floor next to number five.

She raised her hand to knock; heard laughter within and changed her mind; pushed the door open and walked in.

The bedsitter was almost bare. There was a sink in the corner, a table and chairs, two armchairs with the stuffing showing through, and a single bed.

On the single bed, two startled teenage girls were laughing helplessly as they threw enormous quantities of five pound notes over each other.

'It's a fiver short, I'm afraid,' said Rosie with amazing calm. 'Hiya Josephine. And you must be Ruth?'

She didn't know what reaction she'd been expecting. For certain it wasn't that the two of them would stare up at her with wide, anxious eyes and both, simultaneously, burst into tears.

*

'Did you follow us back, then?' Josephine asked.

They'd opened a bottle of champagne · they'd been keeping warm for the occasion. But the drink hadn't lifted their spirits, even when the three of them had lifted their chipped mugs and toasted 'Crime'. Josephine persisted gloomily: 'How did you know it was us?'

'I suppose you're gonna take me back, are ya?' asked the girl with black spiky hair. She kept fiddling with the black sheath encasing her index-finger. In her dyed hair-do and caked-on make-up she bore as little superficial resemblance to a fair girl in a photograph on the Green-fields' mantelpiece as Carol had to, well, Carol when Rosie's daughter was dressed in a white sheet and had lipstick all over her cheeks.

'Say something, for God's sake,' said Josephine, curled up in an armchair, sulky and withdrawn. 'Tell us how you found us.'

'I didn't follow you,' said Rosie. 'I just guessed it was you.'

'How?'

Rosie sat forward on the sofa and tried to shake off her torpor. 'Straight off I thought, maybe Ruth was here. Where else,' turning to her, 'where else would you find somewhere to stay? If you hadn't really been kidnapped? But all that cider-drinking and Josephine sounding like your mother — that put me off the scent.' Banana and onion and sweet cider. And now warm champagne with the taste of old coffee lingering in the mug. 'So for a while I started to believe in the real kidnapping. I had loads of suspects: me top of the list.' Which didn't raise a smile. Take the money, she felt like saying. I've got my clever solution: now run, go on, I'll close my eyes.

'Then,' she went on, 'I got to wondering about the voice. The foreign voice. It wasn't consistent in the end. And I thought back — to when me and Margie were at the flat upstairs. There was a moment when Margie was gonna clean under the bed . . .'

'I thought I was a goner then,' said Ruth, still squatting on the bed amidst the money, picking it up and putting it down, fiddling with her finger-sheath. 'Cheer up, Josie.'

Josie didn't react. She looked dangerously as if she was going to cry. 'And then,' Rosie went rapidly on, 'then I thought back to your mother losing her purse. She kept rambling on about it. As if, in spite of the pills and everything, she wasn't the sort of person who'd just lose it. Unless it was nicked. By someone who might be short of cash. And then I saw my daughter — she's eleven — all dressed up and it took me a while but I thought about how different girls can look. Without even meaning to be disguised.'

'I thought I'd die,' said Ruth. 'When you were asking me those questions about shares and I kept asking my invisible feller what he thought.'

'You were very good.' Damn it, Rosie, you've solved a crime, why can't you feel pleased with yourself? 'And then: then the fingertip came. For your father that was proof that some evil monster had you in their grip. And for me it was sorta the opposite. 'Cause I'd heard this story about you and the Nazis. About you stubbing a cigarette out on yourself. And — eh, I know I shouldn't encourage you but, has either of you got a ciggy?'

They didn't. It was bad for their health.

So was staying in a place like this where there were damp patches on the walls and somehow the sunlight didn't penetrate.

Still, maybe fifty thousand quid had been going to change all that. For a villa in Spain, maybe?

'So what's gonna happen, missus?' Josephine asked sadly.

I don't know. I just don't know. 'I've talked enough,'

said Rosie. 'Why don't you two talk? Tell me about it?'

Silence. Josephine staring into space and Ruth fiddling with £49,995 in fivers.

And silence.

So Rosie went on talking, just because she couldn't bear the silence of their sadness and disappointment. She talked about how everybody wanted to leave home sometimes. She talked about the time she'd run away for a night and how she wished she'd had the wit and invention to think of ransoming herself except that her dad didn't have any money. She talked about fathers. No response. She talked about how something happened to fathers when their daughters got to a certain age (a glance between the two girls, nothing more) and how they sometimes blamed it on the daughters. She talked about having to sneak out of the house in her party clothes and her make-up when she was Ruth's age and her father didn't approve. She talked about how she saw now, all these years later, that her father was afraid of something in her, something that was growing away from him and the family; and that he was afraid of something in himself, seeing her become adult and separate. She talked about how problems that might seem enormous and insoluble when you were young could all be sorted out if. . . .

She stopped talking. Josephine was crying and Ruth had gone to hold her hand and was whispering something to her.

Rosie picked up the champagne bottle and re-filled their mugs.

'No,' Josephine was hissing audibly, 'no.'

'I'm not giving up now,' said Ruth, who for some reason was undoing the belt of her jeans. 'Come on.'

And suddenly, caught with the bottle in one hand and her mug in the other, Rosie was grabbed, one girl to each arm. Before she could react they were pulling her hands together behind her and binding them with the belt. 'No!' Rosie said commandingly. 'You won't get away with it!' she was saying with startling originality.

And then they were binding her feet together with the belt from Josephine's jeans. 'I really think we should talk about this,' said Rosie reasonably.

And then they were knotting together two handkerchiefs and using them for a gag. 'Honestly, I think it would be better if we discussed this further,' Rosie insisted.

She tried to insist. 'Mf mf mf mf mf,' was what actually emerged from her gagged lips.

And then the girls were arguing with each other about what to do. Ruth was for going to London like they'd apparently planned, leaving Rosie here. Josephine wanted them to phone up somebody to release the cow (hm). 'Mf mf,' said Rosie in agreement with the sentiment, if not with the description of herself. But Ruth said that the old bat (hm) knew they'd got the money so they couldn't afford to have her on the loose. 'What are we gonna do with her, then?' asked Josephine. 'Kill her?'

'Mf mf,' said Rosie. 'Mf mf,' she repeated meaningfully.

While Rosie entirely accepted that everyone had to die some time, she didn't see why it had to be her, here, now. I've got, she wanted to plead, two children and a messy love-life to support. And a little brother whose VAT is in a mess.

'Mf mf,' she heard her pathetic little voice saying.

Meanwhile she surreptitiously got to work on the belt round her wrists.

Ruth had finally concluded, however, that killing wasn't a desirable option. 'I think we should tell her,' she said to her sister as they tidied the money back into the rucksacks.

Put the money in something else, they'll be on the lookout for the rucksacks, said the criminal part of Rosie's mind.

Don't help people who consider killing you, Rosie.

Josephine: 'I don't think we should.'

'She seems all right,' said Ruth in a surprising flash of insight. 'Maybe if we tell her, *she* won't tell. On us.'

If you think I'm going to sit here and be tied up and threatened with premature burial and then not tell even a dishonest cop which so-called kidnappers had the effrontery to do this to me then you've got another think ...

The girls sat on either side of her, on the sofa. 'Go on, Josie,' said Ruth.

Whatever it was, the older girl was very reluctant to tell it. 'I've never told anyone but you.'

'Go on. Like we said we'd tell, if we got away. Go on, tell her.'

Josephine didn't look at Rosie. She cleared her throat elaborately. She took a sip of champagne. She glanced at her little sister. She sighed.

At last, she began: 'It started when I was ten. I didn't know it was wrong. He said Mum didn't love him any more but I loved him didn't I? So he'd come in my bed and, and. . . . '

Ruth reached across Rosie for Josephine's hand. Rosie had a terrible feeling she was going to vomit. There's no need, she wanted to say. There's no need to tell me this. Look, I forgive the murder threats, I forgive the tying-up. If you'll tell me it's just an adventure, just a teenage girls' escapade and you can go back to mum and dad and still live happily ever after, then I'll forgive everything. No, don't go on, don't say —

'He said it was love but it hurt me. But he kept coming and doing it and telling me he loved me. He always said that, when he hurt me, that it was 'cause he loved me. And that it was a special secret between us and if anyone else found out they wouldn't understand. And then, I mean years after, then I'd heard things at school and I tried to tell him to stop and then he started telling me that it was *my* fault, that I was evil and I'd be punished. And then — then he stopped coming. Because. . . . '

And she'd thought Ruth was the strong one but now it was the younger girl, on the other side of Rosie, who was crying. Josephine reached across but Ruth pulled away. 'It sounds mad I know,' the older girl went on, 'but even though I'd wanted it to stop I was, I dunno. Jealous. Empty. So I — so I left — left home.'

Rosie had freed her hands behind her now. But she didn't dare move. She had an impulse to clasp the girls to her. But it felt like the story would all go wrong now, if she moved. As if they wouldn't wind up here, free, amid £49,995 of their father's money, within reach of a happy ending, unless she stayed still and listened:

'I didn't know, y'see,' Ruth, sobbing, took up the story, not looking at her sister, 'I didn't know, if only I'd known . . .'

'I wish I'd told you,' her sister cut in but Ruth went on:

'No, no, I don't blame you, but when he came and — and did the same to me, he said I was the only one and, it was always threats with me. I was mad and I'd be locked up, he said. I was bad and I'd be punished. I was evil and God'd get me. I was dangerous and the police'd take me away. It was like a nightmare that you wake up from. And you're still in it. For years. And then Josie came back that day, that Sunday. . . .'

'I just came to say,' said her sister, 'I'd thought about it and I just came to say: I forgive him. Maybe, I wanted to say, maybe I could come back and see them again because I forgave him. But he didn't wanna listen. He just ranted at me, called me names. . . .'

'And I listened,' said Ruth, 'I was supposed to be sent to my room but I crept downstairs and I listened. And I knew. He'd done it to both of us. So I sneaked out after her and she said she'd get me a place. And I packed my bag and I plucked up my courage and I came here. And that was gonna be it, end of story. . . .'

'Till you said,' said Josephine to Rosie, 'till you said about kidnapping that night. That night you came. And we talked about it. And well, I dunno who had the idea first but we thought: that'll be our revenge. To take his money.'

The afternoon sun had begun to filter through the dirty windows and tawdry curtains. Dust fluttered in the shaft of light that fell across the three of them. Simply telling their story seemed to have lifted some burden from the two sisters: like the moment Rosie had slipped the ruck-sacks from her shoulders down by Hale Bank. Cautiously she raised her arms from behind her and put an arm around each of the girls. Ruth jumped back: 'Hey, she's . . .'

'It doesn't matter,' said Josephine, suddenly tired again, 'what does it matter? What does she care?'

'Mf mf,' Rosie grunted, nervous that lifting her hand to her gag would frighten them. Ruth reached across to loosen the knotted handkerchiefs and Rosie sighed with relief. 'So whaddya gonna do now?' the girl asked her, the black lines of tears streaking her cheeks. 'Now that you know who you're working for?'

Rosie flexed her hands and cracked her jaw up and down and tried to get her brain moving. She stared at the money, still scattered on the bed. Their father's money, entrusted to Rosie so that Ruth would be returned to him. To the tenderness of the embrace of her 'secret boyfriend'.

Susie had said, too, that Ruth wore an invisible birth-mark. Rosie could see the mark now. But it wasn't from birth, was it?

Happy endings, she wanted to say. How can we make this into a happy springtime ending full, in its turn, of budding beginnings?

Rosie's voice sounded oddly distant to her as she spoke: 'I suppose I was afraid of it all along. But didn't dare to imagine it. What he might have done. It was kind of a hint, I suppose. You talking about Ruth's older man-friend. . . .'

Josephine stared at her angrily. But Ruth was resolute again now, trying to jolly her elder sister along. 'So are you gonna split on us?' she asked defiantly, trying to put some kind of a threat in her voice.

'No,' said Rosie, exhausted, motherly, summoning up her last reserves of hope and imagination, 'I'm not gonna split on you. And there's no need to worry,' her arms still around the girls, incanting to herself, happy endings, happy endings, 'it'll be all right. I'm gonna make every-thing all right.'

Chapter Twenty-Nine

Rosie sat in the Greenfields' living-room, listening to a pneumatic drill hammering at her rib-cage. Or was it by any chance her heart? An answering pulse beat in her temple. B-dum, b-dum. B-dum, b-dum. A stuck needle in a groove.

It seemed as if the party would never get started. Greenfield, without knowing what was going on, had insisted on his solicitor being present. Rosie had insisted on Alice. Now Alice, insisting on Barbara Greenfield being here, was upstairs trying to coax the woman down. Then *she'd* probably insist on her psychiatrist and she/ he'd have to insist on somebody else and they'd have to postpone the whole showdown till tomorrow and all Rosie's determination would have evaporated by then.

No. She wasn't going to let that happen. She and the solicitor Langton had been left alone. She turned to him: 'You and Greenfield must be pretty buddy-buddy then. Down at the gun club and the nineteenth hole. For you to lie for him to the police and nearly land me in jail.'

Langton acted as if he hadn't heard; as if she wasn't there; watching the whisky swirl in his glass as he slowly rotated it in his hand.

Rosie wasn't having that — not when her aggression needed sharpening up. 'And I hear,' she continued sweetly, 'that you're waging your own personal campaign against homosexuals.'

He deigned to reply to that. 'If you mean Michael, as I presume you do,' he answered, looking down those half-glasses of his at her, 'he is simply considering whether his future might not lie, more profitably, in going into business on his own account.'

And that gave Greenfield, coming in from the hall with a fresh whisky bottle, the excuse to start rambling on about the virtues of self-employment and how he'd never looked back since — agh, Rosie couldn't bear to listen. She stared at the photograph on the mantelpiece of a father with his arms around his two daughters. She sat back in the leather chair and refused to be amused or annoyed by the sound it made. She gazed around the unbearably clean and tidy room and remembered talking to the police about the walking vacuum-cleaner Greenfield called his wife.

At last they were all assembled. Barbara Greenfield, her eyes blinking impossibly fast, her hands perpetually twining and untwining round each other as if cleaning something, sat beside Alice Corrigan on the sofa. The men were sipping whisky and the three women were sipping tea from dainty little cups and Greenfield — no first names tonight, true or false — was saying, 'Well? Where's my Ruthie? What's all this about?'

'You're sure,' said Rosie, hearing her voice shake, 'you're sure you want your solicitor to hear all this?'

He waved his whisky glass at her in answer. 'It's not my fault,' his wife suddenly began babbling, 'it's not my fault, it's not my. . . .'

She went quiet at the touch of her sister-in-law's hand on hers. 'It's quite simple really,' said Rosie. 'Your daughter was never kidnapped. She and her sister Josephine . . .'

'I might have known she'd be in on this.'

'. . . are grateful,' she went on resolutely, reaching into her handbag, 'grateful for the money. They've written you this letter. As you can see,' as Greenfield's misty eyes scanned the note hazily, 'they've thanked you for your gift of £50,000, and would never like to see you again.'

'Gift? I'm not giving those little bastards fifty grand!'

£49,995 actually but we'll not get into that now. 'That's entirely up to you,' said Rosie, 'but if you must have your fifty grand back, then you'd better be prepared for the consequences.'

'Like?'

He was leaning forward on his hands, lower lip jutting out: a sulky child. Rosie glanced at Langton nervously. 'Like,' she said, 'like answering allegations about the way you, er, loved your daughters. You sure you want Mr Langton to hear all this?'

Still resolutely not reacting, still sulky: 'I've nothing to hide.'

Rosie glanced nervously at Alice. The older woman nodded a little, still squeezing her sister-in-law's hand. Rosie cleared her throat. 'When Josephine was ten years old. . . .'

*

Of course he denied everything. What had Rosie been expecting? He didn't understand how they dared to allege anything of the sort. He was sure if he could just see his little girls this could all be sorted out. . . .

Langton kept coughing. Just a little cough, at first. It sounded false: Rosie mistook it for a signal to Greenfield to be quiet. But no, the cough kept jumping, unwilled, out of the man. A-ha, a-ha. His adam's apple kept rising and falling. The skin beneath his lower lip was moist with sweat.

Rosie couldn't look at Greenfield. She just couldn't. She kept glancing at the solicitor; then at Greenfield's wife, hands busy, eyes wide, mouth zipped up tight; then at Alice, nodding to her encouragingly. It was when Greenfield was denying everything for the fourth time, and beginning to insinuate that Ruth and Josephine were covering up sexual misdemeanours of their own by accusing him, that Langton's little cough bubbled out of him again. 'I really don't think,' he said with difficulty, 'I really don't think, a-ha, a-ha. . . .'

But he couldn't seem to get any more words out. Nor did he move from his seat; he just sipped at his whisky, and coughed, and listened.

Soon — without the prompting Rosie had expected she'd have to provide — soon Greenfield's denials turned to justifications. He hardly seemed to realise that he was admitting what he'd done and Rosie began to realise just how drunk he was: speaking evenly, unslurred, not swaying, yet with his gaze fixed on some invisible adversary just over Rosie's shoulder. There were, he said, all sorts of reasons. For what he'd done. If he could just explain. Rosie couldn't listen. Yet she couldn't stop listening. His daughters had seduced him. He'd tried to stop himself but he couldn't. Perhaps if Barbara had loved him more. Not that he wanted to blame anyone else but . . . it had been done to him. In the children's home, in his childhood. An older boy. Made him do things. Then a man. And after all he hadn't done them any harm. The girls. He'd always been gentle. Love, he said. They wanted it, he said. It was love, he said.

Rosie shrank down into her seat, trying hopelessly to become part of the furniture. Please, let me be a chair. Let me be wallpaper. Let me, yes now let me turn into a fly. Now I'm in the spider's lair I want to buzz away. I don't want to have to hear Alice, quiet spinster Alice, shouting at him: 'How dare you! When are you going to stop blaming everyone but yourself?'

But her shouting didn't stop him. And the more he went on, the more his whining voice begin to sound like his wife's. He was going to go bankrupt, he said. They couldn't do this to him, he said. Everything he'd worked for, he said: his family, his home: in ruins, he said. It wasn't his fault, it wasn't his fault. . . .

And Alice was standing and shaking her fist at him and shouting, tears rolling down her face (and Langton was coughing and Mrs Greenfield had begun some monologue of her own about how they'd always been good girls), when all at once Greenfield erupted from his sulky, bent posture. He stood up, facing his sister. For a moment it seemed he was going to strike her. Then he turned away; hurled his whisky glass across the room and was saying: 'Okay, if that's what you want, I'll show you all! I'll show you all!'

He ran out of the room. They heard a door slam. Nobody looked at one another. Alice went across to the wall and began quietly to pick up the pieces of broken glass. Langton, not coughing any more, stared into his whisky tumbler. Rosie hardly listened to Barbara Greenfield's meandering speech — the only sound in the room — till she suddenly realised it was becoming more urgent and coherent:

'The guns!' his wife was saying. 'He's gone to his room with the guns! No, Lolly! Not the guns!'

*

Was there always something false, Rosie wondered, about people's hysteria? The man had locked himself in. Within, they could hear him crying. The hurled glass, the locked door, the sobs: they were all out of some melodrama he was imitating.

So, too, was the click of metal that made Rosie decide, imitation or no imitation, to charge the door.

The door came off best.

Alice pushed Rosie to one side. She took a run at the door as Rosie pulled a sobbing Barbara Greenfield out of the way, then kicked at the handle where the latch would be. The door splintered and swung open. Greenfield was sitting facing the doorway, a pistol of some kind cocked and in his hand. He was aiming it at himself. Go on then, said a voice inside Rosie, angry now, flaming angry now, go on, do it, you bastard! You have raped and damaged your daughters for life and I'm not going to tell you this but they are too scared and scarred by what you've done to testify against you and somehow here you are, still managing to make yourself the centre of frigging attention so — go ahead! Shoot!

Then he was aiming the pistol at his sister. And Rosie

186

felt paralysed as Alice shouted at him, 'Go on! Shoot! Go on!'

But he was staring at her, and lowering the pistol, letting it drop to the floor in another gesture that Rosie had seen somewhere before — in some film of some cornered gangster — so she was just about to relax when the gun, hitting the floor, went off and the man's wife, crouching in fear in the corner of the room, screamed and suddenly there was blood on the woman's leg. And Rosie, in the circumstances Rosie did the only melodramatic thing she could think of doing — but was sure she wouldn't do — Rosie fainted.

Chapter Thirty

Some mysteries remain for ever unsolved.

Rosie never knew, for instance, what became of friendship-hungry Anne-Marie, or Jack Fountain and Siggy's big hands, or Harry Allsopp. Nor did she ever find out what had happened to her in between holding Martin's hand one Friday night and waking next to Jerry's back the following morning.

Some things she was sure of, though. She knew, for instance, that they all lived happily ever after.

Except, that is, for. . . .

Well, Jerry happened to be round at Rosie's the night Luke Greenfield confessed. Jerry had finally given up hope of her replying to his letter, he said, and had decided to come and remind her in person of all the advantages to humanity of his becoming a father.

'Fuck fathers,' said Rosie moderately. 'I never want to see you again,' she added, 'and leave the door-key behind you.'

She thought she'd been remarkably affectionate in the circumstances. Jerry, however, seemed to interpret her words as meaning that she never wanted to see him again, and left his key on the table, and went.

Still, apart from Jerry they all lived happily ever after.

Except, that is, for. . . .

Well, Rosie did Paddy's accounts for him and went to see his wife Debbie in hospital. Debbie told her that she was profoundly depressed by the birth of her third child because Paddy had become jealously and wrongly obsessed with the idea that the baby wasn't his but his business partner's. That, indeed, was why his business partner had walked out on him. So Paddy wanted nothing to do with the child. Rosie took a cab straight from the hospital (Margie's little manoeuvre at the entrance to Wallasey Tunnel having finally written off the Mini) round to her brother's house.

'Bugger fathers,' said Rosie quietly. 'I never want to see you again,' she added, in her sisterly way, and went.

— Still, apart from Paddy and Rosie's Mini and Jerry they all lived happily ever after.

Except, that is, for. . . .

Well, once Martin knew that Jerry was out of the running he started suggesting he might stay the night sometimes. And, in between discussing the state of the world, he made small-talk with Rosie about how his ex-wife was bringing up 'his' children all wrong.

'I've had it up to here with fathers,' said Rosie angrily. 'I never want to see you again.'

'You don't really mean that,' said Martin.

Which was, alarmingly, true.

She didn't let him stay the night, though.

Still, apart from Martin and Paddy and Rosie's mini and Jerry they all lived happily ever after.

Except, that is for. . . .

Mike did the firm and principled thing and promised Langton he'd never appear in public espousing the cause of homosexuality ever again. This was, on the face of it, nothing to do with fathers, though Rosie suspected they were behind it somehow. Whoever's fault it was, it saddened her.

— Still, apart from Mike and Martin and Paddy and Rosie's Mini and Jerry they all lived happily ever after.

Yes, some of them did — for a while. Patresi, for instance, opened his theme park based on a Roman salt-mine in Cheshire and moved to the Costa del Sol. Barbara Greenfield only suffered a flesh wound and her husband only suffered a bankruptcy and a nervous breakdown, which Rosie thought was less than he deserved. Of his victims, a few hundred of his old mates from the docks lost several thousand pounds each. But then, they were as low down the pecking order of the Starship Enterprise Culture as Roşie (who never got paid by Greenfield either) so the world didn't care very much.

Greenfield's other victims, Ruth and Josephine, found a safe house in Birmingham off the Incest Crisis Line. Alice Corrigan got a job down there and became their guardian. She sent Rosie a postcard of Stratford-on-Avon where they were having a day out which said:

Girls recovering slowly. Thanks for all your help.

Love Alice.

And finally Rosie got to give Bob his talk about damp patches in the bed and, er, fatherhood. She told him that she wanted him to understand how a moment of desire for a man could become a lifetime of motherhood for the girl. . . .

'I know all that, Mum,' said Bob, embarrassed. 'About sex and all that.'

He was thirteen years old and he knew all that. 'No you don't, love,' Rosie replied, and went on to talk about the terrible things fathers did sometimes, and found herself unaccountably . . .

'Don't cry, Mum,' said Bob, bewildered, hugging her even though it was cissy. 'It'll be all right,' he said, 'whatever it is. It'll be all right.'

— As his mother was fond of saying.

Was this what was making the future meant? Passing on your deluded optimism to the next generation? Rosie the magician remembered how she'd told Ruth and Josephine that everything would be all right, and how she'd managed to make a kidnapping disappear into thin air so that Detective Inspector Norfolk had no crime honestly to investigate — abracadabra! — and said to Bob, 'Okay, sometimes. Sometimes it's all right. But only if you work at it. Hey, and look,' removing the watch from her wrist that she'd been meaning to return·to him for weeks now, 'this is yours . . . '

190

'Haven't you even noticed?' replied Bob in consternation. 'I showed it you once. Me dad gave it,' and he displayed for her, on his wrist, a miniaturised aircraft control panel faintly reminiscent of a timepiece. 'Look, it's even got a database with a memory.'

It didn't keep time very well — gaining three minutes on Greenwich every day, Bob said — but it had a database with a memory. Rosie re-fastened the old watch on her own wrist. Resign yourself, Rosie, she said inwardly — hearing the lack of resignation in her unspoken tone — resign yourself to the faulty shining gifts of fathers and the quiet resignation of mothers.

Rosie sighed, almost resignedly. She wished Bob and Carol were still young enough for her to tell them stories. Then she could kiss her son goodnight now and quietly murmur to him out loud, instead of just whispering it to herself:

'And they all lived happily ever after. . . .'

Warner now offers an exciting range of quality titles by both established and new authors. All of the books in this series are available from:

Little, Brown and Company (UK) Limited,
P.O. Box 11,
Falmouth,
Cornwall TR10 9EN.

Alternatively you may fax your order to the above address. Fax No. 0326 376423.

Payments can be made as follows: cheque, postal order (payable to Little, Brown and Company) or by credit cards, Visa/Access. Do not send cash or currency. UK customers and B.F.P.O. please allow £1.00 for postage and packing for the first book, plus 50p for the second book, plus 30p for each additional book up to a maximum charge of £3.00 (7 books plus).

Overseas customers including Ireland, please allow £2.00 for the first book plus £1.00 for the second book, plus 50p for each additional book.

NAME (Block Letters) ....

....

ADDRESS ....

....

....

☐ I enclose my remittance for _____

☐ I wish to pay by Access/Visa Card

Number ☐☐☐☐☐☐☐☐☐☐☐☐☐☐☐☐

Card Expiry Date ☐☐☐☐